# Secrets at the
# Little Village School

A Little Village School Novel

# GERVASE PHINN

## Secrets at the Little Village School

HODDER

First published in Great Britain in 2016 by Hodder & Stoughton
An Hachette UK company

1

First published in paperback in 2017

A CIP catalogue record for this title is available from the British Library

ISBN 978 1 444 77941 7

Typeset in Plantin Light by Hewer Text UK Ltd, Edinburgh
Printed and bound by Clays Ltd, St Ives plc

Hodder & Stoughton policy is to use papers that are natural, renewable
and recyclable products and made from wood grown in sustainable
forests. The logging and manufacturing processes are expected to
conform to the environmental regulations of the country of origin.

Hodder & Stoughton Ltd
Carmelite House
50 Victoria Embankment
London EC4Y 0DZ

www.hodder.co.uk

For my first and finest teachers,
Pat and Jimmy Phinn

# I

'It is a sad fact,' announced Mrs Robertshaw, teacher of the lower juniors at the village school, 'that there are some in our profession who just do not like children and are singularly unsuited to being teachers, and in my book, this Mrs Humphrey-Snyde is one of them.'

The speaker was sitting in the corner of the staffroom after school on Friday afternoon, nursing a tepid mug of tea on her lap. Such had been the length of her diatribe so far that she had not raised the mug to her lips, and the biscuit on the plate beside her had remained untouched.

'I mean,' she continued, getting into her stride, 'the woman's a supply teacher, for goodness' sake, not a permanent member of staff, and she's been in the school one week – one week, I ask you – and she thinks she owns the place. In my entire teaching career I have never encountered anyone so patronising, self-opinionated and downright ill-mannered as that woman.'

Mrs Robertshaw, a broad individual with a wide face and steely grey hair gathered untidily on her head, was dressed in a brightly coloured floral dress and a shapeless brown cardigan, and wore a rope of pearls and matching earrings. She was normally a jolly, comfortable woman with the ease and confidence of a teacher who had been in the profession for more years than she would like to recall. It was true that she was strong-minded and could be brusque and forthright in her manner, but it was out of character for her to be so impassioned and so critical of another.

Her colleague, a tall, pale-faced man in his thirties, with an explosion of wild, woolly hair and large enquiring eyes, had listened without interruption.

'Well, am I right?' demanded Mrs Robertshaw.

Mr Hornchurch, the teacher of the upper juniors, smiled. 'It's not like you to be so restrained in your views, Elsie,' he said mischievously. 'Why don't you say what you really think about Mrs Humphrey-Snyde?'

'It's all very well you being flippant about it, Rupert,' she replied gravely. 'You heard her in the staffroom the first day of term, when she made her appearance like the wicked fairy at the christening, with her smug self-righteousness, pontificating about education as if she were the Director of Education herself instead of a mere supply teacher. Probably couldn't hold down a permanent job. And I'll tell you this, if she is offered a post in this school, that will be the day I hand in my resignation.'

'I don't think there's much chance of that,' observed her colleague mildly.

'Well, just you wait and see. There is no way I can work with that woman.'

'I meant that it's unlikely our head teacher will want to keep Mrs Humphrey-Snyde on. I should imagine that like you, she is not overly impressed with her.'

'Not overly impressed!' Mrs Robertshaw repeated. 'Huh, that's an understatement if ever I heard one. I sincerely hope that we've seen the back of the dreadful woman and she will not make an appearance next week. Since she's been in the school she has made no effort to fit in and has succeeded in rubbing everyone up the wrong way.'

It was true that the supply teacher had in one week managed to annoy everyone with whom she had come into contact. She had arrived on the Monday morning at the junior site of Barton-with-Urebank Primary School minutes before the beginning of the new spring term, and strode smartly into the entrance trailing melting snow and muddy water behind her from her knee-length black boots.

Mr Gribbon, the caretaker, standing sentinel at the door, shouted after her.

'Excuse me! I've just buffed that floor!'

Mrs Humphrey-Snyde turned. 'Are you by chance speaking to me?' she asked sharply.

'Yes I am,' said the caretaker indignantly. 'In future I should be very much obliged if you would wipe your feet. You're leaving puddles on the parquet floor. I've just gone and buffed it.'

'Is this floor of some priceless architectural interest?' asked the supply teacher sardonically.

'Eh?'

'It is a floor,' she told him, 'and floors are for walking on, are they not? Sometimes they do get wet. It will not have escaped your notice that it is snowing outside.' She began to leave, but stopped and turned. 'And I have to say that the path outside is extremely hazardous. I should have thought that on a morning like this, the first priority of a school janitor would be to clear away the snow, rather than being concerned about a bit of water on his precious floor.'

'Now look here . . .' Mr Gribbon began, bristling.

'I can't waste my time bandying words with you,' said Mrs Humphrey-Snyde. 'I have a class to teach.'

Without another word she walked off briskly in the direction of the school office, leaving the caretaker staring after her open-mouthed.

Mrs Scrimshaw, the school secretary, peered over the top of her unfashionable horn-rimmed spectacles when the supply teacher entered the school office. She brushed a strand of mouse-coloured hair from her forehead, smiled, wished the visitor a good morning and enquired if she could be of help.

'I'm the supply teacher,' Mrs Humphrey-Snyde informed her without so much as a good morning. She was a tall, angular woman with small colourless eyes half hidden below dark lids, and greying hair pulled into a tight bun. Her thin mouth was compressed and unsmiling. She had had a long and arduous journey along icy roads, and was not in the mood for pleasantries. 'Would you tell the head teacher that I have arrived?'

'Mrs Stirling is in her classroom,' the school secretary replied. The smile had left her face. She did not like the woman's offhand manner.

'Well could you find her and tell her that I am here?' The visitor sounded irritated.

'I'm afraid I can't leave the office unattended,' said Mrs Scrimshaw loftily, taking exception to the sharpness in the visitor's voice. 'You will find Mrs Stirling in the second classroom on the left, down the corridor.'

Mrs Humphrey-Snyde remained where she was.

'Is there something else?' enquired the school secretary.

The supply teacher reached into her briefcase, produced a wad of paper and placed it on the desk before her. 'I would like thirty copies of these worksheets and should be grateful if they could be photocopied for tomorrow morning and placed on my desk before the start of school.' With that, she left.

'And pigs might fly,' muttered Mrs Scrimshaw, brushing the papers away with a sweep of her hand.

Mrs Humphrey-Snyde found the head teacher, Elisabeth Stirling, in her classroom, placing dictionaries on each desk.

'Good morning,' she said. 'I'm the supply teacher, Mrs Humphrey-Snyde.'

'Good morning,' replied Elisabeth brightly. 'I'm the head teacher, Elisabeth Stirling. I rather expected you earlier so I could show you around the school, introduce you to the other members of staff and familiarise you with how things work around here.'

'That is not necessary, Mrs Stirling,' replied Mrs Humphrey-Snyde. 'I have been on supply at this school a good few years ago, well before your time of course, during the period when Miss Sowerbutts was head teacher. Therefore I am well acquainted with how things work here. As for not being here earlier, it will not have escaped your notice that there was a heavy downfall of snow last night and it is snowing again this morning. The roads are treacherous. In addition, I do live on the other side of Clayton and it is quite a distance for me to travel.' She paused for a moment before adding, 'I did consider phoning through and saying I couldn't make it, but didn't want to let you down.' The woman clearly thought she was doing everyone a great favour by turning up.

'Well, now you are here, I'll show you to your classroom,' said Elisabeth, rather taken aback by the woman's brusque manner and self-assurance. 'The schemes of work, school prospectus, lesson guidelines and curriculum policy documents are in a folder on your desk.'

Mrs Humphrey-Snyde gave a dry little smile. 'I have been a supply teacher now for over twenty years, Mrs Stirling,' she told the head teacher in a rather condescending tone of voice, 'so I am fully conversant with the requirements of the primary curriculum. I produce all my own materials, so I will not need any lesson guidelines. I have found from experience that it is a much more effective approach if I use my own resources rather than relying on other people's.'

'I see,' said Elisabeth. 'Well, I will let you make a start. You will be teaching a lower junior class. The seven-to-nine-year-olds. The classroom is just across the corridor.'

Mrs Humphrey-Snyde, attired in a heavy black skirt, grey cardigan and prim white blouse buttoned high at the neck,

arrived at the staffroom at morning break on that first day of
the new term to find Mr Hornchurch by the sink, whistling to
himself. He stopped and beamed widely when she entered.
He was a happy, good-natured young man who seemed to
have a smile permanently etched on his face.

'Good morning,' he said brightly. 'Just in time.'

'I beg your pardon?' replied the supply teacher.

'I've just made a pot of tea. I'm sure you would welcome a
cup. I'm Rupert Hornchurch, by the way, teacher of one of
the upper junior classes.'

'Mrs Humphrey-Snyde,' she told him, sitting down, resting
a capacious handbag on her knee and placing her briefcase
next to her.

'Do you take milk and sugar?' she was asked.

'I bring my own beverage, thank you,' she replied. 'I only
drink herbal tea and I use my own receptacle.' She produced
a large china mug from her bag. 'Travelling around schools as
I do, I prefer to use my own mug. One never knows what one
may catch from other people's crockery.'

'Well, we managed to eradicate the Black Death here last
term,' said Mr Hornchurch amiably. His attempt at humour
was clearly lost on the supply teacher, who raised an eyebrow
and stared back blankly, then rose to make herself a drink.

'And how are you finding your class?' asked Mr Hornchurch.

Mrs Humphrey-Snyde approached the sink, which she
examined like some public health inspector. She poured boiling water into the mug and popped in a tea bag, which she
agitated vigorously, having carefully rubbed the spoon on a
tea towel. 'It's early days,' she replied, 'but they seem a docile
lot.'

Docile? thought Mr Hornchurch. Not a word I would use.

'I don't doubt that when they get to know me,' continued
Mrs Humphrey-Snyde, 'the class comedian will make his
presence felt and some of them will try things on. It always

happens with a new teacher. I do, however, know how to deal with cheeky and misbehaving children. I have been in the business a long time.' She drank from her mug with little bird-like sips before resuming her seat.

'Actually they're a decent set of kids,' Mr Hornchurch told her. 'I don't think you'll have any problems with them.'

'Oh indeed I shall not,' she answered. 'As I have said, I have been in this business for a long time and know how children's minds work. Some children are very adept at exploiting a teacher's weakness. I make no apology for being of the old school, one who believes in discipline and good order.' She took another sip of her herbal tea.

'I see,' murmured Rupert, taking a dislike to this dogmatic woman.

'I don't recall there being a staffroom when I was here before,' the supply teacher remarked.

'This was the previous head teacher's room,' Rupert told her. 'Mrs Stirling had it converted into a staffroom.'

'So where is her room?'

'She doesn't have one. She works from her classroom.'

'And she teaches?'

'Yes.'

'Her predecessor, Miss Sowerbutts, didn't teach.'

'So I gather.'

'Who is in the room next to mine?' she asked.

'That's Mrs Robertshaw.'

'She clearly likes a noisy classroom,' remarked the supply teacher. 'I tend to be old-fashioned in that I like children to get on with their work quietly.'

'Really?' said Rupert. 'Did you know that there is no evidence to suggest that working in a quiet atmosphere is any more efficacious, educationally speaking, than in a noisy one?'

'No, I did not know,' replied Mrs Humphrey-Snyde, 'and in my considered opinion that is quite plainly wrong. Children work much better in a quiet environment. The noise from the next-door classroom was most disturbing.'

'Mrs Robertshaw would be doing drama,' Mr Hornchurch told her, and then added, 'Drama does tend to be a bit boisterous at times.'

'Well I won't be doing any drama, and that's for sure,' said Mrs Humphrey-Snyde. 'I think there is quite enough drama in schools without encouraging any more. It winds children up. I am of the considered opinion that such things as drama and poetry and art decorate the margins of the more serious business of study. Not my words, but those of the former head teacher here. Miss Sowerbutts was, like me, one of the old school, and believed in the basics – spelling, punctuation, grammar and neat writing. I agreed with her. Children should know how to add up, know their times tables and master arithmetic.'

'It's called number work now,' Mr Hornchurch informed her.

'Yes, well as I said, I tend to be old-fashioned. I still call it arithmetic. In my experience, trends in education come and go. Everything comes around. It won't be long before arithmetic makes its appearance again.' She raised the mug to her lips.

'I believe that drama, poetry and art – and, of course, music – are essential parts of a broad and balanced curriculum,' said Mr Hornchurch, 'and add immensely to the quality of one's life. Would you not agree?'

'No,' she replied, 'I wouldn't.' The woman's face twisted into a half-smile. 'I guess that is what the colleges of education are teaching these days. In my considered opinion, one can indulge in such subjects when the children can all read and write and add up.'

'Well I'll let you enjoy your herbal tea,' said Mr Hornchurch, wearying of her doctrinaire opinions. And with that, he left the room, shaking his head.

At lunchtime, Mrs Robertshaw found the supply teacher sitting in the corner of the staffroom, eating a sandwich.

'Oh hello,' she said. 'You must be Mrs Humphrey-Snyde. I'm Elsie Robertshaw. I missed you at morning break because I was on yard duty. It was freezing cold out there. I'll be glad when we see the back of all this dreadful weather.'

'Yes, it is cold,' agreed Mrs Humphrey-Snyde before taking a small bite out of her sandwich.

'I say, you don't need to bring your own food,' said Mrs Robertshaw. 'The staff eat with the children.'

'I don't,' replied the supply teacher. 'I'm afraid I can't stomach school meals and prefer to have a break. I see quite enough of the children during the day without giving up my lunch hour.'

Mrs Robertshaw bristled. She didn't like this woman, with her tight little mouth, sharp features and tiny eyes. She didn't like her abrupt manner either. 'During lunchtimes,' she said, 'it's a good opportunity to meet the children more informally. It's a nice social occasion.'

'That may be your view, Mrs . . .'

'Robertshaw.'

'That may be your view, Mrs Robertshaw,' answered Mrs Humphrey-Snyde before dabbing the corners of her mouth with a napkin, 'but I don't share it. I need some respite in my lunch hour.'

'Well I'll let you enjoy your sandwich and your respite,' said Mrs Robertshaw. And with that, she strode angrily to the door.

For the remainder of the week, Mrs Humphrey-Snyde decided to spend her breaks and lunchtimes in her classroom. She did not find the atmosphere in the staffroom conducive. To use one of her frequently uttered phrases, in her considered opinion, the Robertshaw woman was full of her own importance,

spouting her fancy ideas about education and letting the children run riot in her classroom. The other teacher, the man
with the earring and the hair like a mass of wire wool, was
friendly enough but decidedly odd. His classroom was so
jam-packed and cluttered, it looked like a junk shop. No doubt
he allowed his pupils to get away with murder and, like his
colleague, had adopted all the fashionable fads and fancy
initiatives the government saw fit to burden teachers with. No,
she thought to herself, not the sort of colleagues she warmed
to. Miss Sowerbutts would never have countenanced such
teachers when she was the head here. She believed in standards, good old-fashioned discipline, a traditional curriculum
and hard work.

It was on the Tuesday lunchtime that Elisabeth found the
opportunity to speak to the supply teacher. She found her in
her classroom, reading the newspaper.

'I wonder if I might have a word with you, Mrs Humphrey-
Snyde,' she said, walking in to join her.

'Yes, of course,' replied the supply teacher. She folded the
paper carefully into a neat square and turned to face the head
teacher. 'I welcome this opportunity of having a word with
you too.'

'I noticed that you were not in assembly this morning.'

'No, I was preparing my lessons for the day.'

'I do like all members of staff to join the children in the
assembly,' said Elisabeth good-humouredly. 'It's an excellent
opportunity for all of us in the school to be together, to start
the day with a prayer and a hymn and to hear the notices.'

'At the last school where I did supply work, the head teacher
gave the staff the opportunity of preparing their lessons while
he took the assembly.'

'Well in this school I do like all the teachers to attend. I
believe that lessons should be prepared in the teacher's own
time.'

'I see,' said Mrs Humphrey-Snyde. 'Teachers do have a life outside school, Mrs Stirling. I don't intend spending all my evenings doing school work.'

Elisabeth decided not to argue the point but would certainly tackle the teacher again if she failed to turn up for assembly the following day. 'I noticed two pupils standing outside your door this morning,' she said.

'Yes, the Norton boy and that silly Norman Stubbins,' replied Mrs Humphrey-Snyde. 'They are both impudent and lazy. I will not tolerate children answering me back. The Norton boy didn't get on with his work and disrupted the other children in getting on with theirs, and he was impertinent.'

'What did he say?' asked Elisabeth.

'I told him that I could see a coat on the floor and asked if he would care to pick it up, and he replied, "Not really", so I sent him out.'

'And what about Norman Stubbins?'

'Oh, that silly boy! He kept on jumping up and down in his chair, and when I ordered him to sit, he started barking.'

'I see,' said Elisabeth. 'I shall have a word with both boys, but I would ask you, Mrs Humphrey-Snyde, if you have trouble with a pupil, to send him to me and I will occupy him with some appropriate work. I am not in favour of a child standing aimlessly outside a classroom.'

'I was not having trouble with him, Mrs Stirling,' retorted the teacher sharply. 'I have been teaching for over twenty-five years and do know how to deal with troublesome children. I made both boys stand outside to cool off and to think about their unacceptable behaviour.'

'Nevertheless,' Elisabeth answered, 'I should be grateful if in future you would send any child you feel should "cool off" to me.'

'When I was at this school before,' said the supply teacher, not prepared to let the matter rest, 'the head teacher, Miss

Sowerbutts, was very much in favour of taking a disruptive pupil out of the classroom environment so that others could get on with their work, and when I undertook supply work at Urebank Primary School, the headmaster, Mr Robinson, also regularly had badly behaved pupils standing outside his door.'

'Miss Sowerbutts is no longer the head teacher here,' Elisabeth reminded her, 'and Urebank was amalgamated with this school.'

'Yes, I am aware of that,' replied the supply teacher.

'So in future please do not have pupils standing in the corridor. I do not approve of the practice.'

'Is that everything?' asked Mrs Humphrey-Snyde, pursing her lips.

'I would also appreciate it if you joined the children for lunch.'

The supply teacher sighed. 'I believe I am entitled to a lunch hour, Mrs Stirling,' she said. 'I don't recall there being anything in my contract that stipulates I have to eat with the pupils.'

'No, there isn't,' agreed Elisabeth, 'but I think it is a valuable experience for the children to sit with their teachers over lunch. It's a pleasant social occasion. However, if you feel you do not wish to, then that is up to you. Now I believe you wished to have a word with me.'

'I have to say that I am not entirely happy with things in this school,' said the supply teacher. She sounded like a school inspector delivering a critical report.

'Really?' said Elisabeth.

'No, I'm not. Yesterday I asked the secretary to copy some worksheets for me for this morning and put them on my desk, but she has failed to do so, and when I asked why, she was very offhand and told me it was not her job to produce materials for the teachers. I also find the janitor very abrupt and uncooperative. I like my classroom clean and tidy, with everything in its proper place, unlike one of the other teachers I could mention. I asked the janitor yesterday to dust the top of some shelves. He has still not seen fit to do so.'

'Well, Mrs Humphrey-Snyde,' Elisabeth told her. 'I am sorry to hear that Mrs Scrimshaw appeared to you to be rude. It's certainly out of character, for I have always found her cheerful and very helpful. I should say, though, that she has quite enough on with the work I ask her to do, particularly at the beginning of term, without doing jobs for the teachers. As for Mr Gribbon, the caretaker, he is without a cleaner at the moment – she starts next week – and so he has much to do, particularly in this bad weather when he needs to clear the paths of snow. However, I will have a word with them both. Now, if you will excuse me.'

Some moments after Elisabeth had gone, Mrs Humphrey-Snyde became aware of a small boy standing at the door. He was a bright-eyed, rosy-cheeked child of about ten, with clear brown eyes and hair cut in the short-back-and-sides variety and with a neat parting. His hands were clasped behind his back. He looked like a little old man.

'What do you want?' she asked him.

'I just thought I'd pop in and say hello,' said the boy cheerfully. 'I'm Oscar and I'm in Mr Hornchurch's class. You must be the new teacher, Mrs Humphrey-Snyde.'

'Yes I am,' she replied. What a strangely old-fashioned-looking boy, she thought, and with such a curiously mature way of speaking for one so young. 'What is it you want?'

'Oh, nothing in particular,' said the boy casually. He approached the teacher's desk. 'We had a hamster called Humphrey once. He was a little rascal and was always escaping from his cage. Once, my father had to pull up the floorboards because he had found his way under the house – the hamster, that is, not my father.'

'Shouldn't you be out in the playground with all the other children?' asked Mrs Humphrey-Snyde.

'I've been tidying the books in the library,' said Oscar.

'That's what your classroom needs,' said the supply teacher. 'A good tidy.'

'Oh, Mr Hornchurch prefers it the way it is,' the boy replied.

'Really?'

'He says that genius is seldom tidy. He's quite a character.'

'Yes, he is,' muttered the supply teacher.

Oscar shook his head and chuckled. 'Once, when we went away for Christmas,' he said, 'we put Humphrey in the conservatory, and when we got back home he was all stiff and lifeless, curled up in the corner of his cage. We thought he was dead and buried him in a pot in the back garden. Then our neighbour told us he might just have gone into a sort of temporary hibernation because it was so cold, so we dug him up, and do you know, when we warmed him up, he came back to life. Isn't that incredible? My mother said it was a little miracle and that we should rename him Lazarus. He was a person in the Bible who came back to life.'

'I do know who Lazarus was,' said Mrs Humphrey-Snyde. 'Now, I am very busy, so you go about your business.'

'Righty-ho,' said Oscar, heading for the door. 'I'll no doubt catch up with you later.'

'Precocious child,' she muttered before returning to her crossword.

By Friday lunchtime, Mrs Humphrey-Snyde had had quite enough. Nothing in the school suited her – the head teacher, the teaching staff, the ancillaries, the children or the ways of working. How different it had been in Miss Sowerbutts' time. *She* had never insisted on the teachers attending assembly or having to eat with the children. She was every inch the head teacher, with her prim white blouse and air of authority. Many was the time she had children standing outside her room for misbehaving in class. And she would have hammered the basics, not indulged those teachers who wished to teach such fanciful subjects as drama and have classrooms like landfill sites. No, thought Mrs Humphrey-Snyde, it had been a most unpleasant week and she determined that she would not be returning to the school the following Monday. She allowed herself a small smile of quiet satisfaction. Let Mrs Stirling try and get another supply teacher at such short notice.

'Hello again.' Oscar appeared at the door.

Mrs Humphrey-Snyde sighed. 'Oh not him again,' she muttered. 'I haven't the time to listen to your stories today,' she told the boy curtly. 'I am far too busy. Now be about your business and don't bother me.'

'I was just going to tell you, Mrs Humphrey-Snyde—' began Oscar.

'Well don't.'

'But I need to tell you—' tried the boy again.

'Did you not hear me, young man?' asked the supply teacher, raising her voice. 'I do not wish to hear it. Now off you go.'

'Oh very well,' said Oscar.

One minute before the end of school on Friday, Mrs Humphrey-Snyde packed her bag, deposited the unmarked worksheets in the bin, put on her coat and lined the children up by the door. She intended to spend no more time in Barton-with-Urebank Primary School.

'Are you coming back next week?' asked Norman Stubbins glumly.

'No, I am not,' replied the supply teacher sharply. 'I have had quite enough of lazy and impertinent children like you.'

'And I've had enough of rotten teachers like you,' muttered the boy.

Mrs Humphrey-Snyde was about to respond when the shrill ringing of the bell indicated it was home time. She pushed her way through the melee of children, strode across the corridor to Elisabeth's room and put her head around the classroom door. 'Just to let you know, Mrs Stirling,' she said, 'I won't be coming in next week.'

If the head teacher was surprised, she certainly didn't show it. 'Thank you for letting me know,' she said calmly.

'I am afraid this school doesn't suit me,' said the supply teacher.

'I think we can agree on that,' Elisabeth replied. 'I am sure you will be a lot happier in another school.'

Mrs Humphrey-Snyde was taken aback by this response. She had been expecting the head teacher to enquire why she wished to leave, and perhaps try to persuade her to stay. It was clear that this was not going to happen.

'I think you will find it difficult to get another supply teacher at such short notice,' she said smugly, 'but I really don't feel I could continue working here.'

'I appreciate that,' said Elisabeth, 'and actually it was not that difficult to find another teacher. He starts on Monday.'

'Oh,' was all Mrs Humphrey-Snyde managed to say. It was clear to her then that the head teacher had had no intention of keeping her on.

'Drive safely,' said Elisabeth.

'Well, I'll be off then,' said Mrs Humphrey-Snyde rather feebly. 'Good afternoon.'

As the other teachers gathered in the staffroom for the Friday staff meeting, Mrs Humphrey-Snyde, on her way out, encountered Oscar in the entrance. He was sitting quietly, reading a book, waiting for his mother to collect him. He looked up as she approached and was about to speak, but the teacher ignored him and swept out of the door. A minute later, she returned, in a furious mood.

'I thought you'd be back,' remarked Oscar.

'What!' she snapped.

'I said I thought you would be back.'

'What do you mean?'

'I guess your car won't start,' said Oscar. 'It will be a flat battery. You left your lights on.'

'And how would you know that I left my lights on?' she asked angrily.

'I noticed at lunchtime,' said Oscar.

'Then why didn't you tell me, you silly boy?' demanded Mrs Humphrey-Snyde.

Oscar shook his head and breathed out rather noisily. 'I did try and tell you, a couple of times in fact, but you said you didn't want to hear what I was about to say and told me to go about my business. So that is what I did.'

'This is too much!' exclaimed the supply teacher. She looked at Oscar. 'You can make yourself useful and find the janitor for me, and tell him I need some help in starting my car.'

'I would like to be of assistance, Mrs Humphrey-Snyde,' Oscar replied, 'but I've just seen my mother's car pull up at the school gate. I have my piano lesson at ten minutes past four and Miss Platt, my teacher, is a stickler for punctuality.' He snapped his book shut, jumped to his feet and scurried off. 'I do hope you get your car started!' he shouted as he ran through the door.

In the school office, Mrs Scrimshaw was tidying her desk ready for going home. Mrs Humphrey-Snyde burst in. 'My car won't start,' she announced.

'Oh dear,' said the secretary. She didn't sound in the least bothered, and continued to straighten the papers. Then she placed the cover over her computer.

'I left the lights on and have a flat battery. I should have thought that someone would have mentioned it.'

Mrs Scrimshaw didn't reply.

'Could you tell me where I might find the janitor?' asked Mrs Humphrey-Snyde.

'Who?'

'The caretaker or whatever he is called.'

'You mean Mr Gribbon?'

'Yes, yes, Mr . . . Gribbon,' she said impatiently.

'He'll be in the hall at this time, buffing the floor,' Mrs Scrimshaw said, adding pointedly, 'Mr Gribbon is very proud of his floors.' The caretaker had related to her the exchange that he had had with the supply teacher on Monday morning.

Mrs Humphrey-Snyde hurried off.

Having been told by Mr Gribbon that he knew nothing about cars and didn't drive himself, and that he wouldn't recognise a jump lead if it flew through the window and bit him, an increasingly exasperated Mrs Humphrey-Snyde returned to the school office to find the school secretary putting on her coat.

'Could you give a local garage a ring,' she asked, 'and get someone to come out and get my car started?'

The secretary was placing a woollen hat on her head and fastening a scarf around her neck. 'I'm sorry,' she said, pulling on her gloves, 'I have to dash. I have a Women's Institute meeting this evening. There's the Yellow Pages, by the telephone.'

After ten minutes of fruitless calls to various garages, Mrs Humphrey-Snyde gave up and headed for the staffroom.

Mrs Robertshaw was in mid-sentence when the door was thrown open and the supply teacher stood there red in the face and clearly very agitated. Her unexpected and startling entrance was akin to the pantomime villain entering the stage at just the right moment in the drama. This was usually followed by boos and hisses. Before Mrs Humphrey-Snyde's unforeseen appearance, Elisabeth had just informed her two members of staff that the supply teacher would not be returning to the school the following week.

'Well I can't say I'm sorry to see the back of her,' started Mrs Robertshaw with a gleeful smile on her lips, just as the woman in question threw open the door.

Mrs Humphrey-Snyde looked desperate. Her face was creased with worry and her hair had escaped from her bun and straggled around her face.

'Could someone help me, please?' she said rather pathetically.

# 2

After the departure on Friday afternoon of the supply teacher, Elisabeth had informed her colleagues, much to their delight, that a replacement would be arriving on the Monday morning. She had realised as early as Tuesday that Mrs Humphrey-Snyde was not at all suitable and would not be returning the following week. The supply teacher's views on education were wholly at odds with her own; her teaching was less than satisfactory and she had managed to alienate the whole of the staff. Other arrangements had to be made.

Soon after Elisabeth had taken over as head teacher, Mrs Atticus, the vicar's wife, had trained at the school on the graduate teaching programme through St John's College of Education, and this had proved most successful. Having become a qualified teacher with a distinction in her certificate, she had been appointed to Clayton Junior School and was now the acting deputy head teacher.

Under the school-based programme, a trainee teacher, rather than studying full-time for a year at a university or a college of education, had a placement at a school and was mentored by the head teacher and supervised by a university or college tutor – in other words, learning on the job. At the end of the year, he or she was accorded qualified teacher status should his or her teaching be deemed to be satisfactory. Elisabeth had contacted St John's College to enquire if there was anyone suitable who might wish to train at the school in Barton-in-the-Dale. Unfortunately, she was told, all the trainees had already been allocated schools. However, the lecturer at the university Faculty of Education had some very good news.

'I think I have the ideal person in mind,' he had told Elisabeth. 'He is a very personable and able young man who has had some experience of working with children; a former professional footballer who had to give up his career after a series of accidents on the pitch. He has completed an Open University degree in his spare time and now wishes to teach in the primary phase of education. I am sure you will like him and find him most suitable.'

When Elisabeth heard the young man's name, she shook her head and laughed. 'Thomas Dwyer,' she said. 'Why, I have already met him. He came into school last year to talk to the children about his life as a footballer and encourage them to read. He was a great success.'

'So he wouldn't need to be interviewed by you?' asked the lecturer.

'Not at all. I have every confidence that he will fit in well. I'll give my chairman of governors a ring and clear things with him, and Mr Dwyer can start on Monday.'

On Saturday afternoon, Elisabeth called into the village store to collect her weekly groceries. The proprietor, Mrs Sloughthwaite, a round, red-faced woman with a large fleshy nose, pouchy cheeks and a great bay window of a bust, was the eyes and ears of Barton-in-the-Dale. She made it her business to know about everything and everybody, and no customer left her premises without being subjected to a thorough interrogation. Once gleaned, the information was quickly circulated throughout the village.

'Oh hello, Mrs Stirling,' she said brightly when Elisabeth walked through the door.

'Good afternoon, Mrs Sloughthwaite.'

'This weather doesn't get any better, does it?' She didn't wait for a reply. 'It's been snowing incestuously and now we've got the freezing frost. I can fair hear my bones rattling. And how are you keeping?'

'Very well, thank you,' replied Elisabeth.

'And that husband of yours? How's the good doctor?'

'Michael is in good health too.'

'And what about your two lads? I've not seen them lately.'

'Oh, Danny and James are their usual healthy selves. They are out sledging today.'

'I guess Dr Stirling is kept very busy in this weather, what with all the colds and flu about. Mrs Pocock's in bed with a bug and I hear that old Mrs Widowson is on her last legs. Mind you, she's been on her way out for as long as I can remember. She was at death's door last winter but the doctor managed to pull her through.'

'Well, luckily we are free of any illnesses,' said Elisabeth, keen to be away. 'I've just called in to collect—'

Mrs Sloughthwaite was not going to let her escape so easily. 'Have you heard about the vicar?'

'No, I haven't.'

Mrs Sloughthwaite rested her substantial bosom on the counter and leaned forward.

'Mr Sparshott's leaving,' she said in a confidential tone of voice. 'Mrs Wellbeloved, who was in here this morning and who cleans the church, overheard him talking on the phone. I must say, there'll be very few people in the village who'll be sorry to see him go. He was a very hegotestical man, standing up in his pulpit telling us we were all sinners. Since he became vicar of St Christopher's, he's managed to rub everyone up the wrong way.'

'Well I'm sure—' began Elisabeth.

Mrs Sloughthwaite was not to be interrupted mid-flow and continued, 'Mr Lloyd resigned as a churchwarden, Mrs Fish went over to the Methodists after the vicar criticised her organ playing, and he even banned the Remembrance Day service and the Christmas naivety play. I mean, he'd hardly set foot in the village before he got rid of his curate. And talking of Dr Underwood, Mrs Osbaldiston, when she's out of bed with her kidneys, is getting up a partition to send to the bishop asking if she can come back to St Christopher's as the vicar.' She chuckled. 'Dr Underwood, that is, not Mrs Osbaldiston.'

'Dr Underwood was very popular,' said Elisabeth, 'so let's hope she can return. Now, I must make tracks, so—'

'I hear you have a new teacher starting at the school on Monday,' said the shopkeeper, changing the subject.

My goodness, thought Elisabeth, news travels fast. 'Yes, that's right. However did you know?'

'It's a small village, is Barton-in-the-Dale, Mrs Stirling,' answered Mrs Sloughthwaite, raising her large bosom on the counter and folding her arms. 'You ought to know that by now. Nothing can be kept secret for too long. News travels fast. Mrs O'Connor popped into the shop this morning for her paper and told me. She's Tom Dwyer's aunt.'

'Yes, of course,' said Elisabeth.

Mrs O'Connor had been Dr Stirling's housekeeper until he married Elisabeth, and since then she'd done the cleaning and some baking at Clumber Lodge once a week.

'She was telling me that Tom'll be training to be a teacher at the school,' continued Mrs Sloughthwaite, 'and at the end of the year will be fully matriculated. I should imagine he'll make a very good teacher. He'll certainly be a big hit with the girls, a good-looking young man like that.'

'Yes,' agreed Elisabeth, 'I think he will – make a good teacher, that is.'

There was a tinkling of the doorbell and Major Neville-Gravitas entered.

'Good afternoon, ladies,' he said jovially.

Major Cedric Neville-Gravitas, late of the Royal Engineers, was an opinionated man of haughty bearing. Described by the shopkeeper to her customers as 'a wolf in wolf's clothing', he considered himself someone of importance in Barton-in-the-Dale: parish councillor, magistrate, former Worshipful Grand Master of the Freemasons and past president of the Clayton and District Rotary Club. He was also chairman of governors at the village school.

'Afternoon, Major,' said Mrs Sloughthwaite.

'I trust that both you ladies are in good health.' His voice boomed with false bonhomie.

'I was just saying to Mrs Stirling,' said the shopkeeper, 'that the new teacher will cause quite a stir in the school.'

'New teacher?' repeated the major. 'I wasn't aware there was a new teacher at the school.' He sounded rather affronted and looked pointedly at Elisabeth.

'Not a new teacher as such,' she explained, feeling uncomfortable and annoyed that her chairman of governors should hear about the appointment of Mr Dwyer first from the village gossip. 'The young man is training at the school. Of course, were it to be a permanent appointment of a qualified teacher, I should have involved you and we would have had a formal interview. On this occasion, I really didn't wish to bother you. I do know how very busy you are.' The major continued to stare, looking unconvinced. 'I did telephone you several times to keep you informed, but you were out. I tried again this morning.'

'It's just as well you popped in then, Major,' said the shopkeeper.

'As you know, with the retirement of Mr Jolly,' continued Elisabeth, ignoring the interruption, 'we are short-staffed, and it is difficult to get a supply teacher at short notice, so I thought it expedient to move quickly. I'm sorry if you feel it rather precipitate.'

'Well I do see your point, Mrs Stirling,' conceded the major, sounding mollified. 'I appreciate you wanted to get things sorted quickly, and as you say, I am a very busy man. I had numerous appointments earlier this week, a golf club dinner last night and this morning I had a meeting with my financial adviser. Then I—'

'I gather the supply teacher you had wasn't up to much,' interrupted Mrs Sloughthwaite.

Elisabeth sighed. Was there anything this woman was not privy to? she thought.

'I heard from Mrs Stubbins,' the shopkeeper rattled on, 'that her Norman, who was in the woman's class, told her she was a nasty piece of work, always picking on him and making him stand outside in the corridor.'

'Yes, well Norman now has a new teacher,' said Elisabeth non-committally. 'So where are you off to today then, Major?' she asked, keen to change the subject.

'A luncheon in support of the Army Benevolent Fund,' he replied.

'My father was in the East Anglican Regiment,' said the shopkeeper.

The major sighed. 'Really? Some sort of chaplain, was he?'

The humour was lost on Mrs Sloughthwaite. 'Then he joined the Foreign Legion.'

'The Foreign Legion!' exclaimed the major.

'You know, those old soldiers who march past the Cenotaph on Remembrance Sunday.'

'Oh, I see,' he said. 'You mean the Royal British Legion.'

'My father, God rest his soul, was deaf in his left ear through standing close to the big guns.'

'A packet of my usual panatellas, please, Mrs Sloughthwaite,' said the major, glancing at his watch.

'He had what they call gunner-ear,' said Mrs Sloughthwaite.

'He had what?' asked the major, who was slightly deaf himself and had not been listening to her earlier comment.

'My father. When he was in the army he had gunner-ear,' repeated the shopkeeper.

'Perhaps he should have been a little more careful,' said the major. 'Soldiers away from home are frequently warned about the dangers of getting too friendly with the local girls and contracting what are today termed as STDs.'

'As what?' asked Mrs Sloughthwaite.

'Sexually transmitted diseases,' explained the major.

'My father didn't contact any sexually transmitted disease!' the shopkeeper told him indignantly. 'He was a very clean-living man and never played away from home.'

'But you said he had gonorrhoea,' said the major.

'I said he had gunner-ear,' said Mrs Sloughthwaite. 'He was deaf because of the big guns.'

Elisabeth could not contain her laughter.

The major shook his head and smiled. When he had departed, Mrs Sloughthwaite leaned over the counter.

'I can't be doing with him,' she said. 'Full of himself, he is, all puffed up like a Christmas turkey. Him and his SDTs.' She leaned further over and patted Elisabeth's hand. 'Oh I say, I hope I didn't land you in it for mentioning the new teacher,' she said, smiling.

Mr Gribbon was a gaunt, unprepossessing individual with thinning rust-coloured hair and the glassy, protuberant eyes of a large fish. He was a garrulous and opinionated man who spent much of his life in constant complaint about the excessive amount of work he was expected to do.

It was the following Monday morning, and the caretaker was in the school office, perched on the corner of the secretary's desk with arms folded and a fixed smile of amusement on his face.

'What are you looking so pleased with yourself about?' asked Mrs Scrimshaw. 'You look like the cat that has got the cream.'

'I was just thinking about last Friday, when that supply teacher's car wouldn't start,' he said. He gave a snort. 'I can't help smiling when I think about it.'

'I'm surprised that you didn't see that she'd left her lights on,' said the school secretary. 'I mean, you were clearing snow from the path out there on Friday morning, near where she parked her car.'

'Who said I didn't?' said Mr Gribbon with smiling satisfaction.

'You mean you did see?'

'I might have done,' he said, tapping his long nose.

'And you didn't say anything?'

'I wasn't going to tell her, not after how she spoke to me and how she trailed water all over my buffed floors, and then complaining to Mrs Stirling about the dust in her classroom. Serves her right for being so unpleasant.'

'Well I can't say that I'm sorry she's not coming back,' Mrs Scrimshaw told him. 'I didn't like her the first time I set eyes on her, waltzing into the office with a face like creased-up cardboard and speaking to me as if she owned the place.' She looked down at her newly varnished nails. 'I think her replacement will be a vast improvement.'

'Is that why you're all dolled up?' The caretaker winked.

'Dolled up?' repeated Mrs Scrimshaw, pursing her lips. 'You make me sound like some floozy on a night out in Clayton.'

'I mean you've made a bit of an effort with your appearance this morning,' he said tactlessly. He winked.

'Mr Gribbon, I always make an effort with my appearance,' she replied, reddening, 'and you ought to see someone about that squint of yours.'

Mrs Scrimshaw had indeed made an effort with her appearance that morning. The outfit, a startlingly bright thin cotton
dress that displayed large red poppies on a vivid green background, was quite unsuitable for the time of year. It made her
look like an upholstered sofa. The unruly mousy-brown hair
that usually fell like a curtain across her face had been replaced
by a neat honey-blonde creation trimmed to just below the ears.

The caretaker's smile broadened. 'What I mean is that you
look very well presented. You've had your hair dyed and your
nails done, and that's a new outfit unless I'm mistaken.'

'I have not dyed my hair!' snapped the secretary. 'It has
highlights.'

'And where are your glasses?'

'I happen to be wearing my contact lenses this morning,'
the secretary told him, 'not that it is any of your business.
Look, did you want something?'

'No, nothing in particular.'

'Then stop grinning like a Cheshire cat, leave me in peace
and get on with buffing your floors.'

'Where is he, then?'

'Who?'

'God's gift.'

'Do you mean Mr Dwyer?' she asked.

'Who else would I be talking about? Yes, I mean the new
teacher.'

'He's in with Mrs Stirling. She's explaining things to him.
He arrived early. Now could you get up and let me make a
start on my work.'

'Course you've met him before, haven't you?' remarked the
caretaker, making no effort to move.

'You know very well that I have met him before, so I don't
know why you are bothering to ask. He's a very nice young
man.' A blush rose from the neck of her floral dress to her
blonde hair.

Tom Dwyer had called into the school the previous year and she had been very taken with this tall, handsome young man with the candid blue eyes and winning smile.

'Came to talk to the kids about football,' said the caretaker.

'Why are you telling me something I already know?' asked the school secretary.

'Just reminding you,' said Mr Gribbon, getting up from the desk and stretching. 'It'll be a bit of a change from what he used to do. Professional footballer to teacher. Bit of a come-down is that. I mean, teaching kids! Who'd want to do that these days, the way they behave?'

'They behave very well in this school,' answered Mrs Scrimshaw. 'Certainly a whole lot better than when Miss Sowerbutts was head teacher here. She was always shouting, and had a line of naughty children outside her room every day.'

'Yes, I was glad to see the back of her,' said the caretaker.

And I'll be glad to see the back of you, thought the school secretary, starting to open the letters on her desk.

'Well, I suppose I had better get on,' said Mr Gribbon, reaching into his overall pocket and jangling his keys. 'I've got a lot to do, and it's not easy without a cleaner, I can tell you.'

'What are you moaning about? She starts tomorrow, doesn't she?'

'About time, as well,' he grumbled. 'I can't see why she couldn't have started last Monday.'

'Well you just go careful with this one,' said the secretary impishly. 'You know what happened with the last one.'

The caretaker coloured up. 'Look, I don't know how many times I have to tell you, there was nothing going on between me and Mrs Pugh.'

'That's not what her husband said when he came into school that time. It's a good job you made yourself scarce, otherwise you really would have had something to complain about.'

'I don't wish to discuss it,' answered Mr Gribbon, and with that he departed.

Mrs Scrimshaw smiled with satisfaction. The mention of Mrs Pugh always had the guaranteed effect of getting rid of the caretaker.

So on Monday morning, while the school secretary and the caretaker were discussing him in the office, Tom Dwyer walked with Elisabeth around the school. The building was immaculate: clean and tidy, with highly polished floors, bright paintwork and displays of well-mounted work. Children's paintings and poems, posters, pictures and book jackets covered every available space. Shelves held attractive books, tables were covered in shells, models, photographs and little artefacts and there were coloured drapes at the windows. Outside, the school field stretched down to a small copse of bare trees, beyond which was the undulating frost-covered dale, shimmering in the morning sunlight.

'It's wonderful,' said Tom.

'I think it's important to have an attractive environment for the children,' Elisabeth told him. 'I'm afraid your classroom is rather drab at the moment. Your predecessor, a supply teacher, was only here for a week, so had little time to mount displays.' She could have told him that Mrs Humphrey-Snyde had had no inclination to mount anything, for when encouraged by Elisabeth to make the classroom attractive, she had replied that she had not the time nor the disposition to 'stick children's work up on the wall', which 'in any case has little educational benefit and has the effect of distracting pupils from their work'.

'I'll soon get it looking like the rest of the school,' Tom assured her. He grinned. 'But I might need a little help. I'm not the most artistic person in the world.'

'Mrs Robertshaw, the teacher of the other lower junior class, will, I'm sure, be pleased to help.'

They arrived at Mr Hornchurch's classroom. Elisabeth sighed when she opened the door. The room was like a cluttered attic. There were boxes and stacks of books in a corner, and tables covered in a variety of objects: birds' skulls, a stuffed rabbit, old tins, bits of pottery, coins, little brass figures, curiously shaped pebbles, fossils and shells, faded feathers, dried flowers, rusty keys, a chess set, a cricket bat – a fascinating potpourri of objects.

'This is Mr Hornchurch's classroom,' she said. 'I tend to indulge him because, although his room looks chaotic and is not one I would be happy teaching in, he is one of the best teachers I have come across. It may look to us like a jumble, but he knows where everything is and, surprisingly, so do his pupils. As you might imagine, he is not very popular with the caretaker. You'll like Rupert. He is one of the world's great eccentrics and you can learn a lot from him.'

'I am so looking forward to training here,' said Tom.

'You will miss your football, I guess,' said Elisabeth.

'Yes and no,' he replied. 'Like any professional footballer, I knew that I couldn't keep on playing for ever. The various injuries I sustained finally decided me. I'm afraid I was rather accident-prone when I was on the pitch.'

'You will be in good company,' Elisabeth told him. 'One young man in your class called Norman Stubbins attracts accidents like a magnet attracts iron.'

Norman Stubbins was a smaller version of his elder brother Malcolm, who had been at the school the previous year. He was a big-boned individual with an olive-brown face, tightly curled hair, short sandy eyelashes and very prominent front teeth. Unlike his brother, who could be difficult, disruptive and downright rude to his teachers, Norman was on the whole an amenable, simple soul who struggled with his work but caused little trouble, though he had his moments and could be cheeky at times, as Mrs Humphrey-Snyde had discovered.

The problem was that Norman, as Elisabeth had pointed out to Tom, was staggeringly accident-prone.

'I look forward to meeting him,' said Tom, laughing.

'So what made you choose teaching?' she asked.

'I thought of it because of you,' he answered.

'Me?' exclaimed Elisabeth.

'I'd been studying for a degree in sports science part-time and thought of working in a fitness centre when I gave up football, but when I came into school to talk to the children, I was so taken with things, I thought at the time that if there was a job I would really like to do, it would be teaching. So I applied to the university to do the certificate in education, and here I am.'

Elisabeth had taken to the young man, for he was good-humoured, enthusiastic and willing to learn – just the sort of person who would fit in. 'Well I'm very glad you did,' she said.

In assembly that morning, Elisabeth looked at the quiet and attentive children sitting cross-legged in the school hall. Tom stood at the front next to her, tall, slim and upright and looking open and friendly. She introduced him and saw how some of the older girls were spellbound and wide-eyed.

'Mr Dwyer,' she told the children, 'will be the teacher of one of the lower junior classes. I am sure you will all make him feel very welcome.'


Of course, the first pupil to introduce himself and make the new teacher feel welcome was Oscar.

'Hello,' he said, standing at the door of Tom's classroom at Monday lunchtime, his hands clasped behind his back and his chin in the air.

'Hello, young man,' replied Tom.

'May I come in?'

'Of course.'

'I'm Oscar.'

'And I'm Mr Dwyer.'

'Yes, I know,' said the boy, coming into the classroom and looking around. 'I'm very pleased to meet you. If you want to know where everything is in the school, just ask me.'

'Thank you, I will.'

'Mr Hornchurch is my teacher. He's a very clever man, like a walking encyclopaedia. He speaks Latin and knows a great deal about astronomy and fossils and the environment and history. By the way, astronomy isn't to be confused with astrology. A lot of people don't know the difference. His classroom is a bit disorganised, but that's the way he likes it. You were a footballer, I believe?'

'Yes, I was.'

'Do you miss it?'

'Well I enjoyed it while it lasted, but I think I'll be a lot happier as a teacher.'

Oscar sat at the front desk and rested his hands on the top. 'I can't say that I am one of nature's athletes,' he said, 'and I'm not really a team player. I've never had the inclination to run about a muddy field chasing a leather ball, but as my mother says, each to his own.'

What an unusual young man, thought Tom, so articulate, and old beyond his years.

'Perhaps I might change your mind about football when I start coaching the pupils. And by the way, footballs are no longer made of leather.'

'I doubt you will change my mind,' replied Oscar. 'It must be daunting starting at a new school, with all the different faces.'

Daunting, thought Tom. What child of ten or eleven used a word like that? The boy was like a miniature professor. 'It is a little daunting, but I think I'll soon get to like it here.'

'I hope you do like it here,' answered the boy. 'The last teacher didn't, and I'm afraid her class didn't like her. Between you and me, she didn't make a very good impression.'

'If everyone is as friendly and polite as you, Oscar,' said Tom, 'I reckon I shall be very happy here.'

'Well, I must away,' said Oscar. 'I'm on library duty. Goodbye, Mr Dwyer.'

Tom shook his head and smiled as Oscar made for the door. 'Goodbye, Oscar,' he said.

By the end of the week, Elisabeth's confidence in Tom Dwyer was fully justified, for he was a natural teacher. When she walked past his classroom, she saw children busy with their work or reading quietly or listening to him intently. During breaks, she made a few discreet enquiries of the children.

'I hope you're behaving yourself for Mr Dwyer, Norman Stubbins,' she said, coming across the boy sitting on the playground wall, exploring a nostril with his index finger.

'Course I am, miss,' he replied with a cheeky grin on his face. 'Mr Dwyer is great – not like the last teacher. She were crap.'

'Excuse me!' said Elisabeth sharply.

'Sorry, miss,' said the boy. 'I mean not very nice.'

He had hit the nail on the head there, she thought.

At the Friday staff meeting, Elisabeth asked Tom how he had found his first week.

'Really good,' he replied. 'The children are interested and well behaved and have produced some excellent work, and everyone has made me feel very much at home. I really like it here.'

'No regrets, then?' asked Mrs Robertshaw.

'None at all,' he replied.

'Well, Tom, you've made a very good start,' Elisabeth told him, 'and thank you for agreeing to coach the sports teams. I wonder if you might consider joining Elsie and Rupert on the school trip organised for later in the term. It's just a weekend to the East Yorkshire coast for the lower juniors. Next term it will be the turn of the two top juniors.'

'I'd love to go,' replied Tom.

I wish I could say the same, thought Mrs Robertshaw, who was not looking forward to the experience one bit and felt she had been dragooned into taking on the responsibility of teacher-in-charge. Over the years she had been on many school excursions and could predict the likely problems that would arise. She recalled the occasion when the coach carrying the children to the pantomime had just set off when a girl was sick all over the seat, her coat, her dress, her shoes, several other children and finally the teacher herself. Much to Mrs Robertshaw's embarrassment, the theatre manager had remarked that members of the audience and even some of the actors on stage had complained about the smell emanating from the direction of her party. Then there was the incident when the coach tyre had a puncture and she was stuck on the hard shoulder of the motorway for several hours with thirty whingeing children. And she remembered well the time when one child had wandered off in Scarborough and she had spent two fretful hours at the police station until he was found, cold, wet and minus a shoe. Finally, could she ever forget the occasion when one boy fell off the castle wall and broke an ankle and she had three hours in Casualty at the local hospital? After this calamity, she determined it would be the very last trip she would be going on.

It had taken Elisabeth's most persuasive powers to get her to agree to lead the school trip to the coast. As she listened to the head teacher, Mrs Robertshaw told herself it would inevitably be fraught with mishaps and hazards, and she felt rather peeved that she had been finally pressed into taking charge. It was a big responsibility. Elisabeth had listened to her objections, the main one being that it was a risky business taking the likes of Norman Stubbins and Peter Norton on an excursion to the East Yorkshire coast. Elisabeth had explained that the only weekend the hostel could accommodate them clashed with the school fete at Forest View, the special school her son attended. It was an event she really did not want to miss. Otherwise she would have been happy to go herself. Happy was not a word that came immediately to Mrs Robertshaw's mind. Hazardous, possibly; stressful, most certainly. Elisabeth had been at great pains to point out the educational value of such a visit, and told Mrs Robertshaw that being the assistant head teacher and the most experienced of the three teachers who were going, she was best placed to take charge.

'I am sure Rupert is much better suited than I,' Mrs Robertshaw had said.

Elisabeth had replied that although Mr Hornchurch was undoubtedly an outstanding teacher, with many wonderful ideas and initiatives, she did not feel he would be the right person to be in charge of a school trip. She had told Mrs Robertshaw about an incident that had been related to her by the Director of Education concerning the teacher at his last school. Mr Hornchurch had taken some children on a trip to the wildlife centre at Willowbank and had failed to notice one child climbing into the pond area. After the child got home and had his tea, he was sent upstairs to get ready for bed. His mother, hearing splashing in the bathroom, discovered her son sitting in the bath, surrounded by bubble suds, with a baby penguin paddling away merrily in there with him.

Reluctantly Mrs Robertshaw had agreed. 'But I shall be keeping my eyes on certain pupils,' she had said.

'That's settled then,' said Elisabeth now. 'Elsie will fill you in with all the details.'

'I see you've met Oscar,' said Mrs Robertshaw, turning to Tom.

'Yes indeed, a remarkable young man,' said her young colleague.

Mrs Robertshaw raised an eyebrow. 'He's a pleasant enough young man but he can be rather tiresome at times. He likes to have his finger in every pie does Oscar. I'm glad he'll not be on the trip. I couldn't put up with him all weekend, constantly asking questions and making comments and wanting to know everything.'

'He's my star,' said Mr Hornchurch, leaning back in his chair and resting his head on the back. 'Would that all children were as keen and interested as Oscar.'

'He can be a pain in the neck at times,' said his colleague. 'He has far too much to say for himself.'

'You know, Elsie, it is a fact that many adults – and I number teachers amongst those – do not like prodigies. They find them somehow threatening and have an antipathy to old heads on young shoulders.'

'Well I'm pleased that you get on so well with him, Rupert,' she remarked, thinking that the boy had met his match in her colleague, who, like his star pupil, had a great deal to say for himself.

'There is one girl in my class, Amber, who I think is a very talented writer,' said Tom.

'Oh Amber,' cried Mrs Robertshaw, her expression suddenly changing. She pictured the wide-eyed little girl with round cheeks, closely cropped red hair and the wonderfully fresh, rosy complexion of a daughter of the Dales. 'She's a delightful child. You will find Amber is reserved and quietly spoken, but you are right, she's very capable. She astounded me when she performed "The Solitary Reaper" by William Wordsworth at the County Poetry Competition. She outshone all the other children and came away with the first prize.'

'Then there's Norman Stubbins,' said Tom.

'Oh yes,' said Mrs Robertshaw, her face changing again.
'Then there's Norman Stubbins, a very different kettle of fish.
You want to watch that young man. He's a harmless enough
boy in many ways, but he can be a bit impudent at times and
is always in some kind of scrape. When Mr Jolly was his
teacher, the boy was always having accidents, getting his finger
stuck, falling off the wall bars in the hall, grazing a knee, stuffing the rubber end of a pencil in his ear, swallowing a marble.
Accident-prone is that lad.'

'He's a bit of a character,' said Tom, smiling, 'but I reckon I
can handle him.'

'He's probably biding his time. Just you keep an eye on him.'

'This morning I thought he was being cheeky,' replied Tom,
'but as it turned out, he wasn't.'

'What did he say?' asked Elisabeth.

'He asked me what a penis was,' Tom told her.

'What?' exclaimed Mrs Robertshaw. 'He asked you what?'

'What a penis was.'

'Oh dear,' sighed Elisabeth. 'Was this in front of the whole
class?'

'No, no,' said Tom. 'He had a word with me after the lesson.
Just came out with it. It took me by surprise, I have to admit.
As I said, I thought he was being cheeky, trying to be clever,
you know, to embarrass me.'

'Whatever did you say?' asked Mrs Robertshaw.

'I told him to ask his dad,' replied Tom.

'Very sensible,' said Mrs Robertshaw. 'I would have said the
same.'

'Norman hasn't got a father,' Elisabeth said.

'Yes, he told me,' said Tom, 'and then he asked me again.'

'Well I would have told him to wash his mouth out,' said
Mrs Robertshaw.

'I don't agree, Elsie,' said Mr Hornchurch. 'It might have
been a genuine enquiry. I believe that teachers should be

honest with children. Telling untruths or evading a perfectly reasonable question is wrong. I mean, "penis" is not a rude word, it's the correct biological term, and the boy is of an age when—'

'Rupert, please!' she interrupted, holding up a hand. 'Can we not pursue this discussion any longer?' She looked very uncomfortable and a red tinge was appearing on her face. 'Asking what a penis is, in my opinion, is hardly a perfectly reasonable question. It is obvious the child was being impertinent.'

'Well if it had been me,' persisted Mr Hornchurch, 'I would have explained it to him.'

'The thing is,' said Tom, 'I asked Norman where he had heard the word and he said that you, Mrs Robertshaw, had used it.'

'He said what?' cried Elsie.

'That you had used it in assembly this morning.'

Mrs Robertshaw flushed with anger and embarrassment. 'I think, Elisabeth, you need to have a strong word with that young man. As if I would say such a thing.'

Tom laughed. 'No, I am aware that you didn't use the word,' he said. 'When I asked Norman to explain, he said that Mrs Robertshaw said there was a penis coming into school next week to accompany the choir.'

# 3

Mrs Underwood was a thin-featured woman with a fine-boned face and lifeless mousy-brown hair. She sat stiff-backed facing her daughter, her lean, liver-spotted hands knotted together on her lap, staring incredulously as if she had been accused of some heinous crime.

'I cannot believe what I am hearing, Ashley,' she said. Her face, taut and bleak, twitched then tightened even further. 'It is preposterous that you should consider such a match, quite unthinkable that someone with your background and education and position in the Church should be considering marriage to a man like that.'

The Reverend Dr Ashley Underwood, chaplain to the Bishop of Clayton, made a supreme effort of self-control and told herself to try and keep calm and objective. She could, of course, have predicted what her mother's reaction to the news would be.

'I love him, Mother,' she replied simply.

Mrs Underwood responded with a scornful laugh. 'And what do you know of love?' she asked.

Ashley could have enquired of her mother the same question. She remembered only too well the loveless upbringing she had endured, the arguments, the acrimony and the simmering silences between her parents. She often found herself in the middle of this hostility, a child tugged one way or the other, always resisting her parents' demands to take sides. When her father had left, her mother became bitter and resentful, constantly complaining about the man who had deserted her for another woman and forced her out of their large house to live in 'a poky little flat', as she termed it. Ashley had felt miserable and unloved, believing that neither parent really cared about her. She tried to love her mother but it didn't work; she couldn't love her father for she never heard from him. And so she learnt to hide her feelings, conceal her thoughts. She threw herself into her studies, spending hours in the local library. The small, round-faced nun at the convent high school she attended recognised the talent in this quiet, unconfident, lonely girl. Under Sister Augusta Maria's guidance, Ashley blossomed academically, achieving outstanding results in her examinations and going on to study at Oxford before entering the Church. All her life she had lived with the pain of being a child not loved by her parents. It was ironic, she thought now, that her mother of all people should ask her what she knew about love.

'You made your feelings perfectly clear when I first told you I was seeing Emmet,' said Ashley, 'so it comes as no surprise that you do not approve, but I did think—'

Her mother held up a thin hand and cut her off. 'Did you imagine I would be giddy with excitement? Yes, you are quite right, I have made myself perfectly clear. I imagined that you would see sense. I told you what nobody else would, that seeing this . . . this man was a big mistake. It was my duty to do so. Can't you see how thoughtless you are being? Such a marriage could never work. You will be a laughing stock – a bishop's chaplain, an Anglican priest, consorting with an Irish gypsy.'

Ashley maintained a calm silence.

'It is quite unthinkable,' continued Mrs Underwood, 'that you would consider marrying a man who is so very different in upbringing, background, education and social class and, I should imagine, religion.'

'I love Emmet, Mother,' said her daughter evenly, 'and I am going to marry him.' She was minded to add, 'Can't you, just for once in your life, be happy for me?' but she resisted the temptation, knowing that it would lead to further acrimony.

'And to think of all I have done for you,' said her mother peevishly.

Ashley could have told her mother that she had done very little for her if truth be told. She had received no encouragement in her studies, no fulsome congratulations when she had brought home her glowing school reports. She still recalled the headmistress's comment that 'Here is a gifted student who sets the standard by which the remainder is judged.' She could have mentioned the fact that when she had been accepted on a scholarship to study at All Souls in Oxford, her mother could hardly bring herself to comment and hadn't even bothered to attend the degree ceremony. It had been Sister Augusta Maria who had sat amongst the families. Ashley, seeing her fellow students surrounded by proud and happy parents, had felt deeply her mother's decision not to attend.

'And what do you imagine the bishop will say when you tell him?' asked Mrs Underwood, breaking into her daughter's thoughts.

'Pardon?'

'I said what do you think the bishop's reaction will be when you drop this bombshell?'

'Actually, I think he will be pleased for me.'

Her mother snorted. 'Pleased for you!' she repeated. 'He will be speechless. I shouldn't wonder if you lost your position.'

'Well, we will see,' said Ashley. 'I have an appointment with the assistant bishop tomorrow afternoon.'

Mrs Underwood's eyes widened and her shoulders stiffened. 'You have always been stubborn, Ashley – just like your father. You were a difficult, self-willed girl,' she continued, addressing her daughter as one might a disobedient child, 'and you have not changed. You always wanted your own way. Any advice I might have offered was thrown back in my face.' Her voice suddenly became severe and cold. 'Well you must make your bed and lie in it. Clearly nothing I say will make you reconsider, but let me tell you this, if you go ahead with the marriage, I shall not come to the wedding, and your gypsy husband will not be welcome in my flat.' She turned her head away and closed her eyes as if in pain.

Tears blurred Ashley's eyes. 'I thought perhaps that you might have understood, Mother,' she said, 'but clearly you do not. I have to live my life as I see fit.'

'You have always lived your life as you have seen fit,' replied her mother. 'Nothing I have ever said has had any effect. If you decide to go ahead with this reckless course of action, then there is really nothing more to say.' Mrs Underwood rose regally from her chair. 'It might be better for both of us if you didn't call again, not for a while anyway.'

'Do you really mean that, Mother?' asked Ashley.

'I find your visits very trying.' Mrs Underwood massaged her forehead. 'We seem to do nothing but bicker.'

'If that is what you wish,' replied her daughter sadly.

Emmet O'Malley was a tall, broad-shouldered man with shining eyes and a face the colour of a russet apple. Dressed that evening in a smart shirt and tie and new jacket, he cut a very different figure from when he had first appeared in the village. With his young daughter Roisin he had arrived at Elisabeth's cottage over a year before, looking for somewhere to park his caravan. Then he had been wearing a thick, close-fitting jacket, shapeless corduroy trousers worn at the knees and heavy black boots that had seen better days. Around his neck wound a colourful kerchief, and a hooped earring was fastened to his

ear like a small gold manacle. With his mass of shiny black
curls he looked every inch like the illustration of a gypsy one
might see in a child's picture book.

Despite Mrs Sloughthwaite's persistent efforts to glean
information from Emmet when he first called into the village
store, he had said little about his past life, and it had remained
a mystery.

'Perhaps he's got something to hide,' Mrs Pocock, one of
the regular customers, had remarked to the shopkeeper.

'You mean some sort of secret that he doesn't want anyone
to know about?' the shopkeeper had said.

'If it is a secret, of course he wouldn't want people to know
about it, would he, otherwise it wouldn't be a secret,' the
customer had answered, shaking her head.

'It sounds quite romantic,' Mrs Sloughthwaite had remarked
reflectively. 'Something out of a novel – a handsome, dark-
haired traveller escaping his past who appears out of the blue
and falls in love—'

'Or escaping from the police, more like,' Mrs Pocock had
butted in. 'He could be on the run. There's obviously something dark and sinister in his past, something he's hiding.'

'Or maybe he's just a quiet man who likes to keep himself
to himself,' Mrs O'Connor, another customer, had remarked.

'Being Irish and quiet,' Mrs Pocock had snorted. 'That's a
contradiction in terms if ever I heard one.'

'I beg your pardon!' Mrs O'Connor had exclaimed. 'I
happen to be Irish.'

'Least said,' Mrs Pocock had replied.

'Well he seems a nice young man,' Mrs Sloughthwaite had
told her customers, 'and that little girl of his is a delightful
child.' She had made a note in her head to ask Roisin a few
questions when next she saw her. Children tended to be very
honest, she had thought, and she would soon discover Mr
O'Malley's secret, if there was a secret to discover.

Over the next few weeks, Emmet remained a mystery. This was how it had always been. He would stay in a place for a short time before moving on, making a living by doing odd jobs and evading any questions people might ask about his past life. After a few weeks in Barton-in-the-Dale, however, he knew that his travelling days were over. With its surrounding scattered conifer plantations, pale stone and pantile-roofed cottages and old walls of greenish-white limestone enclosing the solid Norman church, the village had a captivating quality about it. The villagers were friendly too, and there were plenty of odd jobs to be done. More importantly, his young daughter, who had sometimes had a difficult time in the past with her schooling, had settled in well at the village school and begged him to let them stay.

Then he was offered a job as a handyman-cum-gardener at Limebeck House, the imposing home of Lady Wadsworth, so he decided to put down roots. Emmet proved to be good-humoured, honest, hard-working and efficient, and before long, Lady Wadsworth was so impressed with his work that she made him her estate manager, and he and Roisin moved into the gate lodge. There was, of course, another, more pressing reason why he wished to stay, and that reason was Ashley Underwood.

For Emmet, it had been love at first sight. He had been smitten by this strikingly beautiful and gentle-natured woman when he had first met her at Limebeck House. She arrived on a bicycle, and after her meeting with Lady Wadsworth, she discovered that the machine had a punctured tyre. Emmet had mended it for her and they had struck up a conversation. They discovered that they both loved folk music. Later, at a folk concert with his daughter, Emmet had met Ashley again. On that occasion, as they sat by the river, he told her of his past life, how Rowena, Roisin's mother, had died giving birth to her and it was then that he had taken to the road with the baby. He had never spoken to anyone about this before. It was just that Ashley was so very easy to talk to, and he knew she was not the sort of person to repeat what he had told her to all and sundry.

She had listened fascinated as he described how Rowena's parents, scions of a landed Anglo-Irish family, had made it clear from the outset that they strongly disapproved of the association of their daughter with some sort of itinerant, fiddle-playing hippie, and wanted nothing to do with the man their daughter had taken up with. They hoped for a much better match for their only child. After several heated arguments, they had given her the ultimatum that should she continue with the relationship, she would not be welcome in their home. They would disown her. Rowena, always strong-minded, had been defiant and left. After she had died, Emmet called at Castle Morden, her parents' home, with the newborn baby in his arms, but was refused entry and turned away. Since then, he had had no contact with them.

Emmet's attraction to Ashley was reciprocated, for she fell for the softly spoken Irishman with the wide tanned face framed in its mass of black curls. And such eyes! Long-lashed, warm and dark. The relationship between the gypsy and the curate blossomed, and after a brief and secret courtship, he asked her to marry him.

Ashley had agreed to meet Emmet for a meal the evening after the strained conversation with her mother. He had chosen Le Bon Viveur, a smart French restaurant in Clayton, hoping that it would cheer her up after her ordeal. And, of course, he knew that it would be an ordeal, for Mrs Underwood had made it patently clear right from the start that she strongly disapproved of her daughter's relationship. Ashley had told Emmet of her mother's reaction when she had visited her some weeks before.

'I hope you are not forming some sort of attachment to this man,' she had said.

'What a strange turn of phrase that is,' her daughter had replied. 'Forming an attachment. It sounds as if I'm an extension to a house, or some sort of accessory.'

'Don't be silly, Ashley, you know perfectly well what I mean. Are you involved with this man? If you are, it is quite unthinkable that someone with your background and education and a position in the Church should be mixing with someone like that. What would people say?'

'I intend to continue to see him whether you like it or not,' Ashley had said defiantly.

'Headstrong,' her mother had admonished, her face as hard as her words. 'You have always been headstrong.'

Emmet knew that their relationship would, at the very least, cause some raised eyebrows, and sometimes wondered if they would be able to deal with the gossip and the comments. He felt in his heart that Ashley, beautiful, talented, highly educated, was too good for him. Would love be enough?

The owner of Le Bon Viveur, a lean, olive-skinned individual with glossy boot-black hair scraped back on his scalp and large blue-grey eyes, looked up from the small desk behind which he stood.

'*Bonsoir*,' he said, smiling and displaying a set of perfectly even and impressively white teeth. There was the whiff of expensive cologne.

'Good evening,' replied Emmet. 'I have a reservation for seven thirty.'

'And your name, *monsieur*?'

'O'Malley.'

The owner scanned the contents of a red leather-bound book on the desk. He ran a manicured finger down a list of names and nodded. '*Ah, oui.* A reservation for two.'

'That's right,' said Emmet. 'I'm meeting someone.'

Looking around at the elaborate decoration – the ornamen-tal vases, sparkling crystal chandeliers, thick red patterned carpet and walls displaying elegant paintings of exotic French scenes – he felt suddenly uncomfortable and out of place, and wished he had chosen somewhere less grand. He had never been in such a plush restaurant.

'Would you care to wait for your companion at the bar, *monsieur*, or go straight to your table?' he was asked.

'I'll wait at the table, thank you,' replied Emmet, feeling hot under his collar.

'Your table is ready, if you would like to follow me,' said the owner.

The table to which Emmet was shown was covered in a stiff white linen cloth and set with expensive white china plates edged in gold, starched napkins and heavy silver cutlery. There was a single red rose in a slender cut-glass vase.

It was with great relief that he saw Ashley entering the restaurant just as he was about to sit down. 'Ah, here is my friend now,' he said.

The owner sauntered over to Ashley. '*Bonsoir, madame,*' he said, smiling and displaying the set of white teeth. 'Your companion has already arrived.'

Emmet went to meet her, put his arm around her and kissed her lightly on the cheek.

'Thank goodness you're here,' he whispered. 'I feel like a fish out of water in this place.'

'It's lovely,' replied Ashley, taking his arm.

When they had sat down, Emmet leaned across the table and took her hand in his. 'So was it as bad as you thought it would be?'

She nodded. 'I'm afraid so, but it was to be expected.'

'I suppose she doesn't think I am good enough for you. I guess a lot of people will think that.' He sounded sad.

'You *are* good enough for me,' she replied, squeezing his hand, 'and that is all that counts.'

He smiled weakly. 'I love you so much,' he said.

'I know.'

The owner returned with the menu and the wine list. He flashed his teeth at Ashley again.

'Thank you,' said Emmet, taking the enormous leather-bound folders from the Frenchman's hand.

'Now perhaps you would like me to take you through what is on the menu this evening?' said the owner.

'I think we can manage, thank you,' answered Ashley.

'You speak French, *madame*?'

'*Un peu,*' replied Ashley.

'Is there no end to your talents?' Emmet asked her when the owner had departed.

'Schoolgirl French,' said Ashley, being rather economical with the truth.

'So what did your mother say?' he asked.

'I really don't want to talk about it,' said Ashley. 'I wish she could be happy for me, but it is not to be. Now let's enjoy the rest of the evening and forget about it.'

Emmet reached into his pocket and produced a small box. He passed it over the table. 'For you,' he said. 'I was going to wait until after the meal, but . . .'

She opened the box to find a gold ring in the form of two hands clasping a heart and surmounted by a crown. In the centre was a small emerald.

'Oh Emmet, it's lovely,' she said.

'It's a Claddagh ring,' he told her, 'a traditional Irish ring that symbolises love, loyalty and friendship.' He slipped it on her finger. 'The hands represent friendship, the heart represents love and the crown represents loyalty. When I become rich and famous, I'll buy you a big diamond ring.'

'I don't want a big diamond ring,' she replied softly. She reached for his hand and squeezed it. 'This is perfect.'

'I love you, Ashley Underwood,' he said. 'I love you more than I can say.'

The Right Reverend Charles Atticus, suffragan Bishop of Bilsdon, was not a handsome man in any conventional sense, but he had a thoughtful, intelligent face and kindly eyes. His calm, warm and attentive manner endeared him to all those with whom he came into contact. He had been the vicar of Barton-in-the Dale, where Ashley had been his curate, before his preferment to become the Venerable Archdeacon of Clayton. Recently (and much to his wife's delight), he had been elevated to become a bishop, albeit the assistant to the Bishop of Clayton.

It was a cold and sunless Saturday morning when Ashley was shown into the chilly sitting room at the suffragan bishop's residence. The snow, which had thawed overnight, had been replaced by a biting winter frost. Such a cold and gloomy atmosphere reflected her feelings as she crossed over to the window and stared out at the bleak garden. In summer it would no doubt be bursting with life and colour, but it now seemed cheerless, the pond frozen over, drifts of fallen leaves heaped in icy piles and the great copper beech trees with their thick grizzled trunks dark and leafless. A clamouring flock of rooks cawed noisily in the empty grey sky.

Ashley had been summoned to see the bishop and had a gloomy presentiment that the interview would not be a happy one.

'It is so very good to see you, my dear,' said the bishop, striding into the room and smiling widely. He shook her hand vigorously. 'Do make yourself comfortable.' He gestured to a chair. 'I am sure you would welcome a cup of tea.'

'No thank you, Bishop,' replied Ashley. 'I'm taking a service later today and can't stay long.'

'Oh please, let's dispense with the "Bishop", at least in my own home. I've known you long enough for you to call me Charles. I hope you have time to stay and see Marcia. My wife is very keen to catch up on things with you.'

Ashley was cheered by the bishop's bright and welcoming manner, but it was short-lived.

The bishop sat down in a large leather armchair, rested his hands on his lap and looked thoughtful. 'Such a pleasure to see you,' he said at last.

'How is Marcia?' asked Ashley.

'Oh, she is in her element, still teaching art at the junior school here in Clayton. Mr Steel, the school inspector, suggested she should be trying for a deputy headship – she's acting deputy head at the moment, you know – but she feels she needs a few more years' experience in the senior management post before embarking on that. Actually, the school has had a pretty unfortunate time lately, concerning a supply teacher, an infant and a length of masking tape. You might have read about it in the papers.'

'No, I'm afraid not, but it sounds intriguing.'

'Well, I'll let Marcia tell you about it,' he said. 'It was quite a carry-on.' There was a silence. The bishop rubbed his chin and looked as if he was about to broach some sensitive issue.

'And how are you liking your new role?' asked Ashley.

'To be frank, it's less onerous than when I was the archdeacon, or as Mrs Sloughthwaite used to say, "the archdemon".' He gave a small laugh. 'Anyway, I have not invited you here to talk about Marcia or myself. I wish to speak to you on a matter of some import.'

'Well here I am,' said Ashley apprehensively.

The bishop coughed. 'I wanted to see if you had heard the rumours.'

Ashley's heart fluttered like a caged bird. So her relationship with Emmet was now common gossip. 'Rumours?' she repeated.

'In the village. I don't know whether or not they have reached you yet.'

'No, they haven't.'

'Well, when I heard what was being said, and then when I discovered for myself the veracity of these rumours, I have to admit it came as quite a shock. I think in common parlance the phrase is "gobsmacked".'

'Really?'

'Of course, having lived in Barton for many years, I can quite see how tittle-tattle travels so speedily.'

'Did these rumours concern me?' asked Ashley.

'In a way they do have implications for you and could very well affect your position as chaplain to the Bishop of Clayton.'

'In what way?'

'Let me explain—' began the bishop.

'Charles,' interrupted Ashley. 'I love him and I want to marry him and nobody will change my mind, not my mother and not you.'

'Marry him!' exclaimed the bishop. 'That is quite out of the question.'

'Why?' asked Ashley, tears pricking the corners of her eyes. 'Why is it out of the question when two people love each other? I thought that you of all people would understand.'

'But you cannot marry him!' cried the bishop.

'Why?'

'Well, for a start, you have very little in common. His views are very different from your own. Indeed, you have not seen eye to eye with him since he moved to Barton.'

'But that's not true!' cried Ashley.

'I was led to believe that you didn't get on,' said the bishop, looking mystified. 'Anyway, and most importantly, he's a married man and has four children.'

'His wife is dead.'

'But I spoke to her yesterday. Mrs Sparshott was in the best of health.'

'Mrs Sparshott? What has Mrs Sparshott to do with it?'

'I think we have a few crossed wires here, Ashley,' said the bishop. 'Let me start again. There were rumours abroad that the vicar of Barton was intending to leave. These rumours turned out to be true. Mr Sparshott came to see me a week ago to inform me that, after careful consideration, he was resigning from his post as the incumbent of Barton-in-the-Dale. As you are aware, having continued to act as the curate at St Christopher's when I left, he does not exactly relate well to his parishioners.' The bishop, a tactful and sympathetic man, failed to mention that there had been numerous complaints about the vicar. 'Mr Sparshott feels he is unsuitable for the position. He is not a bad man, you know. He is a straight-talking and dedicated priest with strong, uncompromising views that have not gone down too well with his congregation. Village life does not appear to suit him or his wife. Anyway, he has decided that he wants more of a challenge and has decided to undertake missionary work. He intends to take further training in Durham before departing to Africa. So there it is.'

'So the rumours were about Mr Sparshott leaving?' said Ashley.

'Indeed,' answered the bishop. 'I gather one of the parishioners who cleans the church overheard a conversation and mentioned it to Mrs Sloughthwaite in the village store. This, of course, meant the whole of the village soon got to know. I am surprised that the rumours never reached your ears.'

'No, I was unaware,' said Ashley.

'Of course, this means there will be a vacancy at St Christopher's. Mr Sparshott suggested that you might become the vicar there. I know that when you were his curate, you did not see eye to eye on certain matters, but despite his unfortunate manner, he is a good-hearted man with a deep biblical learning and a steadfast belief. He also recognises your undoubted talents and felt there would be no one better suited to become his successor. I have to say that I agree with him. Of course, if you were to consider this position, it would mean giving up your role as the bishop's chaplain.'

Ashley took a handkerchief from her handbag and dabbed her eyes.

'I'm so sorry,' said the bishop, rising from his chair. He rested a hand on Ashley's. 'I didn't imagine that you would take this so hard.'

'I thought the rumours were about me,' she said, sniffing.

'About you? In what way?' asked the bishop.

'That I am to marry. Emmet O'Malley and I are engaged. I imagined that you might disapprove.'

The bishop clapped his long hands together.

'Disapprove? My dear Ashley, I think it is wonderful!' he cried. 'I couldn't be more delighted. I must tell Marcia. You know, she had an inkling when Mr O'Malley drove you home after the concert in Clayton. "You mark my words," she said, "something is going on between those two." ' He rushed to the door, flung it open with a flourish and shouted, 'Marcia! Marcia! Would you come here, my dear, I have some splendid news.'

# 4

The full governing body of Barton-with-Urebank school convened in the staffroom for the first meeting of the new term. Those present were the chairman, Major C. J. Neville-Gravitas, Royal Engineers (retd); Mrs Stirling, the head teacher; Mrs Cosgrove, the parent governor; the Reverend Dr Ashley Underwood, co-opted governor; Lady Helen Wadsworth, the foundation governor; Mrs Robertshaw, the teacher governor, and Councillor Wayne Cooper, the Local Education Authority representative. Mr Nettles, the education officer, representing the Director of Education, was there in his capacity of adviser.

It was a motley group by any standards: the major red-cheeked and watery-eyed, with a bristly moustache and short-cropped hair shooting up from his square head; Ashley Underwood blessed with the deepest of blue eyes, the fairest of complexions and a soft mass of golden hair; Mrs Cosgrove a small, loud, bustling woman whose dark eyes were magnified alarmingly behind thick-lensed glasses; Lady Helen Wadsworth, the imperious grande dame of Barton, an extraordinary-looking woman with hair the colour of brown boot polish, heavy-lidded eyes and a sharp nose, slightly hooked at the end; Mr Nettles a tubby man with thick straw-coloured hair sticking up from his head like tufts of dry grass and wearing small steel-rimmed spectacles; Councillor Cooper a remarkably thin individual who sported a shock of frizzy ginger hair; and Elsie Robertshaw in a brightly coloured floral dress and shapeless brown cardigan.

'Before we look at the agenda,' announced the major, stroking his moustache, 'perhaps I might call upon the head teacher
to give us a run-down of how things are going so far.'

'Of course,' replied Elisabeth. 'Well, the term has started off
very well. We have had an increase in the number of pupils,
the part-time cleaner, Mrs Massey, started this week and—'

'Is this Mrs Massey related to Fred Massey?' interrupted
the major.

'Yes, it's his niece-in-law,' answered Elisabeth.

Fred Massey, a local farmer, was a parsimonious, ill-
tempered old man, disliked by all in the village, for he rarely
had a good word to say about anyone, constantly moaned
about how badly done-to he was and never missed the opportunity of telling all and sundry about his catalogue of ailments.
With his shabby clothes, old boots and unshaven face, he
looked like a penniless vagrant. However, Fred Massey was
far from penniless; he was shrewd, sharp-eyed and opportun-
istic, and he had a tidy sum squirrelled away. He never missed
an opportunity to make money, and often with the least
amount of effort. Most of the work on his smallholding, where
he kept cattle and a few sheep, and the odd jobs that came his
way in the village – repairing walls, pruning trees, killing
vermin, clearing blocked drains – he delegated to his long-
suffering nephew Clarence, who lived at Tanfield Farm with
his wife Bianca and their baby son.

'Well I hope she's a bit more diligent than her uncle-in-law,'
said the major. 'He's a miserable, lazy, good-for-nothing
individual.'

'You're right there,' agreed Mrs Cosgrove. 'The mess his
cattle make on the high street is nobody's business,' she stated
angrily.

'Well, Mrs Massey is doing very well,' said Elisabeth. 'She's
punctual, hard-working and good-natured.'

'I know Bianca,' said Ashley, 'and she's a pleasant young woman.'

Mr Nettles glanced at his watch. 'Might we move on, Mr Chairman?' he said.

'Ah yes,' said the major.

'So, as I was saying,' Elisabeth continued, 'there have been three new additions to the pupils on roll, the part-time cleaner has made an excellent start, and Mr Thomas Dwyer, a new member of staff, has replaced Mr Jolly. Mr Dwyer was formerly a professional footballer, but after a series of injuries he has given up his footballing career and now wishes to become a teacher. He took an Open University degree, studying part-time, and is now training here at the school with supervision given by the university. He has taken over Mr Jolly's lower junior class and already he's made a very favourable impression, relating well to the pupils and the staff. He seems a keen and agreeable young man, and—'

'An Open University degree?' interrupted Mr Nettles. 'Some might be of the view that such a degree is not as demanding and rigorous as one gained through full-time study at a proper university.'

'Well they would be mistaken in such a view,' said Elisabeth. 'I should point out that the Open University is a proper university and the degrees it confers are every bit as demanding and rigorous as any others, perhaps more so.'

'I think it is very commendable,' said Lady Wadsworth, 'for someone to study for a degree and hold down a job at the same time. It shows determination and ambition.'

'If one were to believe being a footballer a proper job,' remarked Mr Nettles condescendingly.

'So what sort of degree have you got?' asked Mrs Cosgrove curtly and, with folded arms, turned to face the education officer.

Mr Nettles gave a small cough. 'Actually I don't possess a degree,' he replied.

'Then you're not in any position to comment on them what do have one, are you?' she demanded.

'Perhaps, Mr Nettles,' added Lady Wadsworth, allowing herself a small wry smile, 'you might consider studying for an Open University degree yourself and then you would see how demanding and rigorous it is.'

'Let us move on,' said the major, keen to get away. He had a golf club dinner that evening.

'Could I ask, Elisabeth,' said Ashley, 'how Robbie Hardy is getting on?' She had met this angry and demanding little boy several times, and often wondered how he was coping in school.

'Ah yes,' sighed the major. 'That wayward young man. Quite a handful, by all accounts.'

'I am pleased to say,' said Elisabeth, 'that there has been a real change for the better in Robbie.' She thought for a moment of the small twig of a boy with the shiny chestnut-brown hair cropped as close as a doormat, the pale freckled face and small upturned nose. She recalled how difficult and challenging the boy had been when he had first started at the school the previous year, how uncooperative and rude. Robbie had been expelled from the neighbouring school, where he had been deemed unteachable. Elisabeth had agreed to accept him. Her philosophy was such that she believed that no child should be written off, and that with time, perseverance and firm handling, the boy's behaviour would improve. Mrs Robertshaw and Mr Jolly, her former colleague, had taken some convincing.

'Robbie is without doubt a problematic child,' she had explained to them at the staff meeting at the beginning of the previous term. 'He's a disturbed, troublesome, unhappy boy with a feeling of being unloved, and has had a great deal to put up with. From what I can gather, his stepfather had little time for him – he used to hit him and verbally abuse him – and Robbie's mother appears a sad and weak character who does exactly what her husband tells her to do. It is no surprise that the boy is mixed up.'

Robbie's conduct had improved greatly over the weeks he had been in the school. Elisabeth's careful and sympathetic treatment of him had borne fruit, and when the child was taken away from his grim home environment and placed with experienced, kindly and supportive foster carers, he became less angry and resentful and started to settle down and behave himself.

'I do like happy endings,' said Ashley now. 'You and the staff should be congratulated, Elisabeth, on giving Robbie a chance and making such a difference in his life.'

'He can, I guess, still be a bit of a handful,' admitted Elisabeth, 'but so far this term he has kept out of trouble.'

'I have to say, Mrs Stirling,' said the education officer, 'that although of course I am pleased to hear that the boy seems to be behaving himself, this might be the lull before the storm. You might find that he shows his true colours before long. In my opinion, kids like this boy are better catered for in a special school, one for those with behavioural problems.'

'He is not an animal,' said Mrs Robertshaw angrily. 'A kid is a baby goat, unless I am mistaken. They are children, not kids, and as far as your comment is concerned, I find it very cynical. I might have agreed with you that Robbie needed to be in a special school when he started here, but Mrs Stirling and the child's teacher, Mr Hornchurch, have worked wonders and deserve thanks, not some dire warning.'

'Let's not pursue this,' said the major. 'We have much to get through. Now, let's look at the agenda.' He consulted the papers on his knee. 'The first item we have been asked to consider is policy documents. We have been asked—'

'Directed, Mr Chairman,' corrected the education officer, clearly unchastened by Mrs Robertshaw's comment.

'What?' snapped Major Neville-Gravitas.

'It is a statutory requirement,' explained Mr Nettles. 'All schools are required to have a raft of policies in place. This is a directive.'

'If I might be allowed to finish,' said the major, clearly irritated at being interrupted. He coughed and continued. 'We have been asked,' he stressed the word, 'by the Director of Education to ensure that the school has the appropriate policies for a whole number of subjects.' He breathed out noisily through his teeth. 'I have to say that these directives seem to come over the Yorkshire Dales like the Plagues of Egypt, and I cannot see the point of some of them.' He ran his finger down a list. 'I can understand why we need to have anti-bullying procedures, health and safety measures and a policy on school trips, but I can't for the life of me see why we need to have a policy on sex education. In my opinion there is a time and a place for everything. I do not feel that it is the time for junior-aged children to learn about sex, and Barton-with-Urebank Primary School is not the place for them to hear about it.'

'Mr Chairman—' began the education officer.

'I agree,' cut in Mrs Cosgrove, the parent governor. 'Why in the world do children need to know about that sort of thing? It will give them ideas. Teaching them about it only encourages them to do it. I certainly don't want my Barnabas and Paige to learn about sex. They see enough of it on the television without having it pushed down their throats at school.'

'It's not a question of pushing it down throats,' said Mr Nettles.

Mrs Cosgrove ignored his interjection.

'I mean,' she continued, 'I knew nothing about sex when I was at school and it never did me any harm. I didn't know what a homosexual was until I married my husband.'

Elisabeth smiled and decided not to enter the discussion for the time being. She was enjoying the exchange.

'No, it was a different age,' said Lady Wadsworth. 'We were very naive and innocent as children, and kept very firmly in the dark about such matters. The "facts of life" when I was growing up was something of a soiled phrase. No one ever talked about it. Perhaps they should have.'

'If I might—' began Mr Nettles.

Lady Wadsworth was not at all used to being interrupted and carried on regardless.

'When my dear brother, who was killed in the last war, God rest his soul, was seven, he asked our father the question curious children frequently ask of their parents: "Where do I come from?" He related the encounter to me when we were adults. My father took him into his study and spent an inordinate amount of time explaining how babies come into the world. "So does that explain where you come from?" he asked. "No," replied my brother simply. "I just wanted to know where I come from. Sebastian, my friend at school, comes from Harrogate." How we laughed.'

'Thank you, Lady Wadsworth,' said the major, stroking his moustache and giving a small smile. 'Most amusing, but we really must press on and discuss the matter in hand.'

'If I might come in here—' began Mr Nettles again.

'I do think it is very important for the older children in the school to know about sexual and related matters,' announced Elisabeth, casting a glance in Mrs Robertshaw's direction. She was thinking of the earlier discussion they had had in the staffroom. 'Unless things are explained clearly and fully and without embarrassment, young people most likely will get the wrong end of the stick. Having said that, I think it is best left to someone with the appropriate knowledge and expertise to speak to the children about such matters. I do know that some teachers,' again she glanced at Mrs Robertshaw, 'might be uncomfortable about broaching the subject.'

'I think children should be told the facts of life early on, with no shilly-shallying,' said Lady Wadsworth. 'Telling them that they were born under a gooseberry bush or delivered by a stork is just plain silly.'

'The thing is—' started Mr Nettles, trying again.

'I think you are right,' agreed Councillor Cooper, nodding enthusiastically. 'When I was at school, I learnt about sex in the playground from the other boys, who knew no more than I did and merely bluffed. There were all sorts of weird and wonderful misconceptions. I was told by one boy, whose sister was expecting a baby, that she became pregnant just through having a bath after the lodger.'

'If I might come in here?' asked Mr Nettles in a piping voice.

'I remember hearing someone at school say that a girl in the class above us was in the pudding club,' said Mrs Cosgrove. 'I had no idea what it meant and asked my mother if I could join this pudding club. I was very partial to spotted dick and bread and butter pudding. My mother told me she'd wash my mouth out with carbolic soap and water if I ever said that again. I had no idea that what I'd said was wrong.'

'That proves my point exactly,' said Councillor Cooper. 'Children should have things explained to them early on.'

'Young girls getting pregnant outside marriage is one of the results of the permissive society in which we live,' stated the major with his usual smug self-righteousness. 'I know full well from my work as a magistrate that there are a growing number of unmarried young women getting pregnant and then falling on the resources of the state to provide them with housing and any number of benefits. The youth of today don't seem to have any moral sense.'

'I think you are being a little hard on the younger genera-tion, Mr Chairman,' said Ashley. 'I feel very optimistic about the young. There are a lot of decent and principled young-sters out there, though it has been ever thus that one genera-tion is always critical of the one that comes after it.'

'I beg to differ here, Dr Underwood,' replied the major. 'I think that moral standards have declined. It was considered a disgrace in my day for a woman to have a child out of wedlock. Nowadays it seems to be the done thing. I think the less young people know about sex the better.'

'Really, Major,' said Elisabeth, 'you surely can't blame underage pregnancies on sex education? Perhaps if these girls were taught about how babies happen, they wouldn't get pregnant.'

'Well I'm not so sure about that,' voiced the major. 'Telling them how to do it might very well encourage them.'

Lady Wadsworth responded with a curt laugh. 'If young people knew about sex,' she said, 'and how to take precautions, then there would not be all these teenage pregnancies that you talk about.'

'This directive—' began Mr Nettles impatiently, endeavouring once again to get a word in.

'Well in my view, if children were kept in the dark a bit longer,' announced Mrs Cosgrove with a disapproving intonation in her voice, 'these girls wouldn't know what to do and they wouldn't get pregnant. I recall when I was a teenager, we girls were told by our teacher Miss Percival not to do it, we were told by the vicar not to do it and we were told by the headmistress where not to do it.'

'I don't see why this discussion centres on girls,' said Mrs Robertshaw. 'What about boys? They have some responsibility in this – in my view much more than girls, of whom they take advantage. Girls don't get pregnant by themselves.'

Mr Nettles produced a large handkerchief and blew his nose with a loud trumpeting sound. This had the effect of silencing the governors, who all turned their faces in his direction. At last he was able to speak.

'Mr Chairman,' he said sonorously, scratching a tuft of hair, 'the government is now insisting on guidelines on sex education, which all schools will be required, by law, to include on the curriculum. England has one of the highest rates of unwanted pregnancies in Europe, and this initiative, amongst other things, aims to warn youngsters of the dangers of unprotected sex and the looming menace of STDs.'

'The looming menace of what?' asked Mrs Cosgrove.

'Sexually transmitted diseases,' explained the education officer.

'A cousin of mine was a bishop of some distant outpost of the Empire,' said Lady Wadsworth, off on a tangent again, 'and he had the letters STD after his name. He was a Doctor of Sacred Theology. I guess he would be rather chary about appending that abbreviation now.' She chuckled.

'That's very interesting,' said the major despairingly, massaging his brow. He was wearying of the endless discussion and could see the meeting dragging on into the evening unless he took firm control.

'There is a portrait of General Sir Leon Wadsworth in the library at Limebeck House,' continued Lady Wadsworth, 'and he has the letters VD after his name. It is, I am reliably informed, the abbreviation for Victorian Decoration. Mind you, old Sir Leon did have something of a reputation with the ladies when he served in India, so—'

'Mr Chairman,' the education officer cut in loudly, 'could we please move on?'

Elisabeth had remained largely quiet and continued to enjoy the entertaining, if irrelevant, discussion, for the school had most of the policies in place already. She would soon feel it appropriate to tell everyone this, but for the moment she sat back, in particular relishing the discomfiture of the education officer. She had little time for Mr Nettles, for he was a man with an inflated idea of his own capacities and blessed with the ability to appear to be very busy whilst actually avoiding much of the work for which he was responsible. He also liked the sound of his own voice. In her dealings with him, he had proved to be evasive and ineffectual.

'I was in the middle of a sentence, young man,' retorted Lady Wadsworth. 'It is most discourteous to interrupt.'

Mr Nettles, getting increasingly hot under the collar, sighed.

'This discussion,' he said, 'albeit interesting, is academic in that the Education Department requires, under the law, I repeat, for all schools to have a sex education policy. As I have endeavoured to explain, it is a statutory requirement. I am prepared to work with the school to produce such a document and—'

Elisabeth interposed smoothly. She had a mischievous light in her eye. 'That won't be necessary, Mr Nettles,' she said. 'We already have all the policies on this list in place, except for the one on sex education, which is in draft. When I have consulted the staff, I shall present it to the governors for their approval.'

'Well that's settled then,' said the major. 'Let's wait until we see the policy.' He consulted the papers on his knee again, shook his head and breathed out noisily. 'Now, the next item on the agenda is dog excrement on school premises. We've been asked,' he stressed the word again, 'by the Education Department to complete a three-page questionnaire asking for details about dog waste: the frequency, size, condition, location, et cetera.' He looked accusingly at Mr Nettles. 'Don't you people have anything better to do than produce ridiculous time-wasting documents like this?' He waved the paper. 'What stupid person is behind such nonsense as this?'

'Well actually, Major,' said the education officer sheepishly, 'I compiled the questionnaire. We have been getting complaints about dogs fouling school fields and we felt it important to ascertain the extent of the problem.'

'And what about the mess Fred Massey's cattle make?' asked Mrs Cosgrove. 'He takes his cows down the high street, leaving behind great splats of manure. It's a good job it's not summer, or the smell would be intolerable.'

'We are not discussing Mr Massey's cattle,' the major told her.

'Yes, well something's got to be done about it,' persisted the parent governor. 'You're on the parish council, Major Gravitas. You need to sort that out.'

'Oh dear,' sighed the major, massaging his brow again. 'I will raise it at the next parish council meeting. Now let's get back to the dog excrement.'

'I'd rather not, if you don't mind,' said Mrs Robertshaw, pulling a face. 'I've heard quite enough about it.'

'When I take Gordon, my Border terrier, out for his constitutional,' remarked Lady Wadsworth, 'I always pick up his little parcels with a plastic bag that I take along with me for the eventuality.'

'You'd need a pretty big bag to do that with Fred Massey's cattle,' said Mrs Cosgrove.

Elisabeth could see this discussion was getting nowhere. 'Dog waste is a concern,' she said, 'for it is not only an environmental pollutant but also a health hazard, so the problem has to be addressed.'

'Thank you, Mrs Stirling,' said the education officer, feeling vindicated.

'However,' she continued, 'at this school we have addressed it. Mr Gribbon, the caretaker, checks around the premises and on the fields each morning and after school.'

'Good,' said the major, 'so we can dispense with this.' He slid the questionnaire in Mr Nettle's direction.

'I would be grateful if it could be completed,' said the education officer.

'Is it a directive?' asked the major. 'Is it a statutory requirement? Do we have to complete it by law?'

'Well, no, but—'

'Then we don't need to do it,' the major told him. 'Let's move on. The next item on the agenda . . .' He paused and looked heavenwards. 'Oh for goodness' sake, it's another bloody directive – this time about nits!'

The figure waited behind the huge oak tree at the front of the school until he saw Elisabeth drive out of the entrance, then he entered the building and found his way down the silent corridor to the office. Mrs Scrimshaw was putting on her coat ready to go home when she was confronted by the man. He was a heavy-set individual with a wide square face, heavy rounded shoulders and a thick neck.

She felt ill at ease alone in the empty school with this intimidating figure, who blocked the office door. A shiver of fear ran through her as he entered the room and stood before her. 'May I help you?' she asked, attempting to sound confident.

'I 'opes so,' replied the man. 'I'm 'ere to see Missis Stirling.' He knew of course that Elisabeth had left. He realised that, like the social worker he had been to see earlier that day, the head teacher would not be coerced into giving him the information he wanted. However, the school secretary just might.

'Well I'm afraid you've just missed her,' said Mrs Scrimshaw, moving back behind her desk. She picked up a staple gun.

'Pity.'

'Perhaps you might like to make an appointment to see her.'

The man ignored the invitation. 'I'm Robin Banks's stepfather,' he said.

'Actually his name is now Robin Hardy,' Mrs Scrimshaw told him. 'He's gone back to his original name.'

''As 'e now?' The man stared at her for a moment with a smile on his lips. It was not a pleasant smile. 'Thing is,' he said, 'I just wants to know 'ow t'lad's gettin' on.'

'Well you would have to speak to Mrs Stirling about that,' said Mrs Scrimshaw. 'I'm not in a position to say.'

'Robin's bein' fostered, I 'ear.'

'Yes, I believe he is.'

'You wouldn't 'appen to know who by?' asked Banks. 'It's just that I'd like to see 'ow t'lad's settlin' in.'

'As I have informed you, I'm afraid I can't give you that information,' said the secretary. 'It's confidential.'

'Even when it's 'is stepfather who's askin'?' He leaned over the desk. 'I only wants to know where t'lad's livin'.'

'Well, as I've said, I can't divulge that sort of information. You would have to see the head teacher. Now, if you would excuse me, I need to get off home.' She was still gripping the staple gun.

The man nodded. 'OK,' he said and ambled off.

Mrs Scrimshaw sighed with relief. She put the staple gun in her desk drawer. Mr Gribbon was supposed to lock the main doors when the staff and children had gone home. She determined to have a sharp word with him the following day.

Banks waited out of sight until he saw the school secretary head off down the path, then went back into the building and wandered around the school. Hearing the jangling of keys, he headed in the direction of the sound and found Mr Gribbon locking the classroom doors.

'Ey up!' said Banks, coming up behind the caretaker.

Mr Gribbon jumped as if he had been drenched in a bucket of icy water. 'Blood and sand!' he cried. He turned to face the man.

'Sorry, mate,' said Banks. 'I didn't mean to scare yer.'

Mr Gribbon, like the secretary, was unsettled by the daunting appearance of the figure. 'C-can I help you?' he stuttered.

'I 'opes so. My name's Banks. I'm Robin Banks's stepfather.'

'Oh yes,' Mr Gribbon replied timidly.

'I've been away workin'. I called in to see how t'lad's gettin' on.'

'V-very well. 'E's a very w-w-well-behaved boy.'

'Dun't sound like our Robin to me,' said the man. "'E's a right little bugger at t'best o' times. I'm telled 'e's bein' fostered.'

'Y-yes, I believe so,' said the caretaker.

'You wouldn't 'appen to know where, by any chance?'

'N-n-no.'

'You're sure about that, are you?' There was a subtle threat in Banks's voice. He positioned his face disconcertingly close to the caretaker's. Mr Gribbon could smell the alcohol on the man's breath. 'It's just that I'd like to go an' see t'lad an' meet the folks who are lookin' after 'im.'

'He's living with a farmer and his wife, I believe,' said Mr Gribbon, 'somewhere at the other side of Clayton. It's a pig farm. That's all I know.'

The man leaned forward, his face now only a couple of inches from the caretaker's. He patted him on the shoulder. 'Tha's been very 'elpful, mate,' he said. 'Very 'elpful.'

'I hope you didn't tell him anything,' said Mrs Scrimshaw to the caretaker the following morning. She had gone in search of Mr Gribbon to complain about his carelessness in not locking the doors at the school entrance, and had been told that he too had been accosted by Robbie's stepfather.

'N-no . . . no, of course I didn't tell him anything,' the caretaker lied. 'What do you take me for? I showed him the door.'

'So you didn't tell him where the boy was living?' she asked.

'What could I have told him? I don't know where the lad lives.'

'Well it's just as well you didn't,' said the secretary, 'because Mrs Stirling would not have been best pleased if you had.' Then she went to report Mr Banks's unwelcome visit to Elisabeth.

# 5

The Reverend Algernon Sparshott, vicar of Barton-in-the-Dale, was not a man who possessed the social skills of those who could speak easily to people. He appeared a strait-laced, self-important and humourless man of uncompromising views, which he was not afraid of expressing. His sermons were of the hellfire-and-damnation kind, and were not well received by the rather sleepy, complacent congregation at St Christopher's. His lack of cordiality and his forthright views had held him back in preferment within the Church; however, the bishop, a generous-natured man, had decided to support him when he applied for the position of vicar at Barton-in-the Dale, vacated when Mr Atticus was elevated to archdeacon. The bishop felt that the cleric, after many years of loyal service, deserved to be given the chance of running his own parish. But sadly, things had not worked out, and life had not been trouble-free for Mr Sparshott. Church attendance had declined, the organist and two churchwardens had left and the bishop had received numerous complaints about this dour, distant and fervent cleric.

The presence of the curate at St Christopher's had not made things any easier. The Reverend Dr Ashley Underwood was so different from the vicar in every way. Mr Sparshott was an unfortunate-looking man: tall and thin, with straight, colourless hair and large pale eyes set wide apart. There was frequently an expression of extreme sanctity on his narrow, bony face. Ashley Underwood, by contrast, was a strikingly beautiful woman, personable, highly intelligent and also very popular in the village. More important than the disparity in their appearance was the fact that they did not agree on many matters relating to the Church. Mr Sparshott, of Low Church persuasion, preferred a plain building devoid of statues and crosses. He favoured a simple service with quiet periods for prayer and contemplation, traditional hymns, readings from the King James Bible and long, moralistic sermons. Ashley liked something altogether more modern: lively contemporary hymns, the Good News Bible and short, uplifting homilies. Their differences could not be reconciled, and so, when the opportunity arose, she had left to become the bishop's chaplain. Her departure was another sore point with the villagers, who blamed the vicar for driving her away.

There was one person in the village, however, who liked the vicar and who had discovered that underneath the carapace of apparent coldness and pomposity was a shy and thoughtful person and at heart a kindly man. This was young Danny Stainthorpe. Danny, a friendly and confident boy of eleven, was a country lad through and through, with a healthy brown complexion, a mop of dusty blonde hair and the bright brown eyes of a fox. Everyone in the village liked this sunny-natured and helpful boy, who seemed to have a permanent smile on his face.

Danny had not always been a happy child. He had lived with his grandfather in a caravan parked in the neighbouring field to Elisabeth's cottage. His father had disappeared before he was born and his mother was killed when he was a baby. He had been raised by his grandfather, and the pair had been inseparable. Soon after Elisabeth had started as head teacher at the village school, the old man had become ill, and after a brief spell in hospital, he had died, leaving Danny alone and grief-stricken. The boy had become confused and anxious, not knowing what would become of him and the once lively and sociable lad grew withdrawn and miserable. However, things had turned out for the best when he was fostered by Dr Stirling, who was currently, along with his new wife, in the process of adopting the boy and rearing him at Clumber Lodge along with James, his own son by his first marriage. Danny was now back to his old self, chatty and cheerful.

Danny had first met Mr Sparshott when he was tidying his grandfather's grave in the churchyard. The vicar immediately took a liking to this polite and helpful boy, and they had struck up a friendship. Danny, who loved the outdoors, became a regular visitor to the churchyard, cutting the grass, weeding and pruning, planting flowers and cleaning the gravestones. As a thank you, the vicar would take him on fishing trips, and as they sat on the riverbank, they chattered. The clergyman found the boy an interested listener, someone he could talk to and share his thoughts and feelings with. How different he found Danny compared with his own two sons. They were away at a prestigious public school and had become moody and demanding, clearly embarrassed by what they considered to be their lowly background, refusing their father's invitation to ask some of their friends to stay during the holidays.

Saturday morning found Danny busy shovelling snow from the path leading to the church. He was dressed in an old waxed jacket frayed at the collar and a woolly hat that had belonged to his grandfather, shapeless corduroy trousers and wellington boots turned down at the top that were a couple of sizes too big for him. He looked a comical figure, puffing and blowing, his face red with the exertion and the cold.

'Hard at work, I see,' said Mr Sparshott, approaching him.

'Ey up, Mester Sparshott,' said the boy cheerfully. 'If tha dunt keep this path clear, the'd be a few brokken bones tomorra when they all come to church.'

The vicar paused for a moment. All come to church? It would be a small congregation indeed on such a cold, cheerless Sunday, he thought.

'It's good of you to do this, Daniel,' he said. 'I meant to do it myself this afternoon.'

'It's no bother. I like being in t'outdoors. Can't stand bein' cooped up.' The boy looked up at the grey sky and sucked in his bottom lip. 'I thowt we'd seen t'back o' this snow, but there was a reight fall last neet. I were watching from mi winder. Gret flakes o' snow fell like goose feathers an' all of t'garden were like one gret sea o' white. It were an 'andsome sight.'

'You're very observant, Daniel,' said the vicar, smiling. 'I think I've said to you before that you're quite the poet.'

'Mi grandad used to say that most people look at everythin' an' see nowt,' replied Danny. 'They just don't see all t'beauty what's around 'em.'

'A wise man,' said Mr Sparshott. ' "A poor life this if, full of care, we have no time to stand and stare." A favourite poet of mine wrote that, Daniel. Now don't you stay out here too long.'

The boy rested on his spade. 'Mester Sparshott, before you go, can I ask thee summat?'

'Yes, of course.'

'Are tha leavin'?'

'News travels fast, Daniel. Where did you hear that?'

'Missis Sloughthwaite's been tellin' folk. Mi grandad used to say she's like t'jungle telegraph. 'E used to say that when tha went in t'shop, it were more of an interrogation than a conversation, an' if tha wanted owt spreadin' then tha should tell Mrs S. There's nowt she misses. Mi grandad used to say she could hear a feather falling on a piece of cotton wool. Is she reight that tha's leavin'?'

'Yes, she is.'

'I'm reight sorry abaat that. Who'll tek me fishin' when tha's gone?'

'I'm sure you'll find someone.'

'Why are tha leavin'?' asked the boy.

'Pastures new, Danny.'

'Pardon?'

'I'm going to Africa.'

'Africa!' exclaimed Danny. 'Blimey!'

'It's what I've always wanted to do, and now I have the chance,' the vicar told him.

'Well, as I said, I'll be sorry to see thee go. I'll miss thee.'

'Thank you, Daniel,' said the vicar, suddenly moved. There would be few others in Barton-in-the-Dale who would miss him, he thought.

'Course you'll not be bothered wi' all this blinkin' snow out theer in Africa, will tha? Tha berrer watch out for t'lions.'

'No, I won't see any snow,' said Mr Sparshott, feeling unaccountably sad. He would miss the boy's bright, affable nature. Never had he met a child with a more ready smile. 'And I'll watch out for the lions.'

'Mester Sparshott,' said Danny. 'Could I ask you summat else?'

'Yes, of course, Daniel. What is it?'

'You remember when we went fishing an' sat on t'riverbank talkin' abaat things an' you said it were allus best to tell t'truth even if it 'urt someone's feelin's?'

'Yes, I do recall saying that.'

'Well what if tellin' t'truth gets somebody else into trouble?'

'That's a bit of a tricky one,' replied the vicar.

'I mean, if tha sees somebody do summat wrong, do you say owt?'

'It really depends, I suppose, as to what the person has done,' said the vicar. 'For example, if you were to witness a serious crime, I think you would have to say something.'

'But if it wasn't a serious crime?'

'If it was something quite trivial, something that didn't hurt another, then that might be perhaps a different matter. Would you like to tell me about it?'

'No, I think I need to think things through for missen.'

'Well if you do, you know where I am,' said the vicar. 'Now, you should be getting off home. You have done quite enough for today.'

When Mr Sparshott had gone, Danny went over to his grandfather's grave. He brushed the snow away from the headstone.

'I wish tha were 'ere, Grandad,' he said. 'To tell us what to do.'

He caught sight of Ashley walking up the path.

'Ey up, Dr Underwood!' he shouted.

'Hello, Danny,' she said, walking towards him. 'Is it you who has cleared the path?'

'Aye, I were tellin' Mester Sparshott that if it weren't cleared afore tomorra's service there'd be a few broken bones. It's still dead slippy, so watch 'ow yer go.'

'And how are you?' she asked.

'I'm champion,' replied the boy. He gave the broadest of grins.

Ashley smiled. 'How are things at the big school?'

Danny had moved up from the village school to the comprehensive in Clayton the previous September. He had never settled.

'It's all reight, I suppose,' he said unconvincingly.

'Oh dear,' she said. 'It doesn't sound as if you like it very much.'

'Well I can't say as 'ow I do, really,' he said. 'I'm in t'bottom group and I 'ate bein' stuck in a classroom behind a desk all day when I want to be outdoors in t'countryside. Schoolin' in't for me.' He was minded to tell her of the trouble he was in at Clayton Comprehensive, how he had been summoned to the head teacher's room and how a letter would be on its way to Clumber Lodge, but he decided not to say anything.

'It's very important to try your best at school, Danny,' Ashley told him.

'Aye, I know. Mester Sparshott told me education is t'most important thing, and to work hard an' pass mi exams.'

That is one thing Mr Sparshott and myself can agree on, thought Ashley.

'If there were exams in ferreting, mole-catching, gardening and birdwatching,' Danny told her, 'I'd be top o' t'class, but as for readin' and writin' and arithmetic, I'm about as thick as champ. I'm just not suited to learnin' what they teach yer at school. Hey, by the way, did you know that Mester Sparshott's leavin'?'

'Yes, I just heard,' said Ashley.

''E's off to Hafrica.'

'So I believe.'

'It'll be a sight warmer out theer.'

'It will,' agreed Ashley. 'I must go, Danny. Give my best wishes to your parents,' she added before heading up the path to the rectory.

Mr Sparshott was surprised to see his visitor standing on the doorstep.

'Dr Underwood,' he said.

'I'm sorry to disturb you, but I did want to have a word with you if it's convenient.'

'Yes, yes, of course,' he replied. 'Do come in. Go into the sitting room. I have lit a fire but it's still very chilly in there.'

The rectory was an unprepossessing residence, erected in the late nineteenth century to replace the imposing grey-stone Georgian mansion that had been destroyed when the Victorian incumbent, Dean Joseph Steerum-Slack, a seasoned drinker and notorious gambler, had burnt the building to the ground with himself and his dogs inside. The present rectory, with its shiny red-brick walls, dark grey slate roof, small square windows, towers and mock turrets and enveloping high black iron fence, resembled a workhouse more than a vicarage. Inside it was cool and unwelcoming, with black and white patterned tiles in the hallway, plain off-white walls and high ceilings. The drawing room was equally cheerless, with its heavy, overbearing furniture and dark oak doors. The place smelled of old wood, damp and lavender floor polish.

Ashley sat in a chair by a feeble fire that gave out more smoke than heat. She warmed her hands.

'My wife is out shopping with the girls this afternoon,' Mr Sparshott explained. 'Would you care for a cup of something?'

'No thank you. I won't stay long. I'm on duty at the hospital later today.'

'Ah yes, you're the assistant chaplain there, aren't you?'

The vicar sat opposite her in a padded leather chair and crossed his thin legs. He rested his hands on his lap and folded them with priestly precision. 'So, what can I do for you?' he asked.

'I saw Bishop Atticus this morning,' she said, 'and he told me you were leaving Barton-in-the Dale.'

'That's right. I'm surprised that the rumours haven't reached you before this. I gather it is a talking point in the village.'

'What made you come to this decision?' asked Ashley.

'I am sure you have some idea, Dr Underwood,' he said. 'As you are no doubt aware, my tenure here has not been an unmitigated success.' He leaned back in the chair. 'I have thought long and hard about it and decided that I shall move to South Africa. Over the years, I have kept in contact with a colleague with whom I studied at theological college, and he has been insistent for some time that I should join him. He is the pastor of a large, very vibrant and dedicated congregation. He tells me there is much to do. It will be challenging but very rewarding work.'

'I see.'

'To be frank, Rosamund and I have not settled here. I soon realised that the role of a country parson was not for me. I am the first to admit that I am not a very sociable person. I find polite conversation tedious, and when so many people are suffering in the world, I have little patience with those who complain about their lot in life. You know, as does the bishop, that I have ruffled quite a few feathers with my views. I think I might be better suited working in South Africa, and maybe more appreciated.'

'And what about your family?' asked Ashley.

'The two boys are at boarding school and will remain there. We will come over to visit them and I guess they will be keen to come out to South Africa to see us. The girls see it as a great adventure. They have not been happy at St Paul's preparatory school. I should have heeded the advice of Mrs Atticus and sent them to the village school. I felt the smaller classes, more individual attention and a traditional curriculum would be better for them. Sadly, I was proved wrong. As to my wife, Rosamund is keener and less apprehensive than I about the move. In fact she's quite thrilled. She has always been most supportive, and I could not have contemplated such a step without her entire agreement. I should say also she will not be at all sorry to leave this very cold and gloomy rectory. She does so like the sun, and there will be plenty of that where we are going.'

'I am sorry that things have not worked out for you here,' said Ashley.

'Oh, I am not a person to feel regrets, Dr Underwood. I count myself very fortunate compared with many in the world.'

'I believe you recommended me to Bishop Atticus; that you hoped I would succeed you as vicar here?'

'I did. I know we have had our differences, but I feel your approach will suit the congregation at St Christopher's much better than mine has.'

'Thank you,' said Ashley. 'That was kind of you.'

'Kind?' he repeated with a slight smile on his thin lips. 'I was just speaking the truth. You will make a far better vicar here than I.'

She got up to go. 'Well, I mustn't keep you.'

'Thank you for calling,' said the cleric, rising to his feet. 'We leave here at the end of the month and will spend some time in Durham, where I have a stand-in position and where I can continue my studies. We sail for South Africa after Easter.'

He extended a long, bony hand, which Ashley shook.

'Good afternoon, Dr Underwood,' he said, and gave another of his rare smiles.

When Danny arrived back at Clumber Lodge, he found Mrs O'Connor, the former housekeeper, in the kitchen. She called in a couple of times a week to do some cleaning and cooking. She was a dumpy, round-faced little woman with the huge liquid brown eyes of a cow and a permanent smile on her lips. There was a large sponge cake cooling on the table.

'Now then, young Danny,' she said, 'where have you been in all this awful weather?'

'Cleanin' t'path in t'churchyard,' replied the boy. He decided not to think about the trouble at school. As his granddad might have said, 'Things have a way of sorting themselves out.' 'Ey up, summat smells good,' he said, raising his head and sniffing the air like a hare in a field sitting up on its hind legs. 'Nob'dy bakes cakes like thee, Missis O'Connor.'

'Get away with you,' she replied, smiling broadly. 'You've got more blarney than the Irish, so you have. Mind you, I have to admit that I do bake a nice cake. "Light as a nun's kiss", as my sainted Grandmother Mullarkey used to say.'

Mrs O'Connor, like many of her nation, embroidered the
English language with the most colourful and original axioms
and expressions, most of which were throwbacks to her grandmother, who'd had a caustic comment, a saying or a snippet
of advice for every occasion.

'What do you want to clear the church path for on a day
like this?' she asked.

'Well someb'dy's got to do it,' the boy answered, eyeing the
cake. 'There'd be a lot of brokken bones tomorra if it din't get
done. All these old people goin' to church. They could fall an'
brek an 'ip. Mi grandad used to say that if tha put all t' metal
together what are in old folks's 'ips, tha cud build a Spitfire.'

'I don't know why you want to put yourself out for that
vicar,' observed Mrs O'Connor tartly. 'He's a po-faced individual if ever there was one, so he is. I'll tell you this, if he died
with a face on him like that, nobody'd wash the corpse.'

'As your sainted Grandmother Mullarkey used to say,'
added Danny, laughing.

'Get away with you, you cheeky rascal.' Mrs O'Connor
chuckled and ruffled the boy's mop of hair. 'Anyway, from
what I've heard, there'll not be that many in his congregation
tomorrow. He's managed to drive most of them away. Nobody
likes the man and none will be sorry to see the back of him.'

'I like 'im,' said Danny, 'an' I'll not be 'appy to see 'im leave.
'E's all reight when tha gets to know 'im.'

'You like everybody, Danny,' said Mrs O'Connor. He was
such a sunny, good-natured boy, she thought, with not a bad
word to say about anyone.

'Mi grandad used to say that if yer can't find summat good
to say abaat someone, then tha shouldn't say it,' replied the
boy. He thought for a moment. 'I can't say as 'ow I liked Miss
Sowerbutts when she were 'ead teacher at t'village school. She
were allus rantin' an' ravin' an' mekkin' kids stand outside 'er
room all day, but she weren't as bad as some med out. When I

cleared t'moles from 'er lawn, she gev me a fiver. Some people are better wi' knowin' 'em, as mi grandad used to say. 'E reckoned she were just a sad an' lonely old woman an' thy 'as to feel sorry for folk like that.'

'Well happen your grandfather was right,' said Mrs O'Connor, 'but if she was sad and lonely she brought it upon herself, so she did. Nobody liked the woman and she was no loss to the village when she moved away.'

'Mrs O'Connor?' said Danny.

'Yes, love?'

'What's t'cake for? Is it a birthday or summat?'

'Have you forgotten what day it is today, Danny Stainthorpe?'

'It's Saturday,' replied the boy.

'But don't you remember what's special about today?'

The boy rubbed his chin. 'I can't say as 'ow I do,' he replied.

'It's this afternoon when Miss Parsons from the Social Services is making a special visit to see Dr and Mrs Stirling and you about your adoption.'

'Oh crikey, yea!' exclaimed Danny. 'I clean forgot.'

'I've baked that cake specially. I think we're in for a bit of a celebration, what with you being officially adopted. After today, Dr and Mrs Stirling won't be your foster carers any more, they'll be your mum and dad, so they will.'

'Do you think everything will be all right?' asked the boy, glancing at her nervously. 'I mean, will Miss Parsons let me be adopted?'

'Course she will,' answered Mrs O'Connor, putting her arm around the boy's shoulder. 'Now you get up them stairs, wash your face, comb your hair and put on a clean shirt. You scrub up well when you make the effort.'

Miss Parsons, Senior Social Worker, was a handsome woman with bright, shrewd eyes easily moved to sympathy and light sandy hair tied back to reveal a finely structured face. Later

that day, she sat with Danny in the sitting room at Clumber
Lodge. Elisabeth and Michael were waiting in the kitchen, for
the social worker had asked to speak to the boy alone.

'Now then,' said Miss Parsons, smiling reassuringly. 'I think
you know why I am here.'

Danny nodded, and fidgeted nervously on the sofa, his
hands locked beneath him. There was a tightness in his chest
and his throat was dry. He felt like crying, but the tears
wouldn't come. He stared at her intently.

'Don't look so frightened, I'm not going to eat you,' said
Miss Parsons. 'We're just going to have a little chat.' She patted
a blue file on her knee. 'Then, if everyone's happy, we have a
few papers to sign.'

Danny remained solemnly still.

'My job,' she told him, 'is to make certain that children like
yourself who are placed in care have the best possible home to
go to, that they feel secure and happy with their new families.
What you want comes first, not what adults necessarily think
should happen to you. Your welfare and your happiness are
the most important considerations. Do you understand that,
Danny?'

'Yes, miss,' he mumbled, and managed a half-smile.

'Now, being adopted is a big step. It's not like being fostered.
It means that you will be with a family permanently. Do you
understand?'

'Yes, miss.'

'So are you happy living with Dr and Mrs Stirling?' she
asked.

'Yes, miss,' he replied quietly.

'And you want to stay here?'

'Yes, miss.'

'You're sure?'

He nodded and looked her straight in the eyes. 'I thowt that
when mi grandad passed away I'd never be 'appy again. I felt

like everythin' in mi life had gone wi' 'im. We did everythin'
together, you see. 'E were mi best friend as well as mi grandad. There'd only ever been 'im an' me. I don't know 'ow to
explain it, but I felt all empty an' alone an' frightened an' sad.
Then Dr Stirlin' said 'e'd look after me, that I could come and
live wi' 'im and James 'ere at Clumber Lodge an' bring mi
ferret wi' me. When 'e got married to Missis Devine, Missis
Stirlin' as she is now, she was 'appy to 'ave me stay 'ere an' all.'
His balled his fists and rubbed his eyes to stem the tears that
now came. 'I'm sorry . . .'

'It's all right, Danny,' Miss Parsons told him gently. 'Just
take your time.'

'Since I've been 'ere, all that 'appiness I used to feel 'as
come back,' he said. 'I'm not good wi' words but I want say
that I love it 'ere and I love Dr Stirlin' and Missis Stirlin'.
They're t'mum and dad I never 'ad. James is t'brother I never
'ad. I wants to stay 'ere, miss, more than anythin' I wants to
stay 'ere. That's all I've got to say.'

Miss Parsons smiled and felt her own eyes pricking with
tears. 'Of course you can stay, Danny. I just needed to make
sure that you are happy. I have the papers here. They just
need signing and then you will be here for ever.'

Before he died, Danny's grandfather had told Elisabeth when
she visited the old man in the hospital that he feared for his
grandson's future. The boy would be taken into care and
maybe placed with a family in the middle of a city, away from
the countryside he so loved.

'It worries me what'll 'appen to Danny when I'm gone,' the
old man had confided. His eyes had filled with tears. ''E's a bit
of a free spirit is Danny, likes t'sun on 'is face, rain in 'is 'air.
'E lives for t'outdoors. 'E's a country lad. Tek 'im away from
t'country and 'e'll be like a caged bird beating its wings agin
t'bars to try an' get out.'

It was true that Danny hated to be indoors, and the day after the adoption papers had been signed and all the family had celebrated with a slice of Mrs O'Connor's cake, he was up bright and early and heading for the woods and the mill dam. He had to think about things. The adoption had of course made him happy, but he could not get out of his head thoughts about the trouble he was in at school and what his new parents would say. If only his grandfather was there to advise him what to do.

Danny took a narrow snow-dusted path through the woods, beneath a canopy of spreading skeletal branches silvered in frost and bordered by prickly sparkling holly bushes, tangles of briar and rank undergrowth. He stopped for a moment to look at a spider's web, lacy between the bushes, then moved on, his breath steaming in the cold air and the crisp snow crunching under his feet. A gusty wind that bent the treetops made his ears and cheeks tingle. He started to shiver and rubbed his hands to keep himself warm. As the path opened out, rays from a watery sun pierced the high feathery clouds, making the snow glow a golden pink. The scene was magical.

At the mill dam, Danny brushed away the settled snow and sat on a dead tree trunk, his legs stretched out before him on a carpet of leaves silvered in hoar frost. He looked out across the frozen water. The huge water wheel, rotten and rusted, was silent and the stone building a crumbling roofless ruin. Riding the air currents, a hawk swept in wide circles in an empty sky, and a flock of crows rose from the treetops, filling the air with the noise of flapping wings and a cacophony of *kaa*s. There was a rustle of movement in the undergrowth and the distinctive red of a fox's coat flashed through the bushes. The animal appeared and observed Danny – fearless, truculent, bright-eyed and unconcerned by his presence.

On these occasions, when he was alone, Danny liked to remember the old man who had brought him up. He could picture his grandfather's weathered face, the colour of bruised parchment, the grizzled smoky-grey hair, the untidy beard and the smiling eyes resting in a net of wrinkles. He could see him in his long-sleeved collarless shirt, open at the neck, baggy corduroy trousers and heavy boots. That morning he wished his grandfather was alive to listen to him and tell him what he should do. Growing up, Danny had always confided in the old man, talked things through with him, asked his advice. He was now faced with a dilemma.

He reached into his pocket and produced a sandy-coloured, pointed-faced little creature with small bright black eyes. He held the animal under its chest, his thumb under one leg towards the ferret's spine, then using the other hand, he gently stroked it down the full length of its body.

'It's a cold un today, in't it, Ferdy?' he said.

The ferret sniffed the air.

Danny turned on hearing a noise behind him. A small boy wrapped up in an old jacket and flat cap appeared through the trees.

'Ey up, Robbie,' said Danny.

'I thought you'd be down here,' said the boy, sitting beside him on the dead tree trunk.

'Bit early for thee, in't it?' Danny put the ferret back in his pocket.

'I couldn't sleep,' Robbie told him, rubbing his hands together to warm them.

'Neither could I. 'Ow are things up at Treetop Farm?'

Robbie, like Danny, was being fostered, and his foster carers were in the process of adopting him. 'It's all right. I really like it there.'

'You're dead lucky livin' on a farm,' said Danny. 'Course I'm not complainin'. I'm 'appy weer I am, but I'd love to be in t'middle o' t'countryside wi' all them animals an' birds.'

'I know I'm dead lucky,' agreed Robbie.

They sat for a moment in silence looking out over the frozen water. The crows wheeled above them in a cold, clear grey sky.

Danny looked up. 'I 'ates them birds,' he said. 'When you see a reight big flock like that, they mek me shiver.'

'Are you adopted yet?' asked Robbie.

'Yea. They signed all t'papers yesterday. I can stay at Cumber Lodge for ever.'

'I hope Mr and Mrs Ross'll adopt me,' said Robbie. 'They said they will.'

'Well if they said they will, then they will.'

'Adults sometimes say things they don't mean,' said Robbie. 'They make promises they never keep. Anyway, I'm trying my best to do what you told me.'

'What were that then?' asked Danny.

'You said to keep out of trouble and behave myself, because if I started kicking off and answering back and being a pain in the bum and causing trouble, then they'd not want me and I would be sent back and end up in one o' them children's homes.'

'Did I say that?' asked Danny.

'You did, and you told me that if I liked where I was fostered and they liked me then they might adopt me. And you were right.' Robbie was thoughtful for a moment. 'I was a right little bugger, wasn't I? Always in some sort of trouble.'

'I'm in a spot of bother at school,' Danny told him.

'What did you do?'

'I din't do nowt,' said Danny. 'I saw this kid throw some eggs at a teacher's car. Nob'dy likes this teacher. 'E's allus shoutin' and callin' kids idiots and rippin' us work out of us books, and 'is lessons are dead borin'.'

'I'd have chucked a brick at his car,' said Robbie, 'if he called me an idiot or ripped my work up.'

'Anyroad,' said Danny, ''eadmaster sent for me and wants me to tell 'im who it was who chucked these eggs, but I'm not gunna.'

'Why, is he a mate of yours?'

'No, I don't like 'im, but I don't think it's reight to tell on 'im.'

'Why should you be in trouble?' asked Robbie. 'You didn't do anything.'

'I know, burrif I don't tell him, 'e's gunna write to mi parents. I might get hexpelled.'

'He wouldn't do that.'

'He might.'

'So why don't you tell him then?'

'Because I'm not a telltale,' replied Danny.

'I wouldn't say anything either,' said Robbie. 'I wouldn't grass anybody up. Nobody likes a sneak.'

'Anyroad, I'll 'ave to face t'music. See what 'appens. But I know one thing for certain, I'm not gunna tell on anybody.'

# 6

Mrs Sloughthwaite was a mistress of the malapropism and the amazingly inventive non sequitur. She managed to mangle the English language like a mincer minced meat, often to the amusement of her customers. She would comment on the colourful enemas that flowered in the tubs by the village green, the Mongolian tree with the beautiful blossoms, the chameleon bush in the churchyard and the creeping hysteria that grew up the wall on the rectory. She would bemoan the fact that the lovely buddleia bush in her back garden was full of atheists. She would enquire of her clientele if they favoured semtex in their tea instead of sugar, if they wanted evacuated milk or the semi-skilled variety and if they preferred orgasmic vegetables instead of the ordinary sort.

Her interest in other people's ailments was legendary.

'Poor Mr Farringdon,' she divulged to her customers, leaning over the counter and lowering her voice conspiratorially, 'is suffering with a large prostrate and his wife is laid up in bed after that nasty fall at the bus stop. Discollated her hip, so I hear. Mrs Widowson's legs are no better. I don't know how the woman manages to remain upright. Mind you, at her age she ought to get down on her knees and thank the good Lord she can still stand up. Fred Massey has been to hospital for an autopsy and Mrs Fish was telling me she has to go in to have a catheter removed from her eye. Evidently she was missing all the notes on the organ at the

Methodist chapel. Everybody seems to be ill with something or other.' She tapped the counter. 'Touch wood I'm keeping well.'

There were two customers in the shop that Monday morning: Mrs Pocock, a tall, thin woman with a pale, melancholy beaked face, and Mrs O'Connor, Dr Stirling's former housekeeper. Mrs Pocock was a gloomy, ill-tempered individual who delighted in the unadmitted pleasure of contemplating other people's misfortunes. In contrast, Mrs O'Connor was a happy, kindly and optimistic soul who looked for the good in everyone. That morning she displayed a particularly impressive head of wavy lilac-tinted hair.

'I see you've had your hair done,' observed the shopkeeper, resting her commodious chest on the counter. Her customer looked as if she was sporting a head of purple broccoli.

'I go to Les Belles,' Mrs O'Connor told her, patting her new perm. 'Les suggested I change the colour. He said it suits my personality.'

'Purple!' said Mrs Sloughthwaite.

'It's not purple,' answered the customer. 'Les calls it a tasteful lavender tint.'

'Les?' exclaimed Mrs Pocock. 'Who's Les?'

'He owns the salon – Les Belles.'

'Les Belles is French,' she was told.

'He doesn't sound French to me. I thought he was from Barnsley.'

'It's French for something or other,' said Mrs Pocock. 'It's not his name.'

'I don't know what you mean.'

'Oh it doesn't matter,' Mrs Pocock told her dismissively.

'How's your nephew getting on at the school then, Bridget?' asked the shopkeeper, keen to glean any gossip. She rested a dimpled elbow on the counter and placed her fleshy chin on her hand.

'Very well,' replied Mrs O'Connor. 'He's taken to teaching like a duck to water.'

'He called in here last week,' said Mrs Sloughthwaite. 'He's a very nice young man, and a bit of a heart-throb. I can see he'll be a big hit with the girls up at the school, and with the mothers too, I shouldn't wonder.'

'Yes, the Dwyers are a good-looking family, so they are,' agreed Mrs O'Connor.

Mrs Sloughthwaite wondered if the young man's aunt was aware of what her nephew used to do to supplement his earnings when he was a footballer. It was a snippet of interesting information she decided not to divulge – for the time being, at any rate. She had been browsing through some old copies of her women's magazine and had come across a full-page advertisement for swimwear. Other less observant readers might have flicked past the picture of the strikingly athletic-looking male model posing on a sandy beach before an azure sea in the briefest of swimming trunks, but Mrs Sloughthwaite, eagle-eyed as ever, immediately recognised the new teacher.

'Tom was after being a priest, you know,' Mrs O'Connor said, 'but he found he was allergic to the incense. Anyway, he loves teaching. Mrs Stirling seems very impressed with him.'

The shopkeeper resisted commenting that if her customer's nephew didn't find teaching to his liking, then he could always go back to modelling skimpy swimming trunks.

'Mrs Stirling has asked him if he would like to go with the other teachers when they take some of the children on a school trip later this month,' Mrs O'Connor told the shopkeeper. 'They are to stay at the hostel near Whitby for the weekend.'

'Well I'll tell you this,' said Mrs Pocock. 'I wouldn't want to take a group of noisy and overexcited children on a school trip, and certainly not overnight in a youth hostel. Just think of the things they might get up to.' The woman had a hard face, a thin, pursed mouth and a habitual frown. She was one of life's malcontents and rarely had a good word to say about anyone. Now in her stride, she moved on to her perennial theme: the poor behaviour of modern youth. 'Kids these days get away with murder,' she announced. 'It was a sad day when they got rid of the cane in schools. My husband was always bending over the headmaster's desk to get "six of the best", and Miss Pratt at my school was a dab hand with a ruler across your knuckles, and it didn't do us any harm.'

That was questionable, mused Mrs Sloughthwaite, thinking of the lazy great lump of a man her customer had married. He hadn't done a day's work in his life and spent most of his time propping up the bar at the Blacksmith's Arms. And as for her son – that sullen-faced, surly boy, who was light-fingered to boot – she wanted to put her own house in order before she started commenting on the behaviour of other people's children.

'I mean, if you try and discipline kids these days,' Mrs Pocock carried on vehemently, 'you end up getting sacked. Look at that teacher at Clayton Juniors. She tried to sort out this violent little infant and was given her marching orders for her pains.'

'There was a piece about it in the *Clayton Gazette*,' said Mrs Sloughthwaite, reaching under the counter to produce the newspaper. She flicked through the pages until she found the article, then read the headline out loud: 'Teacher Suspended by Head.' She read on. 'A supply teacher at Clayton Junior School has been suspended for securing a six-year-old child to a chair using masking tape. Mrs Humphrey-Snyde, 56, from Bestwood Avenue, Clayton, was kicked by the infant, who when chastised told her that it was an accident and he had slipped on the polished floor. The teacher kicked the boy back, saying that she agreed with him that it was a slippery floor. The child then had a tantrum and was restrained by the teacher, who wrapped him in sticky masking tape and fastened him to a chair. The school's head teacher said the punishment was excessive. The parent of the child, Mrs Ruby Prosser, aged 32, said it was barbaric.'

'Children these days,' fulminated Mrs Pocock, 'just don't know how to behave themselves. Course, I blame the parents, letting them get away with murder.'

'Is your Ernest getting on any better at the comprehensive?' asked Mrs Sloughthwaite provocatively.

'No he isn't,' Mrs Pocock answered. 'He's still in the bottom group and says it's terrible boring, not like when he was at the village school. When he was here, he really came on with his work, got in the football team and sang in the choir, and he loved his art. Up at the comprehensive he doesn't seem to be interested in anything and doesn't want to do anything either. He says his teacher is horrible, always shouting and throwing things. He nearly took a lad's eye out with a board rubber. And Malcolm Stubbins is still making his presence known. Always in trouble he is. Evidently this particular teacher told him off, so the next day Malcolm brought half a dozen eggs to school and threw them at the teacher's car. A right old mess he made, all over the windscreen and bonnet.'

'I thought it wouldn't be long before that young man got expelled,' observed Mrs Sloughthwaite.

'The teacher never found out who threw the eggs,' said Mrs Pocock, 'but the headmaster is determined to get to the bottom of it. He reckons that some of the other pupils must have seen who did it and he's speaking to them one at a time. He sent for my Ernest but he told him he didn't see anything.'

The bell on the door tinkled and Major Neville-Gravitas walked briskly into the shop.

'Good morning, ladies,' he said cheerily. He reached into his jacket for his wallet and placed a crisp ten-pound note on the counter. 'A packet of my usual panatellas, please, Mrs Sloughthwaite.'

'I heard from Mrs Cosgrove that you had a lively gover- nors' meeting up at the school,' said the shopkeeper.

'Mrs Cosgrove had no business discussing what was talked about at the meeting,' the major told her haughtily.

'She said you governors went at it hammer and tongs about sex.'

'For your information,' said the major, 'we were consider- ing the sex education policy and not talking about sex per se.'

'Who?'

'Well I don't think kids ought to be taught that sort of thing,' said Mrs Pocock. 'They see quite enough of it on the televi- sion without hearing about it in schools.'

'On that we can be agreed,' said the major. 'In my opinion, far too many young women are getting themselves pregnant outside wedlock, and I put this down partly to sex education in schools.'

'A lot of people don't bother with getting married these days,' remarked Mrs Sloughthwaite. 'They just live together. In my day that was frowned on and called "living over the bush".'

'Brush!' corrected Mrs Pocock. 'Living over the brush.'

'Whatever,' said the shopkeeper. 'As I say, in my day it was frowned upon, but these days there's not the same stigmata attached to couples who decide to live together rather than get married.'

'I mean, take Fred Massey's niece-in-law, that Bianca,' said Mrs Pocock. 'She's a case in question. She can't have been any more than seventeen when she had that baby, and unmar- ried. Young people's morals these days leave a lot to be desired.'

'At least her boyfriend did the right thing,' said Mrs Sloughthwaite. 'Clarence did stand by the lass and marry her, not leave her to bring up the kiddie by herself, and I'll tell you this, no parents could care for that child better than they do.'

'Be that as it may,' said the major, 'I still feel there are far too many unmarried mothers, and not a sign of the feckless young men who got them into this state. It's a sad reflection on the loose morals of the young today.'

Mrs O'Connor, who had remained uncharacteristically quiet during this exchange, patted her new perm and remarked, 'I can't recall that we had any sex education from Sister Pauline-Therese at the convent, but perhaps if Molly Burke had have had, she wouldn't have ended up pregnant with twins.'

Robbie Hardy's young life had been harrowing. A year after the death of his father, his mother, a weak-willed and nervy woman, had married a brute. Loud, domineering and unfeeling, the man had little time for his new wife, who he treated as a drudge, and no time at all for her son. He constantly found fault with the boy, humiliating him, criticising him, shouting at him and hitting him. There was nothing in Robbie's childhood home except bad temper, grumbles and recriminations; there were no saving moments of laughter or shared pleasure. Robbie soon came to realise that his stepfather resented his very presence. He came to realise too that his mother could or would do nothing to alleviate his suffering, so frightened and intimidated was she by her new husband. So the boy, who had an inner strength of character and a remarkable resilience, reacted to his punishing treatment in the most negative of ways. Rather than being subjugated by his situation, he became insolent, angry and disobedient, so badly behaved at home and at school that his parents and teachers found him unmanageable. He was put into care. Then Elisabeth came into his life, agreeing to take this troubled, unruly little boy into her school, and with patience and perseverance she saw Robbie's behaviour slowly begin to improve.

The great change in the boy's life came when he was fostered by a farmer and his wife. Mr and Mrs Ross had fostered many children over the years; few of them, however, had been as difficult and demanding as Robbie. This kindly couple were quick to recognise that the little boy who arrived at the farm tight-lipped and with eyes like arrow slits was in need of help. At first he was suspicious and uncommunicative. They knew it would not be an easy task gaining the confidence of this damaged child, but they had plenty of experience of dealing with disturbed children, and with understanding and support they believed that he would change for the better.

Mr and Mrs Ross were a larger-than-life couple: she a round, red-faced, jolly woman with long grey hair gathered up untidily in a tortoiseshell comb, and large friendly eyes; he a burly man, big and ruddy like a side of beef and with a thick head of woolly hair and copious white whiskers that gave him the appearance of a benevolent, sleepy old lion. They recognised the boy's anger and feeling of resentment, his unhappiness and lack of self-worth, and over the weeks he was with them, through their kindness and encouragement, Robbie became a different boy. Then when his stepfather left and soon afterwards his mother died, his foster carers decided to adopt him.

Treetop Farm was extensive, with sheds, stone outbuildings, huge metal silos and cattle stalls. In one field was a rusting tractor and the remains of an excavator, broken and corroded, a mountain of tangled scrap metal and mounds of stone. In shed after shed, kept in clean, spacious pens with thick plastic slatted floors, were the pigs: pigs squealing and snuffling, pigs of every size and colour.

Robbie took to the pigs from the start. He liked nothing better than accompanying the farmer to see the rumbling trucks arrive up the farm track with the new consignment of squealing piglets – 'little grunters' as Mr Ross called them. He helped unload the animals and usher them into the large pens, then over the next few weeks he would feed and water these lively little weaners and watch them grow healthy and strong, fat and clean and pink. On market days, dressed like the farmer in an almost identical outfit of shapeless blue overalls beneath a waxed jacket with corduroy collar, tweed cap and sturdy brown boots, the boy soon became as knowledgeable about these inquisitive creatures as any pig farmer.

Robbie was desperate to stay at Treetop Farm. He had never felt so safe, secure and happy. His earnest wish was that Mr and Mrs Ross would eventually adopt him. They had promised as much, but he had been let down so many times before in his young life that he still harboured a suspicion that it would never happen. Determined to stay out of trouble, at first he had kept his head down at school. He rarely mixed with the other children, did the minimum amount of work, took little interest in the lessons and, despite his teacher's sterling efforts, contributed little in class. At first he found Mr Hornchurch, this idiosyncratic, untidy and overenthusiastic teacher, annoying, but as the weeks passed, a grudging liking and respect developed. Mr Hornchurch was calm, cheerful and patient; he never shouted or complained or pressured Robbie, and soon the boy began to take more of an interest in his work.

It was one lunchtime that things went wrong for Robbie. Barry Biggerdyke, an unfortunate-looking boy with an unhealthy pasty complexion, crooked teeth and large protruding ears, had caught sight of Oscar and Roisin in the small school library. The two friends were chatting amiably as they tidied the books. Like all bullies, Barry picked on those who were smaller, weaker and more vulnerable than himself, and Oscar was a prime target. Barry disliked Oscar intensely, for he was everything the bigger boy was not: keen and clever, a helpful, curious boy who loved school, one who readily asked questions of the teacher and volunteered answers.

Barry wandered into the library whistling nonchalantly to himself. At first he looked around abstractedly, then began pulling one book after another from the shelves and letting them fall to the floor.

'Please don't do that,' said Oscar sharply. 'I've just put them in order.'

'Bugger off, four eyes!' replied the bully, pulling more books out and letting them drop with a thump.

'It's taken me ages to put them into alphabetical order,' Oscar told him, bending to retrieve the fallen books.

Barry plucked the glasses from the boy's nose and twirled them in his fingers.

'Give me back my glasses!' cried Oscar.

'Give me back my glasses,' mimicked the bully.

'Why are you so horrible?' asked Roisin, snatching the glasses from Barry's hand.

'Shut your dirty gyppo face!' cried the bully, grabbing back the glasses.

'There's really no need to be so unpleasant,' said Oscar.

Barry punched him in the chest and threw the glasses on to a top shelf, out of reach.

Unseen behind one of the shelves, where he was flicking through a book on tractors, Robbie heard this exchange. Barry Biggerdyke had tried to bully him once and came out the worse for it. Since then, he had kept his distance. Robbie recognised in the bully's mocking voice that of the stepfather who had made his life such a misery; the loud, nasty, taunting tones of the tormentor. He emerged from behind the shelf and approached the boy. He showed no fear, despite the fact that Barry was a foot taller and much broader. Physical hurt held no terrors for Robbie, for he had received enough beatings in his young life and learnt to endure the pain. When his stepfather had taken the belt to him, Robbie had refused to cry, which made his abuser even angrier.

'Give the glasses back,' he said quietly, with an expression of fierce determination on his face.

'Bugger off, pig boy!' spat out Barry. Then he made a grunting noise like a pig.

Robbie stared up at the spiteful, smirking face. It was as if at that moment he was back at home facing the hated man who had taken his father's place. Slowly and calmly he raised his fist and with a quick jab hit Barry square on the nose. The bully's large moon face, half hidden behind a fiercely cut gingery fringe, at first conveyed incomprehension. His mouth dropped open like a fish on a slab. Then blood streamed from his nose and he cried out. He raised his fist to retaliate, but Robbie was prepared and hit him again. Barry ran from the library screaming.

'I don't think that was such a good idea,' remarked Oscar. He shook his head like a member of the older generation despairing at the antics of the young. 'I guess there will be repercussions.'

His prediction proved right.

Mr Dwyer, disturbed by the noise, emerged from his classroom to see a pupil running down the corridor spattering blood on the wall and floor. The teacher managed to intercept the boy, sat him down in his classroom and, pinching the bridge of his nose, stemmed the flow of blood. Then he sent Norman Stubbins, who had been kept in over lunchtime to finish his work, to fetch Mrs Stirling. Elisabeth arrived minutes later. Having been reassured by Tom, who in his previous career had suffered a few bloody noses, that the boy's injury was not serious and he would not need to be taken to the hospital, she asked Barry what had happened.

'It was Robbie Hardy,' he told her, sniffing. 'He attacked me.'

'Why did he attack you?' she asked.

'I don't know,' he spluttered. 'He just went barmy and punched me on the nose.'

'I'm sure there was more to it than that. He wouldn't just hit you for no reason.'

'Well he did!' exclaimed the boy, wiping a smear of blood from his lip.

'Please do not use that tone of voice with me,' said Elisabeth crossly.

'I didn't do nothing,' insisted the boy. 'He wants locking up.'

Elisabeth turned to Tom. 'Welcome to life in a school,' she said with a slight smile on her lips. 'Never a dull moment.' Then she asked him if he would go and find Robbie Hardy and tell him to come and see her in her classroom. 'You remain here,' she told Barry.

Elisabeth expected to find Robbie subdued and remorseful when he arrived at her classroom, but he raised his little chin defiantly and stared at her. His expression was unreadable.

'So, Robbie,' she said calmly, 'would you like to tell me what happened? Why did you hit Barry?'

The boy shrugged. 'He deserved it,' he said.

'Is that all you have to say for yourself?' Elisabeth's voice now had an edge to it.

Robbie shrugged again. He stared down mulishly at his feet.

'I see. Well perhaps you ought to sit here for the rest of lunchtime and think about it, and when you are ready to tell me exactly what happened, we will speak again.'

For the remainder of the day Robbie sat at a desk in Elisabeth's classroom tight-lipped and unforthcoming. The class was unusually quiet that afternoon. Several of the pupils glanced surreptitiously at Robbie, and at Barry, whose swollen nose had taken on a bright red sheen. When the bell rang for the end of school, Elisabeth dismissed the class, gave Barry a note to take home to his parents and asked Robbie to wait.

'Now then,' she said, 'have you had time to think about things and tell me what happened?'

Robbie looked down. 'I hit him because he deserved it, miss,' he mumbled.

'And is that all you have to say for yourself?' she asked.

'Yes.'

'You know, Robbie, I have been really pleased with you since you started school this term,' Elisabeth told him. 'You have behaved yourself, and from what your teacher has told me, your work has come along really well. And now this. You know I will not have violence in this school. To hit someone else, particularly in the face, is a very serious thing. Do you understand what I am saying?'

'Yes, miss.'

'Now I will ask you again. Why did you hit Barry?'

Robbie looked at her for a moment. 'Because he deserved it,' he said again.

'Very well,' said Elisabeth. 'I mean to get to the bottom of this, Robbie. Make no mistake about that.' Then she added, 'And I shall be getting in touch with Mr and Mrs Ross. Perhaps they can find out from you why you did it.'

When Robbie got home, he ran up to his room, threw himself on the bed and punched the pillow. 'I've spoilt everything,' he said out loud. 'Everything, I've spoilt everything.'

'Robbie, would you come down here, please?' It was Mrs Ross's voice. She didn't sound her usual cheerful self.

With misery written all over his face and his heart thumping in his chest, he descended the stairs slowly and hovered indecisively in the doorway of the kitchen. The farmer was standing by the black-leaded kitchen range, warming his backside. Robbie had never seen him look so solemn. Mrs Ross, her face soft with concern, went to sit at the kitchen table.

'Sit thee sen down, lad,' said Mr Ross.

The boy perched stiffly upright on the edge of a chair.

The farmer ran a leathery hand through his hair and wrinkled his forehead into a frown. There was a harassed look on his face.

'I reckon tha knows why we wants to see ya,' he said gruffly.

Robbie nodded but remained silent. He kept his head down and stared at the shabby linoleum. He couldn't meet their gazes. Tears began to spring up behind his eyes.

'Mrs Stirling's been on the phone,' Mrs Ross told him. 'It was about what happened at school today.' She didn't sound displeased or angry. It was quite the opposite in fact; her manner was solicitous and kindly.

Robbie made no reply but stared fixedly at the floor.

'What's up wi' thee, Robbie?' asked Mr Ross, raising his voice. 'What made thee do such a madcap thing as thump someone in t'face?'

'You could have really hurt him,' added Mrs Ross. There was calm admonition in her voice.

'Did this lad 'it thee first? Is that why tha punched him?' asked the farmer.

'No, I hit him first,' muttered Robbie.

'Why?'

Robbie held his head down and didn't answer.

''As t'cat got thee tongue, lad?' barked the farmer. He now sounded annoyed. 'Well, why did tha thump 'im?'

Robbie looked up.

'Hamish,' said his wife. 'Shouting does no good. Let's just keep calm. Why did you hit him, Robbie? There must have been some reason.' She looked at the pale, stricken face.

'He made me mad,' muttered the boy.

'Med thee mad!' repeated the farmer, raising his voice again. 'Blood and sand, Robbie, lots o' folk mek me mad, but I don't go around punchin' 'em in t'face.'

'Hamish,' rebuked his wife, 'don't shout. It does no good.' She leaned across the table and put a hand on the boy's, resting it there. 'Is this the boy you had a fight with before? The one who said you smelled?' Robbie nodded. 'Did he say it again?' she asked.

'No.'

'An' can tha remember what we telled thee afore abaat 'ittin' somebody?' asked the farmer.

The boy hung his head and said nothing.

'We telled thee that lashin' out isn't t'answer. 'As tha got cloth ears, or what?'

'No.'

'So why did thy 'it 'im this time?'

Robbie saw the cracks opening beneath his feet, and in the silence that followed, he felt wretched.

'I'd like an answer, lad,' said Mr Ross.

'He called me a pig boy.'

'Blood and sand!' exclaimed the farmer again. 'Is that all? Thy are a pig boy and I'm a pig man. There's nowt wrong wi' that.'

'It was the way he said it,' answered Robbie.

'Tha's got to learn to control that temper o' yourn,' Mr Ross told him, 'or one o' these days it'll get thee into real trouble.'

Mrs Ross sighed. 'Hamish, please,' she said. She looked at Robbie's anxious face. 'Mrs Stirling told me how well you were getting on at school, settling down to your work, staying out of trouble. She's been very good to you, you know that, don't you?'

The boy rubbed his eyes with his fists and nodded.

'She's very upset and disappointed about what happened.'

'I know.'

'I'll tell thee this, Robbie,' said the farmer, 'there's not many who would have been as good to you as Missis Stirling. You know that, don't yer?'

'Yes,' murmured the boy.

'Mrs Stirling thinks you should stay at home for a few days until things calm down,' said Mrs Ross, 'and then she'll decide what to do.'

'I'm suspended?' he asked, looking up. His voice was strained with grief.

'Yes, I suppose you are,' she replied.

'You didn't think she'd be dancin' in t'aisles ovver what tha's done, did tha?' asked the farmer, not expecting a reply. 'She's dead mad wi' what tha did, an' I reckon she feels reight let down.'

Robbie, his face wet with tears, jumped up, pushed the chair back roughly and ran out into the farmyard.

'Robbie!' Mr Ross shouted after him. 'Come back 'ere!'

'Leave him be, love,' said his wife.

'Whatever are we going to do with the lad, Elspeth?' asked the farmer, sighing.

Later that afternoon, when Robbie had not returned to the farmhouse, Mr Ross went in search of him. He found the boy sitting shivering on the cold concrete floor in one of the sheds that housed the pigs. Small and skinny, with his cropped chestnut hair and gangly legs, he looked like a little monkey. The farmer observed him for a moment and considered the words he might use.

'Now then, Robbie,' he said, approaching and trying to sound cheerful.

Robbie didn't look up.

'It's gunna be a bitter neet,' said Mr Ross. He bent down and put his old waxed jacket around the boy's shoulders and sat down next to him. 'Thas'll get tha death o' cowld out 'ere wi' nowt on.' He cleared his throat several times and looked down at his fat red hands. 'I'm sorry I lost mi temper,' he said. 'I shouldn't 'ave raised mi voice. I reckon thee an' me are two peas in t'same pod. We let us tempers get t'better of us.' There was a short silence. 'Thing is, Robbie, losin' tha temper is one thing, but lashin' out is another. Tha could 'ave really 'urt this lad. Tha knows that, dunt tha?'

Robbie continued to look down and remained silent.

'Aye, I reckon tha does,' said the farmer. 'An' I reckon tha regrets what 'appened. Does tha want to tell me abaat it?'

Robbie shook his head.

Mr Ross stood up. 'Don't thee stop out 'ere all neet,' he said, and with that he left the boy.

The farmer and his wife heard the click of the latch on the front door and the footsteps up the stairs a moment later. They knew how upset and confused Robbie must feel, but thought it better not to pursue the matter for the moment.

That evening, as Mr and Mrs Ross discussed what to do about Robbie, Elisabeth and Michael sat with Danny in the sitting room at Clumber Lodge. Dr Stirling held up a letter addressed to 'The Parent or Guardian of Daniel Stainthorpe'.

'This is from your school,' he said.

Danny nodded. 'Aye, I thowt it was. T'headmaster said 'e would be writin'.'

'Would you like to explain, Danny?' said Elisabeth. 'It says here that you witnessed an incident at the school where a pupil threw some eggs at a teacher's car. Is this true?'

'Aye, it's true,' replied Danny.

'And the letter says that you saw the boy who threw these eggs but that you refuse to tell the headmaster who it was.'

'That's reight.'

'Why is that, Danny?' asked Dr Stirling.

'Why I 'aven't said owt?' answered the boy. He scratched his scalp and considered for a moment. 'Well I've thowt abaat it and feel it wun't be the reight thing to do to tell on 'im.'

'Why is that?' asked Elisabeth.

'It's 'ard to hexplain,' the boy told her. 'It's just that I don't think it's reight to do so. I don't think it's reight to get somebody into trouble.'

'Are you afraid that if you tell the headmaster, the boy who threw the eggs would pick on you?' asked Dr Stirling.

'Nay,' Danny laughed. 'I reckon I can tek care of missen. It's not that.'

'Do you not think that if someone does something wrong, they should be punished?' asked Elisabeth.

''Appen,' said Danny.

'And don't you think if someone has information that would help in catching the wrongdoer,' she continued, 'as you have in this case, that they should make it known?'

'Well it depends,' said Danny. 'If it was a murder or summat serious like that, then yea, I think it would be only reight to tell, an' if this 'ad been a brick rather than an egg an' damaged t'car I might 'ave 'ad second thoughts abaat tellin', but it were only a few eggs an' left just a bit of a mess that could be cleaned off. Some might say it were a prank an' not as t'eadmaster said an act o' vandalism. I mean, nob'd'y was 'urt an' no damage was done. And mebbe t'teacher deserved it.'

'Really, Danny, you surprise me,' said Elisabeth. 'I don't think there is any excuse for someone throwing eggs at a teacher's car.'

'It's not something I would do,' Danny answered, 'but I can't say as 'ow I'm goin' to lose sleep ovver it. You see, this teacher's not liked by any of us who are in 'is class. 'E's not bothered abaat us. I don't think 'e likes us. I know that we're in t'bottom group – Special Needs, that's what we're called – and not much good at readin' and writin' an' number work, but we ought to be tret better. 'E 'ardly ever marks us books, shouts at us all t'time and calls us stupid. 'E shouldn't do that. 'E says givin' us 'omework is a waste o' time.'

'Why have you not told us this before, Danny?' asked Dr Stirling.

'Abaat what?'

'About this teacher.'

'I reckon you 'ave enough on yer plate wi'out worryin' abaat me and mi schoolwork,' answered the boy. 'Anyroad, this teacher called t'boy who lobbed t'eggs a waste o' space. 'E said he was thick as a plank o' wood. 'E was really 'orrible to 'im an' ripped t'work out of 'is book. Mebbe they should be askin' why somebody would want to throw eggs at a teacher's car.'

'I still think—' began Elisabeth.

'Were you the only one who saw what happened?' asked Dr Stirling, interrupting.

'No, there were a few of us, but when they were asked by t'eadmaster who did it, they said they didn't see owt. Course they did, but they decided not to tell t'truth.'

'And you did,' said Michael.

'I allus do,' said the boy. There was a kind of defiant look in his eyes. 'Tell t'truth an' shame t'devil, mi grandad used to say.'

'Despite what you say, Danny,' said Elisabeth, 'I think you should say who did it.' There was a gentle reproof in her voice.

The boy pressed his lips together and shook his head. 'I can't do that,' he said stubbornly.

'Well,' she sighed, 'I can't make you, but I hope you will think about it and maybe come to the right decision. I have to say that I am disappointed in you.'

'I think Danny believes he has come to the right decision, Elisabeth,' said Dr Stirling.

'Michael . . .' began his wife.

'I'm sorry, Elisabeth, but I think he's explained himself pretty well. I can see why he's keeping his mouth shut. He's done no wrong and has at least been honest enough to admit that he saw what happened, unlike the other boys. It takes some courage to do that. And as for informing on the lad who threw the eggs, well I think he is right. Nobody likes a sneak.'

'I think we need to talk about this later, Michael,' said Elisabeth, clearly stung by what had been said.

'There's really nothing more to say about it as far as I'm concerned,' he told her. 'So let that be an end to the matter.' He got to his feet and placed the letter in his pocket.

'I didn't mean to cause you to fall out,' Danny said. 'I'm sorry if—'

'Don't worry, Danny,' Elisabeth reassured him. 'We haven't fallen out.' She gave her husband a knowing look. 'It's just a difference of opinion, that's all.'

## 7

The next morning was chilly and overcast. Robbie stood at his bedroom window, looking out over the empty fields dusted in light snow and studded with grey outcrops of rock, and beyond to the bare lonely hills, treeless and austere. The scene reflected his mood. He had never felt so wretched. Living with his mother and stepfather in that dark and miserable home, he had experienced the whole gamut of negative emotions: resentment, anger, hatred, bitterness, depression, the feeling of being unwanted. Most of the time he had felt desperately unhappy. But he had never felt as desolate as he did that morning. He knew he had let Mrs Stirling and his foster carers down. They had been the only ones in his young life who had listened to him, taken an interest in him, tried to help him, the only ones who had shown him any affection, and now he had ruined everything. After what he had done, he knew it was unlikely that he would be allowed to remain at Treetop Farm. He would be put back into care.

He saw the car pull up outside the farmhouse. His heart sank when he recognised the driver. It was Miss Parsons, his social worker. The expression on her face said it all.

At the end of school the previous afternoon, Miss Parsons had telephoned Elisabeth to see how things were going with Robbie. She had sighed heavily when the events of the day had been related to her, saddened to hear that the boy had reverted to his angry and aggressive self.

'I thought it was going so well,' Elisabeth had told her. 'Robbie has made such progress since he has been with Mr and Mrs Ross, less rude and belligerent, more helpful and with a greater willingness to do as he is told. His work has also improved. This attack on another pupil is a real setback.'

'I see,' Miss Parsons had said. 'Did he say why he hit the other boy?'

'No, just that he deserved it,' Elisabeth had replied. 'According to the other boy, it was an unprovoked attack. I have been in touch with Robbie's foster carers and explained the situation and that I will not tolerate any kind of violence in the school. As you might imagine, they were very upset. They were aware that Robbie has been in trouble before about hitting this particular boy, and that he had been warned in no uncertain terms not to do it again. I felt I had no option but to suspend him for a few days. Perhaps when he gets back to school we can decide on what to do.'

'I think I'll give Mr and Mrs Ross a ring,' Miss Parsons had answered, 'and call out to see them tomorrow.'

Now, as Robbie watched the social worker walk down the path to the farmhouse, he was sure that she had come to collect him. He took his case out from under the bed and packed his few things. Then he picked up a small sharp white tusk from the bedside table and studied it. When he first came to Treetop Farm, Mr Ross had told him about a boar he once owned. It was called Boris, a big, nasty-tempered beast that would nudge the farmer if he came near and then turn its bristly head and try to use its tusks. Mr Ross had snapped off one of the tusks with a pair of pliers, but when he tried to do the other, the animal was wise to what was to happen and wouldn't let the farmer near him. In the end, Mr Ross had no option but to shoot Boris. He had given the tusk to Robbie. It was the boy's lucky charm. Now he held it in his hand and ran his fingers across the smooth surface, then placed it back on the bedside table. He would leave it.

Hearing voices downstairs, he crept to the top of the stairs to listen to the conversation that was taking place in the kitchen.

'And how is he this morning?' Miss Parsons asked.

'We've not seen him,' replied Mrs Ross. 'He's stayed up in his room. I called him down for breakfast, but he said he wasn't hungry.'

'It's a rum do, is this,' remarked the farmer, sucking in his bottom lip.

'Did Robbie say why he hit this other pupil at school yesterday?' asked Miss Parsons.

'He said that this lad made him mad and called him names like he did before,' said Mrs Ross. 'We told him that hitting somebody is not the answer. I think he feels bad about what happened.'

'And so he should,' said the social worker. 'Robbie must be made to understand that violence is not the answer and that he is responsible for his actions. He can't go around hitting other children merely because he has been called a name. Sticks and stones. I'm sure you know the rest.'

'Oh I do,' said the farmer's wife. 'I know the rhyme well enough and it's a load of twaddle. Sticks and stones may break your bones, but calling can break your heart. Those like me who were bullied at school know it only too well. I've no doubt that this lad Robbie hit said some very unkind things.'

'But that is no excuse for him to hit the boy in the face,' responded Miss Parsons. 'He could have caused serious damage.'

'Well did 'e?' asked Mr Ross.

'Fortunately not,' replied the social worker, 'but that is really not the point. He should not have hit him.'

'No he shouldn't, and we've told him that,' answered Mrs Ross.

'So where do we go from here?' asked the social worker.

''Ow do ya mean, weer do we go?' asked Mr Ross, looking perplexed.

'Do you still wish Robbie to remain here with you?' asked Miss Parsons. 'Perhaps a few days back at the children's home might be the best thing for him until we sort this out.'

Robbie felt his stomach churn. He gripped the edge of the top step.

'Wish 'im to remain 'ere?' repeated the farmer. 'Course we want t'lad to remain 'ere. 'E's not goin' back to any children's home. Me and t'missus don't give up on kids that easily. Robbie's 'ad a bloody rough time of it growing up wi' a stepfather who 'adn't a good word for 'im an' who took a leather belt to t'lad as soon as look at 'im, an' a mother who, from what I've 'eard, stood by an' let it 'appen. You know as well as I do, Miss Parsons, what that little lad 'as 'ad to purrup wi'. Remain 'ere! Too bloody reight t' lad can stay 'ere.'

'Hamish!' exclaimed his wife. 'Will you stop that swearing at once!'

'I'm sorry, love, but there's no way that lad is leavin' 'ere,' the farmer told her. 'I know Robbie should 'ave bit 'is tongue an' kept 'is fists to 'issen, but at 'eart 'e's not a bad lad. You should see 'im wi' t'grunters—'

'I'm sorry,' interrupted Miss Parsons. 'Grunters?'

'Mi pigs. Robbie's a natural wi' 'em as 'e is wi' all t'animals. They're good judges o' character are animals, an' they've took to Robbie like nobody's business. An' I'll tell thee summat else, Miss Parsons, me and Elspeth have took to t'boy an' all. We likes 'im.' The farmer took a deep breath. 'Nay we don't like him, we love the lad.'

Robbie, sitting at the top of the stairs, sniffed, then his small shoulders heaved and great tears rolled down his small cheeks.

The social worker smiled. 'Well, Mr Ross, that was quite a speech.'

'Aye, mi gob sometimes runs away wi' me,' the farmer told her.

'And having heard it,' continued Miss Parsons, 'I don't think I need to talk to Robbie, do I?'

'No, I reckon you don't,' said the farmer. 'This'll blow ovver. I've allus believed that things 'ave a way of sooarting their sens out.'

When Robbie heard the car engine start and the tyres crunch on the gravel drive, he crept downstairs and out into the farmyard. He followed the sound of the squealing pigs and found Mr Ross filling the feeders in the first shed. He stood by the door.

'Ey up,' said the farmer. 'Look what t'cat's brought in.'

'I'm sorry,' said Robbie with a tremble in his voice. Suddenly the tears came brimming up, spilling over, and he began to cry with great heaving sobs.

'What's all this?' asked Mr Ross, going over to the boy. Robbie fell into the man's arms and hugged him.

'It's all reight, lad,' said the farmer, his own eyes filling with tears. 'It's all reight.'

The following Monday morning, Elisabeth arrived at school earlier than usual. She had the governors' report to write. She sat at her desk and stared at the blank sheet of paper before her. She would have to mention the problem of Robin Hardy, of course, and his suspension, something, amongst other things, that had been preying on her mind all weekend. Added to her worry about the boy's refusal to say what had happened on Friday was Danny's reluctance over the incident with the eggs. He had been obstinate too. And then there was Michael's reaction. During the time they had been married, there had not been a cross word or a disagreement. His taking Danny's side in the matter of the eggs had surprised and saddened her. In her view it was only right and proper that Danny should divulge the identity of the culprit. Michael's stance was as misguided and intractable as that of the boy. When she had tried to raise the matter with her husband at breakfast on the Saturday morning, he had refused to discuss it further and had been quite short with her.

'I'm surprised, Elisabeth,' he had told her, 'that you are unable to respect Danny's viewpoint. It is surely up to him as to whether or not he reveals the identity of this egg thrower. I should have thought that you would have been far more concerned about this incompetent teacher of his than about a pretty harmless prank.'

'It's hardly a harmless prank, Michael,' she had countered.

'Of course it's a prank. That's what schoolboys get up to and this teacher clearly deserved it. I remember when I was at school we put a herring behind the hot pipes at the back of the classroom and stank the place out, we sent a Valentine from one teacher to another, we put a frog in the teacher's desk. No one was hurt and no damage was done.'

'I think this is rather different,' Elisabeth had said.

'Well let's agree to differ,' Michael had replied. 'And leave it at that.'

'Michael, can we talk about this?' she had asked.

'Look, Elisabeth, as far as I am concerned there is nothing to talk about,' he had told her. 'Danny has done no wrong. He didn't throw any eggs and he was truthful, unlike the other lads. Furthermore, he's not a telltale. In fact, I'm rather proud of him.'

'Oh Michael,' she had answered. 'You are not serious. Proud of him?'

'Yes, I am. Now can we let the matter drop?'

When she had endeavoured to respond again, Michael had risen abruptly from the table, pushing back his chair noisily.

He had raised a hand and told her that there was nothing more to say.

It had been their first real disagreement since they had been married. There had been regular and furious arguments and clashes with her first husband, largely over the upbringing and education of their son, John, but until now her relationship with Michael had been perfectly amicable. She had never seen her husband so angry and fervent about anything. Their heated exchange had saddened her greatly. She decided, as he had suggested, to say no more on the matter.

After so many years in education, Elisabeth assumed that she knew how the minds of children worked, but she felt bemused by both boys' reactions. Robbie had made such an improvement since he had been at the school, yet now he seemed to be reverting to his old difficult and wilful self. Why ever had he been so tight-lipped? Then there was Danny. He had always been such an easy-going, obedient and principled boy, and now this stubborn streak had appeared. What was it about adolescent boys? she asked herself. She thought for a moment of her own son, who she had visited the previous Saturday.

John was a student at Forest View residential special school for severely autistic children. His life was so simple compared to the two boys who lived with her. He was a placid, happy child who lived in a world of his own, untroubled by the worries and problems of others. Elisabeth had found him sitting at his favourite table by the window in the classroom, staring intently at a set of large coloured cards that showed pictures of everyday objects: a kettle and cutlery, cups and plates, hats and coats. He had started to sort the cards according to shape and size, his forehead furrowed with concentration. She had sat next to him and watched him for a moment. He was such a good-looking twelve-year-old, she thought, with his large dark eyes, long lashes and curly blonde hair. She had taken his hand in hers and pressed it gently. He had glanced around and smiled and then returned to arranging the cards.

She loved these quiet moments with her son. She could talk freely about things knowing that she would not be interrupted or challenged. John was the best of listeners. How much he understood of what she said, she would never know.

She looked at the blank piece of paper before her now. Unable to concentrate, she decided to leave the report until later. At eight o'clock, as was her custom, she set off around the school, checking that everything was in order for the week ahead.

In the entrance hall, she discovered a distinguished-looking man waiting for her. He was tall and smartly turned out, and smiled warmly as he caught sight of her.

'Mrs Stirling?' he asked.

'That's right,' Elisabeth replied.

'I'm terribly sorry to arrive so early, but I hoped to see you before school. Your caretaker very kindly said I could wait here. I should have made an appointment, I know, but I do wish to get things sorted ASAP. My name is Robinson,' he said, extending a hand, 'Nigel Robinson.'

'How may I help, Mr Robinson?' asked Elisabeth. She felt a twinge of nerves, for the man looked for all the world like a school inspector. Was this a surprise visit? She had heard that HMI were now undertaking what were termed 'dipstick inspections' – unannounced one-day visits. She shook the proffered hand, noticing that the man wore an expensive gold wristwatch and an enormous signet ring on his little finger.

'I am hoping that you will accept my son Jeremy as a pupil here at the village school,' he told her.

Elisabeth sighed.

'Is something amiss?' asked the man.

'No, no,' she replied. 'I thought you might be a school inspector.'

He laughed. 'Do I look so intimidating?' he asked. He took a small gold-edged card out of his top pocket and passed it to Elisabeth. 'I'm a financial adviser for my sins,' he told her, giving a Cheshire-cat smile. 'If you have any spare cash, Mrs Stirling, I am the man to speak to. I can get you a very good return on your investments.'

'I'll bear that in mind,' replied Elisabeth. 'If you would like to come to my classroom, Mr Robinson, we can discuss the entrance requirements.'

Walking down the corridor and looking around her, she was well pleased with what she saw. The paintwork was shining, the floors had a clean and polished look, the brass door handles sparkled and there was not a sign of graffiti or litter. The display boards, which stretched the full length of the corridor, were covered in line drawings, paintings, photographs and children's writing. Everything looked neat and cheerful.

'It's a splendid-looking school,' said the man as he followed Elisabeth along the corridor. 'Most impressive. I was told about the Barton-with-Urebank school by one of my clients, Major Neville-Gravitas. I believe he is chairman of the governors here?'

'Yes, he is.'

'He spoke in very glowing terms of the school, and indeed of you as the head teacher. Said it was the very best school in the area and that you have transformed the place. And I have to say, Mrs Stirling, I am pleasantly surprised to see such a young and attractive head teacher as yourself. The headmistress at the prep school I attended was an ancient, cranky old thing.'

Elisabeth found the man's obsequious smile and flattery rather unsettling.

'So I do hope that Jeremy might attend,' he continued.

'I can't see there being a problem, Mr Robinson,' answered Elisabeth. 'We do have spaces.'

In the classroom, the man explained that his son was currently at St Paul's, the preparatory school in Rushton.

'The thing is, Mrs Stirling, he has not been at all happy there. He never really got on with his teacher, I'm afraid, and made very little progress in his work during the year. I did go and see Mr Arnold, the headmaster, but I have to say, he was very dismissive and said that Jeremy had put in very little effort. My son is a sensitive and intelligent boy and, to be honest, he has tended to coast. A bright child like him needs the challenge of an enthusiastic and interesting teacher, and his teacher at St Paul's, Mr Pritchard, is a very poor—'

'We don't need to go into that, Mr Robinson,' Elisabeth interrupted. She knew it would be unprofessional to discuss the failings of another teacher. 'How old is Jeremy?'

'He's nine, going on fifty-nine,' said his father. 'He is a rather old-fashioned sort of boy, old for his years.' Elisabeth thought of Oscar. 'I think he will be better suited at a school like this.'

'Well, as I said, we have spaces,' she said. 'Jeremy can start tomorrow.'

'Splendid!' said Mr Robinson. 'I am sure he will be very happy here.'

When the parent had gone, Elisabeth headed back to her classroom. As she passed the small school library, she heard a rustling of pages and, looking behind a bookcase, caught sight of Oscar flicking through a large book. She watched him for a moment and smiled. In all her teaching career she had never met such a bright, interested and articulate ten-year-old, so advanced beyond his years. Some teachers, she knew, would find it trying dealing with such an unconventional and preco- cious child, one who frequently asked questions, challenged his teachers and always had a great deal to say for himself. Mr Hornchurch, fortunately, was not that kind of teacher. He delighted in the boy's curiosity, intelligence and acute awareness, and under his guidance and encouragement young Oscar had flourished. The two seemed to be kindred spirits. Mr Hornchurch had himself been a gifted child who, like Oscar, had appeared to his teachers and his peers bookish and eccentric, so he understood more than most about his young pupil's needs.

Of course Elisabeth knew that throughout history there were those who were labelled odd, outspoken and opinionated when young – precocious children – who later went on to achieve great things, gifted individuals endowed with originality and vision. Oscar was such a one. Looking at the boy now, his nose buried in that large tome, she recalled the words of Mr Steel, the school inspector, when he had come across Oscar on his visit to the school. 'Good teachers,' he had said, 'should show children the ropes but should not be surprised or intimidated if some of them can climb higher than they, or that some of their pupils are making ropes of their own.'

'Hello, Oscar,' she said cheerfully. 'I see you are here bright and early as usual.'

'Oh good morning, Mrs Stirling,' replied the boy, closing the book with a snap and getting to his feet. 'I'm just doing a bit of research.'

'And how are you getting on?'

'Pretty well, you know.'

'What are you researching now?' she asked.

'About the Ancient Greeks. Have you heard of Icarus, Mrs Stirling?'

'Yes, I have,' replied Elisabeth. 'He was the character in Greek mythology, wasn't he, who had wings made of wax and came to an unfortunate end when he flew too near the sun.'

'Wax and feathers,' added Oscar, who then took up the story. 'Icarus was warned by his father not to fly too low because the sea's dampness would clog his wings, and not to fly too high because the sun's heat would melt them. He ignored his father's instructions and flew too close to the sun. His wings melted and he fell in the sea and drowned.'

'So it's always best to listen to a parent's advice, isn't it?' said Elisabeth, smiling.

'The Greeks obviously didn't know much about science,' remarked Oscar. 'You see, Icarus would never have got close to the sun, because he would have frozen to death when he entered the stratosphere, which has a temperature below freezing.'

'Do you know, Oscar,' said Elisabeth, 'you are one in a million.'

'I'm sorry, Mrs Stirling,' said the boy, peering over his glasses, 'I don't know what you mean.'

'I mean, if I want cheering up, I talk to you.'

'Oh,' said the boy, smiling.

'And I really appreciate the way you keep the library so tidy.'

'I've just finished putting all the books back in their correct order,' Oscar told her, pulling the disapproving face of a schoolmaster lamenting the waywardness of a naughty child. 'It was quite a job, I can tell you. The library was in rather a state on Friday. And speaking of Friday, I wanted to have a word with you, about the incident. I had to dash off at the end of school for my piano tuition or I would have spoken to you then.'

'The incident?'

'Involving Robbie Hardy and Barry Biggerdyke.'

'And what do you know about that?' asked Elisabeth.

'I'm not usually one to tell tales, Mrs Stirling,' said the boy. 'I mean, no one likes a snitch, do they? On this occasion, however, I feel I have to. I witnessed it all, and so did Roisin.'

'You saw what happened?'

'Oh yes. It took place here in the library.'

Elisabeth sat on one of the small melamine chairs. 'Sit down, Oscar,' she told him.

Oscar placed his book on the shelf, sat down, crossed his legs and folded his hands on his lap.

'Well go ahead,' said Elisabeth. 'You had better tell me all about it.'

Oscar gave a small cough, as if preparing to deliver a lecture. 'I was tidying the books, as I always do at afternoon break on Friday, when Barry Biggerdyke, who is a very unpleasant boy – Mother, who as you know is a psychotherapist, would probably describe him as a problem child – started to throw the library books on the floor. He was being a real nuisance. When I told him to stop, he grabbed my glasses, threw them on top of a shelf and then punched me in the chest.'

'Did he indeed?'

'Roisin told him not to be so horrid and he called her a very offensive name, which I will not repeat.'

'And how did Robin Hardy get involved?' asked Elisabeth.

'Robbie was in the library, quietly reading a book. He came to my rescue, so to speak. He told Barry to give me back my glasses and stop what he was doing. Barry then called him a name.'

'What did he say?'

'Oh, "pig boy" or something beastly like that. You see, Mrs Stirling, Robbie was provoked and only hit Barry in self-defence. I know he can be a bit of a handful at times, but he has got better lately and on this occasion he was not in the wrong.'

'And Roisin saw all this too, did she?' asked Elisabeth.

'Yes,' replied Oscar, 'and will confirm what I have just told you.'

'Thank you for telling me this, Oscar,' said Elisabeth.

'I mean, I don't agree with violence,' said the boy, 'but sometimes it is unavoidable. Don't you think?'

Elisabeth wasn't listening. She was thinking about Robbie. Why had he not told her all this himself? Had he done so, she would not have suspended him, and she would have had a few strong words to say to Barry Biggerdyke.

'Mrs Stirling?' said Oscar.

'I'm sorry,' said Elisabeth.

'You were miles away.'

'What were you saying?'

'I was just remarking that although I don't agree with violence, in this case it is understandable. I do hope you won't be too hard on Robbie. He was only trying to help.'

A short while later, Mr Biggerdyke marched into school with his son in tow.

Barry's unfortunate appearance was now augmented by two shiny black eyes and a nose as red and swollen as a large, over-ripe strawberry, which together with his prominent ears made him look like some exotic tree-climbing creature of the rainforest. He slouched into Elisabeth's classroom behind his father.

'Ah, Mr Biggerdyke,' said Elisabeth in a brisk and cheerful tone of voice before the man could open his mouth. 'I'm glad you have called into school. I was intending to get in touch with you this morning to ask if you wished to see me. Do sit down.'

Mr Biggerdyke was a gaunt, sullen-faced man with the same pallid, unhealthy complexion and large protruding ears as his son. He was unsettled by the jaunty tone of the head teacher and for a moment was rather lost for words. The wind had been taken out of his sails.

'And how are you, Barry?' asked Elisabeth, addressing the morose-looking boy in the same cheerful tone of voice.

The boy touched a plug of dried blood in his nostril. 'All right,' he grunted.

'Do remember to call me "miss", please, Barry,' said Elisabeth pleasantly. 'I have reminded you of this before. Shall we try again?'

'I'm all right, miss,' the boy mumbled.

'I am pleased to hear it,' said Elisabeth. 'I am sure your injury is not quite as serious as it looks.'

Mr Biggerdyke now found his voice. 'It's serious enough!' he cried. 'I mean, look at him! He looks as if he's walked into the back of a bus. I got your letter and I've come in to see you to complain. This sort of thing shouldn't happen in a school. I don't approve of violence.'

'You really don't need to raise your voice, Mr Biggerdyke,' Elisabeth told him. 'I feel certain that we can discuss this in a calm and civilised manner. I agree that this sort of thing should not happen in school, and I too do not approve of violence.'

'He was hit in the face by some hooligan,' said the boy's father. 'I had to take him to the hospital.'

'Nothing serious, I hope,' said Elisabeth.

'Eh?'

'Barry was not seriously hurt?'

'No, but he might have been,' blustered Mr Biggerdyke. 'I mean, look at the state of his face. It's a disgrace.'

'Yes,' agreed Elisabeth, 'it is.'

'So what are you going to do about this lad who thumped him?'

'I shall speak to the boy concerned again when he returns to school. He has been suspended for the moment.'

'Oh well,' said the man, somewhat mollified. 'That's a start. Course I'm considering legal action. This was an unprovoked assault.'

'And I suppose the parents of the boy that Barry hit could do the same,' said Elisabeth.

'Eh?'

'The parents of the boy your son hit.'

'I didn't hit him!' protested Barry. 'He just punched me.' He touched his swollen nose.

'And what about Oscar?' asked Elisabeth. 'Didn't you hit him?'

'I never touched him, miss,' insisted the boy.

'Barry,' said Elisabeth, 'please don't tell lies. You are in just as much trouble as Robin Hardy. As you are well aware, there were two other pupils in the library, Oscar and Roisin O'Malley, and they tell me you provoked this attack.'

'Hang on, hang on!' interrupted Mr Biggerdyke. 'You're making out that Barry was at the bottom of all this.'

'I'm afraid he was,' answered Elisabeth. 'Your son has been very selective with the truth. He threw library books on the floor, took a boy's glasses and then hit him. He also called Roisin a very offensive name, which I will not tolerate. Barry is certainly not blameless in all this and I am considering suspending him over the matter.'

'I know nothing about this,' said the father. He turned to his son. 'Did you hit this other lad?'

'No, I never did. I just pushed him a bit.'

'The truth please, Barry,' said Elisabeth. 'Don't make matters worse.'

'I didn't hurt him, miss.'

'And what about chucking books on the floor?' asked Mr Biggerdyke. 'Did you do that?'

'It was just a bit of fun,' said Barry sullenly.

'And calling this girl names?'

'It wasn't that bad,' mumbled the boy.

'Mr Biggerdyke,' said Elisabeth, 'it is nearly time for the start of school, so unless there is anything further to discuss, I think you might like to leave me to deal with this unfortunate incident. I can assure you it will not happen again. I do not tolerate name-calling, bullying or violence of any kind, and take a very firm line if it occurs. The boy who hit your son was wrong and will be punished for doing so, and Barry too will face the consequences of his actions. I shall have to discuss this with the school governors before I decide if I need to take things further.' She then played her trump card. 'I do hope it will not lead to expulsions.'

'Expulsions!' exclaimed the parent.

'The governors take a very dim view of such matters,' she told him, adopting a solemn countenance.

Of course, Elisabeth had no intention of consulting the governors or considering expelling the two boys. Her bluff had the desired effect.

'It seems to me, Mrs Stirling,' said Mr Biggerdyke, 'that this is six of one and half a dozen of the other. I mean, boys will be boys. I hope you will see your way to asking the governors not to take things further.'

'Very well, Mr Biggerdyke,' said Elisabeth. 'I think we'll leave it at that.'

'Thank you, Mrs Stirling. Thank you very much.'

Then the man who didn't believe in violence clipped his son soundly around the back of the head. 'Next time, tell me the truth, and if I hear any more about you getting in trouble at school, you'll be in twice as much trouble at home. Now say thank you to the head teacher.'

'Thank you, miss,' mouthed the boy.

# 8

The Reverend Mr Sparshott stood in the hallway of the rectory, waiting for the removal van. The black and white patterned tiles his wife had so disliked were hidden beneath crates of books, boxes of crockery and cases packed with clothes. Mrs Sparshott had left that morning for Durham with their two daughters. Her husband was to follow later that day in the removal van. She was pleased to be away from the cold, dark and depressing building. She was pleased also to be away from the insular and claustrophobic community of nosy shopkeepers, disagreeable farmers and unappreciative parishioners. When Mr Sparshott had broached the possibility of leaving and moving halfway across the world, he had anticipated an adverse reaction, so was surprised when she told him she thought the idea an excellent one. She could see herself well settled in the sunny climate of Africa, with a large house and servants, somewhere her husband would be fully appreciated.

Unlike his wife, Mr Sparshott had mixed feelings about leaving. He was saddened that his time in Barton-in-the-Dale had not turned out as he had expected, but excited at the prospect of a new life in Africa.

There was a knock at the door.

On the step stood Danny.

'Ah, Daniel,' said Mr Sparshott. 'Come in, come in.'

'I 'eard tha were leavin' today,' said the boy. 'Missis Sloughthwaite were tellin' folks in t'village store last week.'

'Is there nothing that shopkeeper doesn't know?' asked the vicar, more to himself than a question for his visitor.

'Aye, she don't miss much,' said Danny, laughing.

Mr Sparshott was surprised that anyone should know the day of his departure, for he had been determined to keep it to himself. He wanted to leave quietly. Of course, keeping anything a secret in this village was impossible.

Danny took an envelope from his pocket. 'This is for you,' he said. 'It's a good luck card.'

'That's very thoughtful of you,' said the vicar, taking the envelope from him. 'Go through into the drawing room. I'm afraid it's in a bit of a mess. As you can see, I am all packed up and ready to go. I'm expecting the removal van any minute.'

The drawing room, with its antiquated furniture, worn carpet and thick plain green curtains, had looked cheerless when the rectory was occupied. Now lacking the few pictures and photographs that had adorned the pale walls, it appeared even gloomier.

'I thought tha'd like to know,' said Danny, beaming. 'I've been hadopted, hofficial like. Dr and Mrs Stirling are mi new mam and dad.'

'That's splendid, Daniel,' said the vicar. 'I'm very pleased for you.'

'I sometimes 'ave to pinch missen to mek sure it's real. I'm a lucky lad, aren't I?'

'You are indeed,' said Mr Sparshott, 'and your new parents are fortunate to have you as a son.' He thought for a moment of Rufus and Reuben, his moody and demanding twin sons, away at boarding school. They were so different to this obliging and good-natured boy who radiated such goodwill.

'I'd love to go to Africa,' said Danny, perching on the windowsill.

'Perhaps you will one day,' said the vicar.

'Are you a bit nervous, like, about goin'?'

'Yes, I suppose I am.' He thought for moment. 'But I think I might be happier there than I have been here.'

'I'll tek good care of t'graveyard when you're gone,' said Danny.

'Well I'm sure Dr Underwood will be very grateful for your help. She is to be the new vicar here, you know.'

'Aye, so Missis Sloughthwaite's been tellin' folk,' said Danny.

'You run along now, Daniel,' said Mr Sparshott. 'I'm sure there are lots of things you want to be getting on with.'

Danny remained perched on the windowsill. 'You know when we went fishin' an' we sat on t'riverbank and talked abaat things?' he said.

'I do,' answered the vicar. 'I enjoyed our little chats.'

'I want to ask you something,' said Danny. 'Summat that's been botherin' me.'

'Is this about what we discussed when you were clearing the snow from the church path?' asked the vicar. 'About always telling the truth?'

'Aye, it is,' replied the boy. 'This thing's been on mi mind an' I need to get it off of mi chest. I allus used to chew things ovver wi' mi granddad when I 'ad summat on mi mind but 'e's gone so I need someb'dy to talk to abaat it.'

'And you thought of me?' Mr Sparshott was suddenly touched by the boy's trust in him. Precious few of the villagers had consulted him for his advice.

'Aye, I did,' said Danny.

'Do you think perhaps your parents might be the best people to speak to about it?' asked the vicar.

'No, I reckon you'd be t'best person to tell.'

'Well if I can be of help,' replied Mr Sparshott.

Danny explained his predicament, how he had been asked by the headmaster at the school to make known the name of the pupil who had thrown eggs at the teacher's car. 'Mi mam,

Mrs Stirling that is, says it's the reight thing to tell, but I can't do it. It's 'ard to explain, but I don't feel reight abaat gerrin' somebody into trouble. Do you think I'm wrong?'

'I think it depends on what the person has done,' said the vicar. 'Sometimes it's best not to say anything. Some might think it is your duty to disclose the name, others that your motive for not doing so is admirable. It's what I would call a moral dilemma. In matters such as this, you must decide for yourself. No one else can tell you what to do. If you feel it is right not to reveal the name of the boy, then you must follow your conscience and keep things to yourself. Does that make any sense to you?'

'Aye, it does,' said Danny, smiling. 'I shall miss our talks by the riverbank.'

'Now,' said the vicar, 'I'm glad you've called, because I want you to have my fishing rods and flies. They are in the hall, so take them when you go. I don't think I'll have the opportunity of fly fishing in Africa. And there's a book for you.' He reached for a leather-bound tome that was resting on the mantelpiece and gave it to Danny. 'It's *The Compleat Angler* by Izaak Walton,' he said.

'But you told me once this is your favourite book,' said Danny, stroking the cover.

'It is, or I should say it was, but I can't think of a better person to give it to,' said the vicar. 'Now you run along. I think I can hear the removal van outside. And don't forget the rods.'

When Ashley arrived at the rectory to say goodbye to the former vicar, she found Danny sitting by his grandfather's grave reading the book he had been given.

'Hello, Danny,' she said.

'Oh, 'ello, miss,' replied the boy.

'Aren't you cold sitting out here?' she asked.

'I likes to be outdoors and it's not that cowld.'

'And what's the book you're reading?'

'Tryin' to read more like,' he told her. 'It's a bit 'ard goin'.' He held up the volume.

'*The Compleat Angler* by Izaak Walton,' she read. 'My goodness, that is a difficult book. I think I'd find it hard going too.'

'Mester Sparshott give it me,' the boy told her. 'And he gev me all his fishing rods an' all.'

'That was very kind of him,' said Ashley. 'He was obviously very fond of you. Well don't stay too long out here in the cold.'

'I've bin talkin' to my grandad,' said Danny. He looked down at the square of marble. The inscription on the tombstone was simple: 'Les Stainthorpe, dearly loved grandfather.'

'You still miss him a lot, don't you?' said Ashley.

'Every day I think abaat 'im,' he said. 'I wanted to tell 'im t'good news. I've been hadopted, hofficial like. All t'papers 'ave been signed.'

'Oh Danny, I am pleased,' said Ashley. She bent down and pecked him on the cheek.

The boy coloured up. 'Well, I berrer gerroff,' he said.

'And so must I,' said Ashley. 'I'm just on my way to see Mr Sparshott before he leaves.'

'Tha's missed 'im. 'E left nobbut five minutes ago.'

'Oh dear,' she sighed. 'I wanted to wish him good luck.'

'A lot o' people in the village din't tek to Mester Sparshott,' said Danny. 'But they din't know 'im, not really. I liked him an' I'll miss 'im.'

Fred Massey was a thickset, heavily wrinkled farmer with a ruddy complexion and a mane of ill-cut hair beneath a greasy cap, the inner rim of which was blackened by dirt and sweat. He wore a threadbare jacket, frayed around the collar, and heavy scuffed boots. That morning he was in his usual grumbling bad temper when he called into the village store for his cigarettes. He carried with him the smell of dung and woodsmoke.

'You want to give them up, Fred,' urged Mrs Sloughthwaite, pushing a packet of his usuals across the counter. 'They'll be the death of you.'

'I'll go and see Dr Stirling if I want medical advice, thank you very much,' Fred replied tetchily. 'Anyway, it won't be fags that'll be the death of me, it'll be that Bianca.'

'What's the poor long-suffering lass done now?' asked the shopkeeper.

'Long-suffering? Her? It's me what's long-suffering,' whinged the customer. 'I thought that when her and our Clarence and that baby of theirs moved in with me, she'd take on the washing and cleaning and cook the meals, but she's gone and got a job cleaning at the school, and when she gets home, she sits around all evening watching the television and stuffing her face with chocolates. And that baby never stops whining.'

'Takes after you then,' muttered Mrs Sloughthwaite.

'What?'

'I said that's what babies do.'

'I'll tell you, I've not had a decent night's sleep for as long as I can remember,' said Fred.

'Who looks after the baby when she's at work then?' asked the shopkeeper.

'Her mother,' said Fred, 'and she's another one. Lazy trollop.'

'And how's the celeriac?' asked Mrs Sloughthwaite.

'I'm a celiac, not a bloody vegetable,' the old farmer corrected her gruffly. 'I'm not a well man, not that she cares.'

'Bianca's not been feeding you poisonous mushrooms again, has she?' asked the shopkeeper mischievously. Fred, as he had told all and sundry, had been convinced his niece-in-law had been putting toadstools in his food in the hope of finishing him off and getting her hands on his money. A visit to the hospital, where he was sent for tests, had revealed that the stomach pains he had been experiencing were because he was a celiac. This gave him more reasons to complain, for it meant he could no longer drink beer.

'You've heard that the vicar's leaving today?' said Mrs Sloughthwaite.

Fred brightened up. 'I have,' he said, 'and it's not before time. Stuck-up, pompous little man that he is. Wasn't two minutes in the village before he started throwing his weight about. He stopped me taking my cows down that track by the church and put a big chain and a lock on the gate.'

'You don't need to remind me,' Mrs Sloughthwaite told him. 'I've heard you innumerate times.'

'Now that Dr Underwood is taking over as the new vicar,' said Fred, 'I reckon she'll let me take my cattle down the track. She's a different kettle of fish from old Sparshott. Mind you, she wants to keep her wits about her. That gypsy up at Limebeck House is sniffing around her. I've seen them together. Thick as thieves they were in the Rumbling Tum café last week.'

'Mr O'Malley is not a gypsy, Fred,' said the shopkeeper. 'He's an estate manager and a very nice man.'

'Estate manager my elbow!' cried Fred. 'The bloke's an odd-job man. He can call himself the King of Prussia for all I care, he's still a gypsy and I wouldn't trust him as far as I could throw him. The new vicar doesn't want to be taking up with the likes of him.'

As if on cue, Ashley entered the shop.

'Mr Massey was just talking about you, Dr Underwood,' said Mrs Sloughthwaite impishly. 'Weren't you, Fred?'

The old farmer coloured up. 'Well I was just . . .'

'What was it you were saying?' Ashley asked. 'Nothing bad, I hope.'

'Just that I ... er ... I'm very pleased to hear as how you're to be the new vicar.'

'Thank you, Mr Massey,' said Ashley, giving him one of her most charming smiles. 'Perhaps I might see you in church a bit more often.'

'Oh, I'm not a churchgoer,' replied the old farmer.

'Wasn't there something else, Fred?' persisted Mrs Sloughthwaite provocatively.

'Eh?'

'About Dr Underwood.'

Fred turned to Ashley and smiled, displaying a set of discoloured tombstone teeth. 'I was just saying that now you're up at the rectory, you might consider letting me take my cattle down the path by St Christopher's. Him what's left wouldn't let me. He said my beasts stank and were too noisy.'

'Provided you keep the path clean, Mr Massey,' replied Ashley, 'I have no objection.'

'That's very Christian of you,' said the old farmer.

'What else were you saying, Fred?' persisted the shopkeeper.

'About what?'

'About Dr Underwood.'

'Oh, I can't remember,' said Fred, pulling a face.

'Something about seeing her in the Rumbling Tum café the other week, wasn't it?' probed Mrs Sloughthwaite, enjoying the old farmer's discomfiture.

'I must be off,' said Fred, heading for the door.

'Now what can I do for you, Dr Underwood?' asked Mrs Sloughthwaite when the old farmer had gone.

'Just a good luck card, please,' said Ashley. 'I meant to say goodbye to Mr Sparshott and wish him well in person, but by the time I had got to the rectory he had gone. I was sorry to have missed him.'

'Well I have to say that there's many who won't miss him,' answered the shopkeeper. 'I don't wish to cast dispersions, but he wasn't the most congenital of men.'

As Ashley looked through the selection of cards that had been placed on the counter, Mrs Sloughthwaite, who rarely missed a thing, noticed the ring on her customer's finger.

'That's a most unusual ring, Dr Underwood,' she remarked. 'I don't recall seeing it before.'

'It's a Claddagh ring,' Ashley told her, 'a traditional Irish ring symbolising love, loyalty and friendship.' She twisted it on her finger. 'The hands represent friendship, the heart represents love and the crown represents loyalty.'

'Could I hazard a guess who gave it to you?' asked the shopkeeper.

'Emmet gave it to me.' Ashley smiled coyly. 'I'm sure it's not escaped your attention that it's on my engagement finger.'

'You're not . . .' began the shopkeeper.

Ashley smiled broadly. 'I am, yes,' she said. 'I'm engaged.'

'Well, very many congratulations, Dr Underwood,' said Mrs Sloughthwaite. 'He's a lovely man is Mr O'Malley and I know you'll both be very happy together.' She folded her arms under her voluminous bosom, delighted that she had some new gossip to pass on to her customers. 'Course, as I told you when I read your horoscope when you called in the store a few weeks back, the two of you are perfectly matched, him being a Capricorn and you a Virago. Don't you recall me telling you that those two star signs have an affinity?'

'I do, and as *I* told *you*, I don't believe in horoscopes,' Ashley told her, smiling.

'Well, a lot of the predelictions have come true, I can tell you,' said the shopkeeper. 'Will the wedding be here in St Christopher's?'

'Oh, it's very early days yet,' said Ashley. 'We haven't fixed a date.' She took a purse from her handbag.

'And will you stay at Wisteria Cottage or move into the rectory?' asked the shopkeeper, keen on gleaning as much information as she could.

'I think we'll live at the rectory,' said Ashley. 'I'll take this card, please.' She counted out the correct money on the counter.

'And will it be a big wedding?'

'No, no, just a small, quiet one, I guess. Look, I must rush. I have a meeting this evening in Clayton.'

'Well, it's wonderful news,' said Mrs Sloughthwaite, scooping up the coins and imagining the reactions of some of the villagers when they heard what she had to tell them.

Lady Wadsworth, accompanied by Gordon, her small wire-haired terrier, found Emmet in the walled vegetable garden, vigorously turning over the soil and whistling to himself. Some distance away, a youth with a shaven head was busy cutting back the stalks of some dead vegetation.

The vegetable garden had been a jungle of wild flowers and thistles, choking brambles and rank bushes that might once have been called shrubs. It had been thick with twisting buddleia and sharp-stemmed briars, a crop of dandelions, frothy white cow parsley, clumps of tall stinging nettles and a mass of other weeds. The walls had been swathed in thick ivy and the paths covered in moss. Emmet had transformed the place, which now looked tidy and well tended.

'Someone sounds in a particularly good mood,' said Lady Wadsworth, approaching her estate manager. She was wearing thick brown tweeds, stockings the colour of mud, heavy brogues and a hat in the shape of a flowerpot.

'Good morning, your ladyship,' said Emmet, 'and what a lovely morning it is too.' He bent to pat the dog, which was frisking around his heels.

'And what has occasioned such happiness?' asked Lady Wadsworth.

Emmet stood and leaned on his spade and thought for a moment. 'It's just that things seem to be going so right for me,' he replied. 'I cannot remember a time when I have felt so content.'

'I'm very pleased to hear it,' she said.

'You know, I wonder sometimes if one day I will wake up and find that this has all been a dream.' He sighed.

'I think it's called the luck of the Irish, isn't it?' she asked.

'Well, it was my lucky day when I stopped off here in Barton,' he replied.

'And how is that assistant of yours getting along?' She looked over to the boy, Jason, who was busy chopping away with a pair of shears. She had taken him on to help with the work on the estate. He had been recommended by Mrs Stirling, who had met him when she had visited County Hall and seen how well he tended the gardens there. He had been in trouble with the police and was working for the Parks Department on community service.

'He's getting on very well,' Emmet told her. 'He's keen, punctual and works hard, and I can't ask for more than that.'

'No,' she agreed.

'The lad has green fingers,' Emmet told her. 'Everything he plants seems to flourish. I'm pleased you were willing to give him a chance. It can't be easy to get a job with a criminal record.'

'Everyone should be given a second chance,' she replied. 'I guess we all have things in our past of which we are not that proud and which we would sooner forget. He seems a sound enough young man, though not one of the world's greatest talkers. He's not said above two words to me since he's been here, and if he sees me coming, he scurries off like a frightened rabbit.'

'He's in awe of you, Lady Wadsworth,' Emmet told her. 'I think he finds you a little daunting,' he added tactfully. He could have told her that the boy was not alone in that. Lady Wadsworth was an overwhelming character, a formidable presence in the county, someone who was used to getting her own way and not a person to be crossed. When the village school had been threatened with closure, she had marched into County Hall and berated the Director of Education, and the school remained open. When a housing estate was planned near Barton-in-the-Dale, she had brought her considerable influence to bear and put a stop to it. When Mr Sparshott had refused to agree to the placing of a stained-glass window in the church commemorating her brother, Lady Wadsworth had sent him away with a flea in his ear. Some weeks later the window was duly installed. In all things she invariably emerged triumphant. The word 'daunting' was perhaps something of an understatement in describing the lady of the manor.

'Stuff and nonsense!' she exclaimed now. 'Me daunting?' She chuckled. 'I've never heard such a thing. Well, I must get along. I have a meeting of the Countrywomen's Guild this afternoon, and they do so rely upon me.'

'Before you go, Lady Wadsworth,' said Emmet, 'there's something important I wish to tell you.'

'Please don't tell me you're leaving,' she said. 'That you have found another position.'

'Not at all. I'm very settled here, and so is Roisin. The thing is – I'm to be married.'

'Married!' she exclaimed.

'To Ashley. I've proposed and she's accepted.'

'I had an idea there was something going on between you two,' said Lady Wadsworth, grinning and wagging a long finger. 'Well, this is wonderful news indeed. You make a perfect couple.'

'I guess there will be quite a few in the village who will disagree with that,' said Emmet.

'Tush! Why should you care what other people think? I never have. She is a lovely young woman and I know you will both be very happy. Now, as to the wedding . . .'

'We've not really talked about that yet,' said Emmet.

'Well you must. These things have to be done well in advance. I shall of course take charge. We need to draw up a guest list, send out the invitations in good time, book the church and decide on the bridesmaids. There is so much for us to do. We will have the reception here at Limebeck House, of course. I know some excellent caterers, and there are the flowers to arrange. It's so exciting: a wedding in the village.'

Emmet knew it would be fruitless to argue with this most formidable of women. He smiled wryly and shook his head.

'Have I said something to amuse you?' asked Lady Wadsworth.

Elisabeth found Tom one lunchtime marking books.

'Oh hello,' he said brightly as she entered the classroom.

'I thought I would see how you are getting on,' she said. 'We have all been so very busy lately that I haven't had a chance to ask you. I also wanted to thank you for dealing so well with Barry. He was in quite a state.'

'From what I gather, he rather asked for it,' said Tom.

'I don't think anyone deserves a punch in the face,' said Elisabeth.

Tom laughed. 'Oh, I can think of quite a few people I came across on the football pitch who deserved a punch in the face. I'm not saying they got one, but they merited it. But Robbie shouldn't have hit the lad.'

'Anyhow, it's been sorted out,' said Elisabeth. 'Both boys are on probation to behave themselves. So, how are you getting on?'

'Pretty well, I think,' replied Tom. 'My class is a nice group of kids and I'm really enjoying the teaching. I thought playing football was tiring, but when I get home at night I'm exhausted.

I flop on the settee and fall asleep. It's all the preparation, the lesson planning and the marking.'

'Yes, I'm afraid that does come with the territory,' answered Elisabeth. 'And how is Peter Norton? I hope he's behaving himself.'

'He's quite a lively character is Peter,' said Tom. 'He has a lot to say for himself but he's not been in any trouble. He did start by being a bit cheeky.'

'What did he say?' asked Elisabeth.

'I asked him how old he was and he told me he was nine,' Tom told her. 'I asked him when he would be ten and he said, "On my birthday, of course." ' He smiled. 'Actually I found it quite funny, but I told him any more backchat and he wouldn't be in the football team. He's mad on football, so since then he's been as good as gold.'

'You still need to keep an eye on him when you go on the school trip, and on Norman Stubbins, of course. I can imagine Norman getting stranded on a cliff or being cut off by the tide. He needs to be extra careful. We don't want any accidents when he's away from home.'

'Elsie, I am sure, will be watching him like a hawk,' said Tom, 'but I'll bear in mind what you have said.'

'And how is Norman getting on?' asked Elisabeth.

'OK,' answered Tom. 'He's not one of the brightest buttons in the box, as my mother would say, but he tries his best.'

'His brother was a nuisance when he was here,' Elisabeth told him. 'Malcolm could be very difficult. I believe he's making his presence known up at the comprehensive.'

'Actually, it's not Peter or Norman who worry me,' Tom told her. 'It's the new boy.'

'Jeremy?'

'He's a strange lad. I just can't get the measure of him.'

'He seems a very well-behaved and polite boy,' said Elisabeth, sounding surprised.

It was true that the new boy appeared to her to be a biddable and courteous young man. He always wished her good morning, opened doors for her, helped tidy up after lunch and had a permanent smile on his face. She occasionally found his ingratiating manner a little too much; for example he never missed an opportunity of saying how happy he was at the school and how much better it was than the last one he attended.

'Why do you say that he is strange?' she asked. 'He seems such a cooperative and likeable child.'

Jeremy Robinson was not a likeable child in Mr Dwyer's opinion. Despite his angelic appearance – long blonde hair, large blue eyes and papery white skin – he was far from innocent and inoffensive. He was a bright and perceptive boy and the work came easily to him, but he didn't exert himself and preferred trying to entertain his peers with clever comments and amusing remarks. What intrigued Tom was that his attempts at humour fell on stony ground, for the other pupils never laughed at his wisecracks. He noticed too that his classmates kept their distance. Jeremy didn't mix with the other children in the playground, chatter with them in groups or join in their games. When Tom in one lesson had asked his pupils to work in pairs, nobody wanted to work with Jeremy.

'Oh I'm quite happy to work by myself,' he told the teacher cheerfully. 'Actually I prefer it.' He smiled. 'I like my own company.'

It seemed the other pupils were wary of the boy. Tom could tell that they found him rather odd. Of course what he had not witnessed was an unpleasant side to the pupil's nature. Jeremy could make spiteful comments, and was particularly cutting and sarcastic in his dealings with the less able children in the class, making sure, of course, that he was out of earshot of Mr Dwyer.

'It's not something I can put my finger on,' Tom told Elisabeth. 'He's not cheeky as such, but he disturbs the lessons by asking frivolous questions in the most innocent way and making flippant remarks just bordering on the insolent in an effort to annoy me. He's clever enough to not quite step over the line. Anyway, I reckon I can handle him.'

I think I might have a word with this young man, thought Elisabeth.

The following day, Norman arrived at the classroom during morning break shivering and soaked to the skin.

'What's happened to you?' asked Tom.

'I was pushed in the pond, sir,' he replied glumly.

When Elisabeth had taken over the headship of the village school, she had made a great many changes, including purchasing new tables for each classroom, a bright carpet to replace the faded linoleum in the corridor and large display boards for the walls. The dark corner by the toilets was transformed into a small, attractive library, and a wild garden with a pond in the centre was created at the rear of the school. The appearance of the pond resulted in yet another complaint from the caretaker.

'You mark my words, Mrs Scrimshaw,' he had told the school secretary, 'it'll end in tears. We'll have the kids jumping in and out of it and I shouldn't be surprised if one of them falls in and drowns.' Thankfully he had been proved wrong and there had been no mishaps at the pond – that is, until the day Norman fell in.

'Who pushed you in the pond?' asked Tom. The boy did cut a pathetic figure. There were bits of weed in his dripping hair and his clothes hung off him, soggy and covered in mud. A stubborn snail clung to his neck.

'It was Jeremy Robinson. He pushed me but said he slipped on the ice and didn't do it on purpose,' said Norman morosely.

'You're not hurt, are you?' asked the teacher.

'I'm cold and wet and everyone laughed and Jeremy Robinson called me a stupid prat,' said the boy.

'Well he shouldn't have,' said the teacher. 'I shall be having words with that young man after morning break.'

'And he called me something even ruder,' said the boy. 'He used the "R" word.'

'The "R" word?' repeated the teacher, looking puzzled.

'Arsehole,' Norman answered.

Norman was not the best pupil in the class when it came to spelling.

'Well, you go and get changed into your PE kit,' Tom told him, 'and we'll see about cleaning and drying your clothes.'

'It's not nice to call someone an arsehole, is it, sir?' asked the boy.

'No, it's not,' agreed Tom.

'And he wouldn't have called Robbie Hardy an arsehole, because if he called him an arsehole he would have had his lights punched out like what happened to Barry Biggerdyke.'

Robbie had become something of a hero in the school since he sorted out the bully.

'You don't need to keep on repeating the word, thank you, Norman,' the teacher told him. 'I'm glad you didn't hit him, otherwise you would have been in hot water.' Looking at the soaking wet figure before him and realising what he had said, Tom could not resist a smile. 'Now run along and get changed.'

Norman was not a bad boy, thought the teacher. He tried with his work but wasn't one of the quickest in understanding. In the lesson when Tom had read a short story about a strange-looking animal with a huge mouth, long tongue, protuberant eyes and a curly tail, he'd asked Norman if he could name the creature.

'Brian,' the boy had replied, smirking.

'Dickhead,' mumbled Jeremy.

'What was that, Jeremy?' asked the teacher.

'I was just saying sir that the chameleon has a thick head. They also have very long tongues and can camouflage themselves by changing colour. I think there are over a hundred different species and—'

'Thank you, Jeremy,' said Mr Dwyer. 'That's most informative.'

'If there is anything else you need to know, sir,' responded the boy, 'you just need to ask. I know quite a lot about this species of lizard.'

'That will be quite enough,' said the teacher.

On Friday, Tom asked the boy to remain behind and warned him that his behaviour was unacceptable and he might be better concentrating on his work rather than trying to be clever.

'But I thought that's what pupils should try to be, sir,' Jeremy remarked, looking up with innocent eyes.

'You know perfectly well what I mean,' Tom told him, bending low so his nose was inches from the boy's. 'Any more clever comments from you, young man, and you will remain in every break and every lunchtime until you learn to behave.'

'I'm sure I don't know what you mean, sir,' said the boy.

'I am not deaf, Jeremy,' said the teacher. 'I can hear the difference between "dickhead" and "thick head".' The boy didn't answer, but there was a trace of a smile on his lips. 'Do you know what the word considerate means, Jeremy?' asked Tom.

'Yes, sir,' replied the boy. 'It means kind, caring, nice.'

'And do you think it is considerate to push Norman in the pond and call him names?'

'Push him in the pond!' exclaimed the boy. 'No, no, sir. I slipped on the ice and accidentally knocked into Norman, and he lost his balance and fell in the pond.'

'Really?' said the teacher, unconvinced.

'I think you have noticed, sir,' said Jeremy, 'that when Norman plays football, he's not the most coordinated of players, is he?'

'That will do!' exclaimed Tom. 'I wasn't aware there was any ice.'

'Oh yes, Mr Dwyer, it was really quite icy. I wouldn't deliberately push anyone into a pond.'

'And what about the name-calling?'

'What names would these be, sir?' asked Jeremy. He clearly thought the teacher would not repeat the offensive words.

'What about "prat" and "arsehole"?' asked Tom.

'I wouldn't use language like that, sir,' said the boy. 'Norman must have misheard me.'

'As I must have done,' said Tom.

Jeremy smiled ingratiatingly and then sighed. 'Poor Norman. He does tend to attract bad luck, doesn't he, sir? I do hope he doesn't have an accident on the school trip next weekend.'

'Just watch your step, young man,' warned the teacher, 'or you will not be going on any school trip.'

# 9

'It'll not last,' said the customer, her face as hard as her words. 'You mark my words, it'll not last.'

Mrs Pocock had called into the village store to hear the latest gossip and had just been informed of the engagement of the new vicar and the estate manager. She had treated this information with a snort of derision.

Mrs Sloughthwaite, her corpulence spilling over the counter as she leaned forward, smiled a patient smile of the sort a teacher might employ when she was explaining things to a small child. She was used to the woman's constant criticism of all and sundry, her endless carping and unceasing complaints about the state of the world. Most people would weary of being subjected to such unremitting gripes and grumbles, but the shopkeeper, in a strange way, had, over the years, endured listening to the customer's whingeing. She had found it oddly entertaining and had treated the woman's diatribes with amused tolerance. However, of late, her forbearance was wearing thin.

'One of these days you'll surprise me and say something nice about somebody,' she said, the smile disappearing from her round face.

'I think it's lovely news, so it is,' said Mrs O'Connor, who had arrived at the village store earlier. 'As my Grandmother Mullarkey was wont to say: "A man without a wife is like a horse without a bridle, and a woman's best possession is a loving husband." They'll make a perfect couple.'

'Come on,' said Mrs Pocock, 'it stands to reason it'll never work. They have nothing in common. I mean, what can somebody like her see in somebody like him?'

'True love recognises no barriers,' remarked Mrs O'Connor.

'Twaddle!' snapped the other customer. 'They're as different as chalk and cheese. She'd have been a lot better off marrying someone of her own kind, like that brother of Mrs Stirling's. He was dead keen on her. He was more her type.'

Elisabeth's brother Giles had indeed been very keen on Ashley. On leave from his regiment, the handsome major had been quite bowled over when he first met the stunning young woman with the soft golden hair and dazzling blue eyes. Ashley was on her way to the village following morning service when she caught sight of a tall, fair, very good-looking man staring up at the church.

'May I help you?' she asked.

'I'm sorry?' he muttered, unable to take his eyes off her. It had been love at first sight.

Sadly for Major Ardingly, Ashley had eyes only for Emmet.

Mrs Pocock was still giving the shopkeeper the benefit of her opinion. 'Well his nose will be pushed out of joint when he hears the news.' She laughed mirthlessly.

'Who?'

'Major Whatshisname.'

'He'll get over it,' said Mrs Sloughthwaite. 'I should imagine a fine-looking man like him has women queuing up.'

'So when are the odd couple getting married, then?' asked Mrs Pocock.

'They haven't decided yet.'

'And where are they going to live?'

'At the rectory, I should imagine.'

'And are they to be wed at St Christopher's?'

'I wouldn't know.'

'Well it's not like you to be in the dark,' said Mrs Pocock. 'You're very good at extracting information from your customers.'

'Extracting information!' repeated the shopkeeper. 'You make me sound like the Gazpacho.'

'The what?'

'Those horrible Germans who tortured people in the last war.'

'Gestapo!' cried Mrs Pocock, rolling her eyes.

'Whatever,' said the shopkeeper.

At this point the doorbell tinkled and a customer entered. He was a striking-looking man of about forty, tall and of military bearing, with a large aristocratic nose and a head of thick hair greying around the temples. He was dressed in a well-cut woollen overcoat and wore expensive kid leather gloves.

'Good morning,' he said with a slight accent.

'Morning,' said the shopkeeper. 'How can I be of help?'

'I am looking for a Major Neville-Gravitas,' he replied. 'I am told he lives in zer village.'

'He does, love, yes,' said Mrs Sloughthwaite. 'He has a cottage across the village green, opposite the war memorial. You can't miss it. It's called Normandy Cottage.'

'Thank you,' said the man, bowing slightly.

'He won't be there, though,' said Mrs Pocock. 'He props up the bar this time of day.'

'I'm sorry, I don't understand,' said the man.

'He'll be in the pub,' she explained. 'In the Blacksmith's Arms.'

'It's just along the high street,' added Mrs O'Connor, 'a two-minute walk if you run.'

'Ah, I see. Thank you.' He turned to go, but Mrs Sloughthwaite was not going to let him escape so easily.

'You're not from around these parts?' she said.

'No, I am from Germany. I am just wisiting.'

'The major.'

'That is right.'

'A friend of yours, is he?'

'No, not really. Vell, thank you for your help.'

'Well, what do you make of that?' asked Mrs Pocock when the man had gone. 'I wonder what he wants with the galloping major?'

'I don't know,' replied Mrs Sloughthwaite.

'No, but you soon will,' murmured the customer.

There were few customers in the Blacksmith's Arms that lunchtime. A couple were in earnest conversation at a corner table, two ruddy-faced farmers were engrossed in a lively discussion on the merits of a newly purchased tractor, Fred Massey, a pint of cider in his hand, stood with his back to the fire warming himself, and Major Neville-Gravitas perched on a stool at the end of the bar holding forth to a broad individual with an exceptionally thick neck, vast florid face and small darting eyes.

'So this admiral, standing on the bridge of a ship, sees a light ahead of him,' said the major, 'and orders a message to be sent to the captain of the oncoming vessel to change course. Back comes the reply suggesting that *he* should change course. The admiral gets pretty shirty about this and orders another sharply worded message to be sent instructing the master of the oncoming ship to change course immediately, informing him that if he doesn't, there will be one hell of a collision. Anyhow, back comes the reply saying that it would be advisable if the ship the admiral is on changes course. The old boy is now spitting blood and sends another message to the skipper of the ship heading straight for him to change course and be pretty quick about it, pointing out that he is on the bridge of a battleship, the biggest and most powerful armoured warship in the British Navy, and he can guess who will come

'I'm sorry about that,' said the major. 'It's a sad part of one's life, losing a parent.'

'My mother never spoke about you until she vas nearing her death. Then she told me you ver once very close.'

The major gave a small cough before taking a rather large sip of his whisky.

'We were close, yes,' he replied.

'This is very difficult for me to put into words,' said the man. 'I have thought about vat I might say many times. I think zer best thing to do is to say it straight out.'

'Of course, old chap,' said the major, having no inkling of what was to come. 'You go ahead.'

'Ven my mother married my father, she vas expecting a baby.'

The colour drained from the major's face. 'Ah,' he said.

'She vas carrying your baby, Major Neville-Gravitas,' said the man. 'I am your son.'

Later that day, Fred Massey called into the village store.

'By, but it's cold enough for two pairs of shoelaces today,' he said, rubbing his hands. A dewdrop trembled on the tip of his nose.

'Have you just come from the Blacksmith's Arms?' asked Mrs Sloughthwaite.

'Aye, I have,' replied Fred. 'Why?'

'Did this German man come in looking for Major Neville-Gravitas?'

'Tall bloke in an expensive overcoat and fancy gloves?'

'That's him. I wonder what he wanted with the major.'

'I don't know, but when he spoke to him, old Gravitas went as white as a slab of lard, then ordered a double brandy and downed it in one. Get us my usual fags, will you?'

The shopkeeper reached for the cigarettes and Fred passed over the money.

'Well that's a rum do,' remarked Mrs Sloughthwaite. 'Bit of a mystery.'

It won't be a mystery for long, though, knowing you, thought Fred. She'd soon have all the information at her fingertips.

'By the way, what's wrong with your Clarence?' asked the shopkeeper. 'I saw him yesterday limping down the high street. Is he all right?'

'Clarence!' Fred spat out the name. 'He's about as useful as a washing brick, that good-for-nothing nephew of mine.'

'What's the poor lad done now?'

'You mean what hasn't he done!' snapped Fred. 'I can't trust him to do anything right. He's no use nor ornament. I got this new collie from Hamish Ross and told our Clarence to get it used to the sheep and train it to round them up. You'd think it was a simple enough job, wouldn't you? I gave him a long length of rope and told him to tie one end round the dog's neck and keep a firm hold on t'other so as how he could control the animal. It turns out the sheepdog is as daft as our Clarence. Frightened of its own shadow it is. I have this rogue sheep, a big nasty-tempered Texel. When the collie approached to get it in the pen, the sheep was having none of it and made to butt the dog. Stupid animal shoots back like lightning to our Clarence and runs round and round him with the rope still round its neck, trussing him up. So the daft lad is stood standing there with this rope wrapped right around him, couldn't move a muscle, the useless dog whimpering and shivering behind him and this mad sheep trying to knock him over. And that's why he's limping, if you must know. Serves him right. I was telling the lads at the auction mart, and they had a good laugh about it.'

'Well I don't think it's right making fun of him,' said Mrs Sloughthwaite.

'He'll get over it,' said Fred. 'He can chalk it up to experience.'

Mrs Underwood stood by the window of her flat, looking down at the jade-coloured river, dimpled under the rain, that streamed beneath the stone bridge. It was a dull, overcast day with a blanket of gloomy clouds in the leaden sky. She raised her eyes to look at the great grey cathedral that dominated the city and thought of her daughter. How could she throw everything away, marrying a man so much her inferior in every way? She had not heard from Ashley for over a week. She usually telephoned every Monday and visited each month, but since their last disagreement, there had been no contact. She was such a stubborn girl, thought Mrs Underwood, self-willed, determined to have her own way. It had always been the case. Well, I have no intention of getting in touch with her, she told herself. She must make her bed and lie in it.

Perhaps she should give the apartment another clean, she thought, but she could see as she turned from the window that it didn't need it. The lounge was spotless and tidy, with not a thing out of place. Its clinical appearance always reminded Ashley of the waiting room in some swish medical consultant's practice – expensively equipped but cold and featureless. The cream-painted walls were unadorned save for a couple of insipid watercolours of hills and a river; there was a sofa and matching armchair upholstered in an off-white material, plain light brown curtains, a pale tan carpet, a glass-topped coffee table on stainless-steel legs and in a corner a small television. There were no photographs or ornaments.

The previous day, Mrs Underwood had been invited by Miss Sowerbutts, who lived next door to her in the De Courcey Apartments, to join her for afternoon tea. She had told the former head teacher at the Barton-in-the-Dale village school, someone with whom she felt she had a great deal in common, about her daughter's imprudence in considering marrying a man so beneath her in every way. She had been surprised by the other woman's reaction.

'Your words remind me of what my father said when I told him I wanted to marry a man I met at the teacher training college,' said Miss Sowerbutts. 'Patrick was his name, and he was Irish and from a very different background to my own. "You can do a great deal better than him," my father told me. "I didn't send you to a top private school and give you every advantage to throw yourself away on the first man who takes an interest in you, and certainly not someone like that." I can recall his words to this day. Actually this Mr O'Malley sounds rather like Patrick.'

'He's not a teacher!' snapped Mrs Underwood. 'He's an odd-job man. Before that he was a sort of gypsy who travelled around in a caravan with his daughter. I mean, what kind of life could he offer Ashley? It's unthinkable that she should throw everything away to marry such a man.'

'You are now sounding very much like my father,' said Miss Sowerbutts. 'He said I would be ruining my life taking up with someone like Patrick. We both finished college and Father forbade me to see him again, so I gave him up.'

'Well it was probably for the best,' said Mrs Underwood.

'No, I don't think it was,' replied Miss Sowerbutts. 'I regret it,' she said sadly. 'I was weak. I should have stood up to my father.'

'Are you saying that I should consent to this unsuitable match?' asked Mrs Underwood.

'My dear Ruth,' replied her friend, 'it really doesn't matter whether you consent to it or not; your daughter will go ahead with the marriage with or without your blessing. Is it not perhaps better to accept the inevitable?'

No, thought Mrs Underwood when she had returned to her apartment, I will never accept it.

The telephone rang.

'Hello, Mother,' came a hesitant voice down the line.

'Oh, it's you, Ashley. I wondered when you were going to phone.'

'How are you?'

'As well as can be expected.'

'I thought I might call around tomorrow.'

'You can suit yourself,' she said, refraining from adding that she always did anyway.

'It will be about four o'clock.'

'I'm in all afternoon. I'm not going anywhere,' answered her mother.

The next day Ashley called as arranged. She sat opposite her mother and managed to raise a smile.

'How have you been keeping?' she asked.

'You always ask that, Ashley,' said Mrs Underwood, 'and I always say the same thing. I hardly see anybody from one week to the next, there's nothing for me to do except read and do the crossword and there's never anything to watch on the television. And please don't tell me to get out more. The last thing I want to do is walk the streets in this sort of weather.'

'What about your friend in the apartment next door?'

'Miss Sowerbutts? I can't really call her a friend. I've just had afternoon tea with her.'

'That was nice.'

'Not really. She's very schoolmarmish. I always find that teachers speak to you as if you're a child. I suppose it's all those years spent in the classroom telling others what to do.'

'I've got a new job,' her daughter told her, trying to sound cheerful. Her mother didn't reply. 'I shall be moving back to Barton-in-the-Dale.'

'Isn't the bishop satisfied with your work, then?' asked Mrs Underwood.

'Quite the opposite,' said Ashley. 'I've been offered the position of vicar there.'

'You've not been in your present job above five minutes and now you are off again. Mind you, I suppose a vicar is better than being a glorified secretary to the bishop.'

'As I have told you, there's a bit more to being a bishop's chaplain than secretarial work,' Ashley said. 'Anyway, I shall be returning to St Christopher's in a couple of weeks.'

'You never seem to be settled,' remarked her mother. 'You're always going from one thing to another.'

'I shall be settled back in Barton.' Ashley took a breath and decided to broach the subject that had caused such contention at the last visit. 'Mother, about me getting married . . .' she began.

Her mother held up a hand. 'Please don't, Ashley,' she told her. 'I really do not wish to discuss it. I have made my feelings perfectly clear. Nothing I say will change your mind, I can see that, and nothing you can say to me will change my opinion that this marriage is ill-advised and will end in tears.'

'Very well, Mother,' said Ashley sadly. 'Let's not discuss it further.'

'When we move into the rectory,' asked Roisin, 'will we be able to have a grandfather clock like the one at your cottage that belongs to Mrs Stirling?'

The girl was sitting with Ashley on the sofa in the gate lodge at Limebeck House.

Emmet looked up from the paper he was reading and smiled. 'Look, young lady,' he said in a mock-serious tone of voice, 'don't start getting ideas that we are made of money. They're expensive things are grandfather clocks.'

'I know that, Daddy,' replied the girl, 'but maybe one day.'

'What is it about a grandfather clock that you like?' asked Ashley.

'I do love the sound of the tick-tock and hearing it strike the hour and seeing the little figures dancing on the clock face as if they are alive. Mrs Stirling told me once that when she was a little girl she liked to listen to it ticking away and look at the coloured figures. She used to imagine when she was in bed at night that they came to life and danced on the carpet when everyone else was asleep. One day the clock stopped and Mrs Stirling said she thought it was because her brother put his cricket bat inside, and I don't think it liked that too much because the pendulum stopped swinging, but the lady next door said it was because someone in the family had died.'

'And had somebody in the family died?' asked Emmet.

'An uncle who used to own the clock,' Roisin said.

'It's like the song I used to sing,' he said. 'Do you remember? "My Grandfather's Clock", which stopped, short, never to go again, when the old man died.'

'Well this clock did,' said Roisin. 'When Mrs Stirling moved into Wisteria Cottage, it started working again. It was like magic. She said she thought the clock felt at home. I told her that if we ever stopped travelling, I'd have a big grandfather clock like hers that ticked away every day with little dancing figures on the front, and I'd have a fat black cat and I'd grow lots of flowers and I'd feed the birds.'

'When we move into the rectory,' said Ashley, 'we will get a fat black cat.'

'Really!' cried Roisin.

'And we'll plant lots of flowers and feed the birds.'

'And get a grandfather clock?' said the girl eagerly. She glanced at her father before adding, 'When we can afford it, that is.'

'And get a grandfather clock,' laughed Ashley, 'when we can afford one.'

'Do you promise?'

'Yes, I promise,' said Ashley, kissing the girl's cheek.

When Ashley and Emmet had told Roisin that they were going to get married, they could not have hoped for a better reaction. The little girl had clapped her hands gleefully and then given Ashley a great hug. They had been anxious about how she would respond when they told her, and discussed what they would say: explain that they loved each other and wanted to be together as a family. They had not expected the child to become so pleased and excited.

'Could I be a bridesmaid?' was the first thing she had asked.

'Of course,' said Ashley. 'I shall just have the one, and it will be you.'

'And will I have a new dress?'

'Certainly,' said Ashley.

'Can it be emerald green with matching shoes and can I hold a bouquet and—'

'Slow down,' interrupted her father. 'All in good time. It's early days yet and lots of things haven't been decided. Now, how is school?'

'It's fine,' replied the child, 'although there's been a few shenanigans.'

'A few what?' chuckled Ashley.

'That's what my daddy sometimes says when children don't behave themselves.'

'And who's not behaved themselves?' asked Ashley.

'Robbie Hardy.'

'Oh dear, I hoped it wouldn't be him,' sighed Ashley. 'What has Robbie been up to?'

'He punched a boy called Barry,' Roisin told her.

'Oh Robbie,' sighed Ashley again.

'Why did he hit this boy?' asked Emmet.

'Well, the boy he punched is called Barry Biggerdyke and he's a bully and Robbie hit him because he called me and Oscar names and threw the books on the floor in the library and then took Oscar's glasses and then—'

'Slow down! Slow down!' her father butted in. 'You say he called you names?'

'That doesn't matter,' Roisin told her father, keen to get on with the story.

'It does matter,' said Emmet. 'What did he call you?'

'Oh, being a gypsy and that. I got used to it at my last school and just ignored it. Anyway, Robbie told him to stop, and when he didn't, he hit him right on the nose. There was blood and everything.'

'And what has Mrs Stirling done about it?' asked Ashley.

'She's sorted it all out.'

'Roisin darlin',' said Emmet, 'could you go up to your room and finish your homework, please? I want to have a word with Ashley.'

'Grown-up talk?' she asked, smiling.

When the girl had gone, Emmet came and sat next to Ashley. 'I wonder if people in the village call *me* a gypsy,' he said.

'Does it matter?' asked Ashley.

'It's just that the word has certain connotations, doesn't it? Raggle-taggle gypsies. Travellers are often regarded with suspicion. I spent a few weeks in a gypsy camp back in Ireland, and they were good, honest folk. Some people think they're all thieves and scoundrels, which is just not the case.'

'I know that,' said Ashley.

'But you're different. Roisin had a bad time at one of the schools she attended,' he said. 'She had to put up with a lot of name-calling, and the teachers didn't do much about it. I hope it doesn't start happening again.'

'Children can be very cruel at times,' said Ashley, 'but I wouldn't worry. Elisabeth takes a really hard line on bullying and will have dealt with it. Roisin doesn't seem that upset. I could have a word with Elisabeth, though, if you like. We have a governors' meeting coming up.'

'No, you're right,' he said. 'Roisin doesn't seem too worried. I'm sure she'd say something if she was upset.' He changed the subject. 'So how did you get on with your mother today?' he asked.

'Not very well, I'm afraid,' she told him, 'but I rather expected it would be another difficult visit. I don't think she will ever accept us getting married. I was wasting my breath. Our relationship has never been good and it got worse after my father left. I really have tried, Emmet. I don't know what else to do.'

'You've done your best,' he said.

'I would like her to be at my wedding, but I know she won't come. I feel sorry for her because she's miserable and lonely and still so bitter.'

'Are you still sure you want to marry me?' Emmet said suddenly.

'Of course I am!' she exclaimed. 'Whatever made you think otherwise?'

'I do love you, you know,' he said.

'And I love you. Now let's decide who we are going to invite.'

The following morning, Emmet came across two youths stretched out smoking on a bench before the ornamental pond in the walled vegetable garden at Limebeck House. The first was an unfortunate-looking weasel-faced boy with greased ginger hair that stuck up on his scalp like the spines of a hedgehog. His thin face was full of exploding red acne. He had an assortment of silver rings and studs in the lobes of both ears, and on his knuckles *LOVE* and *HATE* were spelled out in large blue letters. His companion, a thickset, round-shouldered individual with small, mean eyes, had a closely-shaven bullet-shaped head, and like his companion, he sported several large metal rings and studs. His arms were embellished with colourful tattoos of snakes and dragons.

'Can I help you?' asked Emmet.

'We're here to see Jason,' said the weasel-faced youth.

'Who are you?'

'We're mates of his.'

'Jason's busy,' Emmet told him.

'We'll wait,' said the other boy, nonchalantly flicking the ash from his cigarette. 'He'll be having a break soon.'

'No he won't,' Emmet said. 'Jason's working through this morning, so you had better be on your way.'

'Big place you have here,' commented weasel-face. He swept a grubby hand through his greasy hair.

'You are on private property,' said Emmet, 'and you are trespassing, so I suggest you leave right now.'

'And if we don't?' asked the boy. He ran an index finger across the base of his nose to remove a plug of mucus from a nostril.

'Then I shall make you,' replied Emmet calmly.

The bullet-headed boy gave a hollow laugh and stood up. His companion followed suit. 'Oh yeah?' he said.

Before this exchange could escalate, as surely it would have done, Jason appeared. At the sight of the two youths he looked taken aback.

'What are *you* doing here?' he demanded.

'We're here to see you,' said bullet-head.

'I'm working,' Jason told them.

'You can spare a few minutes to see your old mates,' said weasel-face. 'Can't you?'

'No, he can't,' Emmet cut in. 'You heard what he's told you, he's working. I want you off this land. So get moving.'

'You had better go,' added Jason. He looked nervous and embarrassed. 'I'll see you later.'

'You'd better see us later,' said bullet-head.

The two boys ambled off.

'Sorry about that,' said Jason. 'I've told them not to come up here.'

'If I were you, I'd keep clear of those two,' said Emmet. 'I think you can do without friends like that.'

'They're not my friends,' protested the boy. 'I hate them. I don't want anything to do with them, but they won't leave me alone. I wish I'd never met them. It was those two who landed me in trouble with the police in the first place, getting me done for thieving, banged up in the young offenders' slammer for a month and then having to do community service.'

'So how did you get mixed up with those two clowns?' asked Emmet.

'They live down our street,' Jason told him. 'I used to go out most nights, wander the streets to get away from all the rows and shouting in the house. My old man was always having a go at my mam, and if it wasn't her, then it was me or my brothers. He used to come in drunk, shouting the odds. I met those two lads and got into trouble. First it was shoplifting, then more serious stuff, like breaking into cars and houses. There was this bloke. Banks was his name. He was really bad news. He used to get rid of the gear that we nicked. He was a builder and travelled all over the place on jobs, so what we stole was never traced. Anyway, we got caught and Banks disappeared with all the money he owed us. Those two lads who turned up here this morning are looking for him, and when they find him, well I don't fancy his chances.'

'Listen, Jason,' said Emmet. 'Mrs Stirling, who recommended you for this job, and Lady Wadsworth, who let me take you on, have given you a chance to better yourself.'

'I know that, and—'

'Let me finish. You have a good job here, which you like doing. You are punctual and hard-working, you do as you are told and you have made a real effort since you've been here. I've been really pleased at the way that you have applied yourself. You've got prospects and can make something of yourself. But if you keep company with those two villains, then you will throw all that away and let down those of us who have trusted you and given you the opportunity to turn your life around.'

'I know all that!' cried the boy. 'I'm dead grateful for what you've done for me, and Mrs Stirling and Lady Wadsworth. I don't want to get mixed up with them two again, but they won't leave me alone. They keep coming round our house asking my mam where I am, watching and waiting. If I could just get away from them, live somewhere else . . .'

Emmet thought for a moment. 'Well, I might have the solution,' he said.

'How?'

'Roisin and I used to travel around the country in the caravan parked in the paddock behind Limebeck House. It has a small oven, a wood-burning stove and—'

'And I could live there?' exclaimed Jason.

'Hold your horses,' Emmet told him, laughing. 'There's a tap for water in the outhouse, and a toilet, and I could run a cable so you would have electricity. The caravan is comfortable and you could stay there if Lady Wadsworth is agreeable.'

'That's great!' cried Jason. 'I'd love to live there. Thanks, Emmet.'

'You would have to do your own cooking and cleaning,' Emmet said.

'No problem.'

'Then I'll have a word with Lady Wadsworth this afternoon.'

'And you might mention the security of the house to her,' said the boy. 'Or rather the lack of it.'

'In what way?'

'Those two lads wanted information about the house – when there would be no one about, a plan of inside, and where it's easiest to get in.'

'And what have you told them?' asked Emmet.

'Nothing!' exclaimed Jason. 'I've told them nothing, but they keep pestering me. Getting into the house is dead easy,' he continued. 'You might as well leave the front door wide open. There's no security.'

'Yes, I see that,' said Emmet. 'It's been on my mind. I need to do something about it.'

'You want security lights at the front and back of the house,' said Jason, 'double locks on the windows and doors and a burglar alarm. Course the best way of scaring off someone trying to break in is a dog, a big dog like an Alsatian or a Dobermann, not a little terrier like Lady Wadsworth's.'

That afternoon Emmet went to see Lady Wadsworth. He was shown into the kitchen by Watson and was soon joined by the lady of the manor, who was followed by her frisky little dog, its tongue lolling and its tail wagging frantically.

'Thank you for seeing me, your ladyship,' he said.

At Lady Wadsworth's invitation, he took the proffered chair at the large pine table and sat opposite her.

'If it is about the wedding plans,' said Lady Wadsworth, 'let me put your mind at rest. Everything has been arranged this end. I believe Bishop Atticus is officiating?'

'That's right, assisted by Father Daly.'

'And have you picked a best man?'

'I've asked Michael Stirling,' Emmet told her.

'A splendid choice. Now, who will give Ashley away? I believe she doesn't see her father.'

'Sadly not. We're a bit stuck when it comes to choosing someone to walk her down the aisle. I suppose we could ask Major Neville-Gravitas.'

'Yes, I think he would just about fit the bill,' said Lady Wadsworth half-heartedly.

'Actually, your ladyship,' said Emmet, 'it wasn't about the wedding that I wished to see you. It's about security.' He thought of Jason and smiled to himself. 'I've been speaking to a security expert and he feels we need to install a raft of safety measures to make Limebeck House more secure: outdoor lighting, better locks on windows and doors and a burglar alarm. He also suggested getting a guard dog.'

The terrier looked up and cocked its head as if it understood.

Lady Wadsworth bent and tickled the bristly little head. 'Gordon is a great deterrent,' she stated. The dog gave a growl, as if in agreement.

'I don't think he could see off a hardened burglar,' said Emmet.

'You might be surprised,' answered Lady Wadsworth. 'He's a tenacious and intimidating little fellow when he wants to be. Anyway, let me think about the guard dog, but sort the rest out, will you. I think it is about time that we made the house more secure.'

# 10

The frosted glass at the reception desk at Clayton Comprehensive slid back sharply and a thin, hawk-faced woman poked her head through the hatch like a tortoise emerging from its shell. She had a hard, compressed mouth and cold blue eyes magnified behind large black-framed glasses.

'Good morning,' said Michael, smiling.

'May I help you?' asked the secretary, her face remaining dramatically tight-lipped and stern.

'I hope so,' he said pleasantly. 'I have an appointment.'

'Who with?' she asked brusquely.

'The headmaster.'

She began flicking through a large black book. 'At what time?'

'At a quarter to nine.'

She glanced up at the clock on the office wall. 'You're early. Mr Ironside is in a meeting.'

'I don't mind waiting.'

She continued to turn the pages. 'And you are?'

Michael passed through the letter that he had received from the school the week before, addressed to 'The Parent or Guardian of Daniel Stainthorpe'.

'Oh yes,' said the secretary, pulling a face, 'that young man.'

'I'm sorry?' said Michael, getting increasingly angry at the woman's cavalier manner.

'You are the father of the boy who is in trouble.'

'Yes I am,' replied Michael, 'but whether he is in trouble or not is a matter of opinion.'

The woman stared at him for a moment. 'Take a seat,' she instructed, addressing him as one might a disobedient child. 'I will call you when Mr Ironside is available.' She slid the frosted glass shut sharply.

Ten minutes later, Michael was shown into the headmaster's room.

'Mr Stainthorpe,' announced the secretary.

Mr Ironside rose from his desk to greet the visitor. He was a lean, weary-looking individual of indeterminate age, with a pained expression and tired, milky eyes behind wire-framed spectacles. His grey hair, thin and dry, retreated from a red dome of a head. He was dressed in a shapeless grey suit with traces of dandruff on the collar, a white shirt that had seen better days and a loud coloured tie.

'Take a seat, Mr Stainthorpe,' he said, gesturing to a hard-backed chair to the front of his desk.' He leaned back and ran his fingers through his thinning hair.

'Good morning,' said Michael pointedly.

'Ah yes, good morning. Mr Stainthorpe—' began the headmaster.

'Actually I'm not Mr Stainthorpe,' Michael told him. 'My name is Dr Stirling.'

The headmaster sat up, leaned forward and rested his hands on the desktop. His demeanour suddenly changed. 'Dr Stirling?' he said.

'That's right.'

'You are James Stirling's father?'

'Yes, I am.'

The headmaster smiled obsequiously. 'I'm sorry, Dr Stirling, I was expecting another parent.' Removing his glasses, he placed them carefully on the desk before him. His smile was even wider. 'James is doing extremely well,' he said.

'Would that all pupils in the school were like him. He is one of our high-flyers and we expect great things of him. I think in the last standardised verbal reasoning test and the interim mathematics examination James scored particularly highly and—'

'Excuse me, Mr Ironside,' interrupted Michael. 'I am not here about James. I am here about my other son, Daniel.'

'Daniel?'

'Daniel Stainthorpe is my other son.'

The headmaster looked confused.

'He's adopted,' explained Michael.

The headmaster's countenance changed dramatically. 'I see,' he said.

'You wrote asking to see me.'

'I did,' said the headmaster. 'As I explained in my letter, Dr Stirling, Daniel is in very serious trouble.'

'In what way?' asked Michael.

'He witnessed an act of wilful vandalism and refuses to say who the perpetrator is.'

'Yes, I am fully aware of that,' said Michael calmly, 'and I have to say I am surprised at your overreaction. I should hardly think throwing a couple of eggs at a teacher's car could be construed as an act of wilful vandalism.'

The headmaster breathed through his nose like a horse and then placed his spectacles back on his nose. 'This is a very serious matter, Dr Stirling,' he said portentously. 'I will not tolerate behaviour of this sort in this school. I pride myself on exercising firm discipline here at Clayton Comprehensive and—'

'And fair?' asked Michael.

'I'm sorry?'

'Firm but fair.'

'Yes, of course,' he replied. 'Throwing eggs at a teacher's car is a very serious matter in my book.'

'I hardly think it can be described as a very serious matter or an act of wilful vandalism,' answered Michael. 'It's not a capital offence. Of course, if the car had been damaged then this would be a different matter. Anyway, that is by the by. The point is, my son did not throw the eggs. He is an innocent party.'

'Dr Stirling—' began the headmaster.

'If I may finish. From what I gather, Daniel, along with several other boys, merely witnessed the act, but he was the only one who admitted to it. He could quite easily, like the others, have lied and said he had not seen what had happened. But he didn't do this. My son is, above all, a very honest young man. It is in his nature to tell the truth. Refusing to inform upon a schoolmate would be regarded by some as praiseworthy. Nobody likes a sneak.'

'I hardly think it is praiseworthy to conceal something that would bring the wrongdoer to justice,' said the headmaster.

'Well on that we will agree to differ. I will also say this. In my opinion, you might ask why a pupil should throw eggs at a teacher's car. Surely this would not have happened had the teacher in question been liked and respected by those he teaches. Daniel's teacher, from what my son tells me, spends most of his time shouting and telling his pupils how dim-witted they are. He sets no homework and he rarely marks a book.'

Mr Ironside gave a rather pitying smile. 'I have been in education a long time, Dr Stirling,' he said, 'and I have learnt that the things children sometimes say should be taken with a pinch of salt.'

'Really?' retorted Michael. 'Well in my experience, children generally tell the truth, and my son is a particularly truthful young man. Perhaps you might like to spend some time observing some of this teacher's lessons and see if what Daniel says is correct. Actually I am surprised that you as the headmaster are unaware of this teacher's inadequacy. James, as you say, is a bright boy and is doing really well in the top class. He enjoys school, likes his teacher, Miss Waring, and is given a good amount of homework which is well marked. Daniel's teacher is very different. Perhaps you might like to ask Mr Baxter to join us and see what he has to say.'

'Have you quite finished?' said the headmaster, his face flushed with anger. He was not used to being spoken to in such a way.

'No I haven't,' replied Michael evenly. 'The matter of the eggs I think is now closed. I should add, however, that I shall be writing to the Director of Education about this teacher and suggest a school inspector visits to observe his lessons.' He stood and made for the door. 'With that, I wish you a good morning.'

As he walked through the school office, the secretary, who had heard every word, rose from her chair.

'I can see myself out,' he told her.


While this confrontation was taking place, Elisabeth was sitting with Mr and Mrs Ross and Robbie in the staffroom. She had asked Mr Hornchurch to join them.

'Why ever did you not tell me what happened in the library?' she asked the boy.

Robbie remained impassive, staring straight ahead.

'Come on, lad,' prompted Mr Ross. 'Answer Missis Stirling.'

'I just didn't want to,' he said.

'But why?' asked Elisabeth.

'It was between him and me, miss.'

'Oh Robbie,' said Elisabeth with a sigh and a shake of the head. She looked at the boy's pursed mouth and habitual frown. 'What are we going to do with you?'

'I don't know, miss,' he mumbled, giving her a quick, unhappy look.

'This has happened before, hasn't it, Robbie?' Mr Hornchurch reminded him. 'Getting into a fight with Barry? Can you remember what I said to you then?'

The boy nodded.

'I said that violence solves nothing,' Mr Hornchurch continued. 'If someone says something unkind to you, it is best to ignore it, just put it down to the comments of a sad and stupid person who has nothing better to do than hurt other people's feelings.'

'It wasn't just what he said to me,' replied Robbie. 'It was the way he bullied the other kids. I hate bullies.'

'Yes, I am aware that you were trying to help Oscar,' said Elisabeth, 'but it was very wrong hitting someone in the face. You could have really hurt Barry.'

'He knows that, Mrs Stirling,' interrupted Mrs Ross.

'I am not excusing what you did, Robbie,' continued Elisabeth, still addressing the boy, 'but Barry should not have behaved in the way he did. In a way, he is as much to blame as you.' Her voice was warmer than it had been.

'We've had a long talk with him, Mrs Stirling,' said Mrs Ross.

'I think 'e's got t'message,' added her husband, 'and 'e won't be doin' it again, will ya, Robbie?'

'No,' said the boy, his face still tight and unsmiling.

'Then let that be the end of the matter,' said Elisabeth. 'Now you run along, Robbie. I wish to speak to Mr and Mrs Ross.'

'Before tha goes, Robbie, I think tha's got summat to say to Missis Stirlin',' Mr Ross told him.

'I'm sorry, miss,' said the boy.

'He's not a bad lad, you know, Mrs Stirling,' said Mrs Ross when Robbie had gone.

'I know that,' agreed Elisabeth.

'He's had to put up with a lot, growing up with an aggressive stepfather who hadn't a good word to say about him and a mother who didn't seem to care very much.'

'I am aware of that, Mrs Ross,' said Elisabeth, 'but that doesn't excuse his behaviour.'

'Well mebbe it doesn't excuse it,' said Mr Ross, 'but I reckon it explains it. Child brought up wi' violence, who's used to getting t'belt across his backside and a smack around 'is ears, learns to hit out himself. It's t'way 'e was brung up.'

'Robbie has been much better behaved lately,' said Mr Hornchurch, coming to the boy's defence. 'He's made really good progress since he started this term and—'

'I know that, Rupert,' interrupted Elisabeth. 'Nobody knows that better than I, but he still has to learn that he cannot go around hitting other children. Let us hope that this is the last time it happens. We'll put this unfortunate incident behind us.' She turned to Mr and Mrs Ross. 'I do hope that you will impress upon Robbie that he is on probation. Any further misbehaviour will be dealt with most severely.'

'We'll have another talk with him,' said Mrs Ross.

It was at lunchtime later that day that Elisabeth had the opportunity of speaking to Jeremy. He was busy collecting up the plastic trays on which the pupils had their lunch.

'That's very helpful of you, Jeremy,' said Elisabeth, approaching the boy.

'I like to be helpful, Mrs Stirling,' he replied. 'Mr Dwyer says it's good to be considerate.' He gave a small smile.

'And you're getting on well with your teacher?'

'Oh yes. Mr Dwyer is an excellent teacher. I really enjoy his lessons.'

'I'm pleased to hear it. And I hope you are working hard and behaving yourself,' she added.

'Of course,' the boy replied. 'Was there something you wanted, Mrs Stirling?' He looked her directly in the face.

'No, I was just making sure you are happy here at the village school.'

'Very happy,' he replied. He brushed the fringe of blonde hair from his forehead. 'You heard about Norman's unfortunate accident, I suppose.' He knew, of course, that his teacher would have mentioned this to Elisabeth, and also related the conversation he had had with him about it.'

'Yes, I did hear,' said Elisabeth.

'Poor Norman,' said Jeremy. 'He's so accident-prone, isn't he, miss? I do hope he will take more care when we go on the school trip. The coast can be a very dangerous place.'

'I believe that Norman said you pushed him.'

'Oh no, Mrs Stirling,' protested the boy. 'I slipped on the ice. I explained to Mr Dwyer that it was an accident.'

'I hope it *was* an accident,' said Elisabeth, 'because I take a very dim view of bullying.'

'I agree,' he said. 'Having been bullied myself, I do know how it feels.'

'Well, let us hope there are no more accidents,' she said firmly.

'I was sorry to hear about the fight in the library.'

'It wasn't really a fight,' Elisabeth told him.

'Oh, I heard Barry was punched on the nose.'

'He wasn't badly hurt.'

'I'm pleased to hear it,' said the boy. 'It could have been very serious, couldn't it, Mrs Stirling?'

'Yes, it could,' she replied.

There was something about Jeremy's manner and expression, the way he continually smiled and stared her straight in the eyes, that she found rather unnerving. He was unlike any nine-year-old boy she had ever come across.

'And on the school trip,' said Elisabeth, 'I expect you to be on your best behaviour.'

'Of course, Mrs Stirling,' replied the boy. 'I am so looking forward to it. We never had school trips at my last school.'

Their conversation was interrupted by the new part-time cleaner, who came hurrying into the hall. Bianca was a large girl with lank mousy-brown hair, watery blue eyes and prominent front teeth. She was wearing a grey nylon overall, which crackled when she walked, and she carried a mop.

'Could I have a word, Mrs Stirling?' she said breathlessly.

'Yes, of course, Bianca. What is it?'

'Mr Gribbon's sent me to fetch you. There's some writing on the wall.'

'Oh dear,' sighed Elisabeth. 'You had better show me.'

'It's on the outside wall,' said the cleaner. 'Mr Gribbon told me not to clean it off because he thought you would want to see it.'

'There was some writing on the wall at my last school,' said Jeremy, who had heard the exchange. He smiled. 'The headmaster never did find out who did it.'

Elisabeth and Bianca arrived to find Mr Gribbon, hands on hips, shaking his head.

'We've never had this before, Mrs Stirling,' he grumbled. 'Just look at this.'

'What does that word mean?' asked Bianca.

'You don't want to know,' the caretaker told her.

'Well clean it off, Mr Gribbon, please,' said Elisabeth. 'I shall have a word about this in assembly tomorrow.'

'Once this sort of thing starts,' the caretaker remarked, 'it'll be all over the shop. It'll spread like Topsy, you mark my words.'

'That's why it needs to be cleaned off as soon as possible,' said Elisabeth.

On the way back to her room, Elisabeth caught sight of Jeremy sitting on a low wall. Their eyes met. He smiled and gave a small wave. I wonder, she thought, I just wonder.

'St Paul's Preparatory School,' came the voice down the line. 'May I help you?'

School had finished for the day, and Elisabeth had decided that she needed to know a little bit more about Jeremy Robinson.

'Yes,' she replied. 'May I speak to the headmaster, please?'

'Who is this calling?'

'Mrs Stirling, head teacher of Barton-with-Urebank Primary School.'

'One moment, Mrs Stirling,' said the secretary. 'I'll put you through.'

'Hello. Kenneth Arnold speaking.'

'Good afternoon, Mr Arnold,' said Elisabeth. 'You don't know me, but—'

'I have heard of you, though, Mrs Stirling,' interrupted the headmaster. 'Your reputation goes before you. Your children keep winning prizes at county competitions and walking away with the sporting cups. You certainly give us a run for our money. The former deputy headmaster here, Mr Richardson, also mentioned you.'

'I guess not very favourably,' said Elisabeth. 'I am afraid we did not see eye to eye.'

She had had quite a few run-ins with Robin Richardson when he was the headmaster at neighbouring Urebank School. She found the man overbearing and patronising. When Urebank was amalgamated with the village school at Barton, he and Elisabeth had both applied for the headship. She had been offered the position and, feeling bitter and aggrieved, he had left to take up the post of deputy headmaster at the local preparatory school.

'So Mr Richardson is no longer with you,' said Elisabeth.

'No, he's not,' said Mr Arnold. 'I won't go into the details, but just to say that I'm afraid, like you, we didn't see eye to eye. Anyway, Mrs Stirling, what can I do for you?'

'A new boy has recently started at the school,' Elisabeth told him, 'a former pupil of St Paul's, I believe, and I wonder if you might be able to give me some information about him.'

'Yes, of course. What is his name?'

'Jeremy Robinson.' There was a silence. 'Are you still there, Mr Arnold?' asked Elisabeth.

'Yes, yes, I'm still here,' he said. 'I wondered when I would hear about that young man again. Well, let me see, what do I say about Jeremy? He's a rather mixed-up character, I'm afraid. He's intelligent, quick-witted, outwardly very polite and helpful, but he's a devious boy. A loner, too. He had no friends when he was here. In fact the children in his class gave him a wide berth. I think they were a little afraid of him. In the end I had to ask his father to take him away.'

'He was expelled?'

'We don't like to use that word at St Paul's,' said the headmaster. 'We prefer to suggest that the parents find an alternative school, one that is better suited to their child's needs. It is extremely rare that I have to ask a parent to take their child away, but in this instance I felt I had to. Jeremy proved to be a problem. Soon after he arrived, there was a series of incidents in the school. Nothing major at first – pens going missing, exercise books damaged, taps left on in the toilets, a dead mouse found in a child's coat pocket. That sort of thing. Although the finger seemed to point at Jeremy, nothing could be proved. He's a clever boy and was adept at covering his tracks. Then there was his behaviour in lessons. Mr Pritchard, his teacher, found him extremely difficult to handle. It wasn't that he was openly rude or noisy, but he would make snide comments, ask silly questions and say hurtful things about other pupils. Then Mr Pritchard began receiving telephone calls at home. When he picked up the phone, there was clearly someone at the end of the line, for he could hear breathing, but no one spoke. He was convinced it was Jeremy.

'Parents began to complain, saying that their children were put off their work because of Jeremy's behaviour. For much of his time he ended up working outside my room. Then the graffiti started. Although nothing could be proved, I am pretty certain Jeremy was behind it. Some very hurtful and I should say offensive things were written about his teacher and myself on the wall outside, and as soon as it was cleaned off, it appeared again. Mr Pritchard was extremely upset, of course, and it affected his teaching. Things came to a head when Jeremy pushed another pupil over in the playground. Of course he claimed that it was an accident, but the school secretary had seen the whole thing from the classroom window. I asked the boy's father to come and see me, but I'm afraid he refused to accept that there was anything wrong with his son. The father is some important financial adviser, I gather. Rather more money than sense. Anyway, reluctantly I suggested that he find another school for Jeremy. I'm sorry you have been burdened with this, Mrs Stirling. I wish you luck.'

'Thank you, Mr Arnold,' Elisabeth said, before putting down the receiver.

'You look just about done in,' said Michael later that evening. 'Come over by the fire and I'll get you a drink.'

Elisabeth warmed her hands and then sat on the sofa, stretching back and sighing. 'Not for me, thank you,' she said. 'It's been one thing after another at school today.'

'You had better tell me about it,' said Michael, splashing a couple of inches of whisky in his glass.

'No, I'm more interested in what happened at Clayton Comprehensive. I assume you managed to see the headmaster.'

When Elisabeth had told Michael she was minded to go and see the headmaster at the school about the incident with the eggs, Michael had informed her he would like to pursue the matter himself. He knew from the stance his wife had taken over the matter – that Danny should name the culprit

– that she would be more sympathetic than he was to the headmaster's point of view.

'I feel very strongly about this, Elisabeth,' he had told her with uncharacteristic vehemence. 'On this occasion I think it is better if I deal with it.'

Knowing that this was one battle she was unlikely to win, she had reluctantly agreed.

'Oh yes, I saw him all right,' replied Michael now, coming to sit next to her.

'So how did it go?'

Michael took a sip of his whisky and rested his head on the back of the sofa. 'I don't know how that man managed to become a headmaster,' he muttered angrily before taking another sip of his drink. 'He was a scruffy-looking individual for a start, more like a down-at-heel door-to-door salesman than a headmaster.'

Elisabeth could have reminded her husband that he himself had been far from tidy and stylish in the way he dressed when she had first met him. His suit was creased and unfashionable and had seen better days, his shirt was frayed around the collar, his tie crumpled, and his shoes could have done with a good polish. She found herself smiling wistfully.

'You would think a head teacher would know what was going on in the classrooms in his own school,' continued Michael, getting into his stride. 'Unless, of course, he spends all day closeted in his office.' He took another gulp. 'The man's ineffectual. Surely he must be aware that Danny's teacher is incompetent.'

'You would think so,' agreed Elisabeth.

'Something has to be done about this teacher. Anyway, I told Mr Ironside that I shall be writing to the Director of Education to ask her to get the school inspector in. We'll see what she has to say.'

'I don't think it's up to the director to ask HMI to visit the school,' Elisabeth told him. 'They tend to work independently of the local authority.'

'Can't you have a word with the chap who inspected your school?'

'Mr Steel?'

'Surely he can do something.'

'It's not really up to me either to ask an HMI to visit a school, but I will mention something when I next see him.'

'I'll tell you this, Elisabeth,' said Michael, 'if a patient complains about a doctor, something is done about it pretty quick.'

'The school inspectors will report on this teacher when they visit.'

'And then what?'

'He'll probably receive some extra training, be sent on a few courses and possibly monitored in the hope that his teaching will improve. You remember I had a similar situation with Mr Jolly.'

Mr Jolly had taught at the village school for a short time, having been redeployed from Urebank when it was amalgamated with Barton. He was a sad and lonely figure and his teaching was predictable and tedious. With Elisabeth's encouragement and guidance his work had improved – but not markedly. He had jumped at the chance to take early retirement and now ran a health food shop in Whitby.

'Is that it?' said Michael angrily. 'Sent on a few courses and monitored? The man wants sacking.' He finished his whisky in one gulp.

'I'm afraid that's easier said than done,' said his wife. 'He would have to run off with the school fund or behave inappropriately with a pupil to be sacked. It's very difficult to get rid of an incompetent teacher. Usually, though, those teachers who are heavily criticised by the inspectors resign.'

'Let's hope the inspection is sooner than later then,' said Michael, getting up to pour himself another whisky.

'You're drinking too much,' Elisabeth told him.

'Yes, I know,' he replied, 'but like you, I've had a hard day.'

'So what did you say to the headmaster?' asked Elisabeth.

'Just that I took issue with him for singling Danny out as if he was the villain of the piece. I said I admired Danny for sticking to his principles.'

Elisabeth remained silent, not wishing to rekindle the difference of opinion she had had with her husband about Danny's refusal to say anything about the incident.

'I've never known anyone who is so patently honest as Danny,' continued Michael, 'and as good-hearted and tractable. To be honest, Elisabeth, I'm proud of the lad.'

The subject of the conversation stood behind the half-open door and heard everything that had been said. He went back up to his bedroom, his smile hiding his tears.

'Thanks, Dad,' he whispered.

Elisabeth and Michael were ready for bed, snuggled up on the sofa in front of the dying fire.

'Our first tiff,' said Michael. 'Sorry if I got a bit heated, but that Ironside character really made me mad.'

'Let's not talk about it,' said Elisabeth. 'Life's too short.'

There came an urgent banging on the front door.

'Whoever can that be at this time of night?' sighed Michael, getting to his feet.

On the doorstep stood Bianca. The baby in her arms was making a high-pitched moaning sound. Behind her, a tall, gangly lad with wild woolly hair and a flare of red spots on his cheeks looked numb with misery.

'It's the baby,' spluttered the girl, trembling. Her face was taut and bleak, and wet with tears.

'Come in, come in,' said Michael. 'Go into the sitting room.' He ran up to his study to get his medical bag.

'Whatever is it, Bianca?' asked Elisabeth, getting up from the sofa to greet the visitors.

'It's my baby, Mrs Stirling,' cried the girl. 'He's not right at all. I thought it might be the flu what's been going round, but I don't think it is. He looks proper poorly.' She began to cry. 'I'm sorry to have to trouble Dr Stirling, it being so late and all, but I didn't know what else to do and . . .' She broke down, sobbing.

'You did right to bring the baby for the doctor to look at,' Elisabeth reassured her, putting an arm around the young woman's shoulder. 'A good mother trusts her instincts, and if you think your child is unwell, then you must see a doctor.'

Bianca's husband stood listening, his face like a mask.

'Come along in, Clarence,' Elisabeth told him.

Michael hurried into the room with his medical bag. 'Now, let's have a look at the little fellow,' he said, putting the bag on the floor and taking the baby from his mother's arms.

He rested the infant carefully on the sofa and took a stethoscope from his bag, placing it gently against the little chest. He then looked into the baby's eyes and, with an ear probe, took the child's temperature before examining his skin for any signs of a rash.

'What has he been like?' he asked Bianca.

'He's not been feeding proper all afternoon and he doesn't want to be cuddled. He keeps closing his eyes and then opening them, and he's been sick.' She gabbled on. 'Sometimes he just feels sort of floppy and then he starts wriggling, and he's been making these awful moaning sounds, not like proper crying at all. I'm dead worried, Doctor.' She put a hand over her mouth to stifle her crying.

The young man behind her remained silent, with an anguished look on his face.

'We need to get him to hospital,' said Michael. He put the baby back into his mother's arms.

'Oh no!' cried Bianca. There followed a series of great ragged sobs.

Clarence reached for her hand and squeezed it, then spoke for the first time, in a low, tremulous voice. 'Is he really ill, Doctor?' he asked.

As much as he would like to do so, Michael knew it would be wrong to tell the young man not to worry and that everything would be all right, because it was clear to him that the baby was seriously ill and needed urgent medical attention.

'We need to make sure he gets the best care as soon as possible,' he said. 'Now, Clarence, are you able to drive into Clayton, to the Royal Infirmary?'

'Yes, Doctor.'

'I'll come with you,' he said. 'I'll get my coat. I just need a quick word with my wife.' He motioned Elisabeth to come into the hall, out of earshot.

'Ring the hospital, darling, and tell them we are on our way,' he said. 'Tell them about the baby's symptoms.'

Elisabeth put her hand to her throat. 'Is it bad?' she asked.

'I think the child has meningitis,' he told her gravely and in a hushed voice.

'Dear God, no,' she said.

'It may not be, but it looks very much like it,' he said. 'I couldn't find any rash but I'm afraid there are all the other classic symptoms: high temperature, vomiting, drowsiness, fever. The child seems to be drifting in and out of consciousness. Anyway, we must be off. The parents will want to stay at the hospital, so I will get a taxi home.'

'Give me a ring, Michael,' she said, kissing his cheek.

As she watched them drive off, she wiped a tear from her cheek. 'It can't be meningitis,' she said out loud. 'It just can't be.'

In this case, sadly, she was to be proved wrong.

# II

Mrs Robertshaw clapped her hands loudly and waited for the children's chatter to subside. Next to her, standing at the front of the school hall just before lunchtime, were Mr Dwyer and Mr Hornchurch, who would be accompanying her and the two lower junior classes on the school trip the following weekend. When she had everyone's attention, the teacher proceeded.

'All eyes this way, please,' she instructed in a loud, stern voice. 'Sit up smartly and no shuffling. Next weekend, as you all know, we will be going on our school trip.' As she looked at the blank faces before her, she asked herself why had she been persuaded – coerced more like – to give up her precious weekend and take a group of forty-plus children to the coast. She had tried her best to wangle herself out of going, but Elisabeth had been her usual determined self and grudgingly the teacher had given in. So here she was explaining to the children what she expected of them, and she was doing it in no uncertain terms.

'Now that you are all listening,' she said, 'I want to go through with you one or two do's and don'ts. Firstly the do's.' She paused and stared pointedly at an ungainly individual with prominent front teeth who was scratching his scalp and staring at the ceiling. 'Are you listening to me, Norman Stubbins?'

'Yes, miss,' answered the boy.

'You looked as if you were miles away.'

'Honest, miss, I was listening,' replied the boy.

'Because this is particularly applicable to you,' the teacher told him.

'Pardon, miss?'

'We do not – I repeat, do not – want any accidents on this trip. Is that clear?'

'Yes, miss.'

'No falling in the sea, getting stuck on rocks, tumbling over the cliff, slipping on seaweed.'

Jeremy gave a sly smile.

'So stop scratching and staring heavenwards and listen,' the teacher ordered. 'Firstly,' she continued, 'you should all read very carefully the letter I have sent home to your parents. It spells out exactly what you need to wear and what you need to bring along. Make sure that you have the necessary clothing and equipment. It is the responsibility of every one of you to be properly clothed and have adequate footwear. Some of the activities we will be doing involve a great deal of walking, so make sure you have suitable anoraks or waterproof jackets, gloves, scarves, a rucksack and comfortable walking shoes or boots.'

Norman Stubbins, who was now staring vacantly out of the window, caught the teacher's attention again.

'Norman Stubbins!' exclaimed Mrs Robertshaw.

The boy jumped as if poked by a cattle prod. 'Yes, miss?'

'Perhaps you can tell me what ears are for?'

'To wash behind, miss?' he replied. Norman was an ingenuous child and he did not intend the comment to be cheeky. The question was often asked by his mother when he was getting washed in the morning. This was his stock reply.

Mrs Robertshaw clapped her hands again to stem the laughter. 'Be quiet! Norman Stubbins, come down to the front, sit here and pin your ears back. You are a silly boy; what are you?'

'A silly boy, miss,' mumbled Norman.

Mrs Robertshaw sighed, turned to her two colleagues and shook her head. She could tell that she would be having problems with the Stubbins boy. I really don't know why I am doing this, she thought to herself. She looked at the glum faces before her and continued. 'The second rule,' she told the children, 'is to behave yourselves. This goes without saying.' Rupert wondered why she was saying it then, and smiled to himself. Mrs Robertshaw carried on. 'There are plenty of potential dangers on the stretch of coast we will be visiting, so take great care, listen to your teachers and do as you are told.' She caught sight of Jeremy Robinson yawning widely. 'Am I boring you, Jeremy?' she asked.

'Oh no, miss,' he replied sweetly. 'It's very interesting.'

'Perhaps you can tell me what I have just said, then?' she asked him.

'You warned us to take care on the stretch of coast we will be visiting,' he answered, almost repeating her word for word, 'because there are many potential dangers. You also said we should listen to our teachers and do as we are told.'

Too clever by half, that young man, thought Mrs Robertshaw. 'The third thing,' she declared, 'is to bring some money with you, but not a lot. There will be little opportunity for you to buy anything. Five pounds at the most is quite adequate. Number four. Make sure you have all been to the toilet before getting on the coach. There will be only one stop on our journey. Number five. Make sure you arrive on the Saturday morning promptly at seven forty-five a.m. The coach will leave at eight o'clock and it will leave without you if you are not there. Now to the don'ts. Number one, don't make any unnecessary noise on the coach. No shouting, getting out of your seat, talking to the driver, running up and down the aisle, playing loud music or making faces at motorists through the window. Number two. Do not stuff yourselves with crisps, nuts, chocolate bars, biscuits and fizzy drinks before you board the coach. I do not want to have to deal with vomit. When we arrive at the hostel, there will be another set of do's and don'ts.'

Rupert whispered in his colleague's ear. 'I can see this weekend is not going to be a barrel of laughs,' he said.

'Did you wish to add something, Mr Hornchurch?' asked Mrs Robertshaw, swivelling around in his direction.

'I was just wondering if I might tell the children a little about where we are going,' he said.

'Well yes, that seems a good idea,' she replied. 'Sit up, children,' she ordered, 'and listen carefully to Mr Hornchurch.'

'Well now,' said Rupert brightly, determined to be more upbeat than his colleague, who had made an exciting trip to the seaside sound like a visit to a boot camp. 'We shall be staying at a really nice hostel near a quaint little fishing village called Robin Hood's Bay, which is right on the Yorkshire coast. You will be able to hear the sea from your bedrooms and will be woken up by the waves crashing ashore and rattling the shingle, and the cries of the seagulls. The hostel has lots of really fantastic features, including playrooms with puzzles and games, a television, and a library where you can borrow books and listen to stories. The breakfasts and the packed lunches are really good and there is a shop for you to buy souvenirs and sweets.'

'Could I come in here, Mr Hornchurch,' interrupted Mrs Robertshaw, 'and remind them again not to stuff themselves with sweets and make themselves ill, and that they should bring no more than five pounds.'

'Thank you,' said Rupert, before carrying on. 'Around the hostel are woods, picnic areas and gardens that feature a story-telling circle and fairy trails. The beach is on the doorstep, so—'

'So we do not want anyone wandering off into the woods and getting lost,' added his colleague, 'or clambering up the cliffs, or coming off the beach soaking wet and covered in sand.'

'To the southern end of Robin Hood's Bay,' continued Mr Hornchurch, 'is a very special place that we shall be visiting. It's called Boggle Hole, and is a hollowed-out crevice in the coastline, nestling in a narrow wooded cove on the beach.'

The children tittered.

'That will do!' snapped Mrs Robertshaw, casting a beady eye along the rows of children.

'It is a bit of a funny name, isn't it?' chuckled Mr Hornchurch. 'It comes from the word "boggle", a sort of mischievous elf or goblin who is said to live in small caves or holes in cliffsides. In local folklore,' he went on to explain, 'boggles are, if treated kindly, happy to help with household chores, in return for a saucer or two of milk. Mean and ill-tempered householders find them rather less helpful. Stories have been told of boggles smashing dishes or blowing soot from the chimney all over the house. Boggles were often believed to have healing powers, and sometimes the villagers would bring their poorly children to places called "hob holes" where boggles were thought to live, in the hope that the children would be cured. There are some people who believe that the word "boggle" was made up by local smugglers to keep customs officers away.'

'All very interesting, Mr Hornchurch,' said Mrs Robertshaw. 'Shall we move on?' Telling the children about mischievous boggles, she thought, might give them ideas. And as she looked at certain boys sitting before her, she could see a few impish characters of their own.

'Anyway, Boggle Hole is a site of special scientific interest,' said Rupert. 'It was a notorious smugglers' haunt in the past and is full of tales of fishermen's secrets. Many old sailing ships were wrecked off the coast, and we may come across a few timbers poking above the sand, maybe even a rusty anchor, so we need to keep our eyes peeled. It is an amazing and unique place. The foreshore exposes siliceous shales, which contain a range of trace fossils. During much of the year the beach is covered in sand, making collecting fossils very difficult. But sometimes the sea exposes the rocks, especially in the winter months, and fossils can then be collected. So we are lucky going at this time of year. We will be searching for fossils along the beach and exploring the rock pools for aquatic life and—'

'Well thank you, Mr Hornchurch,' said Mrs Robertshaw, cutting him off, 'that sounds very interesting.' From the tone of her voice she didn't sound interested at all; she was clearly more bothered about impressing upon the children health and safety issues than listening to a lecture from her colleague, who, she thought, did have a tendency to rattle on.

'I haven't finished,' replied Rupert. 'I thought I might—'

'Oh I think the children have all heard enough for now, Mr Hornchurch,' Mrs Robertshaw told him. 'It's nearly time for lunch.' She clapped her hands. 'Everyone stand please, and leave the hall quickly and quietly.'

At ten minutes past eight on the day of the school trip, the children, surrounded by cases and rucksacks and chattering excitedly, waited in the lay-by outside the school for the coach. Mrs Robertshaw stood watching the road fixedly for the arrival of the vehicle, tapping a foot in irritation and consulting her watch every few seconds.

'So where is it?' she asked Rupert.

'It'll be along,' he said casually.

'I said seven forty-five,' she said crossly. 'Did I or did I not say seven forty-five?'

'You did,' said Rupert.

'Well where is it then?'

'I guess it's been held up in traffic,' suggested Tom. 'The main road to Clayton gets pretty busy at this time of day, particularly on a Saturday.'

'Well in that case the driver should have made provision for it,' she replied with grating impatience in her voice. 'I cannot stand unpunctuality.' She turned to the pupils. 'Be quiet!' she shouted.

At a quarter past eight, the coach pulled up. The driver, a lugubrious-looking individual with large hooded eyes, a shiny bald head and tufts of sandy hair around his ears, clambered from the driving seat and, in no great hurry, ambled around the front of the bus. He flicked a cigarette stub on to the floor, crushed it with his foot and breathed out a cloud of smoke.

'Morning!' he shouted.

'It's about time,' Mrs Robertshaw told him petulantly, tapping her watch. 'I think I said we should be collected at seven forty-five and be on the road by eight o'clock prompt.'

'Ah well, it's the traffic,' said the driver indifferently. 'It gets congested on the main road on a Saturday.'

'Then perhaps you should have taken account of it,' said the teacher with cold authority, 'and set off earlier. We have been waiting here for half an hour.'

The bus driver looked at her for a moment in a cool, detached way and then shrugged. He had met officious teachers like this one before and did not intend to be intimidated or bossed about all weekend by her. 'For your information, Miss . . .'

'Robertshaw,' she said. 'Mrs Robertshaw.'

'For your information, Mrs Robertshaw—' the driver began again.

'Look, shall we get aboard?' interrupted Rupert. 'The children are getting impatient and it is cold and we do need to be away.' Before either of them could respond, he shepherded the children forward, lined them up at the door of the coach and told them to get on quickly and quietly.

Mrs Robertshaw held up a hand as if stopping traffic, and the queue came to a halt. 'One moment!' she cried. 'Norman

Stubbins, Jeremy Robinson and Peter Norton, you will sit at the front with me. I suggest that you and Mr Dwyer,' she told Rupert, 'sit on the back seat where you can keep an eye on everybody.' Her tone of voice indicated that she would brook no argument.

'Right,' she told the driver imperiously, 'let's get going.'

When the children had settled in their seats, the bus driver approached Mrs Robertshaw.

'Before we go,' he said, 'there are some ground rules I want to make clear to the kids.'

'That will not be necessary,' Mrs Robertshaw pronounced. 'I have already told them about being on their best behaviour.'

'Yes, well I've heard that before,' replied the driver.

'Not from me you haven't,' she told him tetchily. 'I can assure you that the children know exactly what is expected of them.'

'That may be the case, but this coach doesn't move before I've said what I have to say. I've been on trips with school parties before and I know what kids can be like.' Before Mrs Robertshaw could protest, the driver stood in the aisle, legs apart and hands on his hips. 'Right, look this way,' he ordered. 'My name is Mr Bassett and I'm the driver, and before we set off, there are a few things I'm going to tell you. I don't want any mess on my coach. Rubbish should not be dropped on the floor or stuffed behind the seats but put in this.' He produced a large plastic bin-liner from behind a seat. 'If you feel sick, use the bucket, which is here at the front. I don't want anybody throwing up all over my seats. There will be no shouting, jumping up and down, moving about or blocking my rear-view window. I hope that you have all been to the toilet, because I'm only stopping once, and—'

Mrs Robertshaw got to her feet. 'Mr Bassett,' she said, slowly and deliberately, 'I have been through this already, so can we make a move. Please!'

'Well just so long as they know,' answered the driver.

As soon as the coach set off, Mrs Robertshaw comman-
deered the microphone and started to give the children a
blow-by-blow commentary, noting buildings of historical
significance and pointing out scenery of interest. She had
been speaking for barely ten minutes when the driver, wearied
by the strident voice, clicked a switch on his dashboard and
turned her off. The teacher carried on speaking, blissfully
unaware that no one, except poor Norman Stubbins, who sat
next to her, could hear a word she was saying.

It was getting on for late morning when the driver brought the
coach to a juddering halt before a cluster of honey-coloured and
grey-stone buildings. The hostel, which nestled in a steep-sided
wooded cove adjacent to the beach, looked bright and welcoming despite the greyness of the sky and the drizzling rain. The
coach had only just set off from the school when a jagged streak
of lightning had flashed across the sky. This had been followed
seconds later by a grumbling of thunder and a downpour of rain
as thick as umbrella spokes, which lashed fiercely at the windows
of the coach, drummed noisily on the roof and snaked down the
windscreen. The traffic had been heavy and slow-moving, and
to Mrs Robertshaw's annoyance, they had been forced to wait
for some time in a queue on the York ring road.

'If we had set off when we were supposed to,' she told
Rupert irritably when they stopped for a break halfway, 'we
wouldn't have been delayed like this.'

'These things happen,' replied her colleague in a relaxed
tone of voice.

'Well they shouldn't!' she snapped. 'And I hope this weather
improves.'

I hope your temper improves, he thought to himself.

'I'm sure it will,' he replied. 'Just relax and go with the flow,
Elsie.'

'Are you always so laid-back?' she asked, in a rather peevish tone of voice.

Rupert thought for a moment and rubbed his chin. 'Well, I've always believed that getting upset about something that cannot be changed is really a waste of time. It only causes you stress, which is not good for you.'

His reply did nothing to improve Mrs Robertshaw's mood. In fact, it made her more annoyed. 'Well thank you for that *bon mot*, Rupert,' she said, pulling a face. 'I would never have known.'

Tom smiled to himself but said nothing.

The school party was greeted at the door of the hostel by a round-faced, jolly woman with a cheerful smile and friendly eyes. 'Come along in out of the rain,' she said.

The teachers and children gathered in the entrance.

'I'm Mrs Marshall,' said the woman, 'and I will be looking after you while you are here. Welcome to Robin Hood's Bay.' She turned to Mr Hornchurch. 'I was expecting you earlier.'

'We were late getting away,' Mrs Robertshaw told her before Rupert could open his mouth. She glanced malevolently at the driver, who was sheltering in a doorway blowing out a cloud of cigarette smoke. 'Then we were stuck in traffic outside York.'

'Well you're here now, safe and sound,' said Mrs Marshall. 'The weather's been very changeable lately, but I think we are in for a nice day tomorrow.'

'Oh, a little wet weather doesn't deter us,' said Rupert good-humouredly.

Mrs Robertshaw sighed. 'Speak for yourself,' she muttered. Tom's face cracked into a grin. He turned away to conceal his amusement.

After the teachers had introduced themselves and before the children were allocated their rooms, Mrs Robertshaw produced a clipboard from her bag and proceeded to go through another set of do's and don'ts that were listed on a sheet of paper.

'One: boots and outdoor clothing must be left in the tack room at all times,' she said.

'Except when we are wearing them,' ventured Jeremy.

'What?' she snapped.

'Except when we are wearing them, miss – our boots and outdoor clothing,' said the boy.

'I can do without your clever comments, young man,' said the teacher, 'so keep them to yourself.' She continued. 'You must not, I repeat not, wander around the hostel in your boots, leaving muddy footprints all over the floors. Two: when you hear the gong for breakfast and dinner, come down to the dining room promptly. If you are late, you will not get anything to eat. Three: when you are assigned your rooms, collect your cases, make up your beds, unpack, hang your clothes up neatly and keep the room tidy. Four: there will be no going into other people's rooms at any time. Five: lights out at nine thirty, and no talking after that.'

'Perhaps I could show the children where everything is?' Mrs Marshall suggested, interrupting the teacher's flow.

'Yes, of course,' replied Mrs Robertshaw.

The interior of the hostel was clean, bright and colourful, with polished wooden floors of which Mr Gribbon would have been proud and walls full of pictures, prints and photographs. There were comfortable lounges, spotless kitchens, well-equipped lecture rooms and spacious dining areas, and each bedroom was attractively furnished with tubular steel bunk beds and washbasins.

Following the tour of the building, the children were assigned rooms and told to unpack, wash their hands and meet in the dining room for lunch, after which, suitably dressed, they should wait outside the main entrance for the first walk of the weekend.

Rupert, keen that Mrs Robertshaw should not dominate the expedition with another catalogue of rules and more dire warnings of possible disasters, suggested she might like to stay at the hostel that afternoon.

'Tom and I are quite happy to supervise the children,' he said. 'Why don't you stay here and have a well-earned rest?'

Mrs Robertshaw favoured him with the thinnest of smiles and a slight inclination of the head. She peered through the window to see that the weather had not greatly altered. Although the rain had now abated, it was overcast and windy. 'Well if you're sure,' she said.

'Perfectly,' replied Rupert.

Robin Hood's Bay was a small hamlet of tiny old stone cottages with red pantile roofs, narrow interconnecting passageways and steep steps. It crowded around the ravine of King's Beck for protection against the fierce squalls that blew in from the North Sea. This once important fishing village was in times past a haven for smugglers, who moved their illegal contraband of rum, brandy and tobacco through a maze of tunnels and secret passages in an effort to evade the customs men.

For the children's first excursion, there was still a light rain, but now a cold wind whipped up a high tide, sending waves racing up to the bottom of the main street.

Tom looked up anxiously at the gunmetal-grey sky and then at the heaving ocean, which clapped relentlessly against the cliffs. 'I say, Rupert, do you think we should give this trip a miss?' he asked. 'It looks a bit blustery and I don't think, by the looks of it, that the weather is going to improve.'

'Oh we'll be fine,' replied his colleague nonchalantly. 'This wind is bracing and a bit of rain did no one any harm.'

'Nevertheless . . .' began Tom.

Rupert, disregarding his colleague's concerns, turned to the children and rubbed his hands vigorously. 'We aren't going to be put off by a bit of bad weather, are we?' He received a few half-hearted grunts of approval.

'Remember what Mrs Robertshaw said,' Tom told the children, seeing that his colleague was determined to go ahead with the walk. 'Take great care. Stay together and keep well away from the sea and the cliff edge.'

'Oh don't you start,' laughed Rupert. Then, telling the children to follow him, he set off at a cracking pace.

With Rupert leading the way and Tom at the rear, the children trekked up a steep hill to the top of the village, where they stopped, panting, cold and wet.

'Gather around,' said Rupert. 'Now if you look down, we get a superb bird's-eye view of the bay. You might be able to make out the footbridge over Mill Beck beside the hostel, the slipway and the promenade. Notice the graceful curve of the promontory of Ness Point. At low tide, bands of soft shale and hard limestone are revealed to spectacular effect in the shape of curving ridges. The rocky foreshore is a fascinating place to explore.'

'Can't we go back to the hostel?' asked Peter. 'I'm soaking wet.'

'And I'm cold,' said another pupil.

There were several mumbles of agreement.

'My feet hurt,' moaned Norman.

'I'm tired,' said another boy.

'Now come along,' said Rupert. 'My goodness, all this grumbling and griping.'

'Why is it called Robin Hood's Bay, sir?' asked Amber.

'Good question,' said Rupert. 'There are several theories as to why it is named after the famous outlaw. One of the most common is that Robin Hood fled here to escape capture by the Sheriff of Nottingham and disguised himself as a fisherman.'

'Unlikely,' ventured Jeremy.

'Yes, unlikely,' agreed the teacher, 'but it's a good tale.'

'And the story of Robin Hood was complete fantasy,' added the boy.

'Yes, you are probably right,' said Rupert, not reacting to Jeremy's facetious remark. 'Now this stretch of coastline is famous for its storms,' he continued blithely. 'In 1780, the village's main street was washed away, the great surging ocean taking some of the cottages with it, and since then many more houses have been lost. The sea wall, which was built in 1975, keeps the worst of the waves at bay; however, it is only a temporary measure, as the sea continues to eat away at the surrounding cliffs at a rate of five centimetres every year. Interesting, isn't it?'

'Not really,' muttered Jeremy.

'Pardon?' asked Rupert. 'Did you say something?'

'I said it sounds really interesting, Mr Hornchurch,' replied the boy.

'I'm glad you think so,' said the teacher, 'and that you are paying such close attention, because when we get back to the hostel, there will be some work to complete on what I have just said.'

'I look forward to it, sir,' said Jeremy.

Although the rain had stopped for the time being, the wind had not decreased, and Tom was getting increasingly worried. This was neither the time nor the place, he thought, to listen to a lecture. Rupert, however, was consulting his map.

'Now we are going to continue along the cliff-edge path,' he went on, 'which soon leads down into the next ravine of Stoupe Beck, then we will go over a footbridge and along a track to reach Stoupe Bank Farm. We will follow this route straight on and then turn left and head uphill to the left of Home Farm. We will walk along the old railway track bed for about a mile until it drops down to reach a road. Then we will—'

'I think we should be getting back, Mr Hornchurch,' interrupted Tom. 'The weather is getting worse and the children look cold and tired.'

'But we've only just started,' replied Rupert.

'Nevertheless, we should be getting back,' said his colleague in a determined tone of voice. 'We have seen enough for today. Perhaps tomorrow if the weather is fine we can continue the walk.' Before Rupert could protest, he marshalled the children, told them to follow him and set off back to the hostel.

That evening after dinner, worksheets completed, Rupert gathered the children together to outline the route they would be taking the following day. He was still bubbling with enthusiasm.

'Tomorrow we will be following the old railway track through some of the most spectacular countryside, with deep wooded ravines, old railway bridges, streams and footbridges. Then after a vigorous climb uphill we will reach the top of the bank and follow the road to the clifftop before descending back to the village.'

Mrs Robertshaw, when she had discussed the weekend with her two colleagues, had agreed that Rupert, who knew this stretch of coast well, would plan the walks. Listening to him now, however, and having received from Tom an account of the day's trek, she regretted it. There was no way she was going to climb vigorously up hills, trudge over footbridges and hike across muddy fields and along the clifftop in freezing winds and driving rain.

'Rupert,' she said, approaching him later, accompanied by Tom. 'I think your planned outing tomorrow is a tad adventurous. It sounds very interesting, but I don't think we will have time for such a long walk and it does sound rather arduous. What do you think, Tom?' She turned to her colleague and gave him an appealing look that said, 'Please agree with me.'

'I think Elsie is right,' said the other teacher. 'I think it's a bit too challenging and time-consuming. We won't have much time to go on the beach if we do the walk.'

'Exactly,' agreed Mrs Robertshaw before Rupert could object. 'I think a more leisurely walk along the beach looking for fossils and exploring the rock pools might be a better option.'

'Oh, I see,' said Rupert. He didn't sound at all put out. 'Well, if you both think so, we will do that.'

Later that evening, when the children were all tucked up in bed, Mrs Robertshaw did her rounds, patrolling the corridors, checking that all lights had been turned off and there was no noise from the bedrooms. At the end of one corridor she noticed a light shining beneath a door. Assuming that it was one of the rooms allocated to her pupils, she banged loudly on the wood.

'Turn that light off now!' she shouted. 'I said lights out at nine thirty. Do as you are told!'

A moment later, a head appeared around the door. A bemused young man, a geology student from the university, was the occupant of the room.

'Madam,' he said calmly, 'I shall turn off the lights when I see fit! Goodnight.'

And with that he closed the door.

# 12

The following morning, Mrs Robertshaw appeared in the dining room with an expression as stony-faced as some great Easter Island statue. There were dark hammocks of flesh under her eyes, and her uncombed hair was wild and woolly. She looked as if she had struggled up an embankment after a road crash. She decided to sit with Tom. The last thing she wanted was to hear the chirpy chatter of Rupert, who was sitting with a group of pupils enthusing about the trip to the beach later that morning.

'I hardly slept a wink last night,' she complained, pouring herself a mug of tea. 'I can never get settled in a strange bed, and when I did finally drift off, the wretched seagulls began screeching and squawking like there was no tomorrow. Then at seven o'clock in the morning, some stupid child started crunching up and down on the gravel drive outside my bedroom window. I shall have a word with the children about running about in the early hours. I reckon it was Norman, or that Robinson boy, who has far too much to say for himself.' She took a great gulp of tea.

'Ah,' said Tom, 'about the running. That was me.'

'You!' exclaimed Mrs Robertshaw.

'Guilty, I'm afraid. I always go for a run in the morning. Try and keep in shape and all that. I'm sorry I woke you up.'

'Pass the toast, will you,' she said without further comment.

\*　　\*　　\*

After breakfast, the children were divided into three manageable groups, each one with a teacher. They would spend the morning exploring different parts of the beach, studying marine life, coastal geography and geology. Mr Hornchurch had prepared an information booklet with a series of questions for the children to try and answer. Mrs Robertshaw, despite Rupert's assurance that he could cope with the boys, decided that the three potential problem pupils – Norman, Jeremy and Peter – would be in her party, where she could keep an eagle eye on them. She would be the first to admit that her colleague was a dedicated and enthusiastic teacher, but having worked with Rupert Hornchurch, she knew he was not the most reliable when it came to punctuality and health and safety, and he could be quite scatter-brained and *laissez-faire* at times. If the boys were in his group, she could picture one of them – no doubt accident-prone Norman – stranded halfway up a cliff, cut off by the tide or trapped in a cave. No, she thought, they had better stay with me.

Later that morning, she assembled her group on the slipway as the other two groups set off down the beach. Dressed in heavy green rubber boots, a substantial brown duffle coat, thick woolly scarf and gloves and a knitted hat like a tea cosy, with a pom-pom on the top, she would not have looked out of place behind the wet fish stall in Clayton market. She carried a large canvas shopping bag and an umbrella, though she was pleased to see that the weather that morning was bright and clear, and there was no promise of rain. The biting wind of the previous day had been replaced by a gentle breeze, and a watery sun shone with a hard wintry light in a cloudless sky. The sea was like the mill dam in the village.

Mrs Robertshaw, followed by her party, headed in the opposite direction to the others and came to a halt at a patch of clean grey sand a little way away from the detritus that had been washed up by the incoming tide. The other groups could wander off down the beach, she thought; her group would remain in sight of the hostel.

She surveyed the area, looking for potential dangers and noting the looming cliff below which ribs of black rock curled down towards the ocean, fissured and split with long, gaping crevices, some draped in slimy brown seaweed. She told the children to gather around her and listen.

'On your right,' she said, 'you will see the sea.' She paused. 'Have a look.' The children peered out over the pewter-grey water. 'On your left, you will see the cliffs.' She paused. 'Have a look.' Heads swivelled around to gaze up at the dark, looming cliffs. 'In front of you are slippery rocks full of cracks and behind you is rubbish that has been washed up by the tide.'

'Actually it's called flotsam and jetsam, Mrs Robertshaw,' ventured Jeremy bumptiously.

'My goodness, what a knowledgeable young man you are,' she told the boy in a sarcastic tone of voice. 'I shall know who to ask when I want any more useful information.' She turned to the other children. 'Now, as I was saying, behind you is a pile of rubbish. Have a look.' The children turned to view the mound of washed-up material. 'I do not want anyone in the sea, on the rocks, up the cliffs or near the debris. Is that clear?'

'Yes, Mrs Robertshaw,' chorused the children.

'In the summer months this beach is full of holidaymakers, but at this time of year few people venture down on to the sand, so we have it to ourselves. You are all equipped . . .' She stopped mid-sentence. 'Peter Norton, put that down!' she shouted.

'Miss, I thought we had to pick things up,' said the boy.

'I said shells, fossils and interesting pebbles, not great big lumps of rotting driftwood with rusty nails sticking out of them. Put it down at once!'

'Miss, it could be off a Viking longboat or a Spanish galleon,' suggested Norman, waving his hand in the air like a daffodil in a strong wind.

'Don't be silly,' replied the teacher. 'Since when did a Viking longboat or a Spanish galleon have "Produce of Tunisia" written on the side of it? Now pay attention everyone. You are all equipped with your information booklet and a plastic bag in which to put interesting things you might find on the beach, which we will take back to school and display on the nature table. I do not want fish heads, dead crabs, seaweed or anything smelly, and I do not want piles of pebbles either. Peter Norton, if I see you touching that piece of driftwood again, you will go back to the hostel and remain there. Leave it alone. Now I am going to let you explore the beach for half an hour by yourselves. Using the information booklet, see if you can identify some of the things shown and answer the questions. Do not wander too far away from me. And remember, keep away from the sea and the cliffs and don't go near that rubbish that has been washed up.'

'Can we go in the caves, miss?' asked Norman.

'That's where he belongs – in a cave,' muttered Jeremy, nudging the boy next to him. 'Prehistoric Stubbins, the caveman of Boggle Hole.'

'Did you say something, Jeremy?' asked the teacher.

'No, miss,' replied the boy with an innocent expression on his face.

'Your mouth moved.'

'That was my lips wobbling, miss.'

'And why were your lips wobbling?'

'Miss, because I'm cold.'

'Yes, well if you had got well wrapped up as I told everyone to do before coming on the beach, you would not be cold, would you, and your lips would not be wobbling?'

'No, miss.'

'So can we go in the caves, miss?' asked Norman again.

'No you cannot,' answered the teacher. 'The caves are dangerous. These cliffs are very unstable, particularly after

the bad weather we have been having. Mrs Marshall was telling me about a very large lump of rock that fell overnight
from the roof of a cave just last week. Furthermore, I guess
the caves are used as toilets during the summer months and
are likely to be very smelly and unhygienic.'

'Uuuurrrgh!' cried the children.

'Don't be silly, we all have to go to the toilet,' Mrs Robertshaw
told them. 'It's a natural human function. Now stay on the
beach and we will meet back here at eleven. Promptly please.
You may go.'

The children dispersed.

Mrs Robertshaw found a large grey pebble and sat down.
She reached into her shopping bag for her flask of coffee. She
was going to have ten minutes of peace and quiet, breathing
in the fresh salty sea air and looking at the vast panorama,
before setting off down the beach to see how the children
were getting on. Or so she thought.

Five minutes later, a plump, red-faced girl with protuberant blue eyes and giant pink ear muffs came galloping across
the beach kicking sand in every direction like a frantic
donkey.

'Miss! Miss!' she cried. 'You had better come. Peter Norton
is chucking big lumps of smelly seaweed at everybody and
throwing pebbles in the sea and splashing us.'

'I might as well talk to myself,' muttered the teacher. 'Right,
Valerie, go and tell him I want to see him immediately.'

The girl darted off with a smug expression on her face to
fetch the reprobate.

Mrs Robertshaw was halfway through giving Peter a good
telling-off when Norman came rushing up. 'Miss! Miss!' he
cried. 'Come quick!'

'What is it?' demanded the teacher.

'Miss, get up!' shouted the boy, pulling the sleeve of the
teacher's coat. 'You've got to come with me.'

'Will you stop doing that,' ordered Mrs Robertshaw. 'Just calm down and tell me what's wrong.'

'Miss, it's Jeremy Robinson.'

'What about him?'

'He's stuck.'

'Stuck!' repeated the teacher. 'What do you mean, he's stuck?' She rose from the large pebble and began scanning the beach.

'Miss,' said Norman, 'he's stuck in the mud.'

'Oh for goodness' sake,' sighed the teacher, 'whatever next?' Two angry spots showed on her cheeks and it was with difficulty that she controlled herself.

She threw the remains of her coffee on the sand, screwed on the plastic top of her thermos flask and put the container back in her bag.

'You stay with me, Peter Norton,' she told the boy. Then, grumbling to herself, she set off after Norman.

At the end of the beach, the sea lapped gently against an outcrop of black rocks draped in shiny coffee-coloured seaweed. Overhead, in the cloudless slate-grey sky, seagulls wheeled and shrieked. A great mound of sand, clay and gravel mixed with pebbles and rocks had been skimmed off the clifftop in the stormy weather of the previous two days and had slipped down on to the beach. In the middle of this, up to his knees, stood Jeremy, misery written all over his pale face. Surrounding him were the rest of Mrs Robertshaw's group, chattering excitedly.

'He's stuck, miss,' said Valerie, almost gleefully, as the teacher approached. She pointed at the great brown mass of sludge and boulders. 'He's stuck in the mud.'

'I do have eyes,' said the teacher sharply. She advanced towards the boy. 'Get out of there at once, Jeremy Robinson,' she ordered.

'I can't, miss,' he whimpered.

'What do you mean, you can't?' demanded the teacher.

'I can't get out,' he cried. 'I'm stuck.'

'And how in heaven's name did you manage to get stuck?' she asked.

'I was climbing up the side of the cliff,' Jeremy told her. His lips trembled and his eyes filled with tears. 'I was looking for fossils in the clay and I slipped and fell.'

'Did you not hear what I said about keeping away from the cliffs?' asked the teacher. 'I might as well talk to thin air.'

'Can you get me out?' pleaded Jeremy.

'He's sinking, miss,' ventured Valerie.

'Will you be quiet,' Mrs Robertshaw told the girl. She turned back to Jeremy. 'Don't move,' she ordered. 'Stay perfectly still.'

Her mind raced. What could she do? She knew it would be fruitless to try and reach the boy and pull him out, for she would get stuck herself. She needed help, but there was no sign of the other groups, and the beach was deserted.

'Please, miss!' cried the prisoner in the mud. 'Can you get me out? I'm frightened.'

'Just keep calm and remain still,' the teacher told him. 'We'll soon have you out. There's nothing to be frightened about.'

'Miss, there is,' said Valerie. 'The tide's coming in. He could drown or be sucked under the mud.'

Mrs Robertshaw gritted her teeth and bent close to the girl's ear. 'This is the last time I shall tell you – be quiet!'

'I can cut the bottom off my water bottle for him to breathe when the sea goes over his head, miss,' volunteered Peter.

'I don't want the sea to go over my head,' groaned Jeremy. He sank another inch into the mud. 'Please can you get me out, miss?'

Mrs Robertshaw turned to face the children. Beckoning to Peter, who was the best runner in the group, she sent him to the hostel to get help. As he scurried off, she shouted after him, 'Tell Mrs Marshall we will need the emergency services!' It was then that she noticed that one of the children was missing. 'Where's Norman Stubbins?' she asked.

'He's gone, miss,' replied Valerie.

'Gone! Gone where?'

'I don't know, miss,' the girl replied. 'He just ran off.'

'I don't believe this,' muttered Mrs Robertshaw.

There was a small squelching sound and Jeremy sank an inch deeper in the mud. He was now quiet, white-faced and trembling.

'Don't worry, Jeremy,' said Mrs Robertshaw feebly, 'we'll soon have you out. Just stay calm and don't move.'

But even as she spoke, the most terrible thoughts were running through her head. She imagined the incoming tide washing relentlessly up the beach, over the rocky pavement, swirling around the trapped boy, sucking him into the cold grey water. She saw him spluttering and thrashing and choking and finally disappearing beneath the waves. Her heart began beating with slow thumps, like a hammer on a blacksmith's anvil, and her whole body became cold with fear.

At the far end of the beach, Mr Hornchurch, blissfully unaware of the drama being enacted beyond the slipway, was telling the children about some of the things they had discovered on the seashore. The teacher had been out earlier that morning and planted certain interesting items on the sand and in the rock pools for the members of his party to find. He had decided upon this ploy because he knew how disappointing it would be for the children if they searched all morning and found very little of interest.

Mr Hornchurch's philosophy was rooted in the belief that learning should be enjoyable and fun, that his job as a teacher was to nurture curiosity and creativity in the children, to value their questions and contributions and encourage collaboration.

Unlike Mrs Humphrey-Snyde, he was not the sort of educationalist who regarded his pupils as empty vessels to be filled up with information fed to them by a teacher. That morning he was in his element.

'There is a picture of one of these,' he said, holding up a fossil like a coiled snake that one of his pupils had found among the pebbles, 'in your information booklet. Now what sort of creature do you think it was? What do you think it looks like?'

'I think it was a snake all curled up,' said one pupil.

'Or a snail,' suggested another.

Soon the ideas came fast and furious.

'All very good answers,' said the teacher, 'but in fact it's an ammonite, perhaps one of the most widely known fossils. These creatures lived in the seas between two hundred and forty and sixty-five million years ago, when they became extinct along with the dinosaurs. The name "ammonite" originates from the Greek ram-horned god Ammon. Ammonites belong to a group of predators known as cephalopods, which includes their living relatives the octopus, squid, cuttlefish and nautilus.'

'What's this one, sir?' asked a girl holding up a dark grey bullet-shaped object.

'This is a belemnite, which swam in the prehistoric sea millions of years ago,' Mr Hornchurch told her. 'Any ideas what sort of creature it was?' Again the contributions were wide-ranging and inventive.

'Belemnites were part of an extinct group of cephalopods that probably looked like a squid,' the teacher told them. 'They had large eyes and swam quickly, using a form of jet propulsion. Like the octopus, they probably squirted clouds of black ink at their enemies to foil attacks.' He reached into his pocket and produced a small pale orange pebble. 'And this I think I should give to Amber.' He passed it to the girl. 'It looks like a round piece of marble or quartz, but it is Amber's namesake.'

The girl looked puzzled.

'This is a piece of amber,' explained Mr Hornchurch, 'carried all the way down from the Baltic millions of years ago by the ice and dumped here on the beach. It is very hard to find and quite precious.'

The girl smiled and stroked the pebble. 'For me, sir?'

'Of course,' replied the teacher. 'Amber is a beautifully coloured orange resin used to make jewellery, and sometimes it has insects embedded in it. When we get back to the hostel, we will polish it and see if there are any little creatures inside.'

'Sir, can we go and look for some more amber?' asked a boy eagerly.

'Yes, but stay on the beach.'

Mr Hornchurch looked towards the dark, looming cliffs, where there had been a landslip during the storm the previous day. He felt it advisable not to tell the pupils that he had found the piece of amber in the boulder clay that formed huge viscous heaps beneath the overhanging bluff. He did not want them climbing all over the mass of mud. The last thing he needed was for one of them to get stuck in that.

Mrs Robertshaw looked anxiously down the beach, praying that help would soon be coming. Shielding her eyes from the sun, she saw a lone figure running toward her. It was Norman Stubbins

'Where have you been?' she demanded when the boy came within earshot.

'To fetch this, miss,' he replied, patting a length of rope looped on his shoulder.

'A rope?' said the teacher.

'To get Jeremy out, miss,' said Norman. 'I remember seeing that the boats on the slipway were fastened with ropes. We could tie it around him and pull him out.'

'That's very good thinking,' said Mrs Robertshaw. She held her hand out for the rope.

Norman, however, kept hold of it and with surprising presence of mind looped one end and threw it to the boy stuck in the mud. 'Put it around your middle,' he said, 'then we are going to pull you out.'

Jeremy shook his head. 'I don't want to,' he groaned. 'I'm frightened.'

'Come on,' urged Norman. 'It won't hurt.'

Norman turned to the rest of the pupils and picked the four biggest, then told them to take hold of the rope. Jeremy was at last prevailed upon to loop it around his waist, and a few minutes later, swathed in mud and minus his boots, he was sitting on the sand crying gently to himself.

Mrs Robertshaw, who had watched in uncharacteristic silence and let Norman take charge of the situation, gave a great heaving sigh of relief and sat down on the sand next to the distressed boy. She put an arm around his shoulder. 'It's over now, Jeremy,' she told him. 'You're quite safe. We'll take you back to the hostel and you can get cleaned up. Come along.'

'It was a silly thing to do, wasn't it, miss?' remarked Valerie with her hands on her hips.

'We all do silly things at times,' replied the teacher, getting to her feet.

'But that was a really, really silly thing to do,' persisted the girl. 'Especially after you told us not to go near the cliffs.'

'That will do,' said Mrs Robertshaw tersely. 'Come along, Jeremy,' she said, helping the boy to get up.

On their way back to the hostel, the group met Peter running full pelt down the beach towards them. 'The emergency services are on their way!' he cried.

'Well run back and tell them we don't need them any more,' shouted Mrs Robertshaw.

'Pardon, miss?'

'We've got Jeremy out. Run along and tell Mrs Marshall we don't need any help.'

Peter came to a sudden stop. 'But the fire brigade is on its way, and the air-sea rescue.'

'Well we don't need them now. Do as you are told and ask Mrs Marshall to tell them not to come!'

Peter turned on his heel and walked off mumbling to himself. 'I wish she'd make up her flipping mind.'

'And hurry!' barked the teacher after him. She turned to the boy walking next to her. 'You showed great initiative there, Norman,' she said. 'I am very grateful and proud of you. You saved the day.'

Norman's face broke into a great smile. He was unused to receiving praise from his teachers. 'I'd better take the rope back, miss,' he said, setting off with a spring in his step.

Later that afternoon, Mrs Robertshaw, sitting by herself in one of the lounges, anticipated the arrival of the coach for the journey home with a sense of overpowering relief. Never in her life had she experienced such naked terror, and she still trembled at the thought of what might have happened on the beach. She glanced at her watch and counted down the minutes to three o'clock, when they would be departing.

'All packed and ready for the off?' said Rupert, joining her. He was in his usual cheerful good humour.

'Are you always so maddeningly jolly and carefree, Rupert?' she asked, grimacing.

'I try to be positive,' he replied, looking into his colleague's pinched and deeply lined face. 'You know they say it takes twenty-six muscles to smile and sixty-two to frown.'

'You don't say,' said Mrs Robertshaw, wondering how many muscles it would take to give him a smack.

'I heard what happened,' said Rupert.

'Did you?'

'You had quite an exciting time on the beach, I gather.'

'You could call it that,' Mrs Robertshaw answered tersely.

'It must have been a pretty frightening experience.'

'Pretty frightening?' she repeated. 'That's putting it mildly. It was petrifying. It was the worst experience of my life.'

'Well you know, Elsie,' remarked Rupert, patting her arm as a parent might do to comfort a child, 'everything has turned out for the best, and that's the main thing.' His comment was guaranteed to annoy his listener, who gritted her teeth and glared at him. 'These things happen,' he added.

'No, Rupert!' snapped Mrs Robertshaw. 'These things do not happen! How many times have you heard of a child getting stuck in twenty feet of mud and sinking as the tide is coming in?'

'Not many,' he replied. He thought for a moment. 'Actually, never.'

'Exactly, and if that silly Robinson boy had done as he was told, he wouldn't have ended up in that predicament.'

'I hear Norman came to the rescue.'

'It's ironic really,' said Mrs Robertshaw, calming down, 'that the boy who is more accident-prone than any other child I have encountered in my entire teaching career should show such common sense and initiative.'

'I always think that something constructive can emerge from such distressing experiences,' mused Rupert.

'Constructive!' cried his colleague, returning to her angry mood. 'And pray tell me how the outcome of a child being nearly swallowed up in a big mound of mud could possibly be regarded as constructive?'

'For a start, it will be a salutary lesson for the children to always be very cautious when on the beach. It will teach them to be extra careful on future trips to the coast.'

Mrs Robertshaw snorted. 'Future trips to the coast! I can assure you that this will be the last time I shall be taking children to the coast – the very last time.'

'Another positive thing to emerge from this is that the experience will offer a wonderful stimulus for creative writing when we get back to school.'

Mrs Robertshaw breathed in noisily but said nothing.


Wishing to avoid the wrath of the virago in charge of the school trip, the bus driver arrived at the hostel at three o'clock prompt. The children, having packed and tidied their rooms, lined up quietly by the coach in an orderly fashion and were counted aboard by Rupert.

'Did you have a good time then, Mrs R?' the bus driver asked Mrs Robertshaw.

'No,' she replied without elaboration, clambering up the steps and positioning herself on the front seat.

'Weather wasn't that bad, was it?' he asked.

Mrs Robertshaw was not in the mood for polite conversation; she was keen to get home. 'Could we make a move, please, Mr Bassett,' she replied.

'Before we do,' said the driver, 'could I have a quick word?'

'If it's to tell the children to keep your coach tidy, please don't bother,' replied the teacher. 'They have already been told.'

'No, it wasn't that,' he answered. 'It's just that over the years, I've taken parties of school kids on countless journeys, and I always have the devil's own job cleaning up after them – cans and bottles and crisp packets and sweet wrappers and chewing gum all over the place.'

Mrs Robertshaw sighed. 'And the point you are trying to make?' she asked.

'Just that when your kids got off my coach at the hostel, it was spotless.'

'That is good to hear,' the teacher replied, not sounding particularly pleased with the compliment.

'These kids are a credit to you, Mrs R,' the driver told her. 'If more teachers were like you, we wouldn't have all these problems what we have with young people today.'

Mrs Robertshaw cast a sideways glance at Jeremy, who was sitting opposite her. He felt her eyes boring into him and kept his head down.

# 13

The Blacksmith's Arms hadn't been updated in years, and that was the way the locals, who were resistant to change of any sort, liked it. In contrast to the other public house in the village, the Mucky Duck – once called the Dog and Duck – which was bright and brash, this country hostelry looked ramshackle, with its dull red-brick walls, muddy brown-painted windows and sagging roof. The interior was as run-down as the outside. In the dim and smoky public bar, reeking of beer and woodsmoke, a few dark, sticky-topped tables and an odd assortment of chairs were arranged on the grey flagstone floor. The walls were bare save for a set of faded hunting prints, some cracked blue Willow Pattern plates, a pair of old bellows, a few farming implements and a couple of antique shotguns.

Whereas the Mucky Duck, with its booming music, games machines, karaoke nights, happy hours and pub quizzes, attracted the 'off-comed uns' and the young, the Blacksmith's Arms was largely frequented by local farmers, shopkeepers and businessmen, who gathered in the evening and at Sunday lunchtimes to argue about sport and politics.

That lunchtime the pub was unusually busy. A crowd of hardy ramblers had broken off their walk and were chatting noisily with the landlord before the blazing fire that crackled in the inglenook fireplace. It was the landlord's boast that the fire had been kept burning in the grate for over a century. All the tables were occupied by a group of boisterous leather-clad bikers.

Perched on his favoured bar stool, Major Neville-Gravitas was deep in thought, oblivious to the noise around him. He was thinking over the events of the previous week and how his life had changed so dramatically overnight. At the other end of the bar sat Fred Massey, uncharacteristically quiet and equally as pensive. Both men stared down at their drinks.

The major was just coming to terms with the revelation that he had a son. He had spent the previous day at the hotel in Clayton with Max, eager to learn all about him and his life. He discovered that his son was a company director, with a wife and two children, and that he often visited England on business and was keen to keep in contact. He hoped that the major would visit him in Germany and meet his family.

Talking to Max, the major had felt embarrassed and ashamed.

'I must sound to you like a bit of a cad,' he had said, 'upping and leaving like that, but I had no idea Elsa was pregnant. However, there is really no excuse for my actions. They were heady days; I was a young man straight out of Sandhurst, away from home, in a foreign country. I met Elsa and we were genuinely fond of each other. Perhaps we knew deep down, though, that there was no future in it. I suppose we both regarded it as a bit of a youthful fling. Then I was posted back in the UK and given short notice. I tried to contact Elsa. I left messages. Time moved on. We never saw each other again. I hope you believe me when I tell you that I have often regretted that.'

'My mother didn't blame you,' Max had told him. 'She got married, and my father – my German father, that is – took me as his own child. They ver happy together and I had a wery happy childhood.'

'Perhaps it might have been better if your mother hadn't

mentioned me,' the major had said. 'It must have been as big a shock to you as it has been for me. Sometimes it's best to let sleeping dogs lie, if you follow my drift.'

'No. I am glad she told me,' Max had said. He thought for a moment. 'Do you vish that she hadn't?'

'Good God, no!' the major had exclaimed, grasping his son's hand. 'Dear boy, I'm so very, very pleased you came to find me.'

At the airport, the major had watched as the son he never knew he had went through into the departure lounge, and his eyes filled up. He began to cry.

'Are you all right?' a young woman had asked, resting a hand on his arm.

'Yes, yes, I'm fine, thank you, my dear.' He had wiped the tears from his cheeks.

'It's always an emotional time, isn't it, saying goodbye?' the young woman had said.

'It is.'

'Was that your son?' the young woman had asked.

'Yes,' the major had replied, sniffing, 'that was my son.'

'Another whisky?' asked the landlord, breaking into the major's reverie. He had deserted the ramblers to serve his regular customers.

'Yes,' replied the major, not looking up. 'Another whisky, please, and make it a double.'

'You don't seem your usual self today,' remarked the landlord, pouring the drink.

'No, I'm not my usual self,' agreed the major.

'Not bad news, I hope. Have your shares taken a tumble?'

'No, no,' replied the major. 'They are doing very well.'

'What about you, Fred?' asked the landlord, turning his attention to the old farmer and shouting down the bar.

'What about me?'

'Do you want another drink?'

'No, I've not finished this one yet,' mumbled Fred. He ran a hand through his hair and wrinkled his forehead into a frown.

'This must be a record,' said the landlord. 'You've usually downed a good few pints by now and put the world to rights. You look as if you've lost a shilling and found a penny. You haven't said so much as a word since you've come in. What's up?'

'Eh?'

'Why so miserable?'

'If you must know,' said the old farmer, 'I'm worried.'

'Not your wretched cows again?'

'No. I'm worried about our Clarence's baby. He's in the hospital.'

'I'm sorry to hear that, Fred,' said the landlord, coming to join him. 'Is he going to be all right?'

'Little un's got meningitis,' said Fred. 'It's touch and go whether he'll live or not.'

'Hey, Fred, that's rotten news.'

The old farmer scratched his scalp. 'Baby's in some Critical Care Unit. I've just come back and there's no change. Poor little mite's got tubes and drips and I don't know what attached to him. It's just a matter of waiting now. They're doing all they can.' He rubbed his eyes with a fist. 'I know I go on about our Clarence and Bianca and how the baby is always crying and me not having a minute's peace since they've been living with me, but I love that little lad and I'll be heartbroken if anything should happen to him. His parents are still at the hospital, staying over, and Tanfield Farm is so cold and empty without them.' He stopped and rubbed his eyes again.

Major Neville-Gravitas came down the bar and rested his hand on the old man's shoulder. 'If there is anything I can do, Mr Massey . . .' he said.

'There's not much any of us can do, except hope and pray,' said Fred despondently.

The shiny black taxi pulled up with a crunch of gravel at the front of Limebeck House.

Lady Wadsworth, who was in the middle of delivering instructions to the site manager, stopped mid-sentence, raised her face like a beagle picking up the scent of a fox and looked in the direction of the vehicle. The lady of the manor was a large, rather ungainly woman, too tall and stark to be considered handsome. She had inherited from her forebears her heavy-lidded eyes, thin legs and a large nose that curved savagely like a bent bow. That morning she was dressed in a shabby dark green coat with poacher's pockets, which had belonged to her father, and she stood legs apart in heavy green rubber boots.

Her visitor, an elegant woman of indeterminate age but clearly from her attire one who had taste and money, emerged from the car. She adjusted her jacket and smoothed the creases from her skirt before having a word with the driver, telling him to wait.

'Is this Limebeck House?' she asked the site manager imperiously.

'It is,' replied Lady Wadsworth, before the man could reply. 'May I help you?' She spoke with a cut-glass voice containing echoes of the elegance and comfort brought by wealth and breeding, of crystal chandeliers and silver salvers, nursemaids and governesses.

'I wish to see Lady Helen Wadsworth,' the woman told her haughtily.

'I am she,' replied Lady Wadsworth in an equally high-handed tone of voice.

The woman's eyes widened with surprise. 'You are Lady Wadsworth?'

'I am.'

The woman allowed a small smile to cross her face. 'Ah,' she said, approaching, 'I wonder if I might prevail upon you for a few moments of your time?'

'What?'

'Could I speak to you?'

'Are you selling something?' asked Lady Wadsworth bluntly.

'Certainly not!' replied the visitor, sounding peeved.

'You are not some sort of religious fanatic attempting to convert me?'

'Not at all,' said the woman. She had an unpleasantly clipped and penetrating voice.

'I am very busy at present. I'm having some renovations done.'

'So I see,' said the woman. 'I did try and telephone you, but—'

'I'm ex-directory,' Lady Wadsworth told her. 'I can't be doing with all and sundry phoning me up at all hours of the day, and those wretched salespeople trying to sell me double glazing and kitchens and I don't know what. You should speak to my butler and make an appointment.' She turned back to the site manager.

'I should be most grateful if you could see your way to sparing me a few minutes now,' said the woman.

Lady Wadsworth sighed.

'It is rather important, and I have travelled some considerable distance.'

'Oh very well.' Lady Wadsworth spoke to the site manager. 'So tell your men to desist from using such language in future, Mr Purdy. I have never used such words myself, and neither did my parents nor my brother, God rest their souls. The air was blue with expletives yesterday. It would have made a seasoned sailor blush.'

'I will have a word with them, your ladyship,' replied the man, touching his forelock.

'And tell them to be especially careful when they put the statues back around the lake. I don't want them ending up minus their arms. The statues, I mean, not the workmen.'

The man nodded. 'Of course, your ladyship. Just as soon as the lad has finished cleaning them, I shall supervise their return myself.'

'Please do.' She turned to face the visitor. 'If you would care to follow me,' she said, before striding up a flight of worn stone steps flanked by stone pillars to the great black door of the house.

The visitor followed Lady Wadsworth into a cool and spacious entrance hall painted in pale yellow and blue. The ceiling was a jungle of decorative plasterwork, the intricate twisting designs standing out from the darker background. Bits were flaking off. A series of matching panels was set into the walls, interspersed with large gilt-framed oil paintings, also showing signs of wear and tear, depicting various animals: long-horned shaggy-coated cattle, fat pink pigs on stumpy legs, grazing sheep, leaping horses and packs of hounds. The stuffed heads of foxes, hares, deer and wild boar gazed down from the walls. Above the ornate marble fireplace hung a full-length portrait in dark oils of a severe-looking bewhiskered man posing in military uniform and bearing a remarkable resemblance to the lady of the house. The visitor noted that everything was in need of urgent restoration.

Suddenly a small wire-haired Border terrier trotted around the corner. It eyed the visitor for a moment and then skittered across the wooden floor toward her, barking madly, its nails scratching noisily. The woman froze.

'Behave yourself, Gordon!' commanded Lady Wadsworth. 'He's all bark and no bite,' she reassured the visitor. 'Well, he did bite the postman once, the little scamp, but the man deserved it.' The dog had come to an abrupt halt and now flopped on to its stomach, burying its head between its front paws.

The butler appeared.

'Ah, Watson. Take this lady . . .' Lady Wadsworth began. 'I'm sorry, I didn't catch your name.'

'Lady Urquhart,' the woman told her.

'Show Lady Urquhart into the library, and ask Mrs Fish to arrange for some refreshments. I expect you would like a cup of tea?' she asked the woman.

'If it is not too much trouble,' replied Lady Urquhart, patting her blue-tinted hair. She gave a thin smile and followed the butler, while Lady Wadsworth departed to smarten herself up.

The room was too ostentatious and colourful for a library, thought the visitor, taking in the faded burgundy velvet drapes, the patterned Persian silk carpet, the deep plum-red armchairs and the inlaid tables. Two walls were lined with highly polished decorative mahogany shelves, which were crammed with leather-bound books. From a wall bracket a marble bust of a man with a big nose and hooded eyes glowered at her. Lady Urquhart ran a long gloved finger across the books and examined the dust that had adhered. She gave a small grimace. Turning, she noted the soft chartreuse-patterned Chinese wallpaper, discoloured in places and showing signs of damp, and the impressive carved marble fireplace, bearing an elaborate coat of arms, above which a huge Chippendale-style mirror caught the reflected light from the dusty chandeliers.

Dominating the room was an enormous portrait in oils of the man in the painting displayed in the hall. He gazed conde-scendingly back at her. A fat man with heavy-lidded eyes and surprisingly spindly legs, he posed awkwardly, one hand on his hip, in a tight-fitting Prussian-blue jacket and white silk waistcoat, stockings and britches, a scarlet robe draped around his shoulders. At his feet were two lazy-looking liver and white German pointers.

The butler arrived with a silver tray on which had been arranged a fluted china teapot, two delicate china cups and saucers and a jug, sugar bowl, tongs and spoons. Lady Urquhart noticed that the cups were chipped around the edges and the jug had a hairline crack.

Presently Lady Wadsworth made her entrance. She had changed for the meeting and was wearing a long multicoloured cotton skirt, a Chinese silk jacket buttoned up to the neck and red pumps, and had decorated herself with a variety of expensive-looking jewellery. With her wave of bright russet-coloured hair and lipstick as thick and red as congealed blood, she looked like some large exotic bird.

The butler poured the tea and handed a cup to Lady Urquhart, who examined it closely as if it might contain something disagreeable.

'Thank you, Watson, that will be all,' Lady Wadsworth told him. She picked up her own cup and turned to her visitor. 'I was at school with an Urquhart. Fiona-Jean Urquhart, a large girl with red hair and a face full of fierce freckles. Her father was some sort of laird and owned half of Scotland. Any relation?'

'Possibly some distant relative of my husband's,' replied the visitor, fingering the coral necklace at her throat and smiling in a vapid way. 'His ancestors moved from Scotland to County Antrim in the seventeenth century. It was when many Scots settled in Ireland. The first baronet built the house by Lough Moy.'

'And is your husband with you?' asked Lady Wadsworth.

'Sadly Sir Eustace died last year. The title, the house and the estate have passed to his cousin Hubert. I am in the process of moving to England. There is nothing to keep me in Ireland now.'

'I never married,' Lady Wadsworth told her. She took a gulp of tea. 'I have friends in Ireland – the Coulson-Gaunts of

Connislough Castle. I was there a few months ago. Beautiful setting, overlooking a lake. You may know them. Lady Coulson-Gaunt is the cousin of the Throckmortons of Wexford. Her daughter Leonie is a famous artist. She exhibits in the Royal Academy.'

'I am afraid not,' replied the visitor.

'Perhaps you know Lady Molly Denham-Smith. Her grandmother was a great friend of the second Viscountess Wadsworth, from whom I am descended. Sadly my father was the last viscount. The title died with him.'

'I assumed your father was an earl,' said Lady Urquhart.

'No,' replied Lady Wadsworth. 'Whatever gave you that idea?'

'But the daughter of a viscount, unless I am mistaken, is titled "the honourable",' said the visitor.

'Very true,' replied her host. 'However, I have a life peerage. I'm a baroness in my own right. Does that clarify matters for you?' She was getting irritated by the cross-examination, and her annoyance could be seen in her expression and heard in her tone of voice. She placed the teacup down on the tray with a clatter. 'So what is it you wish to see me about, Lady Urquhart?'

'This is a somewhat delicate matter,' admitted the visitor. She sipped her tea and then placed her cup carefully on the small occasional table near her chair.

'Do tell,' said Lady Wadsworth.

'I believe you have a Mr O'Malley in your employ,' said the visitor.

'Yes, I do. He manages my estate – such as it is.'

'Your estate?' said Lady Urquhart. Her eyes widened with surprise. 'Mr O'Malley is your estate manager?'

'That is what I said,' Lady Wadsworth told her. She raised her own teacup to her lips and took a sip. 'As you no doubt observed, I am having some extensive renovations undertaken at Limebeck House. Mr O'Malley is overseeing those and getting the gardens, the lake and the parkland in order. May I ask what interest you have in him?'

'And he has a child with him?' asked Lady Urquhart, ignoring the enquiry.

'He does. Roisin, his young daughter, is a delightful little girl: clever, well behaved and quite a talented flautist. May I ask again what your interest is in Mr O'Malley?'

'The child is my granddaughter.'

'Really?' Lady Wadsworth was silent for a moment, pondering on the revelation. She put the cup down again.

'Perhaps I should explain.'

'Perhaps you should,' said Lady Wadsworth.

'Sir Eustace and I had a daughter. Rowena was given every opportunity one could give a child: she was sent to a prestigious independent girls' boarding school, taken abroad regularly, had equestrian lessons and music tuition and private examination coaching during the holidays. She wanted for nothing.' Lady Urquhart smiled ruefully. 'Sadly, she became a wilful young woman, stubborn and argumentative. We just did not know what got into her.'

'She sounds like a normal teenager to me,' said Lady Wadsworth. 'I know I could be petulant and sulky when I was young and felt my parents were always finding fault with me.'

'It was more than adolescent moodiness,' said Lady Urquhart. 'Rowena seemed to oppose all that my husband and I stood for, scorning her background, mixing with the most unsuitable locals and staying out until all hours, attending folk concerts, beach parties and the like. It was very distressing, particularly for my husband, coming from an established and prominent family as he did. He had a position to uphold in the community and felt such disappointment and shame. When he remonstrated with our daughter about her lifestyle and behaviour, it degenerated into the most disagreeable quarrel, following which Rowena left and set up with this Mr O'Malley. I have never met the man, but my husband and I saw them once in town and he looked like one of those bohemian types – long hair, earrings, shabby clothes.'

'I have always considered that an unconventional lifestyle holds a strong appeal to those who long to escape the stifling bounds of bourgeois society,' said Lady Wadsworth nonchalantly. It was a sweetly damning reply. 'I myself was, and still am, somewhat unconventional.'

'But not so unconventional, I venture to suggest, that you turned your back on your family, with all its traditions and responsibilities. I am sure you will understand, Lady Wadsworth, being from a similar background as my own, that for someone of my daughter's social standing to step out of her class and live with such a man, she might just as well have cohabited with someone of a different colour.'

'I think you do Mr O'Malley an injustice,' said Lady Wadsworth sharply. 'He is a man of strong principles, most trustworthy and very hard-working.'

'But not of our class,' replied Lady Urquhart, smiling archly. She clearly believed that what she was spouting was eminently reasonable, and that her listener would concur with these ridiculous views.

Lady Wadsworth raised an eyebrow, amused by the folly of her visitor's social pretension. She was moved to respond to the asinine observation, but resisted the temptation, not wishing to enter into an argument with this affected woman.

Lady Urquhart gave a heaving sigh. 'The next thing we heard was that our daughter was with child, which in particular deeply upset my husband, who had such high hopes for her.'

'And him coming from such an old-established and prominent family,' said Lady Wadsworth sardonically. 'The shame of an illegitimate child must have been a great affront to him.'

The sarcasm sailed airily over Lady Urquhart's head.

'Indeed, and I am sure that all the stress brought about by this brouhaha occasioned his stroke, from which he never really recovered,' she continued. 'Rowena came to Castle Morden, our residence, to tell us she was with child, but my husband refused to see her. He had determined to have nothing more to do with her.'

'How very sad,' observed Lady Wadsworth.

Lady Urquhart took a small lace-trimmed handkerchief from her handbag and dabbed her eyes, which were the colour of a sunless sea. 'Rowena died in childbirth,' she said, sniffing.

'Dear me,' said Lady Wadsworth, shaking her head.

'Mr O'Malley did contact us after her death, but Sir Eustace would not speak to him and forbade me to have any communication with him. My husband refused to attend our daughter's funeral. It was as if Rowena had never existed. The next thing we heard was that Mr O'Malley had left Ireland with the child. I made every effort to persuade my husband to try and discover where they had gone, but he was resolute and would hear none of it. His health then went into decline, leading eventually to his untimely death.'

'I see,' said Lady Wadsworth. 'So he died never having seen his daughter again or set eyes upon his granddaughter?'

Lady Urquhart nodded and dabbed her eyes again.

Lady Wadsworth stared at her with incredulity. 'I find his attitude unimaginable,' she said, shaking her head again. 'So I take it you now want to make contact with Mr O'Malley and your granddaughter?'

'I do,' said Lady Urquhart. 'When my husband died, I hired a private detective to try and trace them, but every time he came close to discovering where they were, they had moved on. They travelled the country in a caravan. Eventually they were tracked down here to Barton-in-the-Dale. The woman in the village store was most helpful and informative and told me that Mr O'Malley worked for you at Limebeck House; hence the reason for my visit.'

'As I said, Lady Urquhart, I have never married,' said Lady Wadsworth, 'so in consequence I have not been blessed with children. My parents are long gone and my dear brother was killed in the last war. I have no living relatives. I am the last of the Wadsworths. How I wish I had a grandchild like little Roisin. I have to say that I find it inconceivable that your husband should have disowned his own daughter and turned his back on his grandchild, and I should add that I am astonished it has taken you ten years to get in contact with her.'

'My husband was of the old school,' replied Lady Urquhart, sounding affronted. 'Old-fashioned he may have been in some people's eyes, but he believed in standards, certain moral values, acceptable ways of behaving. He was a forceful and determined man and just could not come to terms with our daughter's improper conduct.'

What sort of mother was this woman? thought Lady Wadsworth. Weak in the face of a domineering husband, sitting there with her hard, narrow-eyed look. Humility, forgiveness, compassion clearly did not feature in her life, so wrapped up was she in her old-world complacency. Now old and alone, she wanted to possess her granddaughter, a child she had not bothered with for a decade. Lady Wadsworth almost felt a stab of pity for her, but she had heard enough and was keen to conclude this disagreeable meeting.

'I guess you now think it is better late than never,' she said with more than a hint of sarcasm. 'So you are here to see the child, and presumably you wish me to arrange a meeting with Mr O'Malley.'

'I should be most grateful if you would.'

'Of course, after the treatment he has received at your hands, he may not wish to see you.' There was a coldness in her voice.

'I think as Roisin's grandmother, I have a right to see the child.'

'Not so,' Lady Wadsworth told her sharply. 'From what I can gather, grandparents have no legal right to see their grandchildren and have no recourse should the parents decide to deny them access.'

'That may be the case if Mr O'Malley is indeed the child's father.'

'There are doubts?' asked Lady Wadsworth.

'Such was my daughter's lifestyle,' replied Lady Urquhart, 'that it is not beyond the realms of possibility that he is not the father, in which case I, as the only blood relation, would presumably have custody of her. I have consulted the family solicitor and he is of the opinion that I have a strong case and that I should pursue the matter.' She stared ahead of her for a moment.

'You mean that you, a woman she doesn't even know, wish to take the child away from a loving father who has cared for her all her life?' asked Lady Wadsworth. 'This is unimaginable.'

'As I have said,' replied Lady Urquhart, 'if indeed he is her father. My solicitor is most anxious to act for me and—'

'Well of course he is,' replied Lady Wadsworth. 'Where there's a chance of a fat fee, there's always a lawyer hovering in the background rubbing his hands together.'

'He is putting the wheels in motion,' Lady Urquhart told her.

'Well you should be very careful that the wheels you are setting in motion don't come flying off and you end up flat on your face in a ditch,' said Lady Wadsworth. 'I would warn you not to go down that road. Should you exacerbate the situation by going to law and adding insult to injury, you may find that you never see your granddaughter again.'

'Nevertheless—' began Lady Urquhart.

Her host rose from her chair and said with a note of finality in her voice, 'I shall ask Mr O'Malley if he wishes to see you.' She rang the small bell next to her. 'You can telephone here tomorrow, and if he is willing, then I shall arrange the meeting. Watson will give you the number. Now, if you will excuse me, I have to see how my gardener is getting on cleaning the statues.'

'You rang, your ladyship?' said the lugubrious-faced butler, appearing at the door.

'Please show Lady Urquhart out, will you, Watson,' she said.

Then the last of the Wadsworths swept from the room.

# 14

Elisabeth arrived at Forest View Special School feeling nervous. When John's teacher had suggested that it would be a valuable experience for her son if he were taken out to the seaside for the day, she had expressed strong reservations. Surely, away from the security of the school and its routines and having to cope with so many new faces and crowds, he would find it disorientating and distressing.

'His teacher is right,' Michael had told her. 'It will be good for him. I think John is ready for something a bit more challenging. He's been coming to Clumber Lodge for the last few Saturdays and has got used to the different environment and to us and the boys, and is doing really well. I think it's worth taking the risk of a trip to the coast.'

'That's what I'm worried about,' Elisabeth had replied. 'The risks.'

'You know better than anyone,' Michael had said, 'that you don't make any real progress in anything unless you take a few measured risks. Look what you've achieved at the school. You've never really played it safe, have you? The number of times you've chanced your arm.'

The boys were keen on taking John out for the day, saying they would look after him, so Elisabeth had finally been persuaded.

That morning, before setting off for Forest View, Michael had telephoned the hospital to ask after the baby. He was informed that the child had, as feared, a strain of meningitis

and there had been no change. He was still in the Critical
Care Unit, seriously ill but stable, and everything possible was
being done.

Elisabeth and Michael were greeted in the school entrance
by Mr Williams, the head teacher, a small, dark- complex-
ioned, silver-haired Welshman with shining eyes.

'Dr and Mrs Stirling,' he said brightly. 'A very good morning to you. I hear you are to take your son out for the day?'

'That's right,' replied Elisabeth. 'I must admit to being a
little apprehensive.'

'Oh, John will be fine,' said the head teacher. 'By the way, I
wanted to thank you both for coming to the fete. Sadly, I'm
afraid some parents didn't manage to make it. I am very grateful to those who did. We raised four thousand pounds which
will be well used.'

Elisabeth smiled, feeling vindicated in putting the fete
before the school trip.

At Forest View Elisabeth found John, dressed for his trip
out, sitting at his favourite table by the window. He was
humming to himself and tapping the table top rhythmically as
he posted various shapes into a box with matching openings.
His forehead was furrowed with concentration. Elisabeth sat
next to him and watched him for a moment. She took his
hand in hers and pressed it gently. He glanced around, then
returned to arranging and posting the shapes.

She kissed his cheek. He turned and smiled. How different
he was now from when he had first started at the school. Then
he had been painfully withdrawn, oblivious to his surround-
ings. He would rock back and forth in his own private world
and react adversely if touched, jerking his hand away and
looking upset. He had never been violent except for on one
occasion when he had been sorting out some coloured beads,
putting them in order of size and colour. When one of the
other children had touched them, John had got into quite a

state and lashed out. But over the weeks, with the care and patience of the teachers, he had made significant progress not only educationally but in the way he responded to others. He was now becoming much more self-confident and sociable.

'It's such a lovely sunny day,' Elisabeth said to him. 'I thought we might go to the seaside.' John continued to sort the shapes. 'Michael and the boys are in the car.' She stroked his hand. 'We'll walk along the sand, paddle in the sea, watch the boats and hear the seagulls screeching overhead, and then we are going on a train ride.'

'Hello, Mrs Stirling.' John's teacher, a young man with a wide smile and china-blue eyes, came to join her. 'I see you have come to take this lad off my hands for the day.' He rested a hand on John's shoulder. The boy looked up and smiled.

'Oh hello, Mr Campsmount,' Elisabeth replied. 'I'm feeling a bit anxious. Do you think he'll be all right?'

'He'll be fine,' the teacher reassured her. 'He's all wrapped up and ready to go. Have you brought a change of clothes?'

'I have.'

'Because when John sees the sea, there will be no stopping him. You know what happens when he sees water.'

The teacher had told Elisabeth on one of her visits how he had taken her son to the park on a rainy day, and how John had suddenly discovered puddles and started jumping into them, amusing the people out walking their dogs.

Elisabeth had once heard a speaker at an education conference say that teachers took on the most important role in society because a good teacher changed the lives of children for the better. Perhaps, she thought at the time, doctors like Michael, and nurses, had that top position because they saved lives, but teachers came a good second. This young teacher had certainly changed the life of her son for the better. She'd once told him that she could see he loved his job. He had replied, his eyes shining with enthusiasm, that he had always wanted to teach. For him it was the best job in the world, and working in a special school with young people like John was the most rewarding thing of all.

'Thank you for all you are doing for John,' she said now. There was a slight tremble in her voice. She could feel tears springing up behind her eyes. 'He's so happy here.'

In the car, John sandwiched himself between the two boys on the back seat and started rocking slowly backwards and forwards, but as soon as they set off and the world outside began to flash past the window, he stopped and stared.

At Whitby, Michael parked high above the town. The air was cold and fresh, but a bright sun shone in a cloudless sky. They walked through the arch formed by two massive whale-bones and down a flight of steep steps leading to the harbour. John held Elisabeth's hand tightly. They ambled along the quayside, past the fish market and whelk stalls, the amusement arcades and cafés, the small fortune-teller's booth and the shop windows crammed with all manner of goods. There was the smell of fish and chips and candyfloss and seaweed in the air. In one shop window was a dummy dressed in a black cape. Fake blood dribbled down his chin.

'I think we'll give the Dracula Experience a miss,' said Michael.

Across the bridge, Elisabeth suddenly stopped and looked in the window of a small, brightly painted shop.

'Wait a moment,' she said to the others.

'We haven't time for shopping,' said Michael. 'The boys want to go back and see the sea.'

'You go on,' she said. 'I'll catch you up. I'll just be a minute.'

The window was crammed with all manner of foodstuffs and merchandise: nuts and seeds, grains and cereals, herbs and spices, dried fruits and herbal teas, and even skin-and hair-care products. Above the door, a sign proclaimed in bold red lettering: 'Jolly's Health Foods'. Inside, the shop was bustling with people, and there behind the counter, dressed in a striped apron and sporting a straw boater, was Mr Jolly himself, smiling and chatting to his customers. He looked a different man from the bony individual with lank hair that Elisabeth remembered, a man with a tragic expression permanently etched on his sallow face. He had been a lacklustre teacher, ill-suited to being in charge of children, but he had had the courage to admit his shortcomings and the good sense to accept early retirement when it was offered. Elisabeth smiled. Seeing how happy the man was now, she realised that he had found his vocation.

'Well done, Donald,' she murmured before hurrying off to catch up with Michael and the boys.

As soon as John saw the ocean, he stopped and stared in wonder. Then a flash of pure pleasure lit up his face. Never in his life had he seen such a vast stretch of water. The oily grey sea was calm, and in the ankle-deep water on the shoreline some hardy children were paddling. John broke away from Elisabeth's grasp, and before she could stop him, he was on the sand and running to the water's edge with James and Danny sprinting after him. At first he stood and gazed at the great mass of water, before touching it tentatively with the toe of his trainer. Then he was in the sea, kicking and splashing and slapping and scooping up handfuls of water. The little paddlers stopped and stared. Some giggled. People walking along the beach pointed and laughed and waved. Elisabeth made a move to run on to the beach and try and stop him, but Michael held her back.

'No, leave him,' he said. 'He's enjoying himself. The boys will make sure he doesn't go any further in.'

And so they sat on the small wall overlooking the beach and watched.

\*　　\*　　\*

After a change of clothes, John, his cheeks red with the cold and exertion, sat on the sand with James and Danny, eating a huge nest of candyfloss on a stick. His mouth was bright pink. Danny was devouring a mound of chips from a polystyrene tray and James was tucking into a hamburger. It wasn't long before a flock of seagulls gathered around them. They looked huge and threatening, with their sharp yellow beaks and piercing black eyes. The boldest of the birds came closer and with lightning speed pecked up a chip that Danny had dropped at his feet, then flew off.

John started to laugh, which set off the other two boys.

'Hello, Dr Stirling.' An elderly woman in a thick headscarf and heavy black coat approached with a group of women of similar age and appearance in tow. 'You probably won't remember me. I'm Mrs Irene Bullock. I was president of the Barton-in-the-Dale Women's Institute. You came and gave us a talk.'

'Ah yes, Mrs Bullock,' replied Michael, standing and brushing the sand off his trousers.

'You need to be careful of those seagulls,' she said. 'They're a real nuisance. One has just flown off with Mrs Harrison's ham and mustard sandwich. Took it right out of her hands it did. We've been eating our lunches under towels. Is this your wife?'

'Yes, this is my wife Elisabeth, and these are my boys,' Michael told her. 'We're having a day at the seaside.'

'I've heard all about you, Mrs Stirling,' said the woman. 'Mrs Scrimshaw is a stalwart of the WI. She's always singing your praises.'

'That's nice to hear,' replied Elisabeth.

'I'm here with a WI outing,' the woman told her. She turned to her companions. 'You remember Dr Stirling, ladies, don't you? He came to one of our meetings to speak to us.' She looked at the three boys with their mouths full of candyfloss, chips and hamburger. 'It was a talk on healthy eating,' she said.

It was on the platform at Pickering station that John began to get anxious. When he saw the shiny green monster thundering down the track towards him breathing great clouds of smoke and steam, he began to whine and cover his face.

'It's all right, John,' Danny told him, putting an arm around his shoulder. 'It's just a train. It won't hurt you.'

The engine came to a noisy halt.

'I think we will give this a miss,' said Elisabeth. 'He's getting upset.'

'Let's give it a try,' said Michael. 'You get aboard and try and encourage him to follow you. I'll be right behind him.'

'I don't know, Michael,' she said apprehensively.

'I'm sure that once he's on the train and it sets off, he'll be fine. Trust me.'

John was rooted to the spot, still with his hands over his face.

A squat, thick-chested man, his arms decorated with unusually colourful tattoos of snakes and other fearsome-looking creatures, approached. His nose and ears sported an assortment of silver rings and studs and his head was shaved save for a bright blue Mohican fringe.

'What's up, mate?' he asked Danny.

'We can't get 'im in t'train,' he was told. ''E's not seen one before an' he's frit. 'E 'as special needs, tha see.'

An old woman with a round red face and dyed black hair pushed her way forward, craning her neck to see what the delay was.

'Are we getting on or what?' she demanded crossly.

'Hold your horses, missis,' said the Mohican. 'They're just trying to get the kid on board.'

'Well what's stopping him?' she asked belligerently

'The lad's disabled,' he told her.

'I'll never get a seat if I don't get on now,' she complained. 'Tell them to get a move on.'

'Did you not hear what I said, missis?' asked the Mohican. 'I said the lad's disabled. Just be patient. The train won't go without you.'

'In my opinion they shouldn't be bringing handicapped children like that on a train. It holds everybody up.'

'Why don't you keep your stupid opinions to yourself?' said the Mohican, turning to look into the angry face. 'You miserable, moth-eaten old bag.'

'Well I never!' cried the woman, her face decorated with fury. 'I shall report you to the stationmaster, speaking to me like that.'

'Stationmaster?' laughed the Mohican. 'What century are you in? Stationmasters disappeared in the nineteen fifties.'

The woman stormed off.

During this exchange, Elisabeth had managed to coax John on to the train.

'Thanks,' Danny said to the Mohican.

'No probs, mate,' the man replied, winking.

When the engine began to move, John sat gazing out of the window at the rise and fall of the vast moors as the train sped along, clickety-clacking on the rails.

'How's he doing?' asked the Mohican, who was sitting opposite Danny.

''E's champion,' the boy told him. ''E likes movement.'

'What's up with him then?' the man asked in a whisper.

''E's autistic. It means his brain works in a different way.'

'Well I think it's good to be different,' remarked the man, leaning back in his seat. 'I mean, you can't get much more different than me, can you?'

'Mi grandad used to say that t'woods would be dead boring if all t'birds sang wi' t'same tune,' Danny told him.

'He sounds a clued-up bloke, your grandad,' said the Mohican.

''E was,' replied Danny. He stared at the colourful scorpion on the man's arm. 'I like yer tattoos.'

'A lot of people don't,' said the Mohican, 'but who cares what other people think. I never have.'

John turned from the window and stared at the man.

Michael, who had overheard the conversation, smiled and pointed a finger at Danny. 'Don't you think of getting any tattoos, young man,' he said.

'I might when I'm older an' can please myself,' he replied mischievously.

At the end of the line, the train came to a stop. The Mohican got up to go. He shook Danny and James's hands and patted John on the shoulder. 'Bye, kiddo,' he said.

'Bye,' said John quietly.

'Did you hear that?' cried Elisabeth, jumping in her seat. 'He spoke. Oh Michael, John spoke.'

'Good gracious,' said her husband.

'John,' said Elisabeth breathlessly, reaching for the boy's hand. 'John, can you say hello?'

'Bye,' said the boy almost inaudibly.

'Don't press him, Elisabeth,' said Michael.

'This is miraculous,' said Elisabeth, her eyes blurred with tears.

'We need to tell the school,' said Michael.

'It's wonderful,' she said, resting her head on his shoulder. Michael kissed her cheek and wiped away a tear. 'I never dreamed—'

'Are we getting off the train,' said James, 'or are you two lovebirds staying on?'

'James,' said Elisabeth, 'did you not hear? John spoke.'

'I know,' he said with a sigh. 'He's done it before.'

On the way home, the three boys fell asleep, their heads resting on each other's shoulders.

Elisabeth turned and looked at them. She smiled. 'What a wonderful day it's been,' she said.

'Yes,' agreed Michael, 'it has.'

'You were right, it was worth taking the risk.'

'We shall have to do it again,' he said. 'Today Whitby, tomorrow Disneyland.'

That evening, they had a visitor at Clumber Lodge.

'I'm sorry to disturb you,' Major Neville-Gravitas told Michael as he stood on the doorstep, 'but I wonder if I might have a word with your wife?'

'Yes, of course, come in,' replied Michael. 'She's in the sitting room, go through.'

'Oh, hello,' said Elisabeth, rising to meet the major.

'Good evening, Elisabeth,' he said. 'I hope I'm not interrupting anything.'

'No, not at all. Come along in and sit down.'

'Whisky?' asked Michael.

'Thank you, that would be most acceptable,' replied the major.

'Have you driven here?'

'No, no, I walked. I had a bit of thinking to do.'

Michael poured him a generous measure and gave him the glass. 'Then I think you can manage a double. I'll leave you to it,' he added. 'I guess it's school business you wish to talk about.' He left the room.

The major sat and stroked his moustache thoughtfully. 'So tell me, how is the young teacher getting along?'

'Mr Dwyer is doing really well,' Elisabeth told him. 'He's a born teacher. He works hard, the children like him and he gets on famously with his colleagues.'

'Quite a change from playing football for a living.'

'Yes.'

'It's good to hear that he's doing well.' The major took a sip of his drink. 'And what about Mr Hornchurch? How is he?'

'Fine,' replied Elisabeth, wondering why the major had called. Surely it wasn't to ask about the teachers; he had done that at the last governors' meeting. There was clearly something else on his mind. The major's lips twitched as if he was about to say something more, but he remained silent and stared fixedly at the whisky in his glass.

'Was there something in particular you wished to speak to me about?' she asked.

'There was, yes,' he replied. He stroked his moustache again and took a deep breath. 'I felt I ought to come and see you,' he said, 'to put you in the picture, if you follow my drift, before it gets out. You know what the jungle telegraph in the village is like.'

He fell silent again.

'Gets out?' repeated Elisabeth. 'That sounds a bit ominous. Perhaps you ought to explain.'

'My commanding officer when I was in the army, Brigadier Kerr-Plunkett, told us young officers that people will always doubt what you say but believe what you do,' he said.

'That's very true,' agreed Elisabeth, wishing he would come to the point. 'So what is it you wish to see me about?'

'To be honest, I feel rather a hypocrite.' Elisabeth raised an inquisitive eyebrow and waited for him to explain. 'The thing is . . . Oh I say, this is rather difficult.' He took another sip of whisky.

'In my experience, it's always best just to come out with it,' said Elisabeth. 'I'm sure what you have to tell me isn't that bad.'

'We all have things in our pasts of which we are not that proud,' he said, 'things we wish had never happened, secrets that are sometimes revealed.'

'I'm sure you are right.'

'Well then, those at the governors' meeting will, no doubt, remind me of my words when they know the truth.'

'The truth?' repeated Elisabeth. 'This sounds worrying.'

'I wouldn't exactly describe it as worrying,' said the major. 'Surprising certainly, maybe shocking to some people.'

Elisabeth sighed. 'I wish you would tell me,' she said.

'You will recall that I had a deal to say at the last governors' meeting about unmarried mothers, girls getting pregnant outside marriage and the lax morals of the young. I said it was considered a disgrace in my day for a woman to have a child out of wedlock. Mrs Robertshaw pointed out that men have some responsibility in this by taking advantage of young women.'

'And how does that make you a hypocrite?' asked Elisabeth.

The major breathed in noisily and then gulped down the remainder of his drink. 'It will soon be common knowledge,' he said. 'One can't keep anything secret in this village. The top and bottom of it is that . . . I say, might I have another whisky?'

'Of course,' said Elisabeth, glancing surreptitiously at her watch. She had had a tiring day and was ready for bed. She refilled the major's glass and handed it to him. 'You were saying?' she said.

The major raised the glass and drank before speaking, as if wanting to consider what to say. 'Some years ago, as a young army officer,' he said at last, 'I spent some time in Germany. I was away from home, feeling pretty lonely, and . . . I had a sort of liaison, if you follow my drift.'

'I see,' said Elisabeth. 'Why do you feel the need to tell me this?'

'It was a young German girl,' said the major, not answering the question. Clearly, now it came to it, he had rehearsed what he was about to say. 'Her name was Elsa and we were very fond of each other – rather more than fond – and one thing led to another.' He coughed nervously. 'I don't think I need to spell it out. Anyway, the long and short of it is, I have just discovered after all these years that the young woman in question – did I say her name was Elsa? – had a baby after I had been posted back to the UK. The child was mine. I have a son.'

'Oh,' said Elisabeth.

'His name is Max,' said the major. 'He has two children. I'm a grandfather.'

'Congratulations,' was all Elisabeth could think of saying.

As the major told Elisabeth about the son he never knew existed, and how a visit to Germany was planned for him to meet his new family, Bianca, Clarence and Fred sat at a corner table in the hospital café, unspeaking, with impassive expressions on their faces. They were all thinking of the baby, who they knew might not make it through the night.

Ashley, on duty as the hospital's assistant chaplain, sat down and rested her hand on Bianca's. 'How are things?' she asked.

'There's not been any change,' said the girl, her eyes beginning to brim with tears. She sniffed and grasped Ashley's hand. 'Oh Dr Underwood, he looks so poorly and helpless with all these tubes and wires. We're so worried.'

'The doctor told us to go and have a coffee while they look at him again,' said Clarence. It was clear from his pale and drawn face that he had had little sleep.

'I hope the little un's going to be all right,' said Fred. The old man looked desperate.

At times like this, Ashley was at a loss what to say that could give any real comfort. She couldn't say that everything would be all right, because sometimes it wouldn't be. All she could do was tell the young couple that the baby was getting the best attention possible and to remain hopeful and say a prayer. It sounded feeble.

'It's a good sign if he is stable,' she said, trying to reassure them.

'I suppose so,' said Bianca.

'Have you eaten?' Ashley asked.

'No,' Clarence answered. 'We couldn't eat anything.'

'I'm going to get you all a sandwich,' said Ashley. 'You must keep up your strength.'

'Here, let me give you some money,' said Fred, reaching into his coat. It was a rare occasion when Fred offered to pay for anything.

'That's all right, Mr Massey,' replied Ashley. 'I think I can just about manage a few sandwiches.'

'I've never been one to pray,' said Bianca when Ashley returned from the counter, 'but I've been asking God to let Brandon come through this.' She stared at the sandwich. 'Do you think He's listening to me?'

'I'm sure He is,' replied Ashley.

'Could we say a prayer?' asked Bianca.

'Of course,' said Ashley. She held both parents' hands. 'Dear Jesus, healer of the sick, we turn to you in this time of illness. Hear our prayers for baby Brandon. We ask you to restore him to health again. May his parents find consolation in your healing presence. Alleviate their worries with your gentle love and give them strength to accept this burden. We ask this through the Lord Jesus, who healed those who believed. Amen.'

'Thank you,' said Clarence, wiping his eyes with his fists.

'Will you stay with us, Dr Underwood?' asked Bianca.

'Of course I will,' replied Ashley. 'For as long as you want.'

Fred went off to buy some cigarettes.

'Your uncle's taking it hard,' Ashley said to Clarence.

'I've never seen him like this,' he replied. He thought for a moment. 'People in the village don't like Uncle Fred. Nobody has a good word to say for him. I know he can be mean and bad-tempered and moody and is always looking to make money, but we've seen another side to him over this. He's been really good since Brandon was taken ill. Can't do enough for us.'

'He is a bit grumpy, isn't he?' said Ashley with a little smile, 'but I know that he loves you and the baby, although perhaps he doesn't show it all that often. At times like this, the love, support and comfort of family is so important.' As she said this, she thought of her own mother, from whom she had received precious little love, support or comfort.

'Uncle Fred's been in a real state,' said Bianca, 'and he's been with us to the hospital and paid for taxis and everything.'

Clarence smiled weakly. 'Course, he's always liked you, Dr Underwood. He doesn't have much time for most folk in the village, but he says that you're a real Christian, letting him take his cows down the track by St Christopher's. He says there ought to be more people in the world like you.'

Fred returned and sat down. 'I hear you're getting wed then, Reverend?' he said.

'That's right.'

'I reckon it'll be a big do.'

'No,' answered Ashley, 'quite a small affair actually. James Stirling and Danny Stainthorpe will be ushers, and there will be just the one bridesmaid, Emmet's daughter Roisin.'

'I see that little girl around school,' said Bianca. 'She's always smiling and has nice manners.'

'Aye, I wish there were more kids like that,' grumbled Fred, sounding more like his old self. 'They run riot these days. There's no discipline in schools any more. I mean, I read in the paper that some poor teacher was sacked for putting a bit of masking tape around a naughty child to keep him quiet after he'd kicked her. She did right. When I was at school, we had to behave ourselves. Our headmaster, Mr Petty, stood no nonsense. He was of the old school. He must have used more canes up than I've had hot dinners.'

'You told me you hated school and couldn't wait to leave,' Clarence told him.

'I might not have liked my schooling,' replied his uncle, 'but I behaved myself.'

'I don't think hitting children with a stick or trussing them up with masking tape is at all acceptable, Mr Massey,' said Ashley.

'I think the less said about being trussed up, the better,' said Fred, looking at his nephew. He was thinking of the incident when poor Clarence had been tied up by the sheepdog and butted by the ill-natured, maverick sheep.

'So who is going to be the best man, Dr Underwood?' asked Bianca.

'Michael Stirling.'

'And is your father giving you away?'

'Sadly not,' replied Ashley. 'He lives in Canada.'

'Well if you're looking for someone to walk you down the aisle,' said Fred, 'I'll be happy to do it.'

'That's very kind of you, Mr Massey,' replied Ashley, 'but Major Neville-Gravitas has offered to do it.'

'Oh has he?' grunted Fred. 'Typical. That man's never been backwards in coming forwards.'

A nurse approached the table. 'Mr and Mrs Massey?' she asked.

'Yes,' they said in unison.

'Would you come with me? The doctor would like to have a word with you both.'

Bianca clutched Ashley's arm. 'Will you come with us?' she asked, desperation in her voice. 'Please.'

'Of course I will,' replied Ashley, saying a silent prayer.

# 15

Mrs Scrimshaw was tidying her desk ready to go home when Mr Gribbon appeared at the door of the office with a gloomy expression on his long face. He shook his head unhappily.

'Well it's a bloody nightmare and no mistake,' said the caretaker. 'Pardon my French.'

'What is?' she asked.

'Having to clean all this graffiti off,' he told her, jangling his keys and leaning on the door frame.

'Listening to you, anyone would think the school is covered in it,' said Mrs Scrimshaw. 'How much is there?'

'Well at the moment there's just the one piece of graffiti, but it can spread like Topsy if it's not nipped in the bud. And it takes some shifting, I can tell you,' he complained. 'I don't know what gets into kids these days, defacing and vandalising things.'

'What does it say?' asked Mrs Scrimshaw.

'Never mind what it says,' said the caretaker with a pained expression. 'It's not for your eyes and I'm not repeating it. Beats me how he does it without being seen.'

A small voice could be heard in the corridor.

'Excuse me, Mr Gribbon, I'm sorry to interrupt your conversation, but I couldn't help but hear what you were saying.'

The caretaker moved away from the door to let the new arrival into the office, then rolled his eyes and grimaced as he saw who it was.

'Oh it's you,' he said. 'Little Mr Know-it-all, turning up like a bad penny. What are you doing listening in to private conversations?'

'I couldn't avoid overhearing you, Mr Gribbon,' said Oscar. 'You were speaking so loudly, you could be heard down the corridor. You have a voice that tends to carry.'

'What do you want?' barked the caretaker.

'I have a suggestion to make,' said the boy.

'About what?'

'The graffiti.'

'Well keep your suggestions to yourself and stop earwigging on other people's conversations.'

'Hasn't your mother arrived to collect you yet, Oscar?' asked the school secretary.

'No, not yet, Mrs Scrimshaw,' replied the child cheerfully, 'but I am sure she will be here directly. She often works late. I did say to her that I am quite capable of making my own way home now that I'm in the top class, but she says it is better for me to be collected because there are some suspicious characters lurking about looking to abduct children. You can't be too careful these days.'

'Huh!' huffed Mr Gribbon. 'Anybody who abducted you would want his head examining.'

'Anyway, about the graffiti,' said Oscar. 'First of all, I thought you might like to know that you can't have one piece of graffiti.'

'What are you talking about?' asked Mr Gribbon.

'I heard you say that there was one piece of graffiti. If you just have the one, it's graffito. Graffiti is the plural, you see. It's a Latin word that means "scratching", and there are examples from classical times. Mr Hornchurch was telling us that it appears in Ancient Egypt and Ancient Rome, and there are instances of it—'

'Look!' cried the caretaker. 'I don't want a history lesson. I just want to know who the delinquent responsible is so we can stop it. I wouldn't be at all surprised if it was you and that teacher of yours has been putting ideas in your head.'

'Actually, Mr Gribbon, if it were me, and of course it is not, then I should spell the words correctly. The culprit is not that good at spelling. Now it seems to me that whoever does it picks a time when he can't be observed.'

'Well thank you for pointing out the glaringly obvious,' said the caretaker. 'Of course he does it when nobody's around.'

'So,' said Oscar, 'it has to be early on, before people start arriving at school, or after everyone's gone home. Now, I arrive early and usually go home after most people, so I could keep a very close lookout, do a sort of stake-out.'

'Look, if I want your help, I'll ask for it,' said the caretaker, angry red spots appearing on his cheekbones.

'Yes, well I have to get home,' Mrs Scrimshaw told them both sharply, glancing at the clock on the wall. 'I've got my WI meeting tonight.'

'Oh, and by the way, Mr Gribbon,' said Oscar brightly, 'I did notice another piece of graffito in the boys' toilets that needs removing. There's a rather rude drawing with it as well. I think it's supposed to be you.'

The caretaker opened his mouth to reply but the boy smiled widely and said, 'Well, I think I can see my mother waiting in her car at the gate, so I had better be off.'

'Goodbye, Oscar,' said the school secretary, giving a fleeting smile as she caught sight of the caretaker's scowling face.

At that very moment, a hooded figure was busy at work with a felt pen at the back of the school.

Mr Gribbon cornered Elisabeth as soon as she arrived at school the following morning.

'Something's got to be done, Mrs Stirling,' he said. 'As soon as I clear one lot off, another appears. And now I'm without a cleaner to help me. I mean, she's only just started and she's having time off.'

'Mr Gribbon,' Elisabeth cut in sharply, 'I have told Bianca not to come into school for the time being. You might understand that the only thing on her mind at the moment is her baby son, who is seriously ill in hospital, and not the writing on the school wall.'

'Well, yes . . .' the caretaker began.

'A bit of graffiti is of insignificant importance compared to what Bianca and her husband are going through at the moment. I should have thought you would have shown a little more sympathy, rather than complain about her being off work.'

The caretaker felt suitably chastened. 'I'm sorry, Mrs Stirling,' he said, 'it's just that it's getting beyond a joke, and . . .' His voice tailed off when he saw the fixed expression on the head teacher's face.

'I will endeavour to get to the bottom of it,' Elisabeth told him. 'Now I am sure you have things to do.'

Mrs Robertshaw was sitting with Tom and Rupert in the staffroom later that day, giving her colleagues the benefit of her opinion. 'I reckon it's that Jeremy Robinson who's responsible,' she remarked. 'It's too much of a coincidence that the graffiti only started appearing with his arrival. From what you've told me, Tom, and what happened at Boggle Hole – least said about that – he's a very strange and sly child who doesn't mix with the other pupils. He walks around all day with that silly smile on his face and is too clever by half. I've met devious children like him before. He needs watching.'

'Actually,' Tom told her, 'since what happened on the school trip, Jeremy's been fine. I still find him a bit strange, but he's been less vocal and certainly better behaved. It was a salutary experience he had on the beach.'

'Salutary!' snapped Mrs Robertshaw. 'Terrifying more like. I shall never get over it. It wouldn't have happened if that silly boy had done as he was told. You know how many times I warned the children about the potential dangers on the beach.'

'Oh yes,' agreed Rupert, raising his eyebrows and exchanging a look with Tom, 'you certainly didn't miss an opportunity to warn them.'

'I bet it was him who wrote things about me on the wall. I've had a word with Elisabeth and she's going to see him at afternoon break. Of course it could be Robin Hardy. I've had run-ins with that young man as well. He seems to be starting up on his old ways again, punching another child in the face. He's another one who needs watching.'

'I'm not saying that Robbie should have punched the other boy,' replied Tom, 'but he was provoked, and from what I've heard, he's had a pretty rough life. Actually I feel sorry for him.'

'Look, Tom,' said Mrs Robertshaw, 'you're new to the profession. I've been in it for more years than I'd like to recall. If I may give you some advice: don't get sentimental about children. They need a strong hand and to be kept firmly under control, otherwise they will run rings around you.'

' "I believe it is better to restrain children by feelings of shame and by kindness than by fear",' said Rupert. 'Not my words, but those of Terence.'

'Terence who?' asked Mrs Robertshaw.

'The Roman philosopher and playwright,' explained Rupert.

'Yes, well this Terence individual plainly never had to deal with the likes of Robin Hardy, Peter Norton and Jeremy Robinson. You start as you mean to go on, Tom, and show them who's boss.'

'I'll bear that in mind, Elsie,' he replied.

'About this graffiti,' said Rupert. 'I have an idea that I am in some way responsible for its appearance.'

'You!' exclaimed Mrs Robertshaw.

'Well you see, I was telling my class about graffiti that dates back many hundreds of years, from thirty-thousand-year-old line drawings in France to Ancient Rome to the Crusaders and to the colourful street art we often see today. It could be argued that there is something profoundly human about the age-old art form, that it gives people a voice, one that can be subversive, revolutionary and playful. I recall when I was at Oxford, a tutor had pinned on the noticeboard outside her office instructions about handing in our essays. It said, "Get it done by Friday". Some wag had written underneath, "Signed, Robinson Crusoe".' He chuckled. 'I thought it very witty.'

'There is nothing witty, Rupert,' said his colleague, 'about writing on a wall that says, "Old Ma Robertshaw is a fat old bag".'

'No,' agreed her colleague, 'I guess not.'

'You wanted to see me, Mrs Stirling,' said Jeremy.

Since his frightening experience at Boggle Hole, the boy had been unusually quiet and well behaved. No longer did he make clever comments in class, and he got on with his work diligently. The whole incident had clearly affected him. 'Taken the wind clean out of his sails,' as Mr Dwyer had remarked when Elisabeth had been told what had happened on the beach. She had spent time talking to Jeremy and to Mrs Robertshaw about what had taken place. Jeremy had been distressed and embarrassed when giving his account of the incident; Mrs Robertshaw had complained indignantly about the boy's blatant disregard of what she had said about keeping away from the cliffs, and vowed never to go on another school trip.

Elisabeth had written to Jeremy's parents explaining what had happened, and was thankful that they did not wish to pursue the matter. Had they done so, it would have proved extremely difficult for the school. An article in the newspaper with a massive headline of 'BOY NEARLY DIED ON SCHOOL TRIP!' would have brought unwelcome publicity. In fact, Jeremy's father had sounded most reasonable when he telephoned. He had taken the opportunity while on the phone of reminding Elisabeth that should she wish to invest any of her savings, he would be delighted to give her some advice. 'You must forgive me, Mrs Stirling,' he had told her, laughing, 'but I never miss an opportunity of getting more clients.'

'So, Jeremy,' said Elisabeth now, 'how are you getting on?'

'I'm getting on fine, miss,' replied the boy. He was not his usual cocky self.

'It was quite a scary time you had on the school trip.'

'Yes, it was.'

'It could have been a whole lot worse.'

'Yes, it could.'

There was a quiet moment.

'Why do you want to see me, miss?' asked the boy.

'Do you know anything about the graffiti on the wall and in the boys' toilets?' Elisabeth asked.

Jeremy looked astounded. 'Do I know anything, miss?' he asked.

'That is what I asked you.'

'Of course not, Mrs Stirling,' he said. 'Why would you think I know anything about it?'

'I'm speaking to a lot of the pupils, so don't think I'm singling you out,' she said. She was minded to tell the boy that the graffiti had only appeared since he had arrived at the school, and there was the incident at St Paul's she could have raised, but she thought better of it.

'So you know nothing about it?' she asked.

The boy looked hurt. Elisabeth wondered if he was genuinely upset or if he was a practised and accomplished actor. 'I could never do such a thing, miss,' he declared. 'I hope you don't think I did.'

'Do you know who might have done it?'

'No,' replied the boy, 'but if I do find out, I shall tell you.'

'Well, we'll leave it at that,' Elisabeth said.

At the end of the day, Oscar appeared in Elisabeth's classroom.

'I've been doing a bit of sleuthing, Mrs Stirling,' he told the head teacher.

'A bit of what?' asked Elisabeth.

'Investigating the curious case of the phantom graffiti writer,' the boy told her.

'It sounds like a story by Conan Doyle,' said Elisabeth.

'It's funny you should mention Conan Doyle, Mrs Stirling,' said the boy, 'because I've been reading one of his Sherlock Holmes stories. It's about a secret weapon. Sherlock Holmes was very good at detecting things because he looked at the facts very closely, which always gave clues. Now here are the facts in this case. Firstly, the culprit is tall, because the writing is high up. It couldn't be done by someone small. Secondly, he can't spell. For example, he's written "basted" instead of—'

'Thank you, Oscar,' interrupted Elisabeth. 'I think I know what word was meant.'

'The other thing is that the writing is unusual because it's a mixture of large and small letters.'

'That's very interesting,' said Elisabeth. To be honest, none of this had occurred to her.

'I'm going to do a bit of surveillance tomorrow,' he said. 'Then I might have more to report.'

'You do that, Oscar,' she said. 'Thank you for your help.'

'Actually I'm finding this really quite exciting,' said the boy.

When Oscar had gone, Elisabeth thought about what he had said. Maybe there was something in it. Perhaps Jeremy was not the guilty party after all. He was small for his age, and from what she had seen of his work, he was a good speller and a neat writer. Then again, perhaps he was clever enough to disguise his writing. She decided, to use Oscar's word, that she would do a bit of sleuthing herself.

As she drove home later that afternoon, Elisabeth caught sight of two of her former pupils waiting at the bus stop: Bianca's sister Chardonnay, a large, cheerful girl with bright ginger hair and a round saucer face, and her friend Chantelle, who sported huge bunches of mousy-brown hair that stuck out like giant earmuffs. The girls had moved up to Clayton Comprehensive the previous September. Elisabeth recalled how Chardonnay had entertained her class at the village school with a detailed and vivid description of the birth of baby Brandon, which she had witnessed. It had been Christmas Day, and her parents had gone out to the pub, leaving Chardonnay and a heavily pregnant Bianca on their own. The class had sat in stunned silence as Chardonnay related how she had fetched a neighbour when Bianca had gone into labour, then watched as the baby was born. Without the slight-est embarrassment, she had described the event in graphic detail and at great speed, illustrating the account with facial expressions and actions.

'Hello, you two,' said Elisabeth, pulling over to the kerb.

'Hi, miss!' replied the girls in unison.

'I'm glad I saw you, Chardonnay,' said Elisabeth. 'I was wondering if your little nephew is any better.' Michael had telephoned the hospital the previous day and had been told there was no change.

'No, miss,' said Chardonnay. 'Brandon's not good at all. My sister's really worried. We're off to the hospital now to see him.'

'Jump in,' Elisabeth told them, 'and I'll drive you there.'

'Oh ta, miss,' said the girl.

On the way to the hospital, it was non-stop chatter from the two girls on the back seat.

'So how are you two getting on at the big school?' asked Elisabeth.

'It's rubbish, miss,' said Chardonnay.

'We used to like school when we was at the village school,' added Chantelle.

'I hear there was a bit of trouble with one of the pupils throwing some eggs at a teacher's car.'

'That were Malcolm Stubbins,' Chardonnay told her. 'He's always in trouble.'

'Oh, so they discovered who it was?'

'Everybody knew it was Malcolm,' said Chardonnay. 'He used to brag about it. Anyway, one of the dinner ladies heard him telling another kid that he had done it, and she reported him to the headmaster. Malcolm's been suspended.'

'And when he was walking out of school,' said Chantelle, 'he made a rude sign and chucked another egg, this time at the headmaster's car.'

'He behaved himself when he was with you, miss, didn't he?' remarked Chardonnay.

It had been quite a battle, Elisabeth remembered, keeping Malcolm out of trouble when he was a pupil at the village school, but she had managed it. Obviously the boy had gone back to his old ways at secondary school.

'How is your singing coming along?' she asked. She had discovered when the girl was her pupil that Chardonnay possessed a lovely singing voice, high and clear and with unusual power in one so young. She had performed in school concerts and plays and sung at the Methodist chapel, and her ambition had been to become a professional singer.

'I don't do it any more, miss,' replied the girl. 'There's no choir up at the big school, and they don't do plays and concerts.'

'That's a pity,' said Elisabeth. 'And what about you, Chantelle? Do you still play football?' She had discovered another hidden talent in Chardonnay's friend. The girl was strong and fast, and as good as any of the boys at football. She was the star of the school team.

'Girls don't play football up at the comp,' Chantelle replied. 'We only do netball and hockey, and I'm rubbish at both.'

'That's disappointing,' said Elisabeth. The more she heard about the secondary school, the less she liked it.

'Here!' said Chantelle suddenly. 'Tell miss about the flasher.'

'The flasher?' repeated Elisabeth.

'We were playing hockey on the top field and this flasher came out of the woods and started flashing.'

'Dear me,' said Elisabeth, 'that's shocking. You must have been horrified.'

'Not really, miss,' replied Chardonnay in a matter-of-fact voice.

'Whatever did you do?'

'Well,' said Chardonnay, 'all the other girls started scream-ing and running off, but I told Chantelle to go and fetch the sports mistress and I would keep the flasher talking.'

'You did what?' exclaimed Elisabeth, braking and bringing the car to a halt. She turned off the engine and turned to face the girl.

'I kept the flasher talking,' said Chardonnay.

'That was a very foolish thing to do.'

'He seemed quite nice,' said the girl casually.

'I don't think that was a very good idea,' said Elisabeth. 'You could have put yourself in some danger.'

'Naw, miss,' said the girl. 'He was only a little bloke, bit like my granddad, and anyway, I had my hockey stick and if he had tried anything on I would have whacked him where the sun don't shine. When the teacher come running across the field, he scarpered.'

Elisabeth shook her head and chuckled. 'Oh Chardonnay,' she said. 'I do miss you.'

'The police come to interview me, miss,' the girl continued. 'They wanted me to tell them what the flasher looked like. I was able to give them a really good description.' She nodded. 'A *really* good description.'

'Well *I* heard it from the horse's mouth,' the shopkeeper informed the two customers who had called in to the village store for the weekly gossip. They were discussing the recent revelation regarding Major Neville-Gravitas.

'I don't know about the horse's mouth,' replied Mrs O'Connor, chuckling, 'but he's a dark horse, so he is. Fancy, you would never have guessed, what with him being so upright and proper and all.'

'Telling everybody how to behave,' said Mrs Pocock, with a downturn of the mouth, 'when he should be looking at his own shameful behaviour.' She pursed her lips. 'People in glass houses and all that.'

'Well it's a real turn-up for the books,' remarked Mrs Sloughthwaite. 'As I'm stood standing here, he just upped and came out with it as bold as brass. I couldn't believe my ears.'

Mrs Pocock hadn't finished. 'Bare-faced, that's what he is, going around the village like the lord of the manor, holding forth about all and sundry and their immoral conduct, and all the while he's been carrying on, sowing his wild oats. We don't know how many other children he's sired. There could be lots of them, all over the world.'

'I was just—' the shopkeeper began, trying to get a word in, but her customer was now in full flow. Mrs Pocock had always disliked the major, and now she was relishing his disgrace.

'And speaking of horses,' she said, 'he blows hot air out of his mouth like a broken-down carthorse. He'll not be so full of himself when folk learn he's got an illegitimate child. Oh yes, I've always thought the man to be two-faced, and this proves it.'

'As my Grandmother Mullarkey used to say, "The sin is not in the sinning but in the being found out",' Mrs O'Connor remarked.

'Yes, well now he's been found out and seen for what he is – a charlatan,' said the other customer.

'I don't think you should be too hard on him,' said Mrs Sloughthwaite. 'After all, we all have skellingtons in our cupboards that sometimes come back to haunt us.'

'Speak for yourself!' snapped Mrs Pocock. 'There's no skeletons in my cupboard, I'll have you know.'

Mrs Sloughthwaite raised an eyebrow.

'As my grandmother used to remark,' said Mrs O'Connor, ' "The person who makes no mistakes doesn't usually make anything." '

'Bridget O'Connor!' exclaimed Mrs Pocock. 'Can you spare us any more of your grandmother's homespun wisdom. I'm sick and tired of hearing all this stuff she used to come out with. She sounds a pain in the neck, endlessly giving everyone the benefit of her advice. I would have consigned her to an old folks' home, where nobody would listen to her.'

'As my dear and very much-loved Irish grandmother used to say,' said Mrs O'Connor, undeterred by the interruption, "Let every herring hang by its own tail." '

'And what's that supposed to mean?' asked Mrs Pocock.

'Everyone must be responsible for their own actions,' explained the other woman.

'Anyway,' said Mrs Sloughthwaite, wearying of this badinage, 'the major's as happy as a sandbox and going off to Germany to meet his son's wife and children. I've never see him so excited.'

'Well let's hope he stays there,' said Mrs Pocock, having the last word on the matter.

Major Neville-Gravitas had called into the village store the day after having spoken to Elisabeth. She had reassured him that no one would think badly of him. However, she did suggest he might be a little less vociferous about unmarried mothers in the future. As he left Clumber Lodge that night, rather the worse for drink, he felt a happy man and thought it was time to let others know. And who better to broadcast the news than the very fount of all information and gossip, the proprietor of the village store?

'You are looking very chipper this morning, Major,' the shopkeeper said, reaching to the shelf for his panatellas.

'I am feeling chipper, my dear lady,' he replied, a smile broadening on his face.

'Have you come into some money, then?' she asked.

'Something far more valuable than money,' the major told her.

'I don't know what's more valuable than money,' said the shopkeeper. 'I know I could do with a bit and no mistake.'

'Family, my dear Mrs Sloughthwaite, family,' said the major. 'Having all the riches of the world cannot compare with having a family.'

'Well I guess they'll agree with you there,' she said.

'I'm sorry. Who will?'

'Bianca and Clarence. Isn't that who you're talking about? Did you not know that their baby is very ill?'

'Oh yes,' said the major, becoming more sombre. 'Mr Massey did mention it in the Blacksmith's Arms. There has been no change, I take it?'

'No, the baby's still in the Extensive Care Unit at the hospital.' She shook her head sadly. 'I gather it's touch and go whether he'll live, poor little mite. What they must be going through. It must be terrible to lose a child.'

And I have gained one, thought the major. 'Yes, terrible indeed.'

'By the way, did that German gentleman manage to find you?' asked Mrs Sloughthwaite.

'Yes, yes, he found me,' he replied.

'A very polite man he was, and he spoke very good English for a foreigner. A friend of yours, is he, Major?' she probed.

'No, not a friend, my dear lady.' He placed a ten-pound note on the counter for his cigars. 'That was my son.'

'Mr O'Malley,' announced the butler, showing Emmet into the library at Limebeck House.

Lady Wadsworth rose from behind a delicate inlaid desk with gold-tasselled drawers to greet her estate manager.

'Ah, do come in,' she said. 'That will be all, thank you, Watson.'

'You wished to see me, your ladyship,' said Emmet, standing nervously by the door.

'I did indeed.' She gestured to a deep plum-red armchair. 'Do take a seat.'

Emmet perched on the edge of the chair, his knees pressed together and his hands clasped on his lap. He had very rarely been in the library before and was overawed by the faded opulence of the room: the great marble fireplace and high ornate ceiling, the deep mahogany shelving and the massive mirror, the marble statuettes and the walls crowded with gilt-framed portraits in oils of Lady Wadsworth's ancestors. If his employer wished to speak to him, it was always outside, in his office or in the kitchen. Being invited into the library filled him with some apprehension. He ran a hand through his thick black curls and wondered why he had been summoned.

'Have they moved the statues back by the lake?' asked the lady of the manor.

'Not yet, your ladyship. They are still being cleaned,' replied Emmet. 'I'll get Jason to hurry up. It's proving a longer job than we thought.'

'If you could,' said Lady Wadsworth. 'It was a pity that Mr Massingham, of Massingham and Makepeace Fine Arts Auction House, was not interested in them. I thought they might be worth something. Of course they are not marble like the others I sold. Those were brought back from Italy by the wastrel son of Sir William Wadsworth, one of my forebears. Tristram was the black sheep of the family, a playboy who spent his time gallivanting around Europe, gambling and womanising and drinking himself into an early grave.'

Emmet had heard the story of this prodigal ancestor at least half a dozen times, but he knew how much Lady Wadsworth enjoyed the telling of it, so he smiled weakly and indulged his employer. 'He sounds quite a character,' he said.

'He was.' Lady Wadsworth thought for a moment. 'Mind you, I guess there are a few of us who have done things that, with hindsight, we regret.' She was thinking of Lady Urquhart, although she wondered whether the stiff-backed, stern-faced woman really did feel any remorse for her actions.

'Yes,' Emmet agreed. He sensed that she was leading up to something. 'Was there anything else, Lady Wadsworth?' he asked. 'It's just that I have a very busy morning ahead.'

'Emmet,' she said. 'I've had a visitor, a rather unwelcome visitor if truth be told – a Lady Urquhart.'

'Oh dear,' he sighed. The smile had disappeared and the colour had drained from his face.

'She was here about her granddaughter.'

'I see,' said Emmet, looking at his feet. 'I wondered how long it would be before they tracked me down.'

'She wants to see Roisin.'

'And is Sir Eustace with her?' he asked.

'Her husband died last year,' he was told.

'I would be a hypocrite if I were to say that I was sorry,' Emmet replied. 'He was an unpleasant and obdurate man who made his daughter's life a misery.'

'Yes, I gathered from Lady Urquhart that he was a bitter and unforgiving individual.'

'He was,' agreed Emmet. 'A sad man in many ways.'

'Will you let your daughter see Lady Urquhart?' she asked.

'Yes, of course,' he replied without any hesitation. 'She is Roisin's grandmother, after all.'

'There may be a problem,' said Lady Wadsworth.

'Oh?'

'She has it in mind to challenge your right to look after Roisin.'

He shook his head and sighed. 'Yes, I thought she would eventually get around to it. Rowena foresaw as much before she died.'

'Well of course the woman is tilting at windmills,' stated Lady Wadsworth. 'She has not the slightest claim. She can't just appear out of the blue and demand to take your child away.'

'Rowena made me promise that if anything happened to her, I would not let them bring Roisin up,' said Emmet.

'I don't quite understand,' said Lady Wadsworth. 'How could she think they could do so?' Emmet didn't answer, but looked down at his feet. 'Lady Urquhart did say that she thought you might not be Roisin's father. Stuff and nonsense, of course.'

Emmet breathed out noisily. 'I'm not,' he answered.

'You're not!' Lady Wadsworth was clearly stunned by his revelation.

'No,' replied Emmet.

'You mean you might not be?' she asked.

'I mean, Lady Wadsworth, that I am not.'

'Not her father!'

'No.'

'Good gracious me, I had no idea. Does the child know?'

'Yes, she knows,' said Emmet. 'I've always been honest with her. Of course, it's made no difference to either Roisin or myself. I've always been her father, she's always been my daughter.'

'And is that why you took to the road, the fear that you might lose her?'

'The Urquharts have a lot of influence in their part of the world. I didn't think it would be long before they applied for custody and pulled some strings.'

'But how is it that you are not Roisin's father?' Lady Wadsworth asked.

'Rowena had a relationship with someone before she met me,' Emmet told her. 'He left, I met her, we fell in love and I agreed to bring Roisin up as my own. She did try and contact the father, but he didn't want to know, denied the child was his.'

'This puts rather a different complexion on things,' said Lady Wadsworth, 'of which I am sure you are aware. I guess that if Roisin's grandmother pursues this action, her solicitor will request a DNA test, which—'

'Will prove that I am not the father,' said Emmet.

'This is vexatious,' admitted Lady Wadsworth. 'However, if Lady Urquhart does decide to go to court, I am sure that any right-minded judge would not take Roisin away from you. After all, you have cared for her for ten years. I am not au fait with the machinations of the Social Services, but I gather the child's opinion is considered the most important factor, and your daughter would certainly not wish to live with anyone else.'

'I couldn't be parted from her,' he said, a small tremble in his voice. 'Rowena begged me to look after her. The last thing she wanted was for her own child to have the sort of rigid and repressive childhood she had had.' He went suddenly quiet.

'Did your wife write anything down to this effect?' asked Lady Wadsworth.

'No, she didn't.' He massaged his brow as if he had a headache. 'There's something else,' he said.

'Dear me, this is a day for revelations.'

'Rowena and I were never married.'

'Oh. You were never married. I am so sorry, Emmet,' she said, 'that things have turned out like this. Quite a pickle you are in. Had you stayed on the road, Lady Urquhart might never have found you.'

'No, but I fell in love,' he said.

'Ah yes, dear Ashley. I assume she knows all about this.'

'No, I've never told her,' answered Emmet.

'My goodness, Emmet, you must!' exclaimed Lady Wadsworth. 'It would not be at all fair to keep her in the dark.'

'I know.'

'Why ever have you kept it a secret?'

'I've just been putting it off. I've meant to tell her, but . . .' His voiced tailed off.

'So what are you going to do?' asked Lady Wadsworth.

'I need to think,' said Emmet. 'I had better go.' He stood up.

'Let me assure you, there will be an army of people testifying to your competence as a father and to the love you bear that child – Dr and Mrs Stirling, your Ashley and, of course, myself and I guess many others.' She stood and took his hand.

'Thank you, Lady Wadsworth, I appreciate that.'

'We shall face this situation if it comes. I shall be with you all the way, and I do pride myself on having a fair bit of influence in these parts. Bear up. I very much doubt that anything will transpire.' But from the tone of her voice, she sounded to Emmet unconvinced.

# 16

Mrs Underwood sat straight-backed in the waiting room at the suffragan bishop's residence. She had thought long and hard about whether or not she should consult the cleric, and decided that it was her duty as a mother to raise her objections to the marriage of her daughter and to seek the bishop's assistance.

The bishop appeared. 'Mrs Underwood?' he asked. He smiled and held out a long hand, which she shook.

'Yes, that's right.'

'Do come through.'

The bishop's study was large and high-ceilinged, with long windows. Dark wood panelling covered most of the walls. It was an unwelcoming room, bleakly decorated and sparsely furnished with a faded coffee-coloured carpet and heavy curtains of similar hue, a few framed prints of a religious nature and two heavy oak bookcases filled with leather-bound books. In front of a cold white marble fireplace was a huge oak desk on which sat a neat pile of paper, a large bible and a simple wooden cross.

The bishop indicated a chair and asked his visitor to take a seat. He then sat behind his desk and rested his hands on the top.

'It's very good of you to see me, Bishop,' said Mrs Underwood, sitting down and crossing her legs. 'Thank you for responding to my letter so promptly. I am sure you are a very busy man.'

'Never too busy to meet Dr Underwood's mother,' replied the bishop. He was about to say that her daughter had told him all about her, but in truth, Ashley had never mentioned either of her parents. 'I am sure you are very proud of Ashley,' he said.

'Proud of her?'

'With her new appointment as the vicar of Barton-in-the-Dale. Quite a feather in her cap for one so young, but of course she's very talented and highly regarded, and the preferment is well deserved.'

'Oh, oh yes,' said Mrs Underwood rather dismissively.

'She is quite a remarkable young woman,' continued the bishop, 'and I have an idea that she will be sitting in this chair one day.'

'Sitting in your chair?' Mrs Underwood looked perplexed.

'As one of the Church's bishops. I have great hopes for Ashley.'

'Oh, I see.'

'She has no doubt told you she is to be made a minor canon at the cathedral for her splendid work in the diocese,' said the bishop.

'No,' said Mrs Underwood, 'she never mentioned it.'

'And of course she is a chaplain at the hospital. She never seems to stop. She tells me she is to be married.'

Mrs Underwood leaned forward in her chair. 'That is why I have requested this interview,' she answered, 'in the hope that you may make her see sense. I am afraid my words have fallen on deaf ears. My daughter can be very stubborn. Perhaps someone in your position can persuade her to reconsider this reckless course of action.'

'I'm sorry,' said the bishop, genuinely at a loss as to what she was talking about. 'I don't quite follow.'

'About this proposed marriage,' she explained. 'I would like you to impress upon her the unsuitability of such a match.'

'And why should I see fit to do that?' asked the bishop.

'Well I am sure that it will not be very well received by her superiors. To be frank, Bishop, I am not at all happy with the relationship Ashley has formed with . . . well, with a man so clearly below her social standing.' The clergyman remained silent, too astonished to speak. 'I would not be doing my duty as a mother if I did not point out to her how rash and irresponsible this planned alliance is. You are probably not aware that the person she wishes to marry is quite unsuitable in every way. He is from an entirely different background, intellectually her inferior, has few prospects and, being Irish, is probably a Roman Catholic. He, no doubt, has taken advantage of her. She might have all the qualifications in the world, but she is still very naïve.' When Bishop Atticus remained silent, she continued, 'I am sure you can see why this association is imprudent, and I hope you will impress this upon my daughter.'

The bishop thought for a moment before speaking. He interlaced his long fingers slowly and then set them just below his chin in an attitude of a child at prayer. 'No, Mrs Underwood, I will do no such thing,' he said. 'Your daughter knows her own mind and I am delighted she is marrying the man she clearly loves. I came to know Mr O'Malley when I was the vicar in Barton-in-the-Dale, and you do him an injustice. He is a decent, honest and hard-working man and will make your daughter a most suitable husband. I find your attitude surprising, to say the least.' He stood, indicating that the interview was at an end. 'And now, if you will excuse me, I have several more people to see.'

Mrs Underwood sat stunned for a moment and then rose from her chair with an expression on her face that would freeze soup in a pan. She was about to respond to the bishop, but his lordship, as he escorted her out, had the last word. 'By the way,' he told her, 'your daughter has asked me to perform the marriage ceremony and I am delighted to do so. I wish you a good morning.'

Tight-lipped and infuriated, Mrs Underwood left the room.


'You seem in a very pensive mood tonight, Charles,' remarked the bishop's wife that evening, looking up from marking her pupils' exercise books.

Mrs Atticus was a plain woman with a long oval face and skin the colour of the wax candles on the altar in the cathedral, but her redeeming features were the most striking jade-green eyes and her soft Titian hair.

'Indeed I am,' the bishop replied.

'And what are you thinking about so deeply?' she asked.

'About a most unfortunate exchange I have had today with Ashley Underwood's mother.'

'Ashley Underwood's mother?' exclaimed Mrs Atticus.

'That's right.'

'All the time she stayed with us at the rectory when you were vicar of Barton, I cannot recall her ever mentioning her mother.'

'And I am not a bit surprised,' said the bishop.

'What did she want to see you for?'

'She wanted me,' the bishop told his wife, leaning forward and resting his long hands on his knees, 'to persuade her daughter to give up the man she wishes to marry.'

'Ashley wants to marry a man her mother wishes to marry?'

'No, no, Marcia,' said the bishop. 'Mrs Underwood is against her daughter marrying Mr O'Malley.'

'What?' exclaimed Mrs Atticus.

'She doesn't think he is a suitable choice for her daughter,' her husband told her.

'Fiddlesticks!' cried his wife. 'He's a most charming and upright young man, and just right for Ashley. What a nerve the woman has, asking you to intervene. What did you tell her?'

'Mrs Underwood?'

Mrs Atticus sighed. 'Yes, Charles, Mrs Underwood.'

'I told her what you have just said, that Mr O'Malley is eminently suitable.'

'Fancy coming to see you,' said Mrs Atticus. 'Whatever's got into the woman?'

'She seems a very joyless and determined person, and a terrible snob to boot,' remarked the bishop. 'She thinks Ashley could do a lot better for herself.'

Mrs Atticus smiled and thought for a moment. 'I remember my father saying that I could do a lot better for myself when I told him you had asked me to marry you.'

'Yes, I am aware of what your father said. He made his views perfectly obvious.'

The bishop could picture Marcia's father: the narrow, bony face and the wild bushy eyebrows that frequently arched with disapproval. He could hear the deep, resonant voice dripping with condescension and recall the searing blue eyes that had frequently rested upon him when they had disagreed. His father-in-law had been a bishop, and, as Marcia frequently reminded her husband, at the time one of the youngest senior prelates in the Church of England.

'Are you listening, Charles?' asked Mrs Atticus.

'Yes, yes, my dear. I was just thinking of your father.'

'So what else did you say to Mrs Underwood?'

'I told her that I did not concur with her view and that under no circumstances would I approach her daughter on the subject. I told her I was to marry them.'

'Quite right too. Are you going to tell Ashley that her mother came to see you?'

'I think not, my dear,' said the bishop. 'To do so would only distress her.' He leaned back in his chair and looked heavenwards. 'I'm pleased you decided to ignore your father, Marcia,' he said.

'Yes, Charles,' said his wife with a small smile, 'so am I.'

Wearing shapeless blue overalls beneath a waxed jacket with corduroy collar, a tweed cap and sturdy brown boots, Robbie leaned on the gate at Treetop Farm and gazed over the fields dotted with lazy-looking sheep. Rabbits, their white tails bobbing up and down as they cropped the grass, were unaware of the hawk that rode the air currents, sweeping in wide circles above them. Robbie had never felt as content. He had known very little affection or encouragement and precious little laughter since the time his stepfather had come into his life. It had been a dark time of recriminations and maltreatment and deep unhappiness. Now his world couldn't be better. He felt wanted and valued. He felt loved.

The previous day, a cold, clear Friday, he had rushed home from school to help Mr Ross load the pigs on to the trucks to be taken to the abattoir. Then they had cleaned out the sheds, hosing and scrubbing ready for the next consignment. He was now waiting for the new delivery of pigs to arrive. He would help marshal them into the pens housed in the huge sheds, and then together with Mr Ross he would feed and water them. Then it would be back to the farmhouse for a big mug of sweet tea and freshly baked bread and butter with home-made gooseberry jam.

He was heading for the farmhouse to let Mr Ross know that there was no sign yet of the trucks when a large figure appeared from behind the massive metal silo.

''Ello, Robin,' said the man gruffly.

The boy stopped in his tracks. 'What are you doing here?' he asked in a small voice. He backed away, his chest tightening, and tried to stop himself from trembling.

'I've come to see you,' said the man with a self-satisfied smirk on his face. 'After all, I am your dad.'

'You're not my dad!' cried Robbie. 'You never were my dad and you never will be my dad. I don't want you anywhere near me!'

'Come on now, Robin, don't yer be like that.'

'What do you want?'

The man reached into his pocket and took out a crumpled envelope. 'I got this letter,' he said, still smirking. 'It's from t'Social Services to all interested parties an' it says that you're to be adopted.' He waved the envelope in front of him and shook his head slowly. 'I don't think so.'

'You can't stop me!' exclaimed Robbie.

His stepfather took a pace forward, reached out with a hand like a small spade and gripped the boy's arm tightly. 'Oh yes I can,' he growled. 'When I married your mam, I became thy legal guardian.' Robbie could smell the sweat on his body and the stink of beer on his breath. He wriggled, trying to pull away. 'Now your mam left a bit o' money that's rightly mine, but t'solicitor tells me you 'ave it.'

'Get off me!' Robbie shouted. 'I'm not bothered about any money. You can have it. I just want to be left alone. I don't want you anywhere near me. I hate you.'

The man raised his hand threateningly.

'What's all this then?' Mr Ross appeared.

'The name's Banks,' said the man, 'an' I've come to take my lad 'ere 'ome. I'm 'is dad.'

'No you're not!' shouted Robbie. 'He's my stepdad and I hate him.'

'Let t'lad go,' said the farmer, 'an' gerroff of mi land.'

'I'll go,' answered Banks, releasing the boy, 'but I'm tekkin t'lad wi' me.'

'I don't think thy are,' said Mr Ross calmly.

'An' are you goin' to try an' stop me then, pal?'

'I'm no pal o' yourn,' Mr Ross told him, coming closer. 'I've 'eard o' thee, an' wor I've 'eard, I don't like. Tha're a bully an' a brute an' a coward an' all. I know 'ow tha's tret this young lad. Tha're a big man, aren't tha, 'ittin' kids. Now, gerroff mi land.'

Banks breathed out noisily and scowled. He bunched his fingers into fists. Mr Ross stood his ground and watched with an expressionless face as the man approached him. Banks raised his fist as if to land a blow, but the farmer was too quick and swung a punch that met the other man's nose with an audible crunch. Banks looked astonished for a moment, as if in a trance. Then he charged forward, roaring like some maddened beast. Mr Ross waited until the man was in arm's reach. He dodged the blows and then punched him so hard in the chest that Banks fell back, arms flailing in the air, into a mound of steaming pig manure. He attempted to raise himself but kept slipping back into the slurry.

Mr Ross whistled and two collie dogs darted into sight and sat at the farmer's feet. They looked up expectantly.

'Now be off wi' yer!' shouted Mr Ross, pointing to the prone figure, 'or I'll set mi dogs on thee.'

Robbie and the farmer watched as Banks climbed to his feet and trudged off down the farm track, shouting and cursing and threatening to return.

''E'll not be back,' said the farmer nonchalantly. He rubbed his knuckles.

When the figure had disappeared from sight, Mr Ross put his arm around the boy's shoulders.

'Are thy all reight?' he asked.

'Yes,' replied Robbie.

'I've given 'im a taste of 'is own medicine. Thas'll not be bothered wi' 'im ageean. I shall mek sure o' that.'

'Where did you learn to do that?' asked Robbie.

'Do what?'

'Box.'

'In t'army, lad,' said Mr Ross. 'I was Warrant Officer Class 2 Hamish Ross, First Battalion of t'Royal Scottish Regiment.'

'I didn't know that,' said Robbie.

'There's a lot o' things tha dun't know abaat me, young fella-mi-lad.' He winked. 'Reight, come on. Let's get summat to eat afore t'trucks arrive.'

'OK,' replied the boy. 'Thanks for not letting him take me.'

The farmer bent down so that his face was close to Robbie's. He looked into the boy's eyes, eyes that were as bright as polished green glass. 'There's no way anybody'll tek thee,' he said. 'Does thy understand that?'

The boy nodded and rubbed his eyes.

They set off towards the farmhouse.

'You know when I got into trouble at school,' said Robbie, 'for hitting that lad?'

'Aye, I do,' replied the farmer, 'an' it's best forgotten.'

'Elspeth said that violence was never the answer and you told me that I had to control my temper and that I shouldn't lash out.'

The farmer stopped and looked down at the boy. 'Aye, I did.'

'But Hamish,' said Robbie, 'didn't you just lose your temper and lash out?'

The farmer scratched his beard. 'Well . . . aye, I did, but that were different.'

'How was it different?'

'Well . . . er . . . that bloke was goin' to 'it me. I 'it 'im in self-defence.'

'The lad I hit was going to hit me and I hit him in self-defence,' said the boy.

The farmer laughed and Robbie's face broke into a broad grin.

'Now look 'ere, Robbie,' said Mr Ross, 'it's best not to mention owt abaat this to Elspeth. She might not understand.'

'OK.'

'An' I wouldn't say owt to Miss Parsons, that social worker, either, or to Missis Stirling.'

'Because they might get the wrong idea,' said Robbie impishly.

'Aye, well just so long as we're clear abaat that. Let it be our little secret, eh?'

'Hamish,' said Robbie.

'Now what?'

'I'm glad you hit him.'

'Aye,' replied the farmer. 'So am I.'

On Monday afternoon, a police car pulled up at the front of the farmhouse at Treetop Farm. A young police officer with dark eyes, a receding chin and colourful acne was accompanied by a pale-faced woman in uniform. They found Mr Ross and Robbie in one of the sheds, feeding the pigs.

'Mr Ross?' said the young officer.

'Aye, that's me,' said the farmer, putting down a bucket of feed.

'Can we have a word?'

'What about?'

The police officer looked around and sniffed the air. 'Could we perhaps go somewhere else?'

'Yer can,' replied the farmer. 'You 'ad better come in t'farmhouse.'

'Shall I come too?' asked Robbie.

'Aye, you 'ad better. I reckon it's summat to do wi' what 'appened on Sat'day.' He looked at the police officer. 'Or am I wrong?'

'No, Mr Ross, it does concern what happened on Saturday.'

In the farmhouse kitchen the young police officer sat at the table opposite Mr Ross and Robbie. He took a small notebook and a pencil from his pocket and placed them in front of him.

His colleague perched on the edge of a chair next to him and stared ahead of her with a blank expression.

'We have had a serious accusation made about you, Mr Ross,' said the young officer.

''Ave yer now?'The farmer didn't look at all perturbed.

The officer flicked open his notebook. 'A Mr Banks claims that you assaulted him. He says he came up to this farm to see his son and you attacked him, causing him actual bodily harm, namely a broken nose and severe bruising, and then threatened to set your dogs on him.'

'Is that what 'e said?' replied the farmer.

'Have you anything to say?'

'Let the lad 'ere tell thee what 'appened. 'E saw it all.'

The young officer turned to Robbie. 'Go on then, son,' he said.

'Mr Banks is my stepfather,' said Robbie, 'and when I lived with him he used to hurt me. I hated it there. I was really unhappy. He used to call me names and hit me, sometimes with a leather belt. I was put into care because the social worker said I was mistreated, and Mr and Mrs Ross started looking after me.'The words spilled out in a rush. 'They're my foster carers. I'm happy here and they want to adopt me. My stepfather came up to the farm and tried to make me go with him. He grabbed hold of me and hurt my arm.' Robbie rubbed his sleeve theatrically. 'Mr Ross tried to stop him and he was attacked so he had to hit him. He was protecting me. It was self-defence.'Then for dramatic effect he began to sniff and rub his eyes. 'I was really frightened.' He began to sob piteously.

'It's all right,' said the woman police officer, her face softening.

'So that is what happened?' her colleague asked Mr Ross.

'Just about,' replied Mr Ross.

'It's rather a different account from Mr Banks's,' said the officer.

'Well it would be, wouldn't it?' said the farmer.

The policeman turned back to Robbie. 'Are you sure that is what happened, son?'

'You 'eard what t'lad said,' answered Mr Ross. ''E was tellin' t'truth. T'wife and me 'ave fostered many a kiddie in our time and it's a fact that some adults don't listen to 'em, don't believe what they've bin told or just ignore 'em. Sometimes when kids 'ave complained to t'police, nowt's been done.'

The woman police officer spoke. 'I'm sure that Robbie is telling the truth,' she said.

Mr Ross had not finished. 'An' I'll tell thee summat else, Hofficer. If Banks comes up 'ere agen, tryin' to abduct this lad – an' that's what it amounts to, an abduction – then I'll 'it 'im agen.'

'I wouldn't make threats, Mr Ross,' said the officer.

''Ave you a family?' asked the farmer.

'I hardly see that that is of any relevance,' replied the young officer.

'Well if you did 'ave a kiddie an' someone tried to mek off wi' 'em, I reckon you'd feight tooth an' nail to stop 'em. That man 'as no legal reight to tek Robbie. T'lad's in my care. Banks was trespassing. He tried to snatch this lad 'ere an' I did what any reight-minded person'd do. I stopped 'im.'

The young police officer rubbed his receding chin and stared at the farmer for a moment. Then he looked at his colleague before snapping shut his notebook.

'Thank you for your time, Mr Ross,' said the female officer, rising from her chair.

'Is that it then?' asked the farmer.

'That's it,' she said.

When the two officers had gone, Mr Ross stroked his beard and looked at Robbie.

'What is it?' asked the boy.

'Tha knaas, that was a reight good performance tha purrup,' he said. 'Tha nearly 'ad me rooarin' mi eyes out.'

The boy gave a small smile.

'If tha gets sick o' looking after pigs, Robbie,' the farmer said, 'tha can allus go on t'stage.'

Fortunately for her husband, Mrs Ross, who had been shopping in Clayton, arrived just as the police car was setting off down the drive.

'What did the police want?' she asked as she bustled into the kitchen.

'They're looking for some pig rustlers,' the farmer told her, winking at Robbie.

'Good morning, Mr O'Malley,' said the butler. 'Lady Wadsworth has asked me to show you into the drawing room.' He grimaced. 'Your visitor has arrived.'

Emmet found Lady Urquhart sitting alone by the window, her fingers clutching the arms of the chair like talons. The room was filled with expensive perfume. He had never met Rowena's mother, but she looked as he'd imagined she would, with her high arching brows, long prominent nose, darting judgemental eyes and thin angular body held stiffly upright in the chair. Her face was as hard as a diamond. She peered at him as if scrutinising a specimen under a microscope.

Emmet had made a real effort with his appearance that morning. Anyone meeting him for the first time would have been taken with his looks and his bearing. He was a striking-looking man, tall and broad-shouldered, and was dressed smartly in a tweed suit and mustard-coloured waistcoat and a pair of smart tan brogues. He looked every inch an estate manager, and not the sort of person the visitor was expecting to meet.

'Good morning,' he said, meeting her gaze steadily.

'Good morning,' replied Lady Urquhart coldly and without getting up. Her manner was aloof and mistrustful. 'Is my granddaughter not with you?'

'No,' replied Emmet. 'I thought it best for me to see you alone. I feel we need to talk about a few things before you meet her.'

'Talk about a few things?' she repeated. Incomprehension crept across her face.

Emmet sat a little away from her and rested his hands on his lap. 'I need to know why you are here.'

'I thought that was evident,' she replied. 'To see my granddaughter.'

'Just to see her?'

'She is my daughter's child and I think it is reasonable that I should meet her and get to know her.'

'If that is all you wish,' said Emmet.

'I beg your pardon?' Her gaze was so level and her expression so mocking it could turn a person to stone.

'Just to meet her and get to know her? It's taken a long time for you to decide to do that.'

'Let me be perfectly clear, Mr O'Malley,' said Lady Urquhart, her voice hardening. 'I think my granddaughter would be better placed with me.' She made Roisin sound like some porcelain figurine to be displayed on a mantelshelf.

'My daughter doesn't know you,' Emmet replied. 'You and your husband saw fit to disown your own daughter and have had nothing to do with your granddaughter, and now, after ten years, you want to uproot Roisin and bring her to live with you. That doesn't sound reasonable to me.'

Lady Urquhart looked uncomfortable and shifted uneasily in her chair. She tweaked at her ring as she always did when she was anxious.

'The circumstances were such at the time that my husband felt it inappropriate to have anything to do with you and the child.'

'Inappropriate?'

'Yes, inappropriate.' Her eyes glinted like polished metal. 'You are perhaps unable to comprehend how very distressing

it was for him when Rowena left home. He was a proud man
from an old, distinguished and highly respected family, and
he had very high hopes for her. He disapproved of the
company she kept and of her lifestyle. When Rowena started
associating with people we felt most undesirable—'

'Such as myself,' added Emmet.

'Well yes, if you wish me to be perfectly candid. When she
began mixing with people not of her class or background, she
became headstrong and opposed to everything my husband
stood for. He was ashamed of her behaviour and very hurt
that she should—'

'Lady Urquhart,' interrupted Emmet, 'I do not wish to hear
any hollow justification of his – or for that matter your –
behaviour. I couldn't understand your attitude then and I
can't understand it now – why parents would disown their
own child and not wish to see their granddaughter. I loved
your daughter. She was a beautiful, intelligent, deeply affectionate woman.'

'Mr O'Malley—' began Lady Urquhart, again twisting the
large ring on her finger.

'One moment!' He cut her off. 'Soon after your daughter's
death, I arrived at Castle Morden holding your newborn
granddaughter – the most beautiful creature in the world – in
my arms. I stood on the steps of your big house while a
member of your staff informed you I was there. I was made to
wait, not even allowed to come inside. Then I was told that Sir
Eustace and Lady Urquhart were not at home to see me. I was
turned away and told not to get in contact again. And that is
what I have done and wish to continue doing.'

'My husband was insistent that this should be so,' said Lady
Urquhart. She sniffed self-righteously. 'He was immovable on
this, and reluctant though I was to accept his decision, I abided
by it. I am not without feeling, Mr O'Malley, and have thought
long and hard about my granddaughter over the years. Now

that Sir Eustace is dead, I do not feel constrained to continue with this estrangement. Indeed, since his death I have made every effort to get in touch with you, employing a private detective.' Her face was rigid with purpose. 'But I have to say that I do not feel your lifestyle of living in a one-room caravan and travelling around the country like a gypsy is at all fitting for a young girl, and that is why I wish her to come and live with me. I can provide her with a more stable and secure environment, where she will have every advantage in life.'

'But I no longer live in a one-room caravan and travel around the country,' he told her, 'and I am to be married.'

'Nevertheless, I am determined that the child should come and live with me.'

'Her name is Roisin, by the way,' said Emmet.

'I am aware of what she is called,' the woman retorted.

'Lady Urquhart,' Emmet told her vehemently. 'Her mother's wish was that she should stay with me. For ten years I have loved that child, nurtured her and raised her. I am her father and I will decide what is best for my daughter.'

'If indeed she is your daughter, Mr O'Malley.' She gave a grim smile of displeasure.

Emmet felt his throat tightening. 'I really don't think there is anything else we need to discuss,' he replied, standing up.

Angry spots showed themselves on Lady Urquhart's cheeks and it was with difficulty that she controlled herself. 'Be under no illusion,' she warned him in a trembling voice, stabbing a finger in his direction, 'this is not the end of the matter. I have the means and the wherewithal and shall pursue this through the courts.'

'You may do as you wish,' said Emmet, and with that he left the room.

# 17

Barry Biggerdyke was sitting on the wall that bordered the school playground, picking his nose, when Oscar joined him.

'Could I have a word?' asked Oscar.

'Bugger off!' barked Barry, continuing to explore a nostril.

'I think we need to talk.'

'I've told you, four-eyes, bugger off!'

'It's about the graffiti,' Oscar told him.

He immediately captured the boy's attention. 'What about it?' Barry asked.

'I know who did it.'

Barry stood up and thrust his face into Oscar's. 'Who?'

'It was you.'

'Liar!' cried Barry. 'I never did nothing.'

Oscar remained perfectly calm. 'I saw you,' he declared. 'You wrote the last lot at twenty minutes past four yesterday afternoon while the teachers were at a staff meeting and the caretaker was having his usual mug of tea in the storeroom. I made a note of the time.'

Barry's vocabulary was not what one would consider very extensive. 'Bugger off!' he said again.

'I have a photograph of you writing on the wall,' announced Oscar.

'Liar!'

'If you don't believe me, I will take the photograph to Mrs Stirling and then you really will be in trouble, especially after what happened in the library. She will probably get in touch with your father and you'll be expelled.'

'Bugger off!' muttered Barry, sounding like a parrot.

'OK,' said Oscar, beginning to walk away.

'Hang on!' said Barry, less aggressively. 'Why are you telling me? Why aren't you going to see Mrs Stirling?'

'Although I don't like you, Barry,' said Oscar, 'I don't want to get you into any more trouble.'

Oscar's mother, a psychotherapist, had often explained to her son that one should feel sorry for difficult and badly behaved children because they were the product of a poor upbringing and a dysfunctional home life. Barry Biggerdyke, with his limited intelligence and unfortunate appearance, to Oscar's mind clearly came into this category.

'So what are you saying?' asked Barry, thrusting out his chin.

'I'm saying that if you stop writing on the wall and in the boys' toilets and stop messing up the books in the library, because I know it's you, then I shall not tell Mrs Stirling, but if you persist—'

'If I what?'

'If you still keep doing it,' said Oscar, 'then I shall.'

'I'll think about it,' muttered the boy.

'Well don't take too long,' replied Oscar. 'And if any more graffiti appears then I shall be forced to tell who is responsible. By the way, there are two g's in "bugger", and "basted" means to have poured hot fat on meat when it is being cooked.'

'Bugger off,' mumbled Barry, having no idea what the boy was talking about.

At the end of the week, as Oscar waited as usual in the school entrance hall for his mother to collect him, he could not help but overhear the conversation taking place in the corridor between the head teacher and the caretaker.

'So you see, Mrs Stirling,' Mr Gribbon was saying smugly, 'it occurred to me that the only time the offender could write this stuff on the walls and in the boys' toilets was when nobody is about, namely before and after school when he can't be observed. Now I've been very vigilant this past week and patrolled the premises regular like, and I reckon that's what's stopped his little game.'

'Well whatever you have done, Mr Gribbon,' said Elisabeth, 'it seems to have done the trick. The graffiti appears to have stopped, so keep up the good work.'

Oscar smiled knowingly to himself.

Emmet stood in the rain on the doorstep at Wisteria Cottage, his wet black hair shining like jet. There was a dark, troubled expression on his face.

'May I come in?' he asked.

'Emmet!' Ashley cried. 'Come in, come in. You're soaking wet. I wasn't expecting you tonight. Go inside and I'll get a towel.' He slipped off his shoes in the hallway as she ran upstairs.

Since renting the cottage from Elisabeth, Ashley had left things very much as they were. The long-case clock ticked reassuringly in the hall, and in the sitting room the solid oak dresser still had pride of place. The pictures on the walls had been replaced with ones of her own – a small watercolour view of All Souls, the Oxford college where she had studied, a scene in oils of York Minster and a framed print of *The Light of the World*, the allegorical painting by William Holman Hunt representing the figure of Jesus preparing to knock on an overgrown and long-unopened door. A few photographs were arranged on a small occasional table, and above the fireplace hung a simple African wooden cross.

Ashley returned with the towel and handed it to Emmet, who rubbed vigorously at his face and hair. She kissed his wet cheek.

'What an awful night,' she said. 'So what brings you out in this weather?'

'I must look like a drowned rat,' he replied. 'I'm sorry I've called so late. I saw the light on and—'

'Here, let me take the towel,' she told him. 'The kettle's just boiled. Would you like a cup of tea? I'm afraid I don't have anything stronger.'

'A cup of tea will be fine.' He followed her into the kitchen.

'Where's Roisin tonight?' Ashley asked, pouring boiling water into the teapot.

'She's staying with a friend on one of these sleepovers.'

'I don't imagine she'll get much sleep,' said Ashley, chuckling. 'They'll be up talking half the night.'

'Yes, I guess so,' he said.

'She seems very settled at the school.'

'Yes, she likes it there.'

Ashley could tell there was something troubling him.

'Emmet,' she asked, 'is there something wrong?'

'I need to speak to you,' he said. He looked utterly dejected. 'I've been sitting all evening trying to think what to say. I need to sort things out.'

'Tell me,' she said, looking anxious. 'What is it?'

'I should have been more honest with you, Ashley,' he said. 'I've kept things from you. I need to tell you now.'

'Go into the sitting room, sit by the fire and I'll bring the tea in,' Ashley told him. Her heart was beating fast and her throat was dry.

'Leave the tea,' he said. 'Just come and sit down.'

She left the mugs on the kitchen table and followed Emmet into the sitting room. He stood by the fire, looking as if he had the whole weight of the world on his shoulders.

'You had better tell me what's wrong,' said Ashley. Her face looked strained. The dreadful thought came into her head that he was going to tell her that he couldn't go through with the marriage, that he didn't love her after all, that he couldn't settle down and was moving on.

'It's just that I need to get things off my chest. You need to know a bit more about me before . . . well, before you commit yourself to marrying me.' He sat on the sofa and looked down at his feet. Ashley could see he was trembling.

'For goodness' sake, Emmet,' she said. 'You're scaring me. Whatever is it?'

'Come and sit down,' he said. She sat next to him on the sofa and he took her hand in his. 'You remember when we met at the folk concert? It was that lovely July evening and we sat by the river.'

Ashley nodded. 'Of course I do. It was when I think I fell in love with you.'

'I fell in love with you the first time we met,' he replied. He sounded sad.

'So you're not going to tell me you have a wife and family back in Ireland and that the wedding's off.' She laughed nervously.

'God, no! I love you. I love you more than I can put into words.'

'In that case, what you are going to tell me can't be that bad.'

'It's bad enough.' Emmet gave a weak smile. 'I told you about Rowena and how she died in childbirth.'

Ashley nodded. 'Yes, I remember.'

'I need to tell you exactly what happened.' He thought for a moment, rehearsing in his head what to say. 'I met Rowena at a folk concert,' he said.

'Yes, you told me,' Ashley said. 'Quite a coincidence wasn't it? It was at a folk concert that I fell for those dark eyes of yours and—'

'I didn't tell you everything,' interrupted Emmet.

'Oh.'

'Rowena was with her boyfriend at the time, a fiddle player called Dermot. He seemed a nice enough chap, a bit full of his own importance, but not the most reliable of men and not one to settle down. They'd lived together for just a couple of months. Neither of them thought of it as leading anywhere, that it was a serious relationship. Anyway, he got the offer of a gig in the States – to play at the big St Patrick's Day celebration in Boston – and was a great hit not only on stage but with all the girls. He wrote to Rowena saying he had met someone and was staying in America.'

'Emmet,' interrupted Ashley, 'why are you telling me all this? What has it got to do with us?'

'Please let me finish,' he said. He sounded tense. 'Anyway, by the time Rowena got the letter, I had seen a lot of her and we had fallen in love. In fact we moved in together a month after Dermot had left for America. We lived in a rusty old caravan with flat tyres, parked in the middle of nowhere, with views of the mountains and pine forests and a lake as soft and blue as a summer sky. It was damp and cold in the caravan but we had this fabulous view and we were happy. Anyway, Rowena discovered that she was pregnant.' He thought for a moment. 'The thing is, the baby wasn't mine.'

'Not yours?' asked Ashley. 'What do you mean? I don't understand.'

'The baby was Dermot's,' Emmet told her, 'but it didn't matter to me and I've loved that child as if she were mine.'

'Roisin's not your daughter?' said Ashley.

'She will always be my daughter,' he said, 'although I'm not her birth father.'

'I see,' said Ashley.

'Anyway,' continued Emmet, 'Rowena got in touch with Dermot to tell him about the child, but he denied that he was the father. He said she had no doubt heard how successful he was now and she was after money. This, of course, was not the case. He really can't have known her very well. She just felt he ought to know. She wanted nothing from him. He was in what he said was a serious relationship and the claim that the child was his was the last thing he needed to hear. He told her not to get in touch again. So we agreed that we would bring up the child together, and I promised Rowena that if anything happened to her, I would look after the baby. The last thing she wanted was for her parents to do it.

'One afternoon I came back to our caravan after fixing the thatch on a neighbour's cottage to find Rowena unconscious. I rushed her to the hospital, and when we got there, I could see that it was serious by the way the nurses gathered around her whispering and then sent for the doctor. Rowena was taken off on a trolley. They sedated her. I think it must have been morphine. I was told by the doctor that it was serious, that Rowena's blood pressure was abnormally high and her temperature was 104 degrees. She was seven months pregnant and all that time she'd been fine. The doctor – I remember he looked too young to be a doctor – said there was little doubt in the diagnosis. It was called eclampsia, a rare, mysterious condition of pregnancy with no known cause. She died, Ashley. She died before she saw her baby. Roisin was born by Caesarean.'

Ashley remained silent. She was having difficulty taking in what she was being told.

'Rowena's parents were from a wealthy and aristocratic family,' Emmet went on, 'members of the ruling elite who owned most of the land in Ireland at one time, proud, overbearing people with entrenched views and assured of their position in society. To say they were snobs would be an understatement. Rowena found living in the big house by the lake cloying and claustrophobic, and she kicked against that sort of privileged existence, all the social events, the hunting and shooting and big dinners and—'

'Yes, you told me all this before,' interrupted Ashley. 'When we first met.'

Emmet brushed the black curls from his forehead. 'There's something else I need to tell you. Rowena wasn't my wife. We never got married.'

'Oh,' was all Ashley could manage to say.

'I should have told you, I know. I meant to, but as time went on and the past faded, it didn't seem all that important.'

'I wish you had told me, Emmet,' she said sadly.

'I know. I'm sorry.'

'Why didn't you?'

'I don't know,' he said. 'If I recall, when we sat by the river after the folk concert, you seemed to assume it. I suppose I thought you might not approve of the life I led, living with someone unmarried, and I so wanted you to approve. Then when I met your mother and she kept on referring to Rowena as my wife, I didn't say anything. I knew she wouldn't take kindly to what I guess she regarded as living in sin.'

'You thought I wouldn't approve?' asked Ashley. 'You don't know me very well, Emmet. I am not like my mother. "Do not judge so that you will not be judged." St Luke. I try very hard not to judge others.'

'Yes, but I had only just met you and wanted to make a good impression. I so much wanted to see you again.'

'The fact that you were not married would have made not a jot of difference to the way I felt . . . that I feel about you.' Emmet said nothing. 'But you've had plenty of time to tell me this. We both need to be open and honest with each other if we are to spend our lives together,' she told him. 'No secrets, Emmet.'

'I know that,' he said.

'Are there any more revelations?' asked Ashley. 'Anything else I need to know?'

'No, there's no more,' he said.

'So you were never married?'

'No, we were never married. We were going to be as soon as the baby was born, but . . . well, you know the rest.'

'Do I know the rest?' she asked.

'As God is my judge there's no more to tell you, just that soon after Rowena's death I went to see her parents but they wanted nothing to do with me or the baby. I was told not to call again and that's when I took to the road.'

'And why are you telling me this now?' asked Ashley.

'Because the past has caught up with me,' he said, his voice apprehensive. 'Rowena's mother has appeared from out of the blue. Her husband's dead and I guess she now wants to get to know Roisin. She's staying at the Royal Hotel in Clayton. I saw her yesterday at Limebeck House. She'd traced me there.'

'But it's good, isn't it, that she wants to make contact and see her granddaughter?' asked Ashley.

'She wants more than that,' Emmet told her. 'She wants Roisin to live with her. For ten years she's never seen or wanted to see her granddaughter, and now she appears like some wicked fairy in a child's story to try and take Roisin away.' He had misery written all over his face. 'I knew in my heart that this day might come.'

'She can't do that,' said Ashley. 'Surely she can't turn up after so long and take the child away. It wouldn't be allowed.'

'She thinks she can,' Emmet told her, 'and she's seen some fancy lawyer and is intent on doing just that.' His voice had increased in pitch and agitation.

'Roisin is such a happy, well-adjusted child and she clearly loves you. You are a wonderful father, Emmet. No one would dream of uprooting her after so long.'

'But I can't be sure. If it goes to court and I have to do one of those DNA tests and it proves I'm not Roisin's father, how would it look – a man living in a one-bedroom caravan with a child who is no blood relation, a man who is some sort of itinerant, roaming around the country with a little girl who moves from school to school. Not the sort of life a judge would think fit and proper for a child when she could live in a huge house with every advantage in life.'

'But you no longer live in a caravan,' said Ashley, 'and you don't roam the country and Roisin is settled at the village school. You have a responsible position now.'

'It won't make any difference to us, Ashley?' he asked. 'Will it?' He sounded like a small child.

She was thoughtful for a moment and stared into the fire. 'If Roisin's grandmother had not appeared, would you have told me all this?'

'I didn't want anything to spoil things,' Emmet said sadly.

'But would you have told me?'

'I don't know.'

'And have you kept Roisin in the dark?' asked Ashley. 'Does she know that you are not her real . . . I mean her birth father?'

'Yes, I've always been honest with her.'

'And did it not occur to you that it would only be a matter of time before I found out?'

'Oh Ashley, I never thought about that. I just wanted to put the past behind me and I couldn't see why it should affect our lives together.'

'But you should have told me, Emmet. Can you not see that? You have not been honest with me. I'm not upset that you were never married or that Roisin is someone else's child. As I've said, that doesn't matter. What has hurt me is that you only decided to tell me this now because Roisin's grandmother has turned up. I'm asking myself would you ever have told me, and are there other things in your past that I don't know anything about?'

'There's nothing else,' he said. 'Nothing else, I promise.'

'All this has come as such a shock,' said Ashley. 'I need to think about what you have said.' She stood. 'We'll talk about things later. Now I think you should go.'

Michael was just on his way upstairs to catch up on his paper-work when the telephone rang.

'Oh dear,' he sighed. 'I hope it's not another emergency call-out.'

He picked up the receiver to hear Ashley's voice.

'Oh hello, Ashley,' he said. 'Yes, I'm fine, and you? Good. I guess it's Elisabeth you wish to speak to. I'll pass her over. It's Ashley,' he said, handing the receiver to his wife, and left the room.

'Are you busy this evening?' asked Ashley.

'No,' replied Elisabeth. 'Michael's got work to do, the boys are busy, I hope, doing their homework upstairs and I'm just about to put my feet up after a hard day at the chalk face.'

'Could I pop around?'

'Yes, of course. It will be good to catch up on things.'

Half an hour later, Ashley arrived at Clumber Lodge.

'I gather there's not been any change in the Massey baby's condition,' said Michael, showing her into the sitting room.

'No, but he's stable,' she replied. 'I was on duty at the hospital today and asked how things were going. The parents, of course, are at their wits' end.'

'I'm sure they are,' said Michael. 'It's a terribly worrying time for them, but children do recover from meningitis and the baby is in very good hands.'

'I'm back at the hospital tomorrow,' Ashley told him. 'I'm hoping there will have been an improvement.'

'Do give Bianca and Clarence our best wishes,' said Michael. 'Say that we are all thinking about them and the baby.'

'I will.'

'Are you all right?' asked Michael. 'You look a bit run-down.'

'Just tired,' she replied.

Elisabeth came into the room. 'Hello, Ashley,' she said. 'Do sit down.'

'I guess I'm not needed,' said Michael, 'so I shall make myself scarce and see how the boys are getting on with their homework.' He chuckled. 'Since I complained to the school that Danny never seems to get any homework, his teacher has piled it on. I don't think Danny is overjoyed.'

Elisabeth listened as Ashley recounted the conversation she had had with Emmet the evening before.

'I feel so confused,' she said. 'Upset, cross, disappointed, worried, sad. My mind is all over the place, which is just not like me. I'm usually so focused.'

'I can quite understand how upset you are that Emmet was not honest with you. He's been very thoughtless and should have told you that he was never married,' said Elisabeth.

'I am upset,' Ashley replied, 'but at heart Emmet's not thoughtless. He's one of the most caring people I know.'

'He was thoughtless in this case,' disagreed Elisabeth, 'keeping a secret like that from you.'

'I suppose so,' said Ashley. She sprang to his defence again. 'When I think about it, though, I can't remember if he ever actually said he was married to Rowena. I know I mentioned the word "wife" to him a few times, but I can't recall him saying it. I just sort of assumed he was married.'

'I think everyone did. I certainly thought so. Whatever was he thinking, not telling you the truth?' asked Elisabeth. 'What was the point of keeping such a secret?'

'He just said he thought I might not approve.'

'I'm sorry if I appear harsh,' said Elisabeth, 'but that sounds pretty feeble to me and shows he doesn't really know you very well. If he had told you that Rowena hadn't been his wife, would it have made a jot of difference to the way you feel about him?'

'No, not at all.'

'I thought not. I've known you long enough to tell that you would have understood. And about Roisin not being his daughter, I'm certain that would not have been a problem for you either.'

'No. Quite the contrary,' said Ashley. 'Emmet's a very loving and dedicated father. I think it is wonderful that he should take on another man's child. That's not the issue. I just feel sort of let down. I suppose it's that this revelation, coming out of the blue like this and just before we are about to be married, makes me wonder if he really knows me, and whether there are other things he has not told me about.'

'That he might have a wife and seven children back in Ireland?' said Elisabeth, smiling.

Her comment raised a smile on Ashley's face too. 'That's what I said to him. No, I'm sure he hasn't. But when I think about it, I know very little about his past, his childhood, his family, what he was like at school, who his friends are, what his life with Rowena was really like. He never talks about it.'

'This sounds rather familiar,' Elisabeth told her. 'To be honest, I know very little about Michael's life before I met him. He rarely talks about his first wife. You know she was killed in a riding accident. It affected him greatly, as it did James, of course, who didn't speak for weeks afterwards. When Michael and I got married and I moved into Clumber Lodge, there wasn't much evidence that his first wife had ever existed. I found this quite bizarre. He had taken everything – her under-wear and scarves, dresses and coats, gloves and shoes, toiletries and hairbrushes – to a charity shop and passed on her jewel-lery to her sister.' She pointed to several photographs in silver frames arranged on a small walnut table. One showed Dr Stirling with his arm around his first wife, a striking-looking woman; another was a more formal portrait of the same woman posing before a horse. 'He even moved these photographs from in here until I insisted that he put them back. He thought them being on display like that might upset me for some reason. I know he loved her very much and was inconsolable for weeks after her death, but it has always seemed strange to me that he doesn't talk about her very much. Perhaps he wants to forget what happened to her, that he thinks it's time to move on . . . I'm sorry, Ashley, here you are wanting to tell me your concerns and I am telling you about mine.'

'I'm just grateful to have a sympathetic ear,' said Ashley.

'I don't think I've been all that sympathetic.'

'You have. You are the one person I feel I can talk to and confide in.'

'Emmet, I guess, feels like Michael, that the past is the past,' said Elisabeth, 'that he wants to move on. The thing is, we can never escape from our past. It is always with us, and sometimes it has a nasty habit of rearing its head.'

'Yes, I suppose so.'

'But in my opinion, for what it is worth, he needs to know how disappointed you are in him.'

'I think he knows that,' replied Ashley.

'Well then,' said Elisabeth, 'I guess you need to put this sorry business behind you. You do love him, of course.'

'Yes, I do.'

'Well, as Mrs O'Connor might say, "the course of true love never did run smooth".' Elisabeth thought for a moment of the tiff she had had recently with Michael.

'I thought that was Shakespeare,' said Ashley, laughing for the first time that evening. 'Anyway, thank you for listening, Elisabeth. It's been good to talk to someone about it and get things off my chest.'

Before Elisabeth could answer, Michael breezed into the room. 'I'm ready for a drink,' he said, rubbing his hands and heading for the dresser and the whisky decanter. 'Will you both join me?'

'No, not for me,' said Elisabeth. 'And I've told you, you need to cut down.'

'Isn't she wonderful when she talks to me like a school-marm?' said Michael. 'I'm just having the one, darling. What about you, Ashley?'

'Not for me,' she replied. 'I must be off.'

'Then I shall drink alone,' he said. 'Now, I can guess what you two have been talking about,' he said. 'Wedding dresses. Am I right?'

'Yes, Michael,' said Elisabeth, shaking her head and looking at Ashley, 'you're right. Wedding dresses.'

Mr Cattermole, owner of Guard Dogs R Us, stood at the bottom of the stone steps leading up to the great entrance door of Limebeck House. He had been told to stay exactly where he was. Standing next to him was the ugliest, most vicious-looking creature Lady Wadsworth had ever set her eyes upon. It was a barrel-bodied, bow-legged bulldog with pinky-white jowls and pale unfriendly eyes. It cocked its fat round head and growled menacingly. Lady Wadsworth, standing at the top of the flight with her terrier at her feet, stared down at the man and his canine companion. Gordon regarded the other dog balefully. Mr Cattermole patted his dog's head lovingly. The monster strained at its lead and growled again, showing a set of impressive teeth.

'She's an old softie really, your ladyship,' he said, 'such a friendly and affectionate animal, well behaved and obedient, and will make a lovely pet and an excellent guard dog.'

'Old softie', 'friendly' and 'affectionate' were not words that readily sprang to the mind of the mistress of Limebeck House. The dog peered up at her with the grey button eyes of a shark and began rumbling like a distant train.

'Now, now, Clarissa,' coaxed Mr Cattermole, patting the animal's head again, 'you be a good girl. Would you care to stroke her, your ladyship?'

'No I most certainly would not!' exclaimed Lady Wadsworth. 'Keep that beast of yours down there on the lead.'

The dog did not need to be told to remain where it was. It stayed rooted to the spot on muscle-bound legs, growling and grimacing and eyeing Lady Wadsworth as if she were some long-lost bone.

'She's a wonderful canine, your ladyship,' Mr Cattermole expounded. 'A pedigree Old English Bulldog, born of impeccable parentage. Like yourself, an aristocrat.'

'I cannot recall ever being compared to a bulldog before, Mr Cattermole,' said Lady Wadsworth.

'Oh no, no, your ladyship,' replied the man, looking flustered. 'I meant she's a thoroughbred, blue-blooded like yourself. Her mother, Wilma, won a blue ribbon for Best of Breed at the Clayton Show a year ago.' He bent down and stroked the fat head. 'She's the most even-tempered, lovable and obedient creature anyone would want.'

'Yes, well I'm not sure that I would want her,' Lady Wadsworth told him, 'and "even-tempered" and "lovable" do not sound to me to be very apposite credentials for a guard dog.'

'That's where you are wrong, your ladyship, if you will excuse the impertinence,' said Mr Cattermole, touching his forelock. 'She'd let anyone walk straight into the house. Wouldn't make a sound. She'd sit there and watch and wait. Course, anyone foolish enough to break in wouldn't get out again. Teeth like metal mantraps she's got. One snap of those iron jaws and she'd not let go. Locks on, you see. Couldn't prise her off with a monkey wrench. Yes, if she grabbed a hand, you'd lose a few of your fingers.'

The dog blinked lazily, lifted its fat face and displayed a set of teeth like tank traps.

'What do you think, Gordon?' asked Lady Wadsworth of the terrier at her feet. The hackles had risen on her dog's back, its ears had pricked up and it too displayed a set of sharp teeth. Before its mistress could stop it, it scuttled down the stone steps, yapping madly. The bulldog stared for a moment, then yanked itself off the lead and shot off down the path, yelping, with Gordon in hot pursuit.

'I really don't think I will be requiring the services of Clarissa,' Lady Wadsworth told an open-mouthed Mr Cattermole.

## 18

Lady Urquhart sat by the window in the drawing room at Limebeck House, straight-backed and stern. She had been summoned by Lady Wadsworth and had assumed, when she received the telephone message at her hotel, that this was her opportunity to meet her granddaughter. She was disabused of this notion when she was shown into the drawing room and there was no sign of the girl.

Lady Wadsworth had dressed for the encounter in her loudest tweeds and heaviest brogues. She had decorated herself with a variety of expensive-looking jewellery and appeared particularly colourful that morning with her wave of copper-tinted hair, rouged cheeks and bright red lipstick. The lady of the manor made her grand entrance accompanied by a tall, distinguished-looking man in his late fifties, with steel-grey hair and a thin, neatly trimmed moustache. He was dressed immaculately in the finest herringbone tweed suit. A gold watch chain and fob dangled from his waistcoat.

'Good morning, Lady Urquhart,' said her host, resisting the etiquette of shaking her visitor's hand. 'Please don't get up. Thank you for coming to see me. May I introduce Sir Robert Mountfield, my solicitor?'

'Good morning,' said Sir Robert, giving a small bow.

Lady Urquhart responded with a slight nod of the head and a quizzical look on her face.

'Sir Robert is acting on behalf of Mr O'Malley in this unfortunate matter,' continued Lady Wadsworth briskly, 'and will be representing his interests should it come to court, which I should add I sincerely hope it will not.'

Lady Urquhart's thin lips tightened. 'I imagined that the point of this meeting was for me to see my granddaughter.' She sounded tetchy and impatient.

'Unfortunately not,' said Lady Wadsworth. 'Since you have seen fit to involve me in this sorry situation, I felt that I should take the initiative and before you depart for home apprise you of what Sir Robert has to say. I should add that Sir Robert advised that the child should not be here to meet you. It might have distressed her.' Lady Urquhart opened her mouth to speak, but Lady Wadsworth held up a hand. She was not one to be interrupted. 'I should further add that Mr O'Malley is ignorant of this meeting. I believe you informed him that you have the means to pursue the matter through the courts. I too have the means and I intend to fully support my estate manager.'

Lady Urquhart's face twitched into a grim smile. 'I really do not wish to hear any more of this.' She rose from her chair and brushed some invisible crumbs from her skirt.

'Since I accorded you the courtesy of seeing you when you called unannounced,' said Lady Wadsworth, 'perhaps you might do me the courtesy of hearing what Sir Robert has to say. He has looked into the matter and is fully conversant with the procedures and processes involved in adopting a child.'

'Very well,' replied Lady Urquhart, resuming her seat, 'but nothing you may say will alter my intention. When I return to Ireland, I propose to put the wheels in motion with my family solicitor to gain custody of my granddaughter. There is nothing you or anyone else might say that will change my mind.'

'Lady Urquhart,' said Sir Robert, 'I think you will agree that the child's happiness and well-being are paramount.'

'Indeed,' she sighed wearily.

'That is exactly what the view of the court will be, that the child should be placed in a safe, secure and happy home. You are, of course, quite at liberty to apply through the courts for an adoption order with regard to your granddaughter,' he said.

'And that I shall most certainly do,' she told him. She twisted the ring on her finger.

'But the judge will take the child's own wishes into serious consideration,' continued the solicitor. 'She will, of course, wish to stay with her father.'

'You don't know that!' snapped Lady Urquhart. She rose from her chair again. 'I do not wish to hear any more. Any further communication with me should be done through my solicitor.'

Sir Robert ignored her intervention. 'I shall be advising Mr O'Malley to contest your claim, of course. Then the legal process will begin.' He paused for effect and took a deep breath. 'I believe that you have some doubts that Mr O'Malley is the child's father?'

'Yes, I do,' replied Lady Urquhart. 'I am afraid my daughter had several . . .' she paused to find the right word, 'liaisons. Where we live is a small community and gossip tends to spread like wildfire. You might imagine how rumours such as these upset my husband and myself. It was my cook who mentioned that he was probably not the father.'

'Proof of paternity can easily be established,' Sir Robert observed. 'That is, if Mr O'Malley were to undergo a DNA test, though I would be very surprised if this were to be directed by the court. I guess it would not be necessary anyway, since his name is on the child's birth certificate. However, even if Mr O'Malley proves not to be the child's biological father, you, as the grandparent, could still apply to the court for a contact order that would enable you to see her on a regular basis. You could also apply for a residence order

for her to live with you. The court would take into account the
advice of professionals such as social workers and psycholo-
gists and would grant custody if it could be proved that the
child is being maltreated, neglected or living in some undesirable circumstances. However, this would not seem to pertain.
From what Lady Wadsworth tells me, the child is very happy
where she is and there are many who will testify to this. It is
therefore most unlikely that a residence order will be granted.'

'I am fully aware of this,' said Lady Urquhart, although she
was not. A defensive defiance blazed in her eyes.

'I tell you this,' continued Sir Robert, 'in an effort to prevent
a great deal of distress and disappointment that will inevitably
occur should you proceed with the course of action you
intend.'

'As I have said, I do have my own family solicitor,' Lady
Urquhart told him, 'who has acquainted me with the facts of
the case. I really do not need you to lecture me. I must go.'

'If I might continue,' said Sir Robert. 'Due to the age of the
child, the length of time Mr O'Malley has cared for her, the
lack of previous interest from her grandparents, the evidence
that she is happy, healthy and well looked after, and the fact
that the man named as her father on her birth certificate has
assumed parental responsibilities and made decisions about
her healthcare and education, it is extremely doubtful if any
court would grant custody to you. More importantly, as long
as the child wishes to remain in Mr O'Malley's care, it would
be difficult to conclude that she would not stay with him. Her
ability to convey her wishes and feelings during the court
process are key. Of course there are many other factors that
would be taken into account and the process could take
months to be resolved. Lady Wadsworth has offered you
advice that I consider to be sound and sensible. By going to
court the situation could become rancorous and you may find
that Mr O'Malley, who is very likely to be successful, will

make it difficult for you to have any access to your grand-daughter. Better perhaps to come to some amicable agreement whereby you are able to see the child on a regular basis. In my experience, going to court is the very last resort.'

'Sir Robert,' replied Lady Urquhart, who had stood through his discourse with a sour expression on her face, 'I am not someone to be bullied, lectured at and remonstrated with.' She twisted the ring on her finger. 'I desire that my grand-daughter lives with me and am determined that it should be so. You will of course be hearing from my solicitor.'

'As you wish,' said Sir Robert.

'Perhaps your butler might show me out,' she said to Lady Wadsworth. 'My taxi is waiting.'

'Well, Sir Robert,' said Lady Wadsworth when Lady Urquhart had departed. 'What did you make of that?'

'A very single-minded woman,' remarked the solicitor, fingering his watch chain.

'I doubt if she will take matters further,' said Lady Wadsworth. 'She would be ill-advised to do so.'

'I would not count on it,' said Sir Robert. 'There was a fierce determination in her eyes. I have seen this many times in my profession – those who doggedly pursue a hopeless case through the courts against all counsel. It will not, I fear, be the last we shall see of that particular lady.'

'But you believe hers is a hopeless case?' asked Lady Wadsworth.

'Undoubtedly,' he replied.

'That is good to hear.'

'And may I be of any further service, Lady Wadsworth?' Sir Robert enquired.

'No, you have been as always most helpful.'

'Then I shall take my leave, your ladyship.' He gave a slight bow. 'By the by, I noticed as I came up the drive that you have discovered yet more statues.'

'Yes, they have been down at the lake for as long as I can recall.' She looked up at a portrait in oils of a large, rather ungainly and serious-faced woman with great black ringlets and a good deal of cleavage. 'My grandmother took against anything that displayed naked flesh and had any paintings with men or women who were not fully clothed consigned to either the attics or one of the empty rooms and put firmly under lock and key. These classical statues, like the others – not to put too fine a point on it – are rather revealing. The old viscountess did not care to have life-sized unclothed figures disporting themselves in the gardens, so banished them to the other side of the lake, out of sight. She thought they might give the servants ideas and corrupt the young. As children, my brother – God rest his soul – and I used to take the rowing boat out and throw pebbles at them. They are green with mould, but Mr O'Malley and his assistant are at present cleaning them up to make them presentable.'

'And are they worth as much as the ones you sent to auction?' asked the solicitor.

'Unfortunately not,' replied Lady Wadsworth, 'and I possess little more of any value to help pay for the completion of the restoration of Limebeck House. Sadly, it is not as if I am *embarras de richesses*, as the French will have it.'

'I see.'

'I did have an art expert to view them, but he said they are crude Victorian replicas, very much the worse for wear and of little value. Still, I rather like them.'

'A pity,' said Sir Robert.

'Speaking of Mr O'Malley, I shall inform him immediately of the outcome of this most agreeable meeting. It will be a great relief to him. He's looked so down of late, worrying about things.'

In the entrance hall, they discovered Lady Urquhart sitting on a hard-backed chair looking austere and uncomfortable.

'Still here?' said Lady Wadsworth.

'The taxi did not wait,' she was informed crossly.

'Perhaps I might be of some assistance,' said Sir Robert. 'I should be only too pleased to drive you back to your hotel.'

'Thank you, no,' replied Lady Urquhart stiffly. 'The butler has rung for another taxi. I shall wait.'

'As you wish,' he said. He bowed to both women and left thinking to himself what a sad, peevish, unsmiling woman Lady Urquhart was, and one with whom no child could ever be happy. On his way down the drive he caught sight of a young man with tattoos and an assortment of rings in his ear, no doubt Mr O'Malley's assistant to whom Lady Wadsworth had referred. The youth was happily scrubbing the plentiful breasts of a marble Venus.

Baby Brandon's parents and Ashley were asked by the nurse at the Royal Infirmary to wait. She told them that the specialist would like to speak to them and would be with them shortly.

'Is he a doctor?' asked Clarence.

'He is,' replied the nurse, 'and a very good one. Dr King is in charge of paediatrics.'

'What's that?'

'Paediatrics is a speciality that manages the medical conditions affecting babies and children. Brandon is under his care.'

'Why does he want to see us?' asked Bianca. The strain showed on her face.

'It's to give you an update on how things are going,' the nurse replied. She smiled reassuringly. She was tempted to tell the mother not to look so worried.

They were shown into a room. Unlike the other areas in the hospital, with their plain pale walls and antiseptic smell, this room had a cosy appearance, with rose-coloured curtains, a small sofa and two matching armchairs. On a wall were three vividly painted seascapes below a large and noisily ticking clock, and a vase of bright flowers on the windowsill made the room look cheerful and welcoming. A selection of magazines and leaflets, the latter warning of the dangers of smoking and drinking and offering advice on healthy eating, covered the top of a coffee table.

Bianca and Clarence looked tired and tense as they sat stiffly on the sofa holding hands. Ashley took a chair. She wished she could tell them that the baby would soon get better, but she knew that this would be idle speculation. As a hospital chaplain she had sat in this very room with distraught parents who had lost children and tried to comfort them. She had found it heartbreaking. Nothing in life, she knew, compared to the tragedy of losing a child. Parents always believed that they would watch their children grow to adulthood, taking their first steps, going to school for the first time, getting married and starting a family, and that inevitably they would die before them. For some this was not to be. As she looked at the frightened, troubled couple sitting opposite her, she prayed that their child might recover.

'Do you think Brandon will be all right?' Clarence broke into Ashley's thoughts.

'I don't know, Clarence,' she replied. 'All we can do is hope and pray. Your baby couldn't be in better hands. I know they are doing everything possible.'

'But why does the doctor want to see us?' asked Bianca. She was clearly thinking the worst.

'As the nurse said,' replied Ashley, 'it's probably just to bring you up to date on Brandon's condition.'

'He looked proper poorly with all them tubes coming out of him,' said Bianca, sniffing.

Clarence put his arm around her and kissed her cheek.

The door opened and the specialist entered the room. Dr King was a broad man, immaculately dressed in a dark brown suit, canary-yellow waistcoat and forest-green bow tie. He sported a fancy silver chain and fob. Kindly eyes were magnified behind rimless spectacles. His wavy pewter-coloured hair was thick and heavy.

Bianca and Clarence stood and looked at him expectantly.

'Do please sit, Mr and Mrs Massey,' said the specialist. He smiled at Ashley. 'Good evening, Dr Underwood.'

'Dr King,' she replied, nodding.

The specialist sat opposite the parents and rested a hand on Bianca's. 'Your baby is going to make a good recovery,' he told her.

'Oh God!' cried Bianca, her eyes brimming with tears. 'Are you sure?'

'Yes, I'm sure.'

'He's going to be all right?' asked Clarence.

'He is,' said Dr King. 'He's a little fighter, your boy, and has responded remarkably well to the treatment.'

'Was it meningitis?' asked Ashley.

'Yes,' replied the specialist. 'It was a type of bacterial menin-gitis.' He turned to Bianca and Clarence. 'He is doing well and will be up and about in no time at all.'

'Can we take him home?' asked Bianca.

'Not for the moment,' the specialist told her. 'He needs to stay in hospital for another week just for us to make certain he is fully recovered. We have given him some antibiotics and cortisone medications, which have done the trick. He just needs a little rest.'

'We've been so worried,' sobbed Bianca. 'We thought he might . . . well . . .'

'If treated promptly,' interrupted Dr King, 'meningitis is less likely to be a life-threatening condition, but it does require rapid admission to hospital and urgent treatment. Your quick action and that of Dr Stirling certainly contributed greatly to the baby's recovery.'

'Thank you so much, Doctor,' said Bianca. 'Could we see him?'

'Of course,' said the specialist. 'Of course you can.'

Ashley left Bianca and Clarence to go and see their baby, and made her way to the chapel to say a prayer of thanksgiving. The hospital chapel was little more than a plain square room with a row of pine pews facing a stained-glass window. Since it was used by patients of different faiths, and none, there were no religious objects. The only occupant this evening was a stiff-backed figure sitting in the very first pew. As Ashley approached, she recognised the woman.

'It's Mrs Pocock, isn't it?' she asked.

The woman looked up. 'Oh, hello, Reverend Underwood,' she replied.

'May I join you?'

'Yes, pull up a pew.' She smiled at the unintentional witticism. 'I mean, yes, do sit down.'

'Are you here visiting?' asked Ashley.

'In a manner of speaking,' said the woman. 'I've just been to say goodbye to my husband. He passed away this afternoon.'

'Oh, I am sorry,' said Ashley.

'Well it was quick, which is a blessing. Heart attack. By the time they got him in the ambulance to take him to the hospital, he was on the other side.'

'I'm sorry,' said Ashley, perplexed. 'The other side?'

'It's a term Mrs Wigglesworth uses when people have died. She's a clairvoyant and psychic and has second sight. I go and see her each month for a consultation. She gets in touch with those who have passed away. She warned me last time that something fateful was going to happen. She'd had this telepathic message from the other side. It was from my Auntie Betty. And she was proved right. I shall try and make contact with my husband when I have my next session.'

'Well I am very sorry for your loss,' said Ashley. She felt this was neither the time nor the place to give her views on the likes of Mrs Wigglesworth and her psychic consultations.

'Of course, the heart attack was bound to happen,' continued Mrs Pocock. 'I mean, my hubby drank like a fish, smoked like a chimney, was way overweight and the only exercise he had was walking to the Blacksmith's Arms and back.' She sighed. 'We had our differences. Mind you, what marriage doesn't have its ups and downs? It's not all plain sailing, I can tell you.'

'No, I guess not,' replied Ashley, suddenly thinking of Emmet.

'But it will be a quiet house now he's gone,' said the widow. 'I shall miss him.'

'I'm sure you will, but your son will be a great comfort to you,' Ashley told her.

'Oh yes, Ernest.'

'And how is he taking the news?'

'I telephoned him earlier to tell him his dad had passed away. He was upset, of course, but he's not one to show his feelings. He's taking it very well. He's off bowling in Clayton with his friends tonight.'

'If there is anything I can do,' said Ashley, 'do ask.'

'There's the funeral,' replied Mrs Pocock. 'I don't want anything fancy. He wouldn't have wanted that. As you know, he wasn't a churchgoer so I don't want anything at St Christopher's. I'd like it at the crematorium. Perhaps you might come along and do the honours.'

'Of course,' answered Ashley.

In the village store the following morning, Mrs Sloughthwaite was discussing the latest death in the village with Mrs O'Connor.

'Well it was to be expected,' observed the shopkeeper. 'I mean, he's been dancing with death for years, what with his drinking and his smoking, and he was vastly overweight.'

Three words came to Mrs O'Connor's mind as she looked at the ample figure behind the counter – 'pan', 'kettle' and 'black' – but she merely nodded in agreement. 'Sure doesn't it come to us all, Mrs Sloughthwaite,' she observed, sighing dramatically.

'What does?'

'Death,' replied the customer. 'The only certainty in life is death. None of us can escape it. However wealthy and powerful you might be, it has a nasty habit of catching up with everyone. It is a great equaliser, so it is. As my Grandmother Mullarkey used to say, "Once the game of life is over, the king and the pawn both go back in the same box." '

The shopkeeper gave a quizzical smile. Mrs O'Connor, she thought, sometimes said the most peculiar things. 'Well Mr Pocock wasn't rich and powerful,' she said. 'Quite the opposite if truth be told. He squandered all his money on drink and cigarettes. Mind you, he has ended up in a box, as we all will one day.'

'As you say, it comes to us all one day, rich and poor, young and old alike, and I'll say this, it holds no terrors for me. I'm prepared to meet my Maker.'

Yes, thought Mrs Sloughthwaite, but is her Maker ready to meet Mrs O'Connor? He would be heartily sick of hearing of the woman's sainted grandmother for a start. Would He even manage to get a word in?

'And how is Mrs Pocock holding up?' asked Mrs O'Connor.

'Oh, very well,' replied the shopkeeper. 'In fact she sounded quite perky on the telephone when she called me from the hospital last night. I don't wish to be unkind, but I can't see her grieving for very long. Her husband led her a merry dance and no mistake. He was always making eyes at Maisie Stainthorpe when she served behind the bar at the Blacksmith's Arms, and I shouldn't wonder, knowing her reputation, if their relationship was more than plutonic. And I'll tell you another thing about that ne'er-do-well husband of hers—'

At that very moment the grieving widow entered the shop. Mrs Pocock was dressed from head to foot in black and had a suitably tragic expression on her face. The shopkeeper's features immediately changed and she adopted the most sympathetic of expressions.

'How are you, love?' she asked with deep concern.

'Oh, I'm not doing so badly,' replied Mrs Pocock in a dramatically morose voice. 'Bearing up, you know.'

'We were very sorry to hear about your loss,' said Mrs O'Connor. 'It must have come as a great shock. I know that when my husband, God rest his soul, entered eternal rest, I struggled to come to terms with it, so I did.'

Mrs Pocock nodded sadly.

'Come through into the parlour,' said the shopkeeper, edging around the counter. 'I'll shut up the shop for a bit and you can have a cup of tea and tell us all about it.' Mrs Sloughthwaite was not one to pass up the opportunity of hearing about a death first hand.

When the three women had retired to the rear of the village store and availed themselves of a cup of tea and a slice of cake, Mrs Pocock related the account of her husband's demise.

'The thing is, I never saw it coming,' she said before taking a sip of her tea. 'It was all so sudden.'

'Ah well, that's death for you,' remarked Mrs O'Connor, nodding sagely. 'It's like a mushroom.'

'Mushroom!' cried the grieving widow. 'How is death like a mushroom?'

'Well sometimes it springs up unexpectedly, like with your husband.'

'I can well do without any more of your grandmother's depressing words of wisdom at a time like this, thank you very much,' said Mrs Pocock scornfully. 'Anyway, as I was saying, it was all very sudden. He came in from the pub complaining about these pains in his chest. He was always grumbling about something being wrong with him. If it wasn't his stiff joints, it was his upset stomach or his bad back. To be honest, I didn't take that much notice until I found him in the kitchen lying prone on the floor.'

'It must have been a terrible shock for the poor fella,' observed Mrs O'Connor.

Mrs Pocock rolled her eyes.

'So what did you do?' asked Mrs Sloughthwaite.

'When I couldn't rouse him,' said the customer, 'I sent for the ambulance, but he had passed away before they got him to the hospital.'

'Well at least it was quick,' observed the shopkeeper, popping a sliver of cake in her mouth. 'He didn't suffer.'

'I mean, he wasn't the best husband in the world,' said Mrs Pocock, sniffing and reaching for a slice of Victoria sponge. 'As I was telling Reverend Underwood, we had our ups and downs, but he had hidden talents.'

I'd like to know what those were, mused the shopkeeper. As far as she was concerned, Mr Pocock was a big lazy lump of a man who never did a day's work in his life.

'Ah well,' said Mrs O'Connor, 'we're very sorry for your loss, so we are.' She sighed. 'As they say, that's another page turned in the book of life.'

'When is the funeral?' asked Mrs Sloughthwaite.

'Next Wednesday,' replied Mrs Pocock. 'He wasn't religiously-inclined so I'm not having a church service. I'm having him cremated. Reverend Underwood is going to say a few words. She was at the hospital and was very thoughtful and understanding. Sat with me for a good half an hour she did, and let me share her taxi home.'

'She's a lovely young woman, so she is,' said Mrs O'Connor.

'A paradigm of virtue is Dr Underwood, if ever there was one,' added Mrs Sloughthwaite.

'Mind you, I still can't get over her going and marrying that odd-job man at Limebeck House,' said Mrs Pocock. 'She could do a whole lot better for herself.'

The shopkeeper sighed. 'Oh don't start on all that again,' she said.

There was a loud banging on the shop door.

'Do you know, I can't get a minute's peace,' said the shop-keeper crossly.

'I shall have to be going,' said Mrs Pocock, getting to her feet. 'I've things to do in town.'

'And I need to be off,' said Mrs O'Connor. 'I've got Father Daly's presbytery to clean.'

Outside, Fred Massey was rattling the door handle and tapping on the glass.

'Hold your horses!' shouted Mrs Sloughthwaite. 'I'm coming.' She opened the door. 'Can you not read, Fred Massey? It says "Closed".'

'Well it shouldn't be at this time of day,' he said. 'It's not your half-day closing.'

'As the proprietor of this establishment,' the shopkeeper told him haughtily, 'I can choose when I open and when I close the premises. What do you want anyway?'

Fred caught sight of the two customers emerging from the back of the shop. 'I just called in to tell you that my great-nephew, Brandon, is getting better. He'll be out of hospital next week, so you can broadcast that around the village.'

'What do you mean, "broadcast"?' replied Mrs Sloughthwaite. 'You make me sound like the news channel.'

'You know what I mean,' said Fred. 'If anyone wants to know anything what's happening in the village, they always come to you.'

'Now you look here, Fred Massey—' began the shopkeeper.

'I'm very pleased to hear that the baby is on the mend,' interrupted Mrs O'Connor. 'I've been praying to St Jude for the little one.'

'Who's St Jude?' asked Mrs Pocock.

'He's the patron saint of desperate cases and lost causes,' replied Mrs O'Connor, smiling.

Mrs Pocock rolled her eyes.

'Well it's very good news that the baby is getting better,' said Mrs Sloughthwaite. 'Do give Bianca and Clarence our very best wishes.'

'I'm going to pop into the Blacksmith's Arms to celebrate,' Fred told them. 'You ladies are welcome to join me. The drinks are on me.'

'My goodness!' cried the shopkeeper. 'Wonders never cease – you buying someone a drink.'

Fred caught sight of the poker face of Mrs Pocock. 'Come on, Mrs P,' he said jovially, 'come and have a drink and help me celebrate. Cheer up. It may never happen.'

Mrs Pocock turned to face him. If looks could maim, Fred Massey would soon be on crutches.

# 19

Tom was staying late at school on Friday to catch up with his marking. Bianca was cleaning his classroom and taking an inordinate amount of time in doing so. She had already wiped down the tables and dusted the windowsills and bookcases twice. Tom noticed that she kept looking surreptitiously in his direction.

'I think you have given the place a good going-over now, Bianca,' he told her, hinting that she should continue her labours elsewhere. 'I guess you have the other classrooms to clean.' He had had quite enough of the young woman's furtive glances; he found them rather discomfiting.

Bianca stopped what she was doing and stared at the teacher.

'Was there something you wished to say?' asked Tom.

'Not really, Mr Dwyer,' she replied. 'It's just that . . . well . . . I can't believe that you're teaching here at this school.'

'Why is that?'

'Well, it's so different from what you used to do. Can I ask you something?'

'Go ahead.'

'Why did you give up something so . . . well, so exciting and glamorous to teach kids?'

'Because I wanted to do something more challenging and interesting,' Tom told her. 'Playing professional football is not all that exciting and glamorous unless you are in the top divisions. And I had a fair few accidents on the pitch and was getting a bit long in the tooth so thought I would call it a day. Then there were all these young players coming on the scene, much fitter than I was.'

'You look very fit to me,' said Bianca, her face turning pink.

'I still try to keep in shape,' said Tom. He too coloured up.

'Yes, I can see.'

'Well I think you've done in here now,' the teacher told her.

'I wasn't talking about you playing football, Mr Dwyer,' she said. 'It was about the other thing you used to do.'

'Ah yes,' said Tom, 'the other thing. What was that?'

'You were a male model, weren't you?'

He winced as if he had been flicked in the face with icy water. This was a part of his life he wanted to put behind him. 'That was in the past,' he told her.

'Some of the lasses in our class at school had your picture on the back of their locker doors,' Bianca told him. 'We thought you were dead dishy.'

Tom was feeling uncomfortable at the way this conversation was leading. 'As I said, it was in the past.'

'I still have some of your pictures.'

'Look, Bianca,' he said. 'Would you do me a big favour?'

'Course.'

'Don't mention what I used to do to anyone.'

'Why?'

'To be frank, it's a bit embarrassing. I was a youngster and was flattered to be asked to do it. But I think it's best to let sleeping dogs lie.'

'What do you mean?'

'Not to say anything.'

'It's not as if you were taking all your kit off or anything,' said Bianca bluntly. 'It was just clothes and swimwear, wasn't it?'

'Yes, it was, but I should still appreciate it if you didn't say anything. All right?'

'OK,' she said. Then, smiling widely, she added, 'I'll keep your little secret.'

'By the way, I was really pleased to hear about your baby. It must have been a terrible time for you and your husband.' He changed the subject adroitly.

'It was,' said the young woman. 'He's better now, though.'

'I'm very glad to hear it,' said the teacher.

Elisabeth appeared at the classroom door.

'If you have finished in here, Bianca,' she said, 'could you give my room a clean, please.' She had noticed that the cleaner spent a deal more time in this classroom than in the others.

The young woman departed. 'Bye, Mr Dwyer,' she said.

'Working late?' Elisabeth asked Tom.

'I wanted to make sure everything is in order before the visitation on Monday morning,' he told her.

'Ah yes, you are to have a visit from your university tutor to see how you are getting along. Have you met him?'

'No.'

'Neither have I,' said Elisabeth. 'When Mrs Atticus trained here, her tutor from St John's called in to introduce herself. I thought yours might have done the same.'

'I have to say that I am a bit nervous,' admitted the teacher. 'This is the first observation, and if I don't pass, it might mean repeating the year.'

'I wouldn't worry too much,' Elisabeth reassured him. 'I shall be giving you a very good reference. In fact, once you are qualified, I hope you will apply for any vacancy that comes up at the school. Of course, it will be up to the governors as to who is appointed, but you will be in with a good chance.'

'I'd love to work here,' Tom replied.

'So what will your lesson on Monday be about?' asked Elisabeth.

'On Monday mornings I generally spend the first part of the lesson asking the children what they have been doing over the weekend. I've been trying to encourage some of the quieter pupils to contribute more and to have the confidence to speak in front of others. I know when I was a youngster I was tongue-tied. The very thought of standing up with all eyes upon me, in the spotlight, and speaking in front of an audience made me sick with fear. I want the less vocal children in the class to overcome their shyness and self-consciousness. Then we are going to do some creative writing.'

'It sounds good,' said Elisabeth. 'I'm sure the lesson will go well.'

On Monday morning, Mr Grimwood, supervisory tutor from the university Faculty of Education, arrived to observe Mr Dwyer's lesson. He was a thin-faced man with a long, prominent nose, a sulky mouth, hooded eyes and an untidy beard. He wore a shapeless tweed jacket, a shirt frayed around the collar, baggy flannel trousers and scuffed shoes. Looking at the dishevelled figure, Elisabeth thought that he could have presented himself rather better. However, as was her custom, she welcomed her visitor with a friendly smile and the offer of a cup of tea. Mr Grimwood did not smile and refused a drink; as he explained, he had an immensely busy day ahead of him.

Having been introduced by Tom to the children, the supervisor sat in the corner of the classroom, took a folder from his briefcase and placed it on his knee. Seeing his pupils looking at him quietly with expectant expressions and the tutor serious-faced and with pen poised in his hand, Tom felt suddenly very nervous. His heart fluttered like a caged bird.

'So, children,' he said with an uneasy smile, 'I hope you all had a really enjoyable weekend.'

'Sir! Sir!' shouted out a small, bright-eyed boy with a crown of close-cropped black hair, large round eyes and equally large round glasses. 'Did you go to watch your old team play on Saturday?' George was one of the liveliest and most self-assured pupils in the class.

'I did, yes,' replied the teacher.

The boy turned to the visitor. 'Mr Dwyer used to play for Clayton United, sir,' he said proudly. 'He was a professional footballer. I want to be a professional footballer when I leave school.' Before the teacher could interject, the pupil continued. 'It was a great match, wasn't it, sir?'

'Yes, George, it was,' said Tom. 'Now shall we—'

'I went with my dad, my Uncle Mike and my cousin Oliver,' the child carried on heedlessly, 'and we went for a pizza afterwards and Oliver sniffed this flaky pepper up his nose and couldn't stop sneezing and everybody looked at him and his dad got really cross because—'

The teacher, keen to encourage the more reticent children in the class, stopped the boy in mid-flow.

'That's very interesting, George,' he said, raising his voice slightly. 'Perhaps we can hear about it a little later.' Several hands were now waving in the air. 'I know you all have lots to say, but I'm going to pick a few pupils who don't get the chance to speak very much and ask them about their weekend first. So, hands down.' He looked at a small, pixie-faced girl sitting right under his nose. 'What about you, Jade? What sort of weekend did you have?'

'All right,' replied the girl in a barely audible voice.

'Did anything interesting happen?'

The child thought for a moment. 'We found a mouse in the pantry, and when we tried to catch it, it ran under the settee in the front room and my mum got the vacuum cleaner and sucked it up.' The class giggled. 'And we could see it jumping up and down inside in the middle of all this dust and fluff. My mum asked my dad to get rid of it but he was a scaredy-cat and said he couldn't, so my mum put the mouse down the toilet and all the dust and fluff got flushed away but when we looked the mouse was still there and it was swimming. My mum got one of these things that we have in the kitchen what we use to put the spaghetti in to get rid of all the water and—'

'Colander,' said Jeremy. 'The utensil you strain spaghetti in is called a colander, isn't it, Mr Dwyer?'

For a few weeks after his frightening experience on the beach at Boggle Hole, the boy had been subdued and better behaved, but of late he had reverted to his usual disagreeable self, with clever comments and flippant remarks.

'That's right, Jeremy,' said Tom. He gave the boy a sharp look. 'Thank you for telling us that.'

'Colander is quite a hard word to spell, isn't it, sir?' the boy persisted.

'It is, yes,' said the teacher. 'Carry on, Jade.'

'Well my mum got this colander thing,' continued the girl, 'and she scooped up the mouse and put it in the garden on the grass in the sunshine so that it would dry out.'

'Well that was good,' said Tom. 'I like happy endings.'

'It wasn't,' said Jade, 'because the next-door neighbour's cat got it and bit its head off.'

The teacher, wishing to move on quickly, looked at a large rosy-cheeked boy with wiry blonde hair. Colin found school a bind and made little effort with work he considered irrelevant. Being from a farming background, he loved the outdoors and hated being confined behind a table all day. He was usually very quiet and unobtrusive in class, unless he was asked about tractors and cows, about which he knew a great deal. He then came to life. Tom knew he was on to a winner with this pupil, for the boy spent most of his weekends helping his father on the farm, and he would be guaranteed to tell the class something of interest.

'Anything happen this weekend, Colin?' Tom asked. 'Something you would like to share with us?'

The pupil stood up as if he were to deliver a lecture. He took a deep breath.

'Aye,' he announced, 'quite a bit 'appened. On Sat'day I 'elped mi dad wi' calvin'. We 'ave Belgian Blues on our farm. They're reight big beeasts, double-muscled an' weigh ovver a ton, and can be ovver five foot 'igh. Ours are blue-grey mottled in colour but yer can 'ave 'em in white an' sometimes in black.'

Jeremy gave a noticeable and audible yawn.

Tom fixed him with an icy stare. 'Carry on, Colin,' he said.

'Yer Belgian Blues are bred for their meat, which is very tender. Now when it comes to calvin', yer can't deliver a pure-bred variety by t'usual method 'cos yer calf is too big to gerrout o' t'cow what wi' its double muscles an' all. T'vet 'as to stand t'cow up what's calvin', give it some sort o' drug so it can't feel owt an' then t'calf is cut out.'

'While the cow is standing?' asked Tom.

'Aye, that's how they do it,' said the boy.

'That's something I didn't know,' said Tom.

'It's by Caesarean, sir,' remarked Jeremy.

'Thank you again, Jeremy, for that snippet of information,' said the teacher, attempting to disguise his annoyance. 'Go on, Colin.'

'That's abaat it really,' said the boy.

'I should think a bull of that size and weight is quite a formidable sight,' said Tom. 'I wouldn't like to be alone in a field with a creature like that.'

'Dairy bulls are more dangerous than bulls bred for their meat,' the farming expert explained.

'So what is the most dangerous breed of bull?' asked the teacher.

'As mi grandad'd likely say, "One what chuffin' kills thee",' replied the boy.

'Can I tell you something, sir?' Norman shouted out.

'Yes, go on then, Norman,' said Tom.

'Some white worms came out of my dog's bottom on Saturday, sir.'

The class made a loud 'Uuuuugggghhh!' noise.

'Quiet, please,' said Tom. 'I don't think we want to hear any more about that.'

'We're taking him to the vet after school today,' said the boy, carrying on regardless.

'Yes, well that's a very good idea—' began the teacher.

'They were tiny white wiggly things,' continued the boy.

'Roundworms,' remarked Jeremy, sounding bored.

Tom remained calm, but he was getting increasingly irritated by the boy's frequent and clever interruptions. On this occasion he decided to ignore it.

'My mum said that lots of dogs get these worms,' said Norman, 'and sometimes human beings can get worms as well if they don't—'

'I think we've heard quite enough about the worms, thank you, Norman,' said the teacher, getting rather hot under the collar. Things were not going as he had planned. He noticed that the tutor was scribbling away in the corner. Tom looked at a frizzy-haired girl with a pale, earnest face. 'What about you, Chelsea?' he said. 'Did anything interesting happen over the weekend?'

'We found a hedgehog on our lawn,' the girl told him.

'That's pretty unusual for this time of year,' said Tom. 'Hedgehogs usually have a long sleep in the cold weather.'

'I think the word you are looking for, sir,' piped up Jeremy, 'is hibernate.'

'That's right,' said Tom. 'Hedgehogs hibernate in winter.' Had the tutor not been listening to the lesson, he would have told the boy to desist from interrupting with his irritating prompts. 'Go on, Chelsea,' he encouraged.

'It came out of the bushes and curled up on the grass. We gave it some bread and milk.'

'Sir!' Peter Norton, sitting at the back, shouted out. 'It's not good to give hedgehogs bread. It makes them swell up.'

'And milk gives them diarrhoea,' added Jeremy.

'That's right,' said Tom. 'Hedgehogs eat insects like grubs, slugs and—'

'And worms,' added Jeremy. 'Don't forget the worms.'

'Sir, you know these white worms I was telling you about . . .' began Norman.

At morning break, Mr Grimwood plonked himself down at the teacher's desk, placed his briefcase on the floor and opened the substantial scarlet folder, on the front of which was written 'Faculty of Education' and 'Confidential' in large black letters. Tom sat before him in a pupil's chair lower than the desk, so that he was obliged to look up at the tutor during the interview. It was the first occasion that a lecturer from the university had observed one of his lessons, and it was important that he passed this initial assessment.

'May I see your curriculum policy document, your schemes of work, your individualised pupils' targets and your lesson plans?' asked Mr Grimwood.

'Ah yes,' said Tom, 'my schemes of work and lesson plans. I'm afraid I haven't got them.'

'Haven't got them?' repeated the tutor brusquely. 'And why is that?'

'I was in such a rush this morning, I left them on the kitchen table.'

Mr Grimwood shook his head and sighed wearily. 'Mr Dwyer,' he said, 'if you wish to be a teacher, you must be well organised, well prepared and your lessons carefully planned.'

'Yes, I appreciate that,' replied Tom, feeling like a naughty child called to see the headmaster for unacceptable behaviour.

'You were aware I was coming in today,' continued Mr Grimwood testily. He drummed his fingers on the desktop and frowned.

'Yes, I was,' replied Tom.

'And that I would need to see all the necessary documentation?' He continued to drum his fingers.

'Yes.'

'This is not a very auspicious start, Mr Dwyer,' said the tutor. 'You will understand that it is difficult for me to assess this lesson unless I know what your aims and objectives were.'

'I can tell you that,' said Tom.

'It is all very well telling me, but I need to see a detailed lesson plan outlining learning aims and objectives with resource implications, a framework for developmental strategies and particulars about pupil follow-on work,' complained Mr Grimwood. 'Please send your documentation to me at the university without delay. Now, what did you envisage the children would learn from the lesson you taught this morning? What did you hope to achieve?'

'Each Monday morning, first thing,' explained Tom, 'I devote half an hour to getting the children to talk about what they have been doing over the weekend. In past lessons I have noted that the more confident and vocal pupils in the class tended to dominate the discussion. I wanted to draw out the reticent children and give them an opportunity to contribute, so I selected several shy pupils to speak first.'

'And do you think you achieved this objective?' asked the tutor.

'Well yes, to some extent,' answered Tom. 'Jade, Colin and Chelsea don't usually contribute very much in class, but this morning they had quite a lot to say. I think the lesson was successful in getting the quieter children to speak.'

'I have to disagree with you,' said the tutor. 'From what I observed, I think the lesson was dominated by two rather boisterous boys.' He opened his file and looked at his notes.

'George and Norman. It seemed to me that the pupils, rather than the teacher, were determining the direction of the lesson.'

Tom felt this to be unfair. George and Norman had had far less to say, he thought, than the other children who spoke. However, he decided to say nothing.

'You also failed to capitalise on the observations of . . .' Mr Grimwood consulted his notes again, 'of Jeremy, the rather perceptive boy, who had some very pertinent points to make.' He closed his file. 'On the whole, I felt the lesson lacked structure and focus. A much more effective approach would have been for you to identify the uncommunicative pupils on Friday, ask them to prepare a short talk over the weekend for Monday, vet what they had planned to say so that inappropriate topics like calving, dead mice and white worms were avoided, then ask them to address the class from the front of the room, without interruptions, and answer questions from the other children and yourself afterwards.' He leaned back in the chair. 'You know, this sort of lesson is rather old hat in my opinion. The days of "show and tell" have largely disappeared in schools in favour of something more innovative and upbeat.'

'Thank you for sharing your opinion,' replied Tom in an ironic tone of voice. 'I did discuss this lesson with Mrs Stirling and she felt it very appropriate.'

Mr Grimwood, not wishing to criticise the head teacher, decided not to respond. He stood, placed the file on the chair and went to look at the display on the classroom wall.

'Displays,' he said, 'should not merely be decorative, such as these. They should be related to the work in hand, and encourage the children to look, read and learn. It is all very well to have colourful pictures and photographs, but displays need to be interactive and relevant.'

'Break time is nearly over,' Tom told him, getting to his feet, 'and I need to prepare for my next lesson. Will you be staying?'

'No, no, I have seen enough, and I do have more students to see today. I shall look forward to receiving the documentation in due course, and I shall call in to see you again after Easter. A detailed assessment of your lesson will be sent to you, and a copy to the head teacher.' With that, Mr Grimwood picked up his briefcase and departed.

Tom flopped in his chair and leaned back with a great sigh.

On his way out, the tutor put his head around Elisabeth's classroom door.

'I am away now, Mrs Stirling,' he told her.

'I'll walk with you to your car,' she said, 'and you can tell me how Mr Dwyer got on.'

'I'm afraid he didn't do very well,' Mr Grimwood informed her as they walked briskly down the corridor.

'In what way?' asked Elisabeth.

'It will be in my report,' the tutor told her. 'You will be receiving a copy in due course.'

'I would like to know now,' she said.

The tutor glanced at his watch. 'His lesson lacked focus and I did not feel it was very apposite. I have judged it to be barely satisfactory. Perhaps in time Mr Dwyer will make an adequate teacher.'

'Adequate!' exclaimed Elisabeth. 'In my opinion, Mr Dwyer will make an outstanding teacher.'

Mr Grimwood gave a weak smile. 'Well not in my opinion. I should add that he did not have his curriculum policy document, schemes of work, individualised pupils' targets or lesson plans available for me to see. It was very thoughtless of him to leave them at home, particularly bearing in mind that I was to visit. I pointed out to him that teachers need to be well prepared, organised and efficient. His forgetfulness is inexcusable. I trust he will not be so careless the next time I call. Now I must make tracks or I will be late for my next appointment, at Clayton Juniors.'

'One moment, Mr Grimwood,' said Elisabeth. 'I have something to say.'

'As I have said, I am in rather a hurry.'

'Please do me the courtesy of listening,' she said.

The tutor stopped in his tracks.

'Forgetting his lesson plan is not a hanging offence, Mr Grimwood,' said Elisabeth, peeved by the man's manner and his criticism of Tom. 'We all forget things at times. I am sure Mr Dwyer had your impending visit on his mind. I have seen his documentation and I can vouch it is all in order.'

'Nevertheless, I still wish to see it. Now I must be off. I have—'

Elisabeth cut him off. 'I haven't finished. I should like to say something in Mr Dwyer's defence.'

The tutor glanced at his watch. 'Very well, if you are quick,' he replied curtly.

'I should like to say that Mr Dwyer is a very dedicated, efficient, organised and enthusiastic teacher who relates well to the children and has very good class control. He arrives at school early, leaves late, coaches two football teams and a swimming club, runs a guitar group and recently gave up his weekend to take the children to the east coast on a geography trip. You will have noted the standard of the children's work when you examined their books, and the progress they are making. I assume you did manage to look at their books?'

'No. I'm afraid I didn't have the opportunity,' replied the tutor awkwardly.

'If you had, you would have seen that they are thoroughly marked and show the great variety of work the children in Mr Dwyer's class have undertaken in the short time he has been teaching in the school. Indeed, I am so impressed with him that were a post available in this school, I should have no hesitation whatsoever in supporting Mr Dwyer's application.'

'My role, Mrs Stirling,' said Mr Grimwood pompously, 'is to moderate the school's judgement of a trainee teacher. Obviously I shall take into account your opinion, but it is the university in the final analysis that awards the certificate in education.'

'I am fully aware of that,' replied Elisabeth. 'I have had a graduate trainee at this school before. She was a student at St John's College and I have to say that she received a great deal more attention from her tutor than Mr Dwyer has received from you. Her supervisor spent several mornings in school, offered the trainee a great deal of advice and support and discussed her work and progress with me. You have only been in once, for what has been a fleeting visit.'

'Perhaps we might discuss this at another time,' said the tutor, keen to be away. 'I shall give you a ring. Now I really must make tracks.'

Elisabeth was not going to let him escape so easily. 'You have observed Mr Dwyer for a little over an hour. I see him day after day. I would ask you to bear that in mind, Mr Grimwood. I will see you out.'

After she had watched the visitor drive, at some speed, out of the gate, she went straight to the office in an angry mood. The man was insufferably self-important and patronising and she intended to make her feelings clear to his superiors.

'I know I don't normally dictate letters, Mrs Scrimshaw,' she told the school secretary, 'but I want this one to go off as soon as possible. It's to the Professor of Education at the university.'

During the lunch hour, Elisabeth found Tom in his classroom looking very down in the mouth.

'I guess you've been told that the lesson didn't go too well,' he said sadly. 'I think the tutor was less than impressed.'

'I was far from impressed with him,' replied Elisabeth. 'He was self-opinionated and condescending and I took exception to the way he was dressed as well as his manner. I seriously question his judgements.'

'Did he tell you that I had forgotten to bring in the schemes of work and lesson plans?' asked Tom.

'Look, we all forget things at times, especially when we have things on our mind. I want you to put this unfortunate experience behind you and carry on as you have been doing. As I told you earlier, I am very pleased with your work.'

'Thank you, Elisabeth,' he replied.

Tom's colleagues were equally supportive and reassuring when he gave them an account of the lesson later in the staffroom.

'So old Grimface is still at the university, is he?' asked Rupert. 'I thought he'd have been put out to pasture by now. When I did my postgraduate certificate there, he was voted the very worst lecturer in the Faculty of Education by the students. He was boring, disorganised and bad-tempered. We got up a petition and he was moved from lecturing to supervising. God help any poor student who is supervised by him. He is clearly as useless at this as he was at lecturing. I wouldn't worry, Tom. I'm sure Elisabeth has got the measure of him.'

'Those who *can*, teach,' remarked Mrs Robertshaw, 'and those who can't, become lecturers, education officers and school inspectors.'

It was later that afternoon that Mr Grimwood reappeared. Elisabeth caught sight of him creeping down the corridor. She intercepted him at the door of Tom's classroom.

'Back so soon, Mr Grimwood?' she said, making the man jump.

'Ah, Mrs Stirling,' he replied sheepishly. 'I just need to pop in and see Mr Dwyer for a moment.'

'You have signed in?' she asked.

'I beg your pardon?'

'I asked if you had signed in at the office and made your presence known to the school secretary.'

'Er . . . no . . . I am just calling in for a minute.'

'The county policy document is quite definite in stating that all visitors to a school must sign in and be given a visitor's badge to identify them. It is to ensure that strangers don't just wander into the school. We have to be very careful in this matter when it comes to child protection.'

'Yes, yes, of course. I'm sorry.'

Tom, seeing the two of them outside in the corridor, opened his classroom door. He held in his hand the tutor's red-backed folder.

'Is this what you are looking for, Mr Grimwood?' he enquired.

Following Elisabeth's strongly worded letter to the Professor of Education at the university's Faculty of Education concerning the behaviour of Mr Grimwood, the man in question did not return to observe any more of the new teacher's lessons. The tutor who replaced him, a former primary school head, was most approving of two of Tom's lessons and agreed with Elisabeth that the young man had great potential and would make a first-rate teacher.

# 20

Emmet was shown into the library at Limebeck House.

Lady Wadsworth, wearing a pair of small gold-rimmed spectacles, sat behind her desk. She smiled and indicated one of the plush armchairs, gesturing for her visitor to take a seat.

Emmet sat down, leaned forward and rested his hands on his lap. He bit his lower lip nervously, for he could sense that Lady Wadsworth had something important to impart. She didn't seem in any great hurry to tell him why he had been summoned, however, and continued looking through some papers that were before her.

'More bills,' she muttered, shaking her head. 'You would not believe the cost of replacing the windows. That is one of the downsides of having a listed building of this size.' She flicked through the papers and sighed.

'The statues have been cleaned and returned to where they were by the lake, your ladyship,' said Emmet, breaking the silence that followed. 'I've arranged for the security firm to fit the alarm and outside lights and cameras next week, and told Mr Cattermole we will not be requiring the guard dog.'

She shook her head. 'More expense,' she sighed.

'And I think we've managed to solve the mole problem, but now it's the rabbits. They are a real nuisance.'

Lady Wadsworth looked up from her papers and removed her spectacles. 'Moles are particularly annoying little creatures. They can spoil a lawn overnight with their wretched burrowing and mounds of soil. We used to have a dedicated mole-catcher in the old days. He did nothing but hunt and kill the little gentlemen in black and hang their corpses on the gate.'

'Roisin has a soft spot for them, I'm afraid,' Emmet replied, 'so I have to deal with them when she's at school and then bury the bodies. Anyway, I think we have seen the back of them.'

'I am heartily glad to hear it,' said Lady Wadsworth. 'As for rabbits, as a child I always felt rather sorry for poor Mr McGregor and had little sympathy for that infuriating Peter Rabbit and his family of greedy burrowing pests. I guess Miss Beatrix Potter never had a vegetable patch of her own, for if she had, she would not have been quite so approving of the voracious creatures.' She straightened the papers on her desk and placed her spectacles on top of them. 'However, it is not the moles or the rabbits I wish to see you about.' She rose from her chair and came to sit next to Emmet. 'I have had a telephone call this morning from Sir Robert.'

Emmet held his breath. 'And there's news?'

'News indeed,' Lady Wadsworth told him. 'Don't look so down in the mouth. It is very good news. I promised you that things would turn out for the best, and indeed they have. I do not wish to sound smug, but I do pride myself on having some influence in the county and knowing the right people, and the Wadsworths have always been in the forefront of fighting injustice.'

Emmet knew his employer did not like to be interrupted when she was in full flow, but he yearned to know the news.

'Sir Robert contacted the Urquhart woman's solicitor,' continued Lady Wadsworth. 'I am afraid I can't bring myself to call her Lady Urquhart, for she is not a lady in my book. A haughtier, more condescending and disagreeable person I have yet to meet. But that is by the by. Sir Robert contacted her solicitor, who seemed a reasonable sort of man, and pointed out certain facts: that you are named as the father on the child's birth certificate, that Roisin has lived with you for ten years in a secure and loving environment vouched for by myself, the vicar and the local head teacher, and that it would be quite inconceivable that Social Services would recommend a child be taken out of her present happy home and placed with an elderly woman she does not even know.'

'And?' Emmet was impatient to hear the outcome and could not resist the urge to interrupt.

Lady Wadsworth held up a hand. 'And as I predicted, the Urquhart woman's solicitor accepted that a court case would prove fruitless and has recommended to his client that she abandon such a foolhardy course of action. So there it is. All sorted.'

'So Lady Urquhart is not proceeding?'

'Isn't that what I have just communicated?'

'I can't tell you how relieved I am,' said Emmet. He bowed his head and felt his eyes filling. 'I couldn't bear the thought of losing Roisin. Thank you, thank you so much for all you have done. I am so grateful.'

'It was the least I could do,' she said. 'Now, there is something else. The Urquhart woman's solicitor made a request on her behalf, one which you are quite at liberty to reject if you so wish.'

Emmet looked up. 'Yes?'

'He has asked if his client might be allowed to see her grand-daughter and keep in contact with her. I guess she is a lonely old widow lacking any other family, and probably without many friends, who wishes, as she nears the end of her life, to have some sort of reconciliation.' Emmet was about to speak, but Lady Wadsworth continued. 'Of course, were it me, I should be minded to tell her that since she has shown not the slightest interest in the child for ten years – not a birthday card or a telephone call – and bearing in mind the unpleasant things she said and her objectionable manner, she can forget it. But that is up to you, of course.'

'I have no objection to her seeing Roisin,' Emmet answered. 'After all, Lady Urquhart is her grandmother. Life is too short to harbour grievances. It's better to move on.'

'I wish I could be as magnanimous,' said the lady of the manor. 'I am afraid it is not in my nature to be forgiving of those who have offended or upset me. The Wadsworths never forget an insult. Indeed, one of my forebears settled such a matter in a duel. I think it was Sir Peregrine Wadsworth, if my memory serves me right. So, shall I tell Sir Robert you are happy to grant the request and set up a meeting?'

'Yes, if you would,' replied Emmet. He stood. 'Lady Wadsworth, I know that without your involvement things might have been a whole lot different.'

She coloured a little at the compliment. 'Tush,' she said and got to her feet. 'Now what are we going to do about these pesky rabbits?'

Lady Urquhart's solicitor lost no time in making contact with Emmet. It was agreed that his client should meet Emmet and Roisin at the Royal Hotel in Clayton on the following Saturday afternoon.

Emmet arrived at Wisteria Cottage. He wanted to tell Ashley the good news but was nervous about the reception he might receive.

Ashley saw him approaching down the path. She had thought long and hard about what he had told her, and what Elisabeth had said. She still felt upset and troubled, but she knew one thing for certain, that she loved the man and wanted to spend her life with him. She took a deep breath and opened the cottage door.

'Hello,' he said sheepishly, standing on the doorstep holding a bunch of flowers. He looked as shy and anxious as a teenager on his first date.

'You had better come in,' she told him. There was no smile on her face.

'I didn't know whether you would want to see me,' he said, coming into the cottage. He placed the flowers on the small table in the hall.

'Don't be silly, Emmet,' she told him. 'Of course I do.' She didn't look to him all that pleased to see him.

He followed her into the sitting room.

'Would you like a drink?' she asked.

'No thanks.' He stood by the fire and twisted his hands nervously. 'I've not slept,' he said.

'Nor me.' She sat on the sofa and rested her hands on her lap.

'I'm so sorry, Ashley,' he managed to say after a silence. 'I should have been honest with you.'

'You should,' she agreed.

'I've hurt you,' he said.

She nodded.

He came and sat next to her and took her hand in his. 'The last thing I want to do is hurt you. I've been a bloody fool.' She looked at him and saw tears in his dark eyes. 'I couldn't bear to lose you.'

'Oh Emmet,' she said, resting her head on his shoulder and squeezing his hand.

'Am I forgiven?' he asked.

'Yes, you're forgiven, but promise me, no more secrets.'

'No more secrets,' he repeated, 'I promise.'

'I'll put the kettle on,' she said.

Later that evening, Emmet related the conversation he had had with Lady Wadsworth earlier in the day.

'I think it's very generous of you to agree to this meeting with Roisin's grandmother,' Ashley told him. 'A lot of people in your position wouldn't.'

'Do you think I'm right?'

'Of course I do.'

'As I told Lady Wadsworth,' he replied, 'it's best to forget what happened. I've got a wonderful life ahead with you and Roisin. I'm looking to the future and putting the past behind me.' He kissed her gently.

'Well I still think you are being very big-hearted.'

'She is Roisin's grandmother, after all,' Emmet told her, 'and I think we need to move on. I have never been one to dwell on the past, and bearing a grudge doesn't help anyone.'

'I agree, of course,' said Ashley. 'Life is too short to harbour resentments and ill will.' She thought of her mother and determined that she would try again to get her to come around.

'I must confess I'm a little nervous,' admitted Emmet. 'I just wonder how Roisin will react at meeting her long-lost grandmother.'

'Have you discussed it with her?' asked Ashley. 'Have you told her why her grandmother hasn't been in touch before now?'

'Yes, of course I have. I've tried to be honest with her and explained the situation,' said Emmet, 'and actually she seems quite excited. Of course I didn't go into all the details. I just said that her grandmother lived a long way away and it had been difficult for her to make contact with us when we were on the road, travelling around the country as we used to do.'

'Perhaps that's being a little too generous,' said Ashley.

'What do you mean?'

'Of course I think it's a good thing that Roisin should get to know the grandmother she has never met, but do you think you really are, as you say, being honest with her?' asked Ashley.

'I still don't know what you mean.'

'I think you underestimate your daughter's intelligence, Emmet, if you think she will be fobbed off with such feeble reasons for her grandmother not bothering to make contact for ten years. Not a birthday card, not a present, not a phone call.'

'I'm not fobbing her off, Ashley,' replied Emmet. 'I just think it's better that she shouldn't know all the details. As I said, I want to put the past behind me.'

'Perhaps you ought to be more candid with her and tell her the real reason. She's old enough to know.'

Emmet was stung by the criticism 'What? Tell her that her grandmother didn't approve of me, disowned her own daughter, wouldn't even attend the funeral or see the baby? I really don't think it will be very helpful to do that,' he said, 'particularly at this time when she is just about to meet her grandmother. Certain things, I feel, are best left unsaid.'

'There were things unsaid that I should have known about, things you kept to yourself. Remember what you just said to me: "No more secrets." I think you should tell Roisin.' Emmet didn't answer. 'Well, it's up to you,' said Ashley, deciding not to pursue the matter. 'You are her father and you should do as you think best. I hope the meeting goes well.'

Lady Urquhart sat in the lounge at the Royal Hotel looking rather pale and drawn. She was dressed in a well-cut dark blue suit with small shiny gold buttons and a cream blouse, and had a lilac silk scarf tied neatly at her neck. Her fingers, wrists, ears and neck had a generous assortment of showy jewellery. As Emmet and Roisin approached, there was the fragrance of expensive perfume in the air.

'Good afternoon,' said Emmet.

Lady Urquhart remained seated. She managed a small smile. 'Good afternoon, Mr O'Malley,' she replied with more civility than at their last meeting. She twisted a large ring on her finger. 'Thank you for coming.'

'Hello,' said Roisin brightly.

'Come over here, my dear,' said Lady Urquhart, 'and let me look at you.' She examined the child as one might scrutinise some rare object in a museum case. 'You look very much like your mother.' Emmet sat down and watched. 'Do you know who I am?' asked Lady Urquhart.

'You're my grandmother,' replied the child. 'Daddy's told me.'

'Yes, I am your grandmother.'

'Why have I not seen you before?' asked Roisin with all the bluntness and honesty of a child.

Lady Urquhart glanced at Emmet. 'Your father has not explained?'

'He said it's because you live far away.'

'Well, there you are then, that explains it.'

'But you could have written, or come and visited,' said Roisin.

'Yes, I guess I could. I'm sorry, but perhaps I can make that up to you now.' She glanced again at Emmet.

'What was my mother like when she was little?' asked Roisin.

'Come and sit by me,' said Lady Urquhart, 'and I shall tell you.'

Roisin sat next to her and took the old lady's hand in hers. Lady Urquhart was taken aback by the child's open affability. She looked on the verge of tears.

'Your mother was a very pretty child,' she said, 'just like you, and she loved to play the piano and sing.'

'I can't sing,' said Roisin, 'but I can play the flute. I like reading and I write poetry.'

'You seem a very clever young lady,' said her grand-mother.

Emmet stood. 'I think I'll leave you two for a while to get to know each other,' he said.

'Thank you,' said Lady Urquhart, and it was obvious that she meant it.

⋆        ⋆        ⋆

On the way home, Emmet asked his daughter what she thought of her grandmother.

'She smelled nice,' said the child, 'and she had lots of lovely rings and bracelets.'

'And did you like her?'

'Yes, I liked her,' replied Roisin. She touched a small gold locket around her neck. 'She gave me this. There's a picture of my mother inside. She said I can come and visit her when she moves to England.'

'And would you like that?'

The child thought for a moment before replying. 'Yes, I think I would. It's nice to have a grandmother. But I still can't understand why it has taken her so long to come and see me. Just because she lives far away doesn't mean she couldn't write to me. Oscar's granny and grandpa live in New York and they send him postcards all the time, and birthday presents, and they talk to him on the telephone and they've visited him and he's been to America to see them. I just don't understand why my grandmother didn't do the same.'

Emmet didn't reply, but kept his eyes fixed on the road.

'Do you like her, Daddy?'

'Well I don't know her all that well,' he answered evasively.

'Did you fall out with her?'

'Yes, I did,' he replied.

'Why?'

'You ask a lot of questions, darling,' he said. 'I think that's enough for one day.'

'Will you tell me why you fell out with her?' persisted his daughter. 'Then I won't ask any more.'

'All right, I'll explain when we get home,' agreed her father, thinking of what Ashley had said.

The following Saturday lunchtime, there was a small reception in the drawing room at Limebeck House. The butler had opened several bottles of vintage champagne, and Mrs Fish, the cook, had prepared a selection of *hors d'oeuvres*. Lady Wadsworth had invited Elisabeth and Michael, Bishop Atticus and his wife, Ashley and Emmet and Major Neville-Gravitas. Mrs O'Connor had agreed to look after the boys back at Clumber Lodge, despite their protests to their parents that they were quite old enough now to be left alone. Roisin had been invited to spend the day at Oscar's house.

'Thank you all for coming to my little *soirée*,' said Lady Wadsworth. 'I wanted you, my dear friends, to help me celebrate the engagement of our vicar and my estate manager. I don't think one could find a better-suited couple and I know they will be very happy together. Everything seems to be on course for an April wedding, which I am sure will be the highlight of the village year.'

Lady Wadsworth had taken charge of the arrangements for the wedding from the start. Neither Ashley nor Emmet had been bold enough to argue with the formidable lady of the manor; in fact they were pleased, both being very busy people, that all the preparations were being taken out of their hands. The ceremony would take place at St Christopher's and the reception would be held at Limebeck House. Bishop Atticus would conduct the nuptials, assisted by Father Daly, and Dr Stirling would act as the best man. The major had agreed to give the bride away. Danny and James would be ushers and little Roisin a bridesmaid. Lady Wadsworth had been surprised to hear from Emmet some weeks earlier that Ashley's mother would not be attending the wedding. She had determined, in her usual redoubtable way, to remedy this.

The week before the Saturday lunchtime gathering, Lady Wadsworth had visited the De Courcey Apartments where Mrs Underwood lived. She had dressed for the occasion in a strikingly colourful tweed suit of mustard yellow with red and green checks, thick green stockings and shoes of the heavy, sensible brogue variety with little leather acorns attached to the laces. To add to the effect, she had worn a wide-brimmed red hat sporting two long pheasant feathers, held in place by a huge silver brooch in the shape of a stag's head, and to complete the outfit she had carried a capacious red leather handbag and an ancient umbrella with a spike at the end and a fox-head handle. She had looked magnificently outlandish.

Mrs Underwood had been quite taken aback by the bizarre-looking figure who stood outside her door.

'May I help you?' she had enquired.

'Indeed you may,' her visitor had replied. 'I am Lady Helen Wadsworth of Limebeck House. I take it you are Mrs Underwood?' Before she had been given an answer, she had continued, 'I trust it is convenient for you to spare me a few moments of your time. What I have to say won't take long.'

'Yes, yes, of course,' Mrs Underwood had replied, dazed by the vision before her. 'You had better come in.'

Lady Wadsworth had entered the apartment, glanced around and taken everything in. It had a cold, brittle, over-manicured appearance, she had thought, not unlike its occupant. She had deposited her large frame in the chair by the window, placed her handbag and umbrella on her lap and rested her hands on them.

'Mrs Underwood,' she had said, 'I won't beat about the bush because I am a woman who speaks her mind. I am a plain talker. Were you to know me, you would be aware that I never shilly-shally but say what has to be said, so I shall come straight to the point. I was surprised, nay astonished, to learn that it is not your intention to attend your daughter's wedding.'

Mrs Underwood had started to speak, but her visitor had held up her gloved hand.

'Permit me to continue,' she had said. 'As I was saying, I am astonished that you have decided not to attend. For a mother to miss her daughter's wedding is unimaginable in my book. I gather you have not seen eye to eye with Ashley over the years, but I am sure, were you to miss the most important day in her life, you would regret it in years to come. Life, Mrs Underwood, is too short.'

'If I may—' Mrs Underwood had begun.

Again the gloved hand had been raised to stop any interruption and Lady Wadsworth had continued as fast and furious as a Gatling gun.

'Your daughter is one of the most delightful, caring and endearing young persons it has been my pleasure and good fortune to meet. She is a great credit to you and you should be immensely proud of her. I never married and therefore have no children, but had I been blessed with a daughter, I should have hoped that she would have turned out like Ashley. She is to marry my estate manager, of whom I gather you do not approve. Mr O'Malley is a man of fine character – trustworthy, hard-working and kind. He will be a most attentive and loving husband, of that I am certain. He is like the son I never had.

'Now I know you will, no doubt, wish to rehearse for me the reasons for your differences with your daughter, but I really do not want to hear them. You will, I guess, regard me as an interfering old woman who has no business getting involved in a family dispute. Well be that as it may. Mrs Underwood, I urge you to reconsider attending the wedding. It would mean so much to Ashley. I shall be having a small get-together next Saturday lunchtime at Limebeck House to celebrate the engagement, to which you are cordially invited. I do hope I might see you there.' Lady Wadsworth had gripped her handbag and umbrella and risen regally from her chair. 'And with that, Mrs Underwood,' she had said, 'I shall leave you and not take up any more of your time.'

When her visitor had departed, Ashley's mother had been too stunned to even move from where she stood at the door.

After a while she had gone to the window of her flat and looked at the great grey cathedral that dominated the city, and thought of the unpleasant interview she had had with the bishop. For some unaccountable reason she had begun to cry. 'This is silly,' she had said out loud, reaching for a small lace handkerchief hidden up her sleeve. She dabbed her eyes. She could not recall the last time she had shed tears. Everyone seemed to see nothing but good in her daughter. Perhaps she had been too hard on Ashley, too tied up in her own grief at being deserted by a feckless husband to pay much attention to her daughter. That evening in her lonely flat she had recalled the words of Lady Wadsworth, of Bishop Atticus and Miss Sowerbutts, all of whom had urged her to accept the situation. 'Oh Ashley,' she had said. 'What am I doing?'

'So I would like you to raise your glasses,' said Lady Wadsworth now, toasting Ashley and Emmet. 'Happy days!'

'Happy days!' everyone chorused.

Lady Wadsworth approached Major Neville-Gravitas, who was standing by the window staring out over the expanse of parkland. Ashley and Emmet were in earnest conversation with the bishop and his wife.

'Breathtaking view,' observed the major. 'You should be congratulated, Lady Wadsworth, on the wonderful transformation you have brought about of the house and gardens.'

'And I believe congratulations are in order to you, Major,' she said, with a mischievous glint in her eye.

'Beg pardon, my dear lady,' replied the major, brushing a hand over his bristled moustache. 'I don't follow your drift.'

'On your news.'

'My news?'

Lady Wadsworth, as she had informed Mrs Underwood, was not one to beat about the bush and came straight to the point. 'I believe you have discovered you have a son,' she said.

The major looked embarrassed and coughed nervously. 'Well, yes, I have . . . er . . . recently learnt I have a son.'

'A youthful fling in Germany, I believe.'

'When I was a young army officer,' replied the major.

'Sowing your wild oats, so to speak.'

'Something like that,' he agreed, not wishing to continue this unsettling conversation.

'The revelation must have come as something of a shock,' remarked Lady Wadsworth, giving a wry smile.

'Yes indeed, but quite a pleasant shock,' replied the major.

'Perhaps this has tempered your view about loose-living young girls getting pregnant outside marriage, and your avowal that the youth of today don't seem to have any moral sense.'

'Yes, I think I was a little too judgemental,' agreed the major.

'I would certainly concur with that. Having a child outside marriage is not always the result of the permissive society you criticised with such fervour at the last governors' meeting, nor of the teaching of sex education in schools,' persisted Lady Wadsworth.

'No, not at all.'

'And as Mrs Robertshaw so convincingly pointed out at the governors' meeting, the man has some responsibility in this and sometimes it is he who takes advantage of an ingenuous young woman.'

The major was minded to tell his host that this had not been so in his case. He had not taken advantage. It had been a case of two young people who loved each other. However, he decided that this was not the time nor the place to discuss his personal life and merely replied meekly, 'I stand corrected, your ladyship.'

'Those in glass houses, Major,' she said, wagging a finger and leaving the proverb unfinished.

'Quite,' he replied.

'Do help yourself to another glass of champagne,' said Lady Wadsworth, enjoying the man's discomfiture. She smiled. 'You look as if you need it.'

While this exchange was taking place, the bishop and Emmet were discussing the wedding, while Mrs Atticus was giving a blow-by-blow account to Elisabeth and Ashley of the difficulties they had experienced at Clayton Juniors with regard to the supply teacher.

'When I arrived in the classroom,' she was saying, 'the scene that greeted me was quite alarming. There were twenty terrified infants, some of whom had wet themselves, others who were cowering by the sandpit, and one child secured to a chair with masking tape. In the middle of this mayhem was the supply teacher, Mrs Humphrey-Snyde, shrieking like a banshee.'

The butler entered and gave a slight bow.

'What is it, Watson?' asked Lady Wadsworth.

'You have a visitor, your ladyship, he said. 'She is waiting in the hall.'

'Is it important?' asked Lady Wadsworth. 'We are in the middle of a party.'

'It appears it is,' replied Watson.

'Well what does she want?'

'She wouldn't say, your ladyship. Just that she wanted to see you.'

'I had better go,' she said, putting down her glass. Then, *sotto voce*, she added, 'I just hope it's not that dreadful Urquhart woman again.'

Lady Wadsworth returned to the drawing room a moment later accompanied by Mrs Underwood.

'I would like you all to meet Ashley's mother,' she announced. There was a faint but unmistakable expression of triumph on her face.

## 21

On Monday morning, Elisabeth was dressed and ready for school as usual. As she sat at the breakfast table, staring out on to the garden, she drifted into a momentary daydream. Snowdrops had pushed up from the soil, buds had appeared on the branches of the trees, and daffodils grew in clusters down the borders. A bright sun shone in an eggshell sky. Spring had finally arrived. On such a clear, crisp day, she felt that everything was right with the world.

'That was a bit of a turn-up for the books,' said Michael, coming into the kitchen.

'What was?' she asked.

'Ashley's mother arriving like that. I thought you told me that her mother was very much against her getting married to Emmet?'

'She was.'

'What changed her mind, then?'

'I have an idea it was Lady Wadsworth,' Elisabeth told him. 'She went to see Mrs Underwood and evidently had a few words to say to her. She has this amazing capacity for changing people's minds to her way of thinking. I recall when they wanted to close the school and she went in to the Education Office all guns blazing and they ended up keeping it open. Then she put a stop to the planned housing estate in the village and sorted out Emmet's problem over the custody of his daughter. She's a formidable presence in Barton, is Lady Wadsworth, not someone to be crossed.'

'I'll not argue with that,' agreed Michael, reaching across the table to take Elisabeth's hand in his. 'Actually, it was Lady Wadsworth who urged me to ask you out. She said we would make a perfect couple.'

'I never knew that!' cried Elisabeth. 'You kept it to yourself. I hope there are no more secrets, Michael Stirling.'

'You never know,' he said, winking.

At school, Elisabeth found Bianca arranging some daffodils in the entrance. 'There's loads of these up at the farm,' she told the head teacher when she caught sight of her. 'My Uncle Fred said you might like a few. They brighten the place up a bit, don't they?'

'They do,' Elisabeth agreed. 'Thank your Uncle Fred, will you?'

'He's in a lot better mood these days,' said the young woman. 'Not half as grumpy and tight with his money. He changed when Brandon come out of the hospital.'

'I'm so very happy that your baby has recovered,' Elisabeth told her. 'He must be a pretty tough little boy.'

'He is,' agreed the girl. 'The doctor said he was a real fighter.'

'It must have been a terribly worrying time for you and your husband. How is Brandon now?'

'He's doing really well,' replied the young woman. 'My mam, who looks after him when I'm at work, says he's a real little handful.' Bianca took Elisabeth's hand in hers. 'Mrs Stirling,' she said, 'the doctor at the hospital said if it hadn't have been for Dr Stirling and you taking such prompt action like, he didn't think that Brandon would have—'

Elisabeth cut her off. 'You really don't need to say anything,' she said. 'We are just so pleased that your baby is better.'

At morning break, Tom found Elisabeth in her classroom.

'May I come in?' he asked.

'Yes, of course,' she said. 'Was there something in particular you wanted to see me about?'

'Well, yes,' said Tom. 'It's about Jeremy Robinson. He's been off school now for over a week, since Mr Grimwood's visit. I was pretty angry with him after the tutor had left. I was feeling rather low about the lesson that had been observed and felt . . . well, I felt it could have gone a whole lot better without Jeremy's clever comments and frequent interruptions. I . . . er . . . I'm afraid I lost my temper. I may have been a bit hard on him.'

'I wouldn't worry too much,' said Elisabeth. 'From what I know of the boy, I don't think being told off will have any great effect.'

'The thing is,' said Tom, 'Mrs Scrimshaw says there has been no call and no note from home explaining his absence. Then this morning I received this rather strange letter.' He held up an envelope. 'It's from Jeremy's father saying that his son will not be coming back to the school. There is no address on it, or contact number, and he doesn't say why Jeremy is leaving. No explanation at all. I feel I may have been responsible.'

'Well, it does sound a bit odd,' agreed Elisabeth. 'I wonder if his leaving might have something to do with what happened on the school trip, although his father seemed very understanding when I spoke to him about it. Do me a favour, Tom, will you. Get the Robinsons' home address from the school office and give Jeremy's father a ring and find out what's at the bottom of this.'

'I've done that already,' said Tom. 'I didn't want to bother you.'

'And?'

'It appears that the telephone has been cut off.'

'Even stranger,' said Elisabeth. 'Anyway, not to worry. I have Mr Robinson's work address and number. He gave me his card when we first met. I'll give him a call later. I wouldn't worry too much. I am sure it has nothing to do with you reprimanding the boy.'

At lunchtime, Elisabeth telephoned the number on the card.

'May I speak to Mr Robinson, please?' she asked.

'He's not here,' said a man's voice down the line. 'Packed up and left last week.'

'Have you a contact address or telephone number for him, please?' asked Elisabeth. 'I do need to speak to him.'

'You and all the others,' answered the man, 'and that includes me. He left without paying for the rental of this office. I hope you're not one of his clients.'

'No, I'm the head teacher of Barton-with-Urebank school, which his son attends.'

'Well I think we've seen the back of Mr Nigel Robinson, that is until the police catch up with him.'

'The police?'

'Look in the *Clayton Gazette*,' said the man. 'There's an article there about him.'

He put down the receiver.

Oscar, perky as ever, found Elisabeth outside, staring out over the playground.

'Hello, Mrs Stirling,' he said, approaching her. 'You look in vacant and pensive mood.'

'Pardon?'

'We've been studying a poem by William Wordsworth with Mr Hornchurch,' Oscar told her. 'It's about daffodils. That's one of the lines: "in vacant or in pensive mood".'

'Oh, I see.'

'May I join you, miss?' asked the boy. Before she could respond, he came and stood next to her, his hands behind his back. 'I say, it must have been really frightening, miss,' he said.

'What must have?' asked Elisabeth.

'Jeremy getting stuck in the mud. It could have been very nasty.'

'Oh, that. Yes, it could.'

'You have to be very careful on the beach, miss,' said Oscar. 'I once went paddling in the sea at Filey and I stood on a weever fish. It's a little sandy-coloured fish that spends most of its life buried in the sand on the sea bed. It has these poison spines on its back. I trod on one and the pain was excruciating. I was rushed by ambulance to hospital in Scarborough and had to put my foot in a bowl of really hot water. That's the way to deal with it, you see. Anyway, my father said there ought to be warnings about these fish, and—'

'Just one moment, Oscar,' interrupted Elisabeth. She had caught sight of Robbie, who was sitting on the wall that bordered the playground. She wanted to have a word with the boy to ask him how he was getting along. 'Was it something special you wanted to see me about?' she asked.

'No, not really, miss,' replied Oscar. 'Just passing the time of day, and to ask if you had heard about the body.'

'I'm sorry, Oscar, I don't know what you are talking about. What body is this?'

'In the mill dam, Mrs Stirling,' he said. 'They've found a body in the water.'

Mrs O'Connor, accompanied by Mrs Pocock, visited the village store and post office on Monday afternoon to collect her pension and inform the shopkeeper of the discovery of the body in the mill dam.

'Yes, I know about it,' said Mrs Sloughthwaite.

'I thought you would,' said Mrs Pocock under her breath.

'Pardon?'

'Nothing much escapes your attention.'

'For your information, I read about it in the *Clayton Gazette*,' the shopkeeper told her.

'Probably drunk,' observed Mrs Pocock, 'or up to no good, I'll be bound.'

Mrs Sloughthwaite sighed. She was becoming weary of late of the customer's constant carping. Over the years she had tolerated the peevish pronouncements, often finding them entertaining and distracting, but lately the woman was becoming increasingly strident and derogatory. She had not a good word to say about anyone. The shopkeeper was about to respond when Mrs O'Connor spoke first.

'Poor man might have taken his own life,' she said.

'I don't know,' said Mrs Sloughthwaite, shaking her head unhappily. 'They're dropping like ninepins.'

'Who are?' asked Mrs Pocock.

'People,' said the shopkeeper. 'First it was Edith Widowson, found dead in her bed as stiff as a board, then your husband launched into eternity with a heart attack, then Mrs Osbaldiston's brother, and now they've found this body floating in the mill dam. It makes you wonder, doesn't it?'

'Makes you wonder what?' asked Mrs Pocock.

'Well, whether there's some sort of curse on the village. It seems a bit coincidental that all these people are dying at the same time. You never know who'll be next at this rate.'

' "Death is but death and we all in time shall die",' said Mrs O'Connor. ' "Death is not a full stop but a comma in the story of life." That is what my—'

'Spare me the words of wisdom from that old Irish grandmother of yours, Bridget O'Connor!' cut in Mrs Pocock, anticipating that she was in for another adage from the woman's Celtic forebear.

'As I was saying,' continued Mrs Sloughthwaite, 'all these fatalities make you think. I can't remember the last time we had so many deaths within a matter of weeks. It seems contigious.'

'Do they know who it was they found in the mill dam?' asked Mrs Pocock.

'I gather his name was Banks and he'd been in the water a good few days, so Mrs Sidcup, who does a bit of cleaning in the funeral director's, told me. Body was in a right old state, she said, all white and bloated – not that she saw it. Just what she was told. It says in the *Clayton Gazette* that the police are leaving no dunghill upturned.'

'Banks,' pondered Mrs O'Connor. 'The name doesn't ring any bells with me.'

'He's not from the village,' Mrs Sloughthwaite told her.

'You'd know, of course,' muttered Mrs Pocock.

'Pardon?'

'Nothing.'

'The corpse was so decomposed, Mrs Sidcup told me when she called in the store,' related the shopkeeper, 'that they were only able to identify the body from details in his wallet.'

'I wonder what he was doing down by the old mill at this time of year,' mused Mrs O'Connor.

'Rabbiting or badger baiting, I shouldn't wonder,' concluded Mrs Pocock. 'As I said, he was probably worse for drink and lost his footing and fell in. Course, in this cold weather he wouldn't have lasted a minute.'

'Well it's a bit of a mystery to me,' remarked the shopkeeper.

Mrs O'Connor looked at Mrs Sloughthwaite for a moment. A slight smile pulled at the corners of her mouth. It won't remain a mystery for long, she thought to herself. She knew the shopkeeper would not give up until she had gleaned every bit of information about the corpse to relay to all those who patronised her shop.

'One bit of good news is that Bianca's little one is better,' said Mrs O'Connor, keen to change the subject. 'I saw mother and baby in the village this morning. The wee lad's out of hospital and has made a full recovery, bless him. He was smiling away in his pram, so he was. So you see, St Jude came up trumps after all, didn't he?'

'It's more due to the efforts of the doctors than it is to some little-known saint,' said Mrs Pocock.

'St Jude was one of the apostles, if you must know,' replied Mrs O'Connor. 'He was not little known and he's always been a great comfort to me in times of need.'

'Well if I was going to pray to a saint, it wouldn't be the patron saint of desperate cases and lost causes,' said the shopkeeper. 'Isn't there a patron saint of babies you could have prayed to?'

'St Philomena is the patron saint of babies, infants and children, and I did say a prayer to her as well,' Mrs O'Connor told her. 'She's also the patron saint of adults who seek to live a life of purity and chastity.'

Mrs Pocock gave a snort. 'Well you'd be hard pressed to find any of those about these days, particularly in this village,' she remarked.

'You sound like that vicar of yours who was always going on about sin,' said Mrs O'Connor. 'Mr Snapshot, wasn't it?'

'Sparshott!' exclaimed the other customer, with a pained expression on her round face. 'And he was no vicar of mine. We were all glad to see the back of him. He's gone off to Africa. He'll go down like a lead balloon with the natives. What I was saying is that there's very few that I could mention who live lives of purity and chastity in Barton-in-the-Dale. I mean, it's become a hotbed of vice and iniquity. Take Major Neville-Gravitas, for instance, going on about loose-living people and him having a secret love child in Germany. Mind you, I always thought he was a hypocrite. Then there's more than meets the eye about Joyce Siddall. She's always got her curtains closed when her husband's at work. And Doris Maynard's no better than she should be. The number of men I've seen coming out of her cottage is nobody's business. And what about Fred Massey? Talk about mean. He'd steal your eyeballs and then come back for the lashes. He's another one about as pure as a mound of mud.'

'It must be nice to be so pure and chaste yourself,' the shop-keeper told her with carefully and cleverly aimed provocation, 'to be so full of virtuosity.'

'I'm not saying that I'm—' began Mrs Pocock.

She was distracted by the sound of the bell as the shop door opened. Clarence, a great smile spread across his face, walked in.

'I shall be off then,' said Mrs Pocock, and with a nod of the head in Clarence's direction, she departed, smarting at the shopkeeper's pointed comment.

'Here comes a happy man,' said Mrs Sloughthwaite as Clarence approached the counter.

'We were so pleased to hear about little Brandon's recovery,' said Mrs O'Connor. 'The wee fella looked the picture of health this morning, so he did.'

'Yes, he's doing champion,' said Clarence. 'Could I have a box of chocolates, please?'

'And who are these for, as if I didn't know?' said Mrs O'Connor.

'How's that leg of yours?' asked Mrs Sloughthwaite.

'My leg?'

'I saw you limping down the high street. Your Uncle Fred told me what happened.'

'Oh, you mean with the sheep. I thought he might have told you. He's told everybody else.'

'What did happen?' asked Mrs O'Connor.

'He had a bit of trouble with a sheep,' Mrs Sloughthwaite told her before Clarence could reply. 'The animal attacked him and his uncle told all and sundry and made fun of the poor lad.'

'I wasn't aware that sheep could be violent,' said Mrs O'Connor. 'I thought they were docile creatures.'

'Not this one,' Clarence told her. 'It's got a real nasty streak, as my Uncle Fred found out last week.'

'So he's had some trouble with it too, has he?' asked the shopkeeper, leaning over the counter.

'The smile's on the other side of his face now,' Clarence told her. 'He's in bed with a bad back and a sore head. Now *he's* the laughing stock at the auction mart.'

'So what's he been up to?' asked the shopkeeper.

The great smile reappeared on Clarence's face. 'Well this sheep we've got up at the farm, the one that I had trouble with, is a real handful. It's got a vicious streak and would as soon knock you over as look at you. The sheepdogs keep their distance and so do the other sheep. My Uncle Fred decided to get rid of it and tried to lasso it with a length of rope. It would have none of it and set off at a fair lick across the field, jumped over the dry-stone wall and raced off down the road. Later that morning Uncle Fred had a phone call from Mrs Osbaldiston at Yew Tree Cottage saying that one of his sheep was in her garden eating her plants. When she went out to shoo it off, it butted her. So Uncle Fred set off in his Land Rover to collect it.

'When he tried to get it in the back of the vehicle, the sheep put up a rare old fight, so he threw his jacket over its head. You see, if an animal can't see, it goes all quiet. When it stopped struggling, my Uncle Fred sat astride of it, grabbed hold of its front legs and tried to lift it into the Land Rover. Now when he got the phone call from Mrs Osbaldiston, he'd rushed out of the house in such a hurry that he didn't have time to put his shirt on, so there he is in his vest next to the main road, with a sheep between his legs and his jacket over its head, and he's puffing and huffing and red in the face as he tries to get it in the back of the Land Rover. You can imagine what it looked like, and Mr Ross, who was passing in his tractor, nearly ended up in a ditch when he saw what was happening. It looked as if—'

'Thank you, Clarence,' Mrs Sloughthwaite cut in sharply. 'I think we have got the idea.'

'As I say,' he continued, 'when word got round, the other farmers had such a laugh at Uncle Fred's expense. "You look a bit sheepish today, Fred," one of them said. "Are you looking for a baaaagain?" said another. They just couldn't stop laughing.'

'Well, he'll get over it,' said the shopkeeper, recalling the old farmer's words. 'He can chalk it up to experience.'

Mrs O'Connor, looking thoroughly mystified, asked innocently, 'Could one of you tell me why trying to get a sheep into the back of a Land Rover is so funny?'

It was just before closing time when Major Neville-Gravitas breezed into the village store.

'I'm glad you've called in, Major,' said Mrs Sloughthwaite. 'There's a man been looking for you.'

'Oh yes?'

'A large man he was, with a thick neck, a loud voice, a red face and little eyes.'

'Ah, that would be Councillor Cyril Smout, a good friend of mine. He's very big in the council. I play golf with him most weeks.'

'Well he didn't look very happy,' said the shopkeeper. 'He said he's been trying to contact you all yesterday and today.'

'I've been very busy,' the major explained. 'I'll give him a ring. May I have a packet of my usual panatellas, please?'

Mrs Sloughthwaite stretched up to a shelf to get the cigars and passed them over the counter. 'Did you hear about the body in the mill dam?' she asked.

'Body?'

She reached under the counter, produced a copy of the *Clayton Gazette* and slid it over to the major. 'Banks was his name. I don't suppose you knew him?'

'No,' answered the major, glancing down at the newspaper. 'The name doesn't ring any bells. Of course we on the parish council have been trying to do something about the mill dam for—' He stopped suddenly as he caught sight of a headline below the article to which the shopkeeper had pointed. He leaned forward to read it with staring eyes and open mouth.

FINANCIAL FRAUDSTER ABSCONDED.

He read on: *Police wish to interview Nigel Robinson (42), a financial adviser, regarding serious irregularities in his business transactions. Robinson left his rented accommodation at Eastgate Lane last Thursday and has not been seen since. Several of his clients, who number some prominent people, including a local councillor, have invested lump sums with Robinson, and now stand to lose considerable amounts of money.*

'Good God!' exclaimed the major.

'Are you all right?' asked Mrs Sloughthwaite.

Without replying, her customer rushed from the shop.

'What about your cigars?' she shouted after him.


The two visitors found the farmer in one of the large sheds, filling the feeders. They looked an odd couple: she tall and slim with shiny blonde hair pulled back into a tight bun; he a small, stout man with a pasty freckled face, gingery eyebrows and thinning hair.

'Mr Ross?' asked the woman.

'Aye, that's me,' replied the farmer, placing a bucket of feed on the floor.

The woman produced a small black wallet from her pocket and flashed her ID. 'I'm Detective Inspector Mason,' she said, 'and this is Sergeant Moorcroft.'

'What does tha want wi' me?' Mr Ross asked.

'Could we have a word?'

'I reckon tha can. What's it abaat, as if I didn't know?'

'Perhaps we might go in the house,' said the police officer.

'Aye, all reight. It dun't smell all that 'eavenly in 'ere, does it? Follow me.' He led the way to the farmhouse. 'Watch thee step. Theer's a lot o' muck abaat.'

The woman, who was wearing expensive-looking shiny knee-length boots, tiptoed after the farmer across the yard, followed by her colleague, who manoeuvred himself around the mud and the mess.

In the kitchen, the farmer, having removed his muddy boots at the door and hung up his coat and cap, sat at the pine table in the centre of the room and rested his large hands on the tabletop. He thrust his chin forward. 'Tek a pew,' he said, pointing to a couple of chairs. 'Nah then. What does tha want wi' me now?'

The police officers sat down. The inspector regarded the farmer with determined eyes but didn't speak. Her colleague took a small notebook from his pocket, licked his index finger and flicked through the pages.

'I believe you know a Mr Banks,' said the sergeant.

'I don't know 'im an' I don't want to know 'im. I 'ave met 'im, though, and no doubt you're well aware o' that since I've 'ad a visit from a couple o' your colleagues.'

'He visited the farm, did he not, some short time ago?'

''E did.'

'And there was an argument?'

'Aye, there was.'

The sergeant looked down at his notes and sucked in his lower lip. 'And you assaulted him?'

''Ang on a minute. As far as I know, t'meanin' o' yon word assault means attack, an' I never attacked 'im. More like 'e attacked me. I punched 'im afore 'e 'ad a chance to land one on me. Banks started it. I were defendin' missen. I told t'other police officers all this when they came up 'ere. Banks was minded to tek his stepson. It's called abduction. I was only protecting t'lad. I'm Robbie's legal guardian an' I were doin' what any reight-minded person'd do. You can ask t'lad what 'appened. 'E were there an' saw it all.'

The inspector continued to regard him with a keen look of enquiry, but she remained silent.

'Yes, we have read a copy of your statement, Mr Ross,' said the sergeant.

'And we are aware of what the boy told us,' added his colleague.

'So why are tha back 'ere questionin' me ageean, then?' asked the farmer. 'Theer's nowt more I can tell thee. Banks is a thug an' a bully. 'E needs lockin' up. 'E med 'is stepson's life a misery, pickin' on 'im, 'ittin' 'im wi' a leather belt an' 'umiliatin' 'im. 'Ave a word wi' Robbie's social worker if tha dun't believe mi.'

'We have already spoken to Miss Parsons,' the sergeant told him.

'Well she'll 'ave telled thee how t'lad was tret.'

'Where is the boy now?' asked the police officer.

'At school weer 'e should be. 'E'll be back at half four. Look, if tha's gunna charge me wi' summat, then do it. I'm a busy man an' I've got two thousand pigs to feed. An' I'll tell thee this, if I do gu to cooart charged wi' assault, it'll be Banks's word agin mine, an' I reckon t'jury'll believe me, what wi' 'is record.'

The police inspector listened quietly until the farmer had finished before speaking herself. 'You will not be facing Mr Banks in court,' she said. 'He's dead.'

Mr Ross breathed out noisily through his teeth and rubbed his exuberant beard. 'Dead, is 'e?'

'Mr Banks's body was found floating in the mill dam,' said the sergeant. 'It had been in the water for over week. We are not yet certain of the circumstances surrounding his death.'

The farmer shrugged dismissively. 'Well, I shan't shed any tears,' he said.

'The police pathologist who conducted the autopsy estimated the time of death as last Tuesday,' the sergeant told him. 'Could you tell us where you were that day, Mr Ross?'

'Weer I allus am. 'Ere ont t'farm.'

'And is there anyone who can collaborate that?' he asked.

'T'wife was 'ere.'

'Anyone else?'

'No.'

'Could we have a word with Mrs Ross?'

'She's out.' The farmer crossed his arms over his chest and looked belligerently across the table.

'Have you ever visited the mill dam at Barton-in-the-Dale?' asked the police inspector.

'No.'

'Are you sure about that?'

'Very sure. Look, do you think I 'ad summat to do wi' 'is death? Is this what it's all abaat?'

'It's for us to ask the questions, Mr Ross,' said the police inspector.

'Well, I've told you all I know, so is that all?'

'For the time being,' she said, getting to her feet. 'We may be in touch again later and ask you to come down to the police station.'

'If we think you can help us further with our enquiries,' added the sergeant.

'Thank you for your time, Mr Ross,' said his superior.

When Robbie arrived home from school, Mr Ross asked him to come into the kitchen.

'Sit thee sen down, lad,' said the farmer. 'I wants a word wi' yer.'

'Have I done something wrong?' asked the boy, eyeing him apprehensively.

The farmer shook his head and laughed. 'Why is it, young Robbie, that when me an' t'missus wants a word wi' yer, yer allus think tha's done summat wrong?'

'It's your voice,' said Robbie. 'You sound dead serious.'

'Well, thy 'asn't done owt wrong, so sit thee sen down and pin yer lugs back.'

Mr Ross looked at the boy, who stared back at him across the table with a sombre and expectant expression on his pale freckled face. Over the weeks he had stayed at the farm, Robbie had flourished, behaving himself and being helpful, but despite what he had overheard when the social worker had called, he still felt insecure and worried that his new life would suddenly end.

'I've 'ad visitors today,' said the farmer. 'Police officers.'

'Was it about you hitting my stepfather?' asked Robbie. His first thought was that he would now go back into care, that he wouldn't be allowed to stay at the farm.

'Aye, summat to do wi' that,' replied Mr Ross.

'I can still stay here, can't I?' the boy asked anxiously.

'Cooarse yer can,' said the farmer. 'I don't know 'ow many times I've 'ad to tell thee that.' He paused, thinking what to say to the lad. Robbie looked at him keenly. 'T'police officers 'ad some news.'

'What about?'

'I reckon there's only one way to tell thee, Robbie,' the farmer said. 'Best is to come straight out wi' it. Yer stepdad's dead.'

'He's dead?' said the boy. He received the news without undue surprise, dismay or pleasure.

'They found 'is body in t'mill dam. They're not sure what 'e were doin' down theer or, as they told me, t'circumstances surrounding 'is death. I never liked t'man, 'e were a brute an' a bully, but I don't rejoice at 'earin' t'news. Drowndin' in a muddy pond is not a good way to go. Anyroad, yer stepdad won't be bothering thee again.'

Robbie nodded thoughtfully but didn't say anything.

'So theer it is,' said the farmer.

'Yes,' murmured Robbie. 'There it is.'

# 22

The first of the three funerals at which Ashley officiated during an unusually cold March week was for Francis Banks. The man's next of kin, his estranged half-brother, who had reluctantly arranged matters when contacted by the police, bore no resemblance to his relative. He was an abnormally thin, nondescript individual with a bony face, sparse stringy hair and myopic eyes. He wore a greasy grey raincoat, flat cap and brown shoes.

Ashley met the man in a small side room in the main crematorium building to discuss with him how they should proceed. She hoped she might learn something good about the deceased so she could at least say a few positive words about him, but she was saddened to hear that the half-brother had nothing pleasant to say about his sibling.

'I would like you to get this over as quickly as possible,' he said in a doleful and plodding voice. 'I never liked my half-brother and haven't seen him in years. He was a nasty piece of work and I can't say that I'm sad he's dead. It might sound a bit unfeeling to you, Vicar, but you didn't know him. He broke our mother's heart. I knew he would come to no good.'

Ashley sighed and wondered what she could say after hearing this. 'So you don't wish to say a few words?' she asked.

'I most certainly would not!' exclaimed the man. 'And I don't want any hymns or sermons either. I'm a busy man and have had to miss a day's work to come up here from Nottingham.' He added, 'And I'm not paying for this.'

'Shall we make a start, then?' asked Ashley.

Clayton Crematorium had a featureless interior of plain oatmeal-painted walls devoid of any religious imagery, functional insipid pine furniture and long windows containing a hint of coloured glass. Bunches of garish plastic flowers in large vases were positioned strategically on the windowsills. The simple coffin rested on two biers before a carpeted stage. The place was empty save for two figures who sat on a pew at the back.

'I don't know who they are,' said Banks's half-brother.

'The young man is his stepson,' Ashley informed him. 'The man is Mr Ross, the boy's foster carer.'

'Yes, I heard Frank got married again. Drove his first wife to drink. She was glad when he left her, I was told. Used to knock her about.'

'Would you like to meet the boy?' asked Ashley.

'No I wouldn't,' replied the man sharply. 'I've got nothing to say to him. Shall we get on with it?'

It was the quickest service at which Ashley had officiated, and as soon as the coffin had disappeared behind the red velvet curtain, accompanied by some suitably sombre organ music, the half-brother was out of the building like a cat with its tail on fire.

Ashley went to speak to Mr Ross and Robbie.

'I'm surprised to see you here,' she said.

'Aye, well, Reverend,' replied the farmer, 't'lad weren't that chuffed abaat comin', but me an' t'missis thowt we should show us faces – not to gloat, mind, or dance on t'man's grave, but just for Robbie' ere to have closure, to put behind 'im one part of 'is life, probably t'worst part, an' to mek a new start.' Mr Ross put his hand on the boy's shoulder.

The second funeral of the week, for Mrs Widowson, was another low-key affair. A few hardy souls, including Mrs Sloughthwaite and her two regular customers, braved the chilly morning to attend. The heating had been turned on and a huge metal contraption blew out great blasts of hot air. The few members of the congregation, who scarcely filled two pews, had wrapped up warmly against the unseasonably frosty weather. As the recorded version of 'The Old Rugged Cross' filled the room, the mourners began divesting themselves of heavy coats, thick scarves and gloves. As Mrs Sloughthwaite remarked later to her customers, perhaps a rendition of 'The Stripper' might have been more appropriate.

The deceased, not having been a churchgoer, was largely unknown to Dr Underwood, and had few friends and no family from whom to glean any information about her. Ashley did her best, speaking of a kind and friendly character who had been the oldest resident in the village, a much-liked woman who had suffered uncomplainingly with numerous ailments. Mrs Sloughthwaite, of course, knew differently, for the woman in question never left the village store without taking all who would listen through a detailed catalogue of her many infirmities. As the shopkeeper once remarked about her aged customer to Mrs Pocock, 'It's a wonder she lasted so long. I've never seen anyone so thin and emancipated.'

It was back to the crematorium on the Thursday for Mrs Sloughthwaite and her regular customers for the funeral service of Mr Pocock. The three women, having endured the almost unbearable heat earlier in the week, decided to leave their outdoor clothing in the entrance, only to find that the heating had been turned off, following complaints from bereaved relatives at the previous funeral. The three of them sat shivering in their pew. Again Ashley tried resolutely to say something positive of a man about whom she knew very little and of whom there was little to commend.

As she made her way to the exit with the other mourners, Mrs Sloughthwaite, out of earshot of the grieving widow, shared her considered assessment of the proceedings with Mrs O'Connor.

'I've never seen such a fandango in all my life,' she whispered to her friend, her hands clasped beneath her solid bosom. 'The place was like an ice box, they nearly dropped the coffin, the miserable-looking undertaker in the top hat and tails who walked before the hearse looked like a Victorian rat-catcher, and I nearly fell full length on those slippery steps at the entrance.'

'You would have thought they'd have put some ashes down,' remarked Mrs O'Connor.

Mrs Sloughthwaite rolled her eyes but decided not to reply.

'And what about the tune that was picked?' continued the doctor's former housekeeper. 'A very peculiar choice, so it was.' The whole congregation had been rather taken aback when the coffin slowly disappeared behind the red velvet curtain accompanied by a loud and spirited rendition of 'New York, New York' by Frank Sinatra.

'Totally unopportune,' agreed the shopkeeper. 'I mean, I don't think the man ever got as far as Scarborough, never mind America. I don't want to sound unkind, but the Pococks were not exactly the best advertisement for maritime bliss. They hardly spoke to each other, and he spent all his time in the Blacksmith's Arms supping pints of ale, propping up the bar or playing darts. Never held down a job in his life. He was about as much use as a chamber pot with a hole in the bottom. Theirs was a marriage of inconvenience if ever there was one. And it's no wonder that lad of theirs has turned out as he has done. You will have noticed he wasn't at the funeral.'

'She looked very upset,' said Mrs O'Connor.

'Who did?'

'Mrs Pocock.'

'Tears of relief, I shouldn't wonder. He led her a right old dance, that husband of hers.'

'Yes, you're probably right,' agreed the customer. 'They say that nothing dries more quickly than a widow's tears.'

The shopkeeper shook her head good-naturedly. Her friend could always be relied upon to draw on her considerable repertoire of sayings when the occasion arose.

'She's having a ring made,' said Mrs O'Connor.

'Who is?'

'Mrs Pocock. She was telling me that they take the ashes of the deceased and make them into a ring that the widow can wear as a keepsake or remembrance.'

Mrs Sloughthwaite gave a hollow laugh. 'It'll be a big ring, the size he was,' she replied.

'Oh, they only take a smidgen,' said Mrs O'Connor.

The shopkeeper shook her head. 'I've never heard the like.'

'And she's after consulting Mrs Wigglesworth, that psychic, to see if she can get in touch with him now he's passed over, as they say.'

'He's not been dead two minutes and she's trying to get in touch with him? She wants to give the man a chance to get there, wherever that might be, before she starts trying to make contact.'

'She said she wants to see how he's settling in.'

'Settling in!' exclaimed the shopkeeper. 'It sounds as if he's starting boarding school.'

'Mrs Pocock was very impressed, don't you recall, when we all went to see Mrs Wigglesworth and she had her tea leaves read. She had quite a shock at what she was told, so she did.'

'And I had quite a shock as well,' grumbled Mrs Sloughthwaite. 'It was left to me to settle the bill and pay thirty-five quid plus VAT. I wish I had never taken her along.'

Mrs Sloughthwaite, who was a great devotee of astrology, fortune-telling, palm reading and clairvoyance, had prevailed upon her two customers to accompany her to what she termed 'a cyclical confrontation' with Mrs Wigglesworth. At the consultation the psychic had revealed to the initially sceptical Mrs Pocock certain things about her past that only her client knew. Convinced that the psychic could genuinely contact the dead and reveal the future, she had made regular visits. Now, as she had told Mrs O'Connor, she was to make an appointment with Mrs Wigglesworth to get in touch with her recently departed spouse.

Following the service, Mrs Sloughthwaite and her two regular customers retired to the parlour of the village store for what the shopkeeper termed 'the funereal tea'. It was fortuitous that Mr Pocock's funeral had taken place on a Thursday afternoon, since it was half-day-closing. The three women, attired in black and with suitably cheerless expressions, got straight down to discussing the two cremations.

'It was a lovely funeral for your husband, so it was,' observed Mrs O'Connor, not really believing this but feeling it was the right thing to say, bearing in mind that the grieving widow was sitting next to her. She took a sip of tea.

The shopkeeper responded with appropriate solemnity, nodding her head dolefully. 'It was,' she lied. 'He had a lovely send-off.'

'Well, the poor man has gone to his just reward now, God rest his soul,' sighed Mrs O'Connor, crossing herself.

'I didn't know your husband was so keen on America,' said Mrs Sloughthwaite, skilfully changing the tenor of the conversation.

'He wasn't,' replied Mrs Pocock, reaching for a salmon paste sandwich. 'He hadn't a good word to say for the Yanks.'

'Well I'm intrigued as to why he went out to "New York, New York",'said the shopkeeper.

'The silly man on the CD player pressed the shuffle button and it went to the next track,' complained Mrs Pocock. 'My husband always was a stubborn man and wanted his own way, so I thought the Frank Sinatra song "My Way" would be appropriate.'

It was providential, thought Mrs O'Connor, that the CD hadn't jumped to another song by the American crooner. It wouldn't have been very fitting for the deceased to depart this earth to 'Smoke Gets in Your Eyes'.

'I noticed Ernest wasn't at the funeral,' said Mrs Sloughthwaite, provocative as ever.

'No, he said he would give it a miss,' replied Mrs Pocock, taking a bite of her sandwich. 'It's games on a Thursday at school and it's the only subject he likes. Course, Ernest never did get on with his father. They were always at loggerheads. To be honest with you, and it's not something I'm proud of saying, I don't think he'll miss his dad very much. Last night he asked who was going to fetch the fish and chips now that he's dead.'

'People grieve in different ways, so they do,' said Mrs O'Connor, a sympathetic look on her face. 'Some show their sorrow, others keep it to themselves. I'm sure that deep down Ernest misses his father.'

I wouldn't be so sure of that, thought the shopkeeper. She knew Ernest Pocock of old. He was a moody, truculent and monosyllabic young man and had to be watched when he came in the store, for things tended to go missing when he was about.

'I wanted my husband to have a church service,' pronounced Mrs Pocock, reaching for another salmon paste sandwich, 'but he wasn't religiously inclined.'

'I'm having a full requiem mass when I meet my Maker,' said Mrs O'Connor. 'I've told Father Daly exactly what I want.'

'Well let's hope the Pope hasn't anything on that day,' said Mrs Pocock, smiling at her own witticism.

*     *     *

The police sergeant with the pasty freckled face, gingery eyebrows and thinning hair, arrived at Treetop Farm just as the farmer and Robbie were finishing their rounds feeding the pigs.

'Mr Ross,' he said, 'might I have a word? I'm Sergeant Morecroft. You remember I called to see you about the death of Francis Banks.'

'Aye, I recall,' sighed the farmer, 'but there's nowt more I can tell thee abaat what 'appened. Banks went for me so I smacked 'im an' that's t'plain truth. I don't know owt abaat t'other matter, 'ow 'e ended up in t'mill dam.'

'We do know that,' said the police officer. 'I've called in to tell you that you will not be required to call at the station.' He looked at Robbie, who was listening intently. 'Could I speak to you in private, Mr Ross?'

'Go an' fettle t'last shed, will tha, Robbie,' the farmer told the boy.

Robbie went off dutifully.

'Now what is it?' asked the farmer.

'We've got to the bottom of Banks's death,' the police sergeant told him. 'The pathologist's report revealed that the victim was killed by a heavy blow to the head and died some distance from the old mill. No water was found in his lungs so it is clear he did not drown. The body was taken and thrown in the mill dam. Two men have admitted to the crime and have been charged. Evidently Banks was involved in receiving stolen goods and not paying the two thieves for what they passed on to him. There was an argument and a subsequent fight when things must have got out of hand.'

'So that's it then?' asked the farmer.

'That is it,' replied the police officer. 'I'll leave it up to you to tell the boy.'

'What did the police want?' asked Robbie later as he sat with Mr Ross at the kitchen table.

'It was about yer stepdad,' the farmer told him. 'T'policeman came to tell me that they've arrested two blokes. Seems they had a bit of an argument with yer stepdad an' it got out of 'and.'

'Did they kill him?' asked Robbie bluntly.

'Aye, it looks like it,' replied the farmer.

'There were times when I wanted to kill him,' said Robbie quietly, 'for what he did to me.'

'Aye, well it's all in t'past now,' said Mr Ross. 'You need to forget about it and gerron wi' yer life.'

'It's hard to forget about it,' said the boy. 'Things were good before he married my mum and when my dad was alive.' He was quiet for a moment. 'I was happy then,' he added thoughtfully. 'I was happy.' He looked up at the farmer. 'I'm happy now.'

When the boy's stepfather had moved in, things had changed for Robbie. It was clear he was not wanted; he was an irritant, a liability, and Banks made his life unbearable. He got rid of most of the things that had belonged to Robbie's father, keeping only those items that he wanted for himself – the fishing rods, the tools, the motorbike and the big leather armchair in the lounge. Every time Robbie saw his stepfather sprawled in the chair, smoking and guzzling a can of lager, he felt incensed, and hatred caught in his throat like a solid lump. There was nothing in the house but recriminations, cruel comments, sarcasm and shouting.

And then came the violence. Many was the time when the boy had gone to bed, his body throbbing from the beating he had received and his heart aching for times past when his father was alive. He would wet the bed and receive another beating for doing so, the smacks making his wet skin sting. Then he was made to sleep in the bath as a punishment. Robbie's mother, totally subjugated by and herself fearful of the brute of a husband she regretted marrying, was powerless and afraid of interfering, which made Robbie feel alone and abandoned. He became an angry and resentful child and a real handful at school as well as at home. Before she died, soon after Banks had deserted her for another unfortunate woman, his mother had told her son how she regretted not standing up to her husband more. In hospital, and near death, she begged Mr and Mrs Ross to look after Robbie, whom she felt she had let down. They had agreed, promising to adopt the boy should anything happen to her. She died a remorseful woman. Over the time Robbie had been living with his foster carers at Treetop Farm, he had flourished and, with care and compassion, become the happy, helpful and well-behaved boy he had been when his father was alive.

'Thy 'as to put t'past behind thee, Robbie,' said Mr Ross now, 'otherwise thas'll end up bitter an' angry all tha life, goin' ovver an' ovver in yer 'ead what 'appened and feelin' badly done to. I told yer when tha first came to live wi' us that we lost our little girl. Gracie was two when she were tekken from us. We was 'eartbrokken. When she died, we didn't think we could go on. It were like our world 'ad come crashin' down. We could 'ave spent t'rest of us lives shakin' a fist at God for lettin' Gracie die; we could 'ave felt cheated that other kids lived an' were growin' up and she wasn't. Course, we'll never forget our little lass, but we've got on with us lives as best we can, and that is what thy 'as to do – get on wi' yer life. Tha's got to move on.'

'I'll try, Hamish,' murmured Robbie, looking down at the tabletop.

'An' speakin' of movin' on, we've 'ad a letter from Miss Parsons of t'Social Services.'

The boy looked up smartly. 'What did she want?' he asked.

'Some papers need signin',' the farmer told him with a smile on his lips. 'Adoption papers.'

Robbie's face lit up. 'Is it really happening?' he asked.

'Course it is,' said Mr Ross.

The boy's face glowed with happiness. He jumped up, ran around the table and gave the farmer a great hug.

With three funerals in as many days, it had been a tiring and demanding week for Ashley. She stared up at the dark brown damp patch and flaking paint above the altar in the side chapel, thinking that she must do something about it. The unsightly stain had been there far too long and was now spreading. As she turned, she caught sight of a hunched figure sitting by the sepulchre of the medieval knight. He was watching her keenly. Bright sunshine shone through the stained-glass window above the tomb and enveloped him in rainbow colours. She walked down the aisle, smiling.

'Hello,' she said brightly, 'may I—' She stopped mid-sentence when the figure looked up and she saw his face. She gripped the side of the nearest pew to steady herself. The sallow, tired face was deeply lined, the grey hair was thin and dry and the pale eyes betrayed a blank desperation. He was no longer the tall, handsome, immaculately dressed man with the bright eyes and the ready smile that she remembered.

'Hello, Ashley,' he said softly. There was a tremble in his voice.

'Hello, Father,' she replied.

She came and sat next to him on the pew, a little way away from him.

'You look well,' he said.

She could not say the same for him; he was clearly an ill man.

Tears welled up in his eyes. He quickly wiped them away with the back of a hand.

'It's so good to see you,' he said, sniffing. 'It's been a long time.'

Ashley couldn't cry. The tears just would not come. She sighed. 'Oh Father,' she murmured. They sat there in silence, bathed in coloured light. She gazed at him as if mesmerised. 'How did you find me?' she asked finally.

'I read the Church Appointments column in *The Times*. It said you had become vicar here at Barton-in-the-Dale.'

'So you knew I had entered the Church?'

'Yes, I knew. You've done well, Ashley, very well. Of course I always knew you would. You were such a clever girl.'

'Why did you never contact me?' she asked flatly.

'I was expecting you to ask me that,' he said sadly. 'I guess any excuse I might give will sound feeble.'

'You're right. Every day I have asked myself why you walked out of my life,' she told him, closing her eyes briefly as if pained. 'I could see why you left my mother. I heard all the rows and recriminations and witnessed the simmering silences and ill-feeling. I couldn't bear to hear you arguing all the time. No child should be subjected to that. I wonder if either of you knew how deeply it was affecting me.'

'I'm sorry,' he murmured.

'I can understand why you left,' she continued, 'but what I can't understand is how you abandoned me so easily. We were so close. I loved you so much. I longed to hear from you. Why did you stop writing to me? Why did I receive not one birthday card after you left? Why at Christmas was there not a present? Why were you not among the proud parents at the graduation ceremony at Oxford when I received my degree?

'I moved to Vancouver,' he said weakly, 'and time moved on. I had a new wife and a child. It wasn't because I didn't care; it wasn't because I stopped loving you. I wanted—'

'It's all very well to say that now,' she interrupted. 'If you really cared, if you truly loved me, you would not have cut me

out of your life. You had the address of the convent school that
I attended, and our new address.'

'I did write,' he said.

'And then the letters suddenly stopped. Why?'

A silence filled the church.

He sighed. 'I guess your mother recognised my writing.'

'You mean she kept your letters from me?'

'I don't know. Maybe,' he said. 'When I received no replies
to my first few letters, I assumed you didn't want any further
contact with me so I stopped writing. I felt guilty, I suppose,
about leaving you. Anyway, that's all in the past.'

'But the past has a habit of catching up with us,' she said.
She thought for a moment of Emmet.

'I know,' he said.

'What is it you want, Father?' she asked.

He avoided looking at her and stared at the tiled floor. 'I
wanted to see you,' he said quietly. His cheeks were wet with
tears.

'Why?'

He looked up at her with a mixture of sorrow and regret.
'Just to see you and talk to you before . . . Just to see you again.
I've thought about you so often and wanted to get in touch,
but Carolyn . . .'

'The woman you left my mother for,' she prompted.

'Carolyn wanted me to sever all contact with my past. She
got quite paranoid if I mentioned my life before I met her, and
if I spoke of you, she would flare up and say I loved you more
than our own child. We had a son. He was killed in a boating
accident. Blake was nine. Carolyn never came to terms with
it.'

'I don't think it is possible for parents to come to terms with
the death of a child,' said Ashley. She thought for a moment of
the bereaved mothers and fathers she had tried to comfort at
the hospital. She thought of Bianca and Clarence.

'She had a breakdown,' her father continued. 'It poisoned our relationship. She never got over his death.'

'I'm sorry,' said Ashley. 'That must have been terrible for both of you. No tragedy in life compares to losing a child. But please don't blame your wife for your failure as a father. And you have failed.'

'I know,' he said.

'You should have stayed in touch. Rather than just give up when you received no letters from me, you should have persevered. You should have tried harder. You cannot imagine how lonely and upset and worthless I felt growing up with a father whom I thought cared nothing for me and a loveless mother for whom nothing was right.'

'Your mother remained bitter?' he asked.

'What do you think?'

'No, of course I shouldn't blame Carolyn,' he replied. 'I should have made more of an effort. I know that now. I've had a lot of time to think about things recently, going over in my mind what I would say to you. I want to say that I'm sorry, I want to say that I very much regret how I behaved, how I treated you. I miss you, Ashley,' he said sadly. 'I never realised how much until these last few months.' He rubbed his eyes. 'I want you back in my life. I want to be part of your life. Can you forgive me? Can you do that?'

'I don't know,' she replied. 'I thought I'd never see you again, and now you turn up.'

'Like the proverbial bad penny,' said her father.

'Yes, I suppose so.' She thought for a moment. 'You must understand that it is hard for me; you must see that. You can't expect to walk back into my life as if nothing has happened. I need time to come to terms with it.'

'I see that.'

'And what about your wife? Does she know you have come looking for me?'

'Carolyn left me,' he said. 'After Blake's death, things got worse and . . . Well, I won't go into details.' He looked at his daughter. 'Do you wish me to leave?' he asked.

'I don't know,' she replied. 'I really don't know.'

'I'm staying at the Royal Hotel in Clayton,' he said, rising to his feet with some difficulty. 'If you do wish to see me again – and I hope that you will – I'll be there for the next few days.'

That evening, Ashley sat in the dark before the crackling fire at the cottage. The silence was only broken by the tick-tock of the long-case clock in the hall. She knew she would go and see her father. She could do no other. How could she talk to her congregation about charity and forgiveness if she turned her back on him? His sudden appearance had been such a shock, though. As she had watched the shambling figure making his weary way down the church path after their meeting, she had felt numb. She had never imagined that he would just walk back into her life. He looked so old and doddery, so different from the father she remembered: that handsome, self-assured, gregarious man. She didn't know him.

The next morning, she found her father in the lounge at the Royal Hotel, sitting by the window staring vacantly out over the gardens. His eyes lit up when he saw her. 'You came,' he said, rising to his feet. He took her hands in his and kissed her cheek.

'Yes, I came,' she replied. They sat opposite each other at a small table.

'Would you like a coffee?' he asked.

'No, I'm fine.'

She wished she could say the same for him, she thought, looking at the ashen face and noticing how his hands trembled. 'You don't look well,' she said.

'Old age, Ashley, it catches up with all of us,' he told her, raising a smile. She knew there was more to it than that.

'There's so much to talk about,' he said. 'I really don't know where to begin.'

'Let's take it slowly,' she said.

'Yes, of course.'

'I'm getting—' she began.

'It's good of you to—' he started.

They stopped nervously, as if they were meeting for the first time.

'After you,' she said.

'No, no, after you,' he replied.

'I'm getting married,' she told him.

'Oh, getting married, eh? Who's the lucky chap?'

'Emmet's the estate manager at the big house near the village. He's Irish.' She stopped, finding the exchange difficult.

'Look, Ashley,' said her father. 'If you feel it would be better for me to leave . . .' He left the sentence unfinished.

She looked into his eyes, which were brimming with tears. 'No, I don't wish you to leave,' she said, feeling her own eyes filling up.

Her father began to cry, great heaving sobs that shook his body. Ashley stood and moved around the table. She put her arms around him and rested her head on his shoulder, and then her own tears came.

## 23

The highlight of the year was the wedding of the vicar and the estate manager of Limebeck House, or, as Mrs Pocock termed it, 'the curious case of the curate and the gypsy'. Ashley and Emmet were married at St Christopher's by Bishop Atticus in the presence of a congregation that filled the church. It was a sunny April morning and it seemed that the entire village had turned out to wish the couple well.

Emmet, looking dashing in a charcoal-grey morning suit, green silk waistcoat and cravat, stood at the altar with Michael at his side, waiting nervously for the arrival of his bride. He glanced around at the congregation. In the front pew sat Ashley's mother, in whispered conversation with Lady Wadsworth. Ashley had not been able to hide her delight on seeing her mother at the reception at Limebeck House and learning that she was to attend the wedding. Now Mrs Underwood was in pride of place. She broke off her conversation with Lady Wadsworth for a moment and glanced at Emmet. When their eyes met, she gave a slight smile.

Major Neville-Gravitas, appearing every inch the retired army officer in his smart blue blazer with brash gold buttons, crisp white shirt and regimental tie, chatted with Mrs Atticus. Behind him sat Bianca and Clarence, next to Fred Massey, who cradled a chortling baby Brandon. Mrs O'Connor, attired in a coat of vivid green, was seated with Mrs Sloughthwaite, who sported a peach-coloured wide-brimmed hat. She was

2

8 Gervase Phinn

scanning the congregation to make a mental note of who was there. As was her wont, she didn't like to miss anything. She turned to give Emmet a small wave when he caught her eye, and smiled broadly. In contrast, her neighbour, Mrs Pocock, sat straight-backed and stony-faced, looking as if she were attending a funeral rather than a wedding.

Danny and James, who were acting as ushers and dressed in matching grey suits, gave the thumbs-up sign at the entrance to the church to indicate that the bride had arrived. Mrs Fish began a rousing rendition of Purcell's 'Trumpet Tune', and the congregation stood.

Ashley looked stunning in a simple white dress and veil. It was clear to all that the bride needed no elaborate silk wedding gown embellished with intricate embroidery and studded with pearls, no fancy necklace or diamond tiara; she needed no long lace train held by pageboys in velvet or a bevy of bridesmaids following her down the aisle. On that bright spring morning, with the sun shining through the stained glass and bathing her in an iridescent light, Ashley was a vision as she walked to the altar on her father's arm, followed by just one little bridesmaid with bright red hair and jade-green eyes who gripped a posy of wild flowers.

Bishop Atticus smiled warmly as the bride and groom stood before him at the altar. They both wore on their faces the dazzled look of two young people very much in love.

'God is love,' the bishop intoned, 'and those who live in love live in God, and God lives in them.'

Prayers were said loudly and hymns sung lustily before the bishop arrived at that part of the ceremony that often gave many a happy couple a tingle of apprehension.

Bishop Atticus stared at the congregation, a serious expression on his long face. His sonorous voice resounded around the church.

'I am required to ask anyone present,' he pronounced solemnly, 'who knows a reason why these persons may not lawfully marry to declare it now.'

In the silence that followed, Ashley's heart gave a little leap.

The bishop addressed the bride and groom.

'The vows you are about to take are to be made in the presence of God, who is judge of all and knows all the secrets of our hearts; therefore if either of you knows a reason why you may not lawfully marry, you must declare it now.'

Again there was a hush in the church.

And when the bishop, addressing the congregation, asked if the family and friends of Ashley and Emmet would support and uphold them in their marriage, the loudest and most vociferous response came from the striking-looking figure who sat regally in the centre of the front pew. 'We will!' thundered Lady Wadsworth.

The following Monday morning, in the village store and post office, the proprietor and her two regular customers held an inquest on the nuptials.

'That was a turn-up for the books,' remarked Mrs Pocock drily.

'What was?' asked Mrs Sloughthwaite, leaning over the counter.

'The bride's father turning up out of the blue like that.'

'Well yes, it was a surprise, I'll give you that,' agreed the shopkeeper. 'As far as I can recall, Dr Underwood's never mentioned him much, and she was very pervasive about her mother as well when I enquired. Just said that he was in Canada and she lived in an apartment in Clayton.'

'Divorced, then,' observed Mrs Pocock.

'When I asked her—' began Mrs Sloughthwaite.

'The poor man, God bless him, didn't look at all well,' remarked Mrs O'Connor, shaking her head sadly. She clearly had not heard a word of the conversation that was taking place next to her. 'As grey in the face as the suit the groom was wearing. It took the poor fellow an effort to get down the aisle, so it did. I don't reckon he's long for this world.'

'As I was saying,' continued Mrs Sloughthwaite, 'Dr Underwood has always been very tight-lipped about her parents. I reckon she was upset that they split up. It can't have been easy for her growing up with no father on the scene. It was lovely that he gave her away, though. I had an idea she had asked Major Neville-Gravitas. She must have changed her mind.'

'Him again,' exclaimed Mrs Pocock. 'He gets in on every act, turning up like a bad penny.'

'Speaking of money,' said Mrs Sloughthwaite, 'I heard he's gone and lost all his savings.'

'Who?'

'Major Neville-Gravitas. Evidently he invested with some charlatan, who's run off with all his money.'

'That explains why he looked so dog-in-the-manger at the wedding,' remarked Mrs Pocock. 'By the way, I didn't see Dr Underwood's mother in the church.'

'Oh she was there,' Mrs Sloughthwaite told her. 'She was the tall woman dressed all in lilac who sat at the front next to Lady Wadsworth.'

'And what a sight she looked!' exclaimed Mrs Pocock.

'I thought she looked quite elegant myself,' said the shop-keeper, 'although lilac is not a colour I would have chosen myself, and I did think the hat was over the top.'

'I don't mean Mrs Underwood,' said Mrs Pocock, irritation in her voice. 'I meant Lady High-and-Mighty. She's always been one to take centre stage given the chance, has Lady Wadsworth, but whatever was she thinking of turning up in that ridiculous outfit. Bright pink dress and yellow jacket, I ask you, at her age. Mutton dressed as lamb. She looked like a slice of Battenberg cake, sitting on the front pew as if she was family. And what about that outlandish pair of feathers on her head? It looked as if a bird was nesting in her hair.'

'They're all the fashion these days, these fornicators,' said the shopkeeper.

'They're called fascinators, actually,' corrected Mrs Pocock. 'And I'll tell you this, two wilting multicoloured feathers sticking up from her head didn't look very fascinating to me.'

'They made a lovely couple, the bride and groom, so they did,' sighed Mrs O'Connor.

'Bridget O'Connor!' snapped the other customer. 'Are you listening to what we are saying? We're not talking about the bride and groom, we're talking about Lady Wadsworth's ridiculous outfit. She looked like the dame out of a panto-mime in that get-up. And what about the bridesmaid?'

'I thought she looked a picture,' said Mrs O'Connor. 'She's such a pretty child, and—'

'Yes, she's not a bad-looking girl,' Mrs Pocock grudgingly allowed, 'but did you see the posy she was holding? It looked like a bunch of weeds, and I didn't think the dress she wore did her any favours. I mean, it was a very unbecoming shade of green, and all ruffled. She looked like a sprout. You would have thought the bride and groom would have had—'

'But speaking of the bride and groom,' said Mrs Sloughthwaite, wearied by the constant carping, 'you have to admit they did make a lovely couple. Course, it was written in the stars. It was predicted in their horoscopes.'

'It was like a fairy-tale wedding,' said Mrs O'Connor.

'Huh!' huffed the other customer. 'Fairy-tale wedding! I've said it before and I'll say it again, it'll not last, you mark my words.' She wagged her forefinger by way of a warning. 'Like daughter, like mother. It'll end in the divorce courts. Cracks will appear in that marriage before too long. It stands to reason. I've never seen a more ill-suited pair.'

'And since when have you been the expert on matrimony?' asked Mrs Sloughthwaite with a grating impatience in her voice. She was fed up of the catalogue of criticisms, and thought of the woman's own less-than-blissful marriage.

'I don't profess to be an expert,' responded the customer. 'I'm just saying that theirs is not exactly an ideal match, despite what their horoscopes say.'

'Why is it that every time you come in my store, you moan about everything and everybody?' asked Mrs Sloughthwaite suddenly. She had wanted to say this for some time now, and after the diatribe to which she and Mrs O'Connor had been subjected, she had had enough of the woman's scathing pronouncements. She leaned over the counter and stared her customer straight in the eye. 'Do you know, I can't recall a time when you have been kindly disposed to anyone. Why don't you have something good to say for once?'

'What?' snapped Mrs Pocock, glaring. She bristled like an angry cat.

'It was a lovely wedding and they made a very handsome couple,' said the shopkeeper. 'Be happy for them, for goodness' sake, and stop finding fault.'

'I am allowed to express an opinion,' retorted Mrs Pocock. She screwed up her face as if tasting something sour. 'I was just saying.'

'Well please don't,' Mrs Sloughthwaite put in. 'I don't want to hear it. I'm sick and tired of having to listen day after day to your disparaging comments. You sat there at the wedding, thin and stiff as a snooker cue and with a face that would curdle milk.'

'I beg your pardon?' retorted the customer angrily. She jutted out her chin in belligerence.

'My grandmother used to say—' began Mrs O'Connor, in an attempt to calm the situation.

'Oh, please, save me from the Irish words of wisdom!' Mrs Pocock exclaimed waspishly.

'There's no need to take that tone,' said the shopkeeper, coming to the defence of the other customer. 'She's entitled to express her opinion just as much as you are.'

'I'm not standing here to be lectured and insulted,' answered Mrs Pocock sharply. 'I've got better things to do.' As a final rejoinder she added, 'And those scones you sold me yesterday were stale.' And with that she strode for the door.

'I think you've just lost a customer,' observed Mrs O'Connor.

'As if I care,' replied Mrs Sloughthwaite. 'Anyway, speaking of the wedding, didn't you think Mrs Stirling looked happy? She was fair blooming. You know, I wouldn't be at all surprised if she wasn't . . .'

Elisabeth was indeed happy, very, very happy. The reason for the elation was that she had a secret, the most wonderful secret. She had waited until Ashley and Emmet's special day was over before she told Michael. Snuggled on the sofa with him the evening after the wedding, she sighed and rested her head on his chest.

'You sound done in,' said Michael.

'I am rather,' she replied, her voice slurry with tiredness. 'It was a lovely wedding. They looked so happy.'

'It's funny how things turn out,' he said.

'How do you mean?' she asked, looking up.

'Well, I was at a pretty low ebb when you came into my life. If you hadn't applied for the position at the village school, we would never have met, and if Emmet had decided not to stay in Barton, he'd never have met Ashley. It's almost as if it was meant to happen, that—'

Elisabeth put a finger over his lips. 'I want to ask you something,' she said.

'I think I know what it is,' he replied.

Elisabeth sat up. 'You know?' she cried.

'I heard you talking to Mrs O'Connor.'

'But I've not told Mrs O'Connor,' she said. 'I've not told anybody.'

'You want a new kitchen, don't you? I heard you telling her last week that you were going to ask me.'

Elisabeth's face cracked into a smile. 'No, silly, it's not a new kitchen.'

'What is it, then?'

'Well, it is something new.'

'Mmmm, let me think. Car? Holiday? Bathroom? I can't guess.'

'Do you consider yourself a good doctor, Michael Stirling?' Elisabeth asked.

'Where's this come from? What sort of question is that?'

'Well, do you?'

'Yes, I do think I'm a good doctor,' he replied. 'Why do you ask?'

'You're good at recognising the various symptoms of a patient, are you?'

'Well I didn't do too badly when it came to little Brandon, did I?'

'That's true.' Elisabeth yawned again. 'Suppose someone felt really tired, suffered from nausea and needed to go to the toilet a lot?'

'Well, it could be anything,' Michael replied. 'These are pretty general symptoms. Anyway, I would need to examine the patient.' He stopped suddenly and sat up. 'Wait a minute,' he said, 'you're not . . .'

'What about having a craving for odd foods, and swollen ankles?' Elisabeth asked.

'You . . . you don't mean . . .' Elisabeth laid the flat of her hand over her stomach and smiled. 'Are you pregnant?' he exclaimed.

'Just a little bit,' she replied.

★　　　★　　　★

The day after the wedding – a bright, sunny Sunday – Elisabeth walked down the high street on her way to the village school. Most Sunday afternoons she spent in her classroom, catching up on all the paperwork and preparing her lessons for the week ahead. She paused at the proud monument built in honour of the second Viscount Wadsworth, the long-dead local squire, which dominated the street, and looked up at the large dull-bronze statue. The figure, attired in military uniform, stood on a large plinth, one hand on his hip, the other holding the hilt of a sword. Elisabeth thought of her brother serving far away in some distant sandy country. She had telephoned him with the news of Ashley's wedding and of the expected baby, and told him that if the child was a boy, they would like to call him Giles.

Elisabeth loved Barton-in-the-Dale, this tranquil village. It had a timeless quality about it. She loved the villagers too. They had made her feel so welcome. They had taken her to their hearts and she had taken them to hers.

As she walked down the high street, she caught sight of familiar faces. There was Bianca, chattering happily with Clarence as she pushed the pram past the Rumbling Tum café, and Elisabeth smiled to see how happy the young couple were after their ordeal at the hospital with their baby. She saw Fred Massey, dressed in his shapeless tweed jacket and greasy flat cap, a cigarette clamped in the corner of his mouth, trying to herd his cows in the field beyond and shouting and cursing at the frisky collie dog at his heels. There was Major Neville-Gravitas, meticulously attired as usual, striding in the direction of the Blacksmith's Arms for his lunchtime tipple, and Mrs Pocock and Mrs O'Connor in earnest conversation outside Everett's butcher's. She waved to Mrs Siddall behind her fruit and vegetable stall at the front of the greengrocer's, and to Mr Farringdon, who, after his prostate operation, was back at work and standing as he always did at the door of his hardware shop, broom held like a bayonet across his chest, ready for a charge. She thought for a moment of Mr Sparshott, the serious and determined former vicar, who had been given to preaching sermons of an inordinate length and who had denounced from his pulpit the iniquity of Sunday trading, not that his admonition had had any effect. Barton-in-the-Dale had not suited the cleric and he had not suited Barton-in-the-Dale. Elisabeth had heard that he had left to become a missionary and, as Mrs Sloughthwaite had termed it, 'was now after converting the heathen hordes in Africa'.

Soon she arrived at the village store and post office. The proprietor stood like a sentinel at the door, her dimpled arms folded under her substantial bust.

'Lovely morning, Mrs Stirling,' she said as Elisabeth approached.

'Yes indeed,' Elisabeth agreed.

'And what a grand wedding. Didn't the couple look a picture?'

'They certainly did.'

'Makes you glad to be alive on a day like this, doesn't it?' Then, with a naughty glint in her eyes, she added, 'Now you mind how you go.'

When she arrived at the school, Elisabeth decided not to go inside for the moment, but sat on the bench by the oak tree. There were so many thoughts running through her mind. Having a baby would certainly change her life, and that of her family. When should she tell her staff? What about her career? How would James and Danny react? What would the baby mean for her relationship with John?

She remembered as if it were yesterday the day John was born. She had held the small bundle in her arms and thought her son was the most perfect child in the world. He had great blue eyes, tiny fingers like sticks and nails pink and shiny as seashells. Simon, his proud father, had held him high in the air and told him he would be a son in a million, handsome, clever and athletic, who would go to Cambridge as he had done and make a name for himself in the world. Sadly, it was not to be. As the days passed, Elisabeth had known that things were not right, and following a meeting with the specialist, which she had insisted upon, her misgivings had been confirmed. When her husband at last understood that his son had a severe disability, he had been devastated. Unable to accept that John would never lead a 'normal' life – going to the local school, passing examinations, finding a job, getting married and having children – he had left.

Elisabeth smiled. That traumatic time was behind her now, and she was looking to the future, to a new and exciting chapter in her life with her husband and son, her two adopted sons and now a new baby. Who could have predicted, she thought, that John would make such progress? She had been told that he would inhabit his own secret world; that he would likely never speak, interact with others, embrace her, kiss her, never understand humour or irony and could be subject to seizures and maybe violent outbursts. She thought of him, settled and secure at Forest View, a gentle and loving boy who smiled at the world around him.

The last time she had sat on this bench in front of the school was when she had come for the interview for the post of head teacher. She remembered seeing for the first time the small, solid stone-built Victorian structure with its high mullioned windows, blue slate roof and large oak-panelled door with the brass knocker in the shape of a ram's head. Set back from the main street, which ran the length of the village, the school was tucked away behind the Norman church of St Christopher and partially hidden by the towering oak tree, its branches reaching skywards like huge arms. It had been an imposing if rather neglected building. The small garden to the front was tidy enough, but apart from a few sad-looking flowers and a couple of overgrown bushes, it was bereft of plants. The paint on the window frames was beginning to flake and the path leading up to the entrance had several cracked and uneven flagstones. There was clearly much to be done, she had thought.

At that time Elisabeth had wondered if she had done the right thing in accepting the position when it had been offered by the rather pompous chair of governors. After she had met the current head teacher, the stony-faced Miss Sowerbutts, and learnt that the school had received a highly critical inspectors' report and that parents were taking their children away, she had become even more convinced that it was not in her best interests to take on such a challenge. But it was in the best interests of her son John, who was a pupil at Forest View, a stone's throw from Barton-in-the-Dale. He was the sole reason for her deciding to apply to this particular school, for moving here would mean he would be in one of the best special schools in the county and she could see a whole lot more of him. And so she became head teacher and started her new and wonderful life.

An elderly woman with a round red face beneath a shapeless woollen hat came and sat on the bench beside her.

'It's a lovely day, isn't it?' she remarked.

'It is,' replied Elisabeth.

'Would you mind if I joined you for a moment?' asked the woman.

'Not at all.'

'I used to sit on this bench when I was young. There's many a young couple used to meet at the old oak.'

'You used to live in the village?'

'I did until I was fifteen, and then I went into service in Northallerton. I was glad to leave if truth be told. Not much happens here. I live in Scarborough now. It's only a small flat, but it has lovely sea views. Do you know, I've not been back to

Barton for donkey's years. I've always meant to, but never got around to it.'

'Has it changed much since your day?' asked Elisabeth.

'Hardly at all, answered the woman. 'St Christopher's is still here, of course, and that dreadful old monument on the high street, which they should have knocked down years ago. We used to throw snowballs at the old viscount when we were kiddies. The Blacksmith's Arms has hardly altered at all and the shops on the high street are very much as they were. The school looks a bit different, though – brighter, more cheerful somehow. There was no garden there in my day, and great black iron railings went all around the building. I'm pleased to see those have gone.'

'So you attended this school, then?' asked Elisabeth.

'I did.'

'What was it like?'

'They say that your schooldays are the happiest time of your life. Well they weren't for me. I hated it and was glad to leave. We had a nasty schoolmaster. Mr Petty was his name. Petty by name and petty by nature. He had a narrow bony face and a great beak of a nose. Like a vulture he was, peering over this big wooden desk with a lid. It was clear he never liked teaching, never liked children. He only bothered with the bright ones who went in for the scholarship exam for the grammar school. I wasn't one of those so I didn't learn that much. Too handy with his cane was Mr Petty. I couldn't put a number on the times young Fred Massey bent over for six of the best. He was always up to something was Fred.'

And he's not changed, thought Elisabeth, smiling.

The old lady chuckled. 'There used to be an open fire in the schoolroom, and every time Fred passed it he would spit into the grate and cause this hissing sound. It drove Mr Petty to distraction. He did get up to some tricks did Fred. Mr Petty used to have a bag of sweets in his desk and he'd suck them all through the lesson. Course *we* weren't allowed to eat in class. One day Fred changed the sweets for laxatives. Teacher was in and out of the privy like a fiddler's elbow. We did laugh.' A smile crinkled the corners of her eyes. 'Another time Fred put a cat in Mr Petty's desk. You should have seen the teacher's face when he lifted up the lid and the cat jumped out. On the last day, Fred snapped the schoolmaster's cane across his knee, emptied all the inkwells on the floor, wrote things not worth repeating on the blackboard and locked Mr Petty in the coal house. He was there for a good few hours, banging and shouting until he was discovered by the vicar. Black as the ace of spades he was, eyes all red, coughing coal dust and screaming blue murder. Adults take a dim view of today's young people and go on about this golden age when bobbies walked the beat and children were well behaved and everything was better. It's just not true. Things are better now, thank goodness. I was just in the village store and talking to the owner. She came to this school as well but was a few years younger. She was telling me it got a new head teacher not that long back, quite a character she said.'

'Really?' said Elisabeth.

'Came for the interview, so I was told, in red shoes and black stockings. Can you credit that? Red shoes and black stockings!'

They sat for a moment in companionable silence.

Elisabeth smiled as she thought of the day of her interview for the headship of the village school. She had dressed for the occasion in a smart, tailored grey suit, cream blouse, black stockings and red shoes with silver heels and had brought the chatter of the governors to an abrupt halt when she had walked through the door of the interview room.

'Good morning,' she had said cheerfully.

The Chairman of the Governors, Major Neville-Gravitas, had moved forward in his chair, stroked his moustache and smiled at her widely. There had been an expression of absolute wonder on his face as if he had discovered a rare and beautiful butterfly on a leaf.

When she had been offered the post, news spread like wildfire throughout the village, fanned by Mrs Sloughthwaite at the village store. All were keen to meet the blonde bombshell, as she was described by Fred Massey, the woman with the startling bright red shoes with silver heels and the black lacy stockings.

'I bet old Mr Petty was spinning in his grave up at the churchyard when she took over,' continued the woman. 'The shopkeeper at the village store said this new head teacher is quite a formidable woman and caused quite a stir in the village. Evidently the school got a terrible report before she came and was due for closure, but she turned things around in a matter of months and now it's one of the best schools in the county, with parents queuing up to get their children in.' The woman thought for a moment. 'Mind you, I guess someone of her undoubted talents won't be here for much longer. I'm afraid Barton-in-the-Dale has always been inward-looking and there's never been much excitement in the village. This new head teacher will no doubt be ambitious and move on to something a lot bigger and better than a little village school.'

Elisabeth closed her eyes and raised her head, feeling the warmth of the sun on her face.

'No,' she replied quietly, 'I really don't think she will.'

# ACKNOWLEDGEMENTS

My profoundest thanks to my patient and greatly supportive editors, Rowena Webb and Emily Kitchin, and to my agent Luigi Bonomi for his invaluable advice and constant encouragement.

How it all began – the first charming instalment in
the *Little Village School* series

GERVASE PHINN

The Little Village School

She was wearing red shoes! With silver heels!

Elisabeth Devine causes quite a stir on her arrival in the
village. No one can understand why the head of a big
inner city school would want to come to sleepy little
Barton-in-the-Dale, to a primary with more problems
than school dinners.

And that's not even counting the challenges the mysterious Elisabeth herself will face: a bitter former head
teacher, a grumpy caretaker and a duplicitous chair of
governors, to name but a few.

Then there's the gossip. After all, a woman who would
wear red shoes to an interview is obviously capable of
anything . . .

Out now in paperback and ebook

HODDER

# GERVASE PHINN

## Out of the Woods But Not Over the Hill

For Gervase Phinn growing old is not about a leisurely walk to the pub for a game of dominoes or snoozing in his favourite armchair. As this sparkling collection of his very best humorous writing shows, he may be 'out of the woods' but he is certainly not 'over the hill'.

Looking back over more than sixty years of family life, teaching, inspecting schools, writing and public speaking, Gervase never fails to unearth humour, character, warmth and wisdom from the most diverse of experiences, whether they be growing up in Rotherham with the most un-Yorkshirelike of names or describing why loud mobile phone users get his goat.

Brimming with nostalgia, gently mocking life's absurdities, never shy of an opinion, this is Gervase Phinn at his wittiest, twinkly eyed best.

Out now in paperback and ebook

HODDER